MW01539143

Every genuine
work of art
has as much
reason for being
as the earth
and the sun.

Ralph Waldo Emerson

Her Reason for Being

a novel

Susan Crossett Dilks

authorHOUSE®

AuthorHouse™
1663 Liberty Drive, Suite 200
Bloomington, IN 47403
www.authorhouse.com
Phone: 1-800-839-8640

This is a work of fiction. Names, characters, places and incidents either
are the product of the author's imagination or are used fictiously.

© 2008 Susan Crossett Dilks. All rights reserved.

No part of this book may be reproduced, stored in a retrieval system, or
transmitted by any means without the written permission of the author.

First published by AuthorHouse   7/28/2008

ISBN: 978-1-4343-6913-0 (sc)

Library of Congress Control Number: 2008904605

Printed in the United States of America
Bloomington, Indiana

This book is printed on acid-free paper.

DEDICATION

To those whose story needed to be written

This is a problem that writers of fiction always have to face in this country. People are literal minded, and they say, "Is it true? If it is true, is it factually accurate? If it isn't factually accurate, why isn't it factually accurate?" Then you tie yourself in knots, because writing a novel in some ways resembles writing a biography, but it really isn't. It is full of invention. If there were no invention, it wouldn't be readable. Invention, freedom. If you need circumstances, you create them in your own mind. But it is obviously not a project for literal-minded people. Habitual readers of fiction have an inkling of that, but so many people do not. I get impatient.

--- Saul Bellow

INTRODUCTION

It is 1899. A man has been shot. His senseless death is of as little concern to us as was his equally irrelevant life. It is the shooter to whom we must turn our attention. More specifically, to the whys that led to that desperate act.

But we speak now of the future, the same future which will see the rise to national prominence of the Larkin Manufacturing Company and its bringing Frank Lloyd Wright to Buffalo to design not only its headquarters but the homes of many of the company's officials. These are also the years that witness the erection of Buffalo's Guaranty Building, designed by the dean of American architects, Louis H. Sullivan, not too coincidentally the early mentor of our Mr. Wright. I mention this last only because of the building's fantastic medallion grille which can represent the interconnection among the lives you must perforce meet within these pages – and of the many complex layers that make up each and every one of us. Some of those, of necessity, remain hidden even to their proprietor.

There's time for all that later.

In May of 1875 John Larkin and his wife moved back to Buffalo, New York, where he established his own business, J. D. Larkin, Manufacturer of Plain and Fancy Soaps. Wright, on the other hand, was just turning eight years old so his story can wait.

It is June twelfth, a Tuesday, in the year of our Lord eighteen hundred and seventy-seven. Margaret Trusler is about to arrive by westbound train. Recently orphaned, the not-quite fifteen-year-old is bringing her younger brother and sister to live with an aunt they have never met.

Meanwhile, across town, Lizzie Knapp, already, at thirty-two, the mother of five, bemoans the extra effort and expense involved in preparing a "Sunday best" dinner for her visiting brother-in-law, Charlie.

The lives and families of the two women, so far apart now, will become inextricably entwined as we follow them across the next four decades.

Her Reason For Being? Strangers with nothing, one might

suppose, in common, these are two women whose lives will ultimately be changed, each by the other. And yet each has already been set on the course her life must inevitably follow.

Ready?

Yes, it's time for the journey to begin.

I

Tuesday, June 12, 1877

The child stood quietly, staring motionlessly at the children before her. Their expressions reflected her curiosity, and her fear. A swaying of the train caused her to momentarily lose her balance. A quick step and, again, the silent watching. Then, slyly, an older boy in the crowd of children winked. She jumped! and hurried back to the safety of her brother and sister.

"Hannah. What have you been up to?" Margaret smoothed her hair as she carefully lifted the young face buried in her lap. Tears were beginning to run down the dirt-stained cheeks. "What happened, dear?"

Bertram laughed. "Hannah was back there with those girls and boys."

Turning in her seat, Margaret glanced toward the rear of their car, seeing at once a group of children, some hardly younger than herself. They squirmed restlessly. She smiled before turning back to her own sister and brother.

"I wish I could be like them," Bert chimed in.

"Why, Bert! Whatever would make you say something like that?"

"Just look how they're dressed," he wailed, "and here I am, wearing this awful heavy suit. There can't ever have been a hotter day!"

"Bertram, we've been through all this. It's the only suit that still fit. I can't help it that you're growing so quickly. Besides, you know how important it is that we always comport as the proper young gentleman and ladies Mama and Papa would have expected us to be."

Hannah giggled at the reference to herself as a young lady.

Having garnered all the attention she was about to receive, her tears ended. Margaret returned to the novel that had fallen into the seat beside her while Bertram again climbed the sill to lean out the open train window. He ducked quickly to avoid the cloud of thick soot pouring toward him. Not fast enough. Coughing, he sheepishly looked around and then returned to the window. The smoke hurt his throat, but what fun to watch the flying cinders, small red fires hurtling through the air.

Ignored, Hannah climbed out of Margaret's lap and, hesitatingly, returned to the group.

This time the winking boy smiled kindly.

"I'm sorry; I didn't mean to frighten you. I'm Robert. What's your name?"

"H-H-Hannah."

"We're going to Nebraska. Where are you going?"

"To B-B-Buffalo." She turned to her sister as if requiring confirmation, saw she was unobserved and turned back to this interesting boy.

"Do you know where Nebraska is?" he asked.

Hannah shook her head

"To tell you the truth, neither do I. But they say it's far away. We're going to be on this train for more than a day."

Fearlessly now, Hannah stepped closer to the group of youngsters.

"Are all of them your brothers and sisters?" she asked.

"Oh, no! Nobody could have that many," Robert laughed. "At least, I don't think they could."

By now a curious Bertram had joined his younger sister, intrigued by the strange story he was hearing.

"Where are your parents? Do they already live in N-Nebraska?"

"Oh, I wish they did," the older boy sighed. "We're all orphans."

A girl, probably the eldest of the group, now turned toward the curious youngsters. "I'm Selma," she volunteered. Hannah and Bert listened intently as she told them of the Orphan Train that was taking them out to the central farmlands. There, she said, the train would stop in each small town, waiting for any family looking for a child or, more than likely, an extra hand.

"Where's your father?" one of the other girls broke in to ask Hannah and her brother.

"He got sick and died," she replied.

"So did our mother," Bertram added officiously.

"I thought that was your mother you were sitting with."

"Oh, no," he giggled. "That's just Margaret, our sister."

"Then," another chimed in, "you must all be orphans, too."

Hannah's lip quivered momentarily before she burst into loud tears.

"Hannah!" Bert nudged her. "Don't be such a crybaby."

"Are we going to have to work on a farm?" she asked.

"No, silly. We'll be living with Aunt Sarah in Buffalo."

"Have you ever been on a farm?" one of the others asked the little girl. "I think a farm sounds like fun. They tell us there'll be lots of animals there."

The sobbing stopped as she turned to this newcomer. "Animals?"

"Yes. Cows and pigs and chickens. Maybe even a goat. Cats, of course. And I hope I have a dog."

"A dog! Oh, wouldn't that be super!" Bertram raced back to Margaret. "Sis, will we have a dog in Buffalo?"

"Goodness, Bert, I don't know. I've never met Aunt Sarah. I don't know what we'll have in Buffalo. But if you want to know what I think, I think we're all – Hannah, and you, and me – very lucky that we have an Aunt Sarah who is willing to give us a home."

She knew all about these orphan trains. Many of the children riding them were foundlings, abandoned at birth. Others were the children of immigrants, rescued from lives of squalor and disease by well-meaning nuns and aid societies. Margaret felt a new sadness as she looked from face to face, wondering which ones would find loving families at the end of their ride. Too many others, she knew, would lead lives little better than that of indentured servants while the rest would be rejected and forced to take the long ride back again.

Hannah returned to her sister's side. "Tell me again about

Aunt Sarah."

Now that the cinders had disappeared Bert was finding the long train ride boring. "Where does she live? Does she have children?"

"Will they be four, like me?" The little girl quickly wiped her nose on her skirt, eager for her questions to be answered.

"I don't believe Aunt Sarah has any children. As for you, Bertram, you who ask so many questions, I really don't know. Father hardly ever mentioned his sister. I don't think Mother liked her very well."

"Will she be mean to us?"

"Let's hope not. Remember, we must try to always be as good as gold. And let's just pray for the best."

II

Tuesday, June 12, 1877

She fought back the tears, uttering a useless prayer, "Oh, God, give me strength."

His house, *his* children, and now *his* brother coming. "Fix 'em dinner, Sunday-like," he'd said, just before he'd hurried out the door. First to work and then off to the depot to meet him. How she'd like to be the visitor just arriving, Jack rushing to meet *her*.

Oh, talk of delicious thoughts! When was the last time Jack paid her that much attention, spending time really listening to what she had to say?

Oh, she knew she'd do it and dinner would be special and he'd be proud of her. He always was.

Truth now. Yes, she did resent his "Sunday-like" command. They had so little, scraping by on a poor workingman's wages. To be expected to sacrifice for a brother. And him rich and still single, certainly better able to afford fine food than she and Jack, particularly them having five little mouths to feed as well.

Her mind quickly turned to what to serve. It was too late for asparagus now. Why hadn't Charlie come six weeks ago if he wanted a feast? Or even a month ago when all the peas – oh! How sweet they were then, just a month ago. Too late even for rhubarb. And too early for the green beans or the sweet corn. Was anything better than corn picked just hours earlier, straight from the fields?

But now? What now?

Thinking of the fresh vegetables reminded Lizzie of the pleasure she always felt shopping at the vegetable stands. The colors and the smells delighted her. She relished the challenge of finding uses for whatever they sold, asking questions of the venders, experimenting, usually pleasing Jack if not the picky younger children, and feeling right proud of her latest accomplishment. Jack, she knew, prided himself on having such a talented wife.

Well, she wouldn't disappoint him now. Not that she'd want to. Charlie was a good sort. He adored their children, loved playing with them all. Bright too, an interesting man. And a good man, like his brother. A fine gentleman. How could one not look forward to sharing the table with another capable of adult conversation?

Nothing wrong with a Sunday dinner midweek. The older girls could help red up the house and keep an eye on the little ones while she chose a menu and started the preparations. Truth be known, food served at her own table really was the best.

Lizzie felt guilty for her earlier outburst. She had been thought a bright woman just out of college when she had married the man of her choice. Oh, my, but Jack had been so dashing. Theirs had been a whirlwind courtship, the stuff of dreams. She still cherished those dreams on occasion.

Only her parents had warned her of the dangers of marrying a man with little but his own burning ambition. She had been used to the finer ways, to having whatever mattered – big homes, trips, fine furs and jewelry – to the point that little had.

She had given it up most willingly and seldom regretted it, certainly never because of Jack. He worked hard. God knows how Mr. Larkin would have gotten as far as he had in these last two years, moving back from Chicago to open his own factory on little more than a wing and a prayer. If the cost just wasn't too high for Jack. And for her.

Children. Housecleaning. Cooking. Planning. Worrying. With five children there were so many fears. Illnesses. And always the danger of an accident. It wasn't that she had an idle moment. Or wanted one.

And yet, with so much – with all this! – something always seemed to be missing.

Was this all there was? Was this what her education had been preparing her to do?

Was this *it?*

Close to tears she wished she had the luxury of time to cry.

No. Not now.

There were better things to do.

III

Tuesday, June 12, 1877

"Hurry, Bertie; we mustn't keep Aunt Sarah waiting."

Margaret struggled with her own precariously balanced portmanteaux as the boy, no bigger than herself, strove to join his sisters. Sniffling, little Hannah, tugging at her sister's skirt, carried her pocketbook with all the importance such responsibility entailed along with her own tousled rag doll.

"Is that Aunt Sarah?" the younger voice chimed.

"No, dear. Or at least I don't think so. I expect she'll come for us with a carriage."

Margaret turned to check on Bertram's progress just in time to see him walk straight into the closer of two well-dressed men, themselves so deep in conversation that neither noticed the lad until it was too late.

"Whoops! Sorry, mister."

She hurried back to the boy, the redness creeping rapidly up his face as his blush turned scarlet.

"Oh, sir, I'm so sorry. So very sorry. He wasn't watching where he was going. So careless of you, wasn't it, Bert?"

"Apologies aren't needed, Miss. If my brother and I hadn't been so involved in conversation of our own, I dare say the collision might have been avoided. Don't blame the boy."

The gentleman reached over, patting the young man on his shoulder. "That's quite a load for one so young. Are you going far?"

"No, sir. We're to wait here for my aunt. I 'spect she'll be along any minute."

"All right then. And good luck to you all."

The men tipped their hats in unison, causing Hannah to giggle as the two continued on their way.

"What fine gentlemen those were, Bertie. And lucky for you so kind as well. I couldn't wish for anything better than that you grow up to be like them."

"A gentleman, and a fine one, too? Do'ya think there's really a chance? I mean, now, with Mum and Dad dead and all."

"Oh, of course; there's always a chance. Just look at those two, will you? Coats, ties just right, hats, looking fresh as a daisy. You wouldn't know by the looks of them that it was such a hot day, now would you?"

. . .

"Did you see those three, Jack?"

"How could one help but notice them? That little girl was a real darling."

"She was indeed. And the boy reminded me of me at his age. You too, I imagine. Remember those heavy suits Mama used to make us wear? How uncomfortable – "

"And unbearably hot! He looked positively miserable. Even before bumping into us."

"But such attractive children. One really appreciates seeing children nicely attired, what with the way so many are dressing nowadays."

"It still bothers me, Charlie: seeing children like that makes one wonder where the world's headed. Tykes like that shouldn't be out on their own. Where do you suppose they're really going?"

"Don't know. But I can see the tragedy. That girl, the blush of childhood still in her face, and already mother of two."

"Oh, I don't think she could be their mother. Take a closer look. Much too young to have a boy that age. And their manners, too. She doesn't look like that type. No, surely not their mother."

"Well, I certainly hope not. The world's already too full of unwanted children. Orphanages overcrowded, children left on parsonage steps to die. And by now we've all heard the horror stories about those Orphan Trains. Tragedy indeed."

"Let's pray they really do have someone to care for them.

Buffalo doesn't need any more unwanted children."

Charlie turned for one last glimpse of the three. "I couldn't agree more."

. . .

The crowd in front of the depot came to a hushed standstill as the carriage approached the curb. It was an uncommon sight, considered rather unmannerly at that, for a woman to be driving her own team but, in this case, it was the driver herself who was the center of all attention. Her plaid dress, cinched to a waist seeming so small as to hardly exist, contrasted sharply with the muted shades on the women passersby, the plume in her hat defiantly larger than any others.

"Look at her, Margaret!"

"Hush, Bert. You know it's impolite to stare." Margaret pulled the children back, hoping to lose herself in the curious crowd. "Hannah, don't point. You know better, too."

"Margaret. Margaret Jane Trusler, is that or is that not you?"

"Aunt Sarah?"

The three edged tentatively forward.

"Oh, what sweet little children you are. You must be Bertram, of course, and here's little Hannah."

"Aunt Sarah?"

"Oh, hush, child. You mustn't call me that. Nobody here in Buffalo knows me by Sarah. Such a dull name. *Sarah?* Never. Not any more. I'm Felicity Joy, *Miss* Felicity Joy. And I've come to welcome you to Buffalo. Now hurry. Oh, dear child. Such a heavy trunk for one so small. And your bags, Margaret. Here, let me help."

Strong as well as beautiful, she easily lifted the suitcases into the back of the buggy as Bertram with an unceremonial shove got Hannah seated beside Margaret in the back.

"M-may I?" He eyed the wide seat his aunt had just left. She climbed back up, reached her arm out and helped the boy up beside her.

"Giddyap, Ballsy. Let's go, Jake. Welcome to your new home, children."

. . .

"My, God, did you see that woman! What a stunning vision!"

"What? Where? Oh – " Jack couldn't keep from chuckling. "Ah, yes, God's gift to the men of Buffalo and a curse, I fear, on all the fair wives."

"You know her?"

"It's not that large a city, Charles. That's our Felicity, Miss Joy, if you will. And *know* her? Know *who* she is – by sight, to nod and say hello to. Nothing more. Still, from what I hear, there's a lot of good in her. Even beyond the stunning looks. It's said she does much to encourage the study of music here. And, to be honest, while Buffalo is growing and, some say, prospering, it still has more than a touch of the frontier. Good music can't hurt."

"Glad to hear you say that."

"Glad to." Jack stopped momentarily to dip in a mock bow to his brother. "In fact, you touched on a subject that's been of concern to me for quite some time."

"And that being?"

"Music. Specifically, music education. I know John Larkin shares my interest."

"I'm afraid I don't catch your drift."

"Yes, I think you do. It's just such a fantastic idea – nobody's ever tried it, at least nobody I know, or Larkin for that matter either. He's already talked of bringing music into the factory – entertainment, relaxation during the employees' dinner hour, that kind of thing. Might even pick out some of our more promising young employees for lessons. Not many, mind you. Soap is our business, not music."

"Or entertainment, I trust."

"Or entertainment. But, you know, things are changing rapidly and, if they continue – God willing – well, who knows what might lie just down the line?"

"Then Larkin's soap business is doing all right? And you too, I gather?" Charlie was relieved. Going into a new business had seemed rather risky, especially with Lizzie and five little ones at home.

"Right. To both your inquiries. In fact, John has just signed the papers to buy two more lots on Seneca Street. He wants to enlarge the company as quickly as possible."

"Good God, man, that is great news! I never suspected selling soap would catch on so fast."

"Neither did I, if you want the truth. It's all because of the slingers."

"The what? I thought you said *slingers*."

"I did. The slingers."

"Don't believe I've ever heard the word."

"My educated brother? My, my now."

"Tease all you want, Jack. Only do go on, please."

"A slinger, dear brother, is the name given to a door-to-door salesman."

"A salesman I quite understand. But where does the name fit in?"

"It's a little shift on the traditional selling job. Our men are instructed to offer the lady of the house free soap."

"*Free?* Where's the profit there?"

"Turns out there's plenty. Our salesman returns a few days later, asks the lady what she tried and how she liked it. Larkin makes a good product. He's sure of that. So there are few complaints. And then our man collects for whatever she's tried and wishes to keep, selling more of course if she's interested."

Charlie turned to face his brother. "And this pays off?"

"Truly, it does. And handsomely, too. Larkin can't keep up with the demand. I imagine, though the plans for the new factories seem immense, that we'll be outgrowing them, too, in no time. In fact he's already talking of hiring women."

"Women! In a factory? Here in Buffalo?"

"Well, yes. That's his plan. Not doing the hard work of course. The men will still handle the mixing and cutting. But women – girls, really, to help with the wrapping and packaging. Heaven knows, the rate the company's going, he'll be hiring everybody he can – and training the rest to be employable."

"May such marvels never cease! For your sake, and for

Lizzie's, too. That's quite a family you have going there."

"Speaking of which here comes the trolley. Jump on, Charlie. Lizzie and the children will be waiting."

"No more eager than I to see your lovely wife and all those sweet nieces and nephews."

IV

Tuesday, June 12, 1877

Margaret was taken aback at the prospect. She'd never shared a bedroom before, never – to be honest – considered the possibility. Oh, of course, that was a requirement of married life, which she knew. But marriage – if ever – was far away from what faced her now. She had a brother and a sister to care for.

Margaret looked around the room. Whatever she had imagined this "new life" might mean, it certainly was not this. One room, three flights up, an aunt seemingly as flummoxed at the idea of having children in her house as the three felt being there.

"Here, this is where you'll sleep. Nice and sunny, don't you think? A little hot right now, I know. Oh! Let me try to get a window open. There now. That should be a little better." Felicity turned from the window to look at her three young charges. "My, you are the quiet ones. Well, so be it. Go ahead and get unpacked. There's a wardrobe in the hall and you're welcome to use the chiffonier over there. If that's all you have, should be plenty of room." She stopped at the door. "Dinner will be ready in forty-five minutes. I'll expect you downstairs then."

With a flourish and deep rustle of her taffeta skirts, Felicity departed the room. A vacuum seemed to exist where she had just stood so commandingly. It was a moment before any of the three could speak.

"Wow!" Hannah summed up their feelings precisely.

"Now what?" echoed Bert.

"Let's listen to Auntie and get unpacked. I'm sure we'll all feel better once we have our own things in place."

Packing only the necessaries and what could fit in her part of the portmanteau, Margaret looked now at the barren room and remembered the painted hobbyhorse with its mane of real horsehair. Left behind with Bert's toy soldiers. Balls. Dolls. Hannah had, of course, brought her rag doll with the curly black hair and she knew Bert had tucked in more toys than he'd been permitted. Margaret hadn't had the heart to stop him.

No sense troubling yourselves over the rest and don't ever forget – and hadn't *that* been drummed into them often enough? – how lucky they were to even have an aunt willing to take them in. Margaret shuddered as she remembered the other orphans.

The manse where they had lived while her father ministered to the Seneca Falls Presbyterians had been a large three-story relic even for its day, affording countless nooks where all three were free to be children. The congregation had been sympathetic about their plight, no one could fault them for that, but still eager to see the youngsters resettled so a new family could be moved in as quickly as possible.

She'd been mother and father these past weeks, accepting the decisions forced upon her, closing up their home, choosing the clothing they'd keep, packing, buying tickets for the train, getting them all this far.

She looked once again around their new room. Occupying the entire third story of Aunt Felicity's, it wasn't cramped. Each had his own bed and room for whatever was needed. Yet it all seemed so strange. A chair none had sat in. Drawers in the heavy chest in the corner yet to be opened.

The old anger welled. So many had died of that awful disease. Hannah still carried traces; Margaret knew the bad coughing caused the little girl pain. Why should they have been spared when both parents were taken? *God's will.* Well, she'd scream if she heard that one more time. She didn't know the god who would take three youngsters away from home and family to deposit them on the third floor of a strange house with an even stranger, for that she had already decided, Aunt Felicity Joy. She wanted only to be reunited with her friends, to share the carefree joys of yesterday and, above all, to be free of all the burdens piled on her now. How utterly stupid for her parents to die.

How many times had she told herself how unfair it all was? And what good had that done? What good at all? Forget it. What was done was done and, God certainly knew, she wasn't able to undo it. So what then? Forget it. Forget . . . as she had so many times before. That was all there was. The forgetting.

Hannah tugged on her sister's skirt. "Is it time for dinner yet?" Indeed, wonderful smells crept up the stairs to entice them.

"Almost. Let's say we go down. Maybe Aunt . . . *Felicity* can use our help."

A quick reprimand from their older sister stopped their racing down the steep stairway. Hesitating on the second floor Margaret noticed the large room she assumed was Aunt Felicity's bedroom. How much different from their own! Theirs was light and airy, the ceiling rising to a central peak, the beds white with light colored bedspreads. This room was dark. Peeking in she could see the heavily carved posts rising from the corners of a bed larger than any she had ever seen, its dark rose satin cover shimmering where tiny flecks of light reached it. A dark carpet, its pattern full of twisting vines she could almost make out, heavy draperies pulled at the windows to keep the room as still as a tomb.

The parlor on the main floor was furnished as ornately. Everything seemed so much heavier, so much darker, than the lovely things she remembered from home. And yet, amid such calm, there was a feeling of welcome, a touch of gaiety even Margaret, no matter how hard she tried, couldn't totally ignore. This was definitely not a family home – and yet people would be comfortable here.

The huge round table in the dining room was set for four. Bert and Hannah were already seated as Felicity pushed open the swinging door, carrying a tray full of steaming bowls.

"I imagine you must all be starved by now. You've had a long day. I hope you like veal cutlets and sautéed eggplant.

I wanted something special for your arrival. But *please*, don't think I'll be able to feed you this lavishly every night."

Hannah's lip quivered as she looked down at the plate Felicity set before her.

"W-W-What's . . . what's eggplant?"

Felicity stopped in mid-spoon, holding the plate she had been dishing up for Bert.

"And what's a veal?"

Her expression was one of bewilderment as she caught Margaret's eye, smiled quickly, and began to explain away her banqueting effort.

. . .

Plates cleaned at last, Hannah was allowed to carry the empty plates to the kitchen while Bert was put in charge of the goblets and silver. Margaret helped carry in the serving dishes. When everything was washed and put away, all joyfully accepted Felicity's suggestion they take a walk – it was such a lovely day after all, and certain to be cooler outside then here in this stuffy house. How about a trip to the ice cream parlor?

Later still, hands and faces cleaned again, Felicity allowed them to join her in her parlor as she stepped to the piano. Margaret delighted in her expert playing, acknowledged, to her aunt's surprise, that she had been taking lessons herself before, before . . . well, you know.

Had Margaret known that her aunt was a teacher of music? That she only accepted a few very special young ladies and gentlemen for her lessons? Perhaps tomorrow Margaret would play for her. In the meantime, did the girl really enjoy being called Margaret? Yes, of course she knew it was her name. But did she *like* it? Personally, her aunt continued, I see you as a fair Maggie. Her shy giggle was accepted as affirmation.

Later the three climbed the stairs back to their garret. Little Hannah had fallen asleep on the sofa while Bertie investigated the picture books he'd found on the lower shelf of a corner table. Maggie now found her aunt more amiable than originally suspected, especially enjoying the wonderful music her fingers made as they glided lightly across the keys.

"Marg – ooh, Maggie?"

"Yes, dear." She carefully tucked the sheets around her sister as she watched her snuggle into the big feather pillow.

"We're going to be all right here, aren't we?

"Whatever makes you ask a question like that, Hannah?"

"I mean, I know Mama and Papa won't come back but she will stay here, won't she?"

"You mean, let us stay? Why, I should suppose so. She's family now, all we've got."

"But nice family; she is, isn't she?"

"Why, yes, dear. I suppose she is."

"I like her, Auntie Fil, I mean."

In his bed Bertie started to giggle.

"She called her a man's name, didn't she?"

"I'm sure she meant no harm."

Maggie smiled down at the now-sleeping child.

Being eight, going on a very grown-up nine, Bert had many more serious issues than his four-year-old sister and insisted each had to be settled before he'd consider closing his eyes.

They talked quietly until, at last, his eyes fluttered shut, fought open one more time before he gave up the battle with a little smile.

Maggie walked to the open window, drew the curtains apart and looked out. She guessed she'd expected green lawns large as they'd played in at home. Here there was little to view but row after row of rooftops, some taller, many shorter, as far as she could see in any direction.

She couldn't change any of the things that had occurred this past month. Everything had happened so quickly but it had happened and it was over now. Fate had brought them to this stranger's house. Actually, she rather cottoned to her Aunt Felicity. The woman was different. Maggie had never seen anyone who dressed like that. Was there even a proper bonnet in the house? And those long curls, redder even than her own! She'd stand out in any crowd. Not so bad, that either. She just might teach Maggie a little, too.

The whimper shook her from her reverie.

"Mama!" the little girl cried out. Maggie hurried to her bed, stroking her head gently as the child woke.

"It's all right, Hannah. I'm here now."

Sitting up Hannah curled easily into her sister's arms.

"Here, let me hold you until you go back to sleep. Is that all right, Hannah?"

"Yes, Marg."

"You just had a bad dream."

"I know. It's all right now." She yawned deeply. "I love you, Margaret."

"And I love you, too."

Still holding the drowsy child, Maggie heard the music start below. What was that song? Did she hear others singing?

"Do you hear the music, Hannah?"

"Hmm, hmm. But I can't tell what they're saying."

"Don't worry about that. Just listen to the pretty music. Pretend they're making it just for you."

Moments later the child was sound asleep again. Maggie stretched her out in the bed and covered her lightly with the sheet.

Undressing quickly she crawled into her own bed. How could she have been unaware earlier of such overwhelming fatigue?

The music below continued, voices joining in rousing choruses, every so often punctuated by a solo baritone or soprano.

Things, she knew, could be a whole lot worse.

But oh! how she wished she could be home again, falling asleep in her own bed, in her own bedroom. The moon would be shining in the alcove window. It wasn't too late in the year for the peepers either. Just an occasional horse's clip-clop and the squeaky wheels of its carriage passing broke the sounds of singing here.

Wouldn't Mama and Papa enjoy the singing?

No use thinking of them, she reminded herself. They were gone.

This was home now.

V

Tuesday, June 12, 1877

The two men had moved to the front parlor to resume their catching up over coffee and a cigar, leaving Lizzie to clean up from dinner undisturbed – and undisturbing.

Lizzie was happy. She recognized the esteem in which each brother held the other, realizing how precious these rare get-togethers had become. God knew how little time Jack had for anything but his work – while Charlie seemed busier every time they talked: his teaching before superintending all the county schools, then studying for and the practice of law, and now his election to the Legislature. They must certainly think well of him down there in Pennsylvania.

Her fine dinner had earned even greater accolades than she'd anticipated. She'd caught the gleam in Jack's eyes and knew he felt she had truly outdone herself this time. She scraped the last ort into the garbage happily. What more could she possibly want?

She remembered how the children had shrieked in delight as Charlie walked through the front door, Grace and Anne immediately vying for his attention. The girls, already seven and eight, were becoming real young ladies, happily swirling their full skirts, eagerly (but politely, she noted) taking turns sitting on his lap, talking of last spring's school lessons and the play they anticipated for the remainder of the summer. They loved to rub their cheeks against his full whiskers, giggling at the tickle, wheedling the promise of one last kiss before being sent to bed.

And Ralph! What a change to have a little boy after the two girls. Lizzie was convinced, no matter what anybody said, that the differences in behavior began at birth. His fascination with ants! And snakes! Funny she mused, testing the water and deciding it was warm enough to add the soap, give Grace or Annie a spool of thread and they'd hie away in search of a needle and scrap of cloth. But let Ralph see the same spool and he'd have it on the floor, pushing it along with the most extraordinary variety of whooshes and bangs and booms.

And Bessie, well, she'd won Charlie over at once. Three's a delightful age for little girls.

The kettle whistled as she finished sudsing the last plate. Rinsing with the boiling water, she reached for a towel as she remembered Charlie and Jack down on the floor, creeping around with baby John. What a bunch of men she had! They'd have him walking in no time. And what good was that going to do her? Better to have him in one place where she could keep an eye on him.

She used the last of the hot water to make new coffee, quietly carrying the glistening silver pot into the parlor, not wanting to interrupt their conversation though, she couldn't help but note, it still seemed to be centered on Jack and their children. Too bad Charlie lived so far away. Coming to Buffalo was a long trek, and, states being what they were, there was little reason for a Pennsylvanian to cross into New York State. She felt happy he was here now.

As she put the food away she checked the icebox. Between the apples and the cream for cereal, there'd be enough breakfast for the girls and the men. The milkman would be by in the morning. She wrote a note and set it out with the empty bottles. The ice cart would come tomorrow afternoon. With this heat she'd be lucky if what they had now lasted until then.

Lizzie set the table for breakfast, plates and bowls out, flatware ready. The silverware from dinner had been dried to its polished finish and put safely away until the next time company came. Jack would have to help tomorrow morning for she had a hard time reaching the top shelf where they kept the china. She had beautiful things and was proud of the lovely table she presented.

Dishrags and towels were hung on the line in the backyard.

This was a part of the dinner she especially enjoyed for it signaled not only the end of the work but gave her a moment, and a quiet one all to herself, to be out of doors. She stopped to listen to the chirruping of the birds. One whistled close by. Moments later she heard the distant echo of its mate. Had they always sung so brilliantly?

The sky remained as bright a blue as it had all day. Let people say what they would about Buffalo, she had never found a lovelier place to call home.

Hunter came running over. Purring loudly he arched against her leg. She'd refill his water dish before going in for the night.

The sun still streamed through the side kitchen window. She pulled her rocking chair over closer to its rays while she mended the clothes set aside after the last laundry. She could turn a collar on Jack's shirts as well as the best of them and, after miserable years of unsteady failures, had learned to make a vest that fit him even better than the ones his mother used to send. Stockings and undergarments now frequently lasted through three or more of the children. It was simply a question of catching the holes while they were tiny. She'd been ready to put her basket away when she spied Jack's newest shirt and the button lying beside it.

Good! That done, she'd iron it in the morning so he'd have it for church on Sunday.

Ready to leave the kitchen Lizzie noticed that the African violet on the windowsill was drooping sadly. Such pretty pink blossoms it had given them through the bleakest days of winter. She always smiled at the funny little gurgle a dry plant made. It was almost as if she were listening to it drink.

She picked up Bessie's doll and John's silver rattle, a gift for the latest baby from her parents. She'd take those upstairs to the children's rooms when she went.

Walking down the hall, she stopped momentarily to listen to the men's voices. Jack gave out a hearty roar, followed immediately by Charlie's laughter. Those two never seemed to run out of subjects to talk about. Or to lack those things which caused such hilarity.

Jack looked up as she passed the parlor door.

"I thought you had gone to bed."

"Just going." She kissed Charlie on his cheek, Jack shyly on the lips, and wished both a good night as she headed for the staircase.

John and Bessie slept soundly in their cribs. Obviously the men had come up earlier to put the little ones to bed.

Ralph, decked out in sporty pajamas, played with a figure of a horse, galloping it over hills created from the tucks in his bedding. His accompanying neighs were kept down so as not to disturb his slumbering baby brother.

Annie and Grace were curled up on Grace's bed, reading their newest storybook. Those two loved to read. Charlie, teacher extraordinaire, had already praised their advanced accomplishments.

Reaching the large room she shared with Jack, Lizzie began to feel the day's fatigue as she slowly undressed, smoothing out the wrinkles as best she could before hanging each garment back in their closet. The rags waited on the dressing table for her to tie up the curls in her hair. One . . . two . . . three, there . . .eighteen . . . just a few more.

The setting sun painted the wall beside her a deep red as she finished.

She glanced at the book that lay on the table beside their bed. A riveting new novel, she'd been eager to return to its pages. She stretched out under the crisp sheet. How good it feels to lie down, she thought, to let my head sink into this soft feather pillow. Rest. Just for a moment.

It was dark and the children were sound asleep by the time Jack blew out the lights and tiptoed quietly upstairs, his passage lighted only by the single candle he carried as he climbed.

"Oh, Lizzie. You really outdid yourself today. Charlie thinks you're the world's best. You would have laughed to have heard the way he went on. Good thing you're already my wife or I'm afraid I'd have a real fight on my hands.

"Charlie always enjoys being here but you know that, don't you? The children were dears tonight, too. And that dinner!

I hope you weren't counting on using any of the scraps for another meal."

His talking continued as he finished undressing.

"Did you hear Charlie's latest plans? There's a movement to get him to run for re-election. Can you imagine?

"Yes, there was much to celebrate today.

"Lizzie?"

Only then did he realize she was not responding.

He climbed into the bed beside her, kissing her slowly on the cheek before blowing out the candle.

"Thank you, dear Lizzie."

It was far too dark for him to see the smile broadening her lips.

VI

Monday, Christmas Eve, 1877

It had been a struggle for Lizzie to get the children to St. Paul's early. She had shepherded the five into the cavernous undercroft, gratefully dropping John in the nursery provided once again this Christmas Eve. Then down the hall to the large Sabbath School room where excited youngsters were already being dressed for the pageant. Five-year-old Ralph had been upgraded to a shepherd while three-year-old Elizabeth was dancingly happy to be out of the nursery and listed as a star. Anne, of course, was serene in her knowledge that she had been selected to play the Virgin. Grace, who had been last year's Mary, would accompany her mother upstairs to the chancel. They'd have to wait for Jack and Charlie who, Lizzie knew, were enduring a struggle of their own to get the large tree up and positioned in the parlor.

After church, as soon as the children were abed, she'd make hot cocoa for the men and then join in the trimming, adding the candles at the last so that they'd be lighted first in the morning. Finally (but please, God, she prayed, don't make it *too* late), they'd place the gaily-wrapped presents beneath.

She realized with a start she had hardly noticed the decorated sanctuary as she and Grace made their way to their pew, automatically dropping to their knees in prayer.

Dear God, give me the strength I need for tonight, and tomorrow. You seem to expect so much.

Oh, dear, I am sorry, God, but I simply cannot do as much as you want. You know – you do, don't you – that it isn't for lack of trying. And now this sickness, too.

When had that begun? She couldn't remember. More to the point anyway, *why* had it begun?

Jack, kissing Grace on the tip of her curly head, and Charlie slipped into the pew beside her. Their smiles were reassurance enough that all was well at home.

She looked up to the chancel, shimmering with the white linens and candlelight and then stared at the large figure of Christ rising over the altar. Here we were, back again, to celebrate his birth.

Had Mary been sick when she carried the Christ Child? Had she ever wished – for even one moment – that she could escape her burden? How had she dealt with all the talk? Lizzie could easily sympathize for no one had to tell her how cruel people could be.

She recalled the hurting letter Mother Knapp had sent after Jack informed her of Lizzie's second pregnancy, remembering with total clarity biting her lip to fight back the hateful tears as she penned the necessarily polite response to her mother-in-law. "Yes, Mother dear," she had written, " 'one a year' is indeed a good many but, if it should be true, I think it calls for your deepest sympathy for me. Let us just hope for the best. Jack and I trust there will be provision for all."

She had shown the beginning of her letter to Jack. Was it really necessary to go on, she'd inquired. Must I be nice to her this time?

But go on she had, writing words no one could hope would become true: "While you know Jack's feelings, I especially hope you will come to stay when I am confined." She paused to take a deep gulp. "We have decided to name our first child Grace Mary," she had continued. "The Grace is a fancy name which we like, and 'Mary' is for yourself."

It was Lizzie who had been taken with the name Grace. Although Jack had favored Mary Elizabeth after his mother and grandmother, he had resigned himself to Grace, providing Lizzie promised to add the Mary. She had with reluctance.

In truth, the second pregnancy had come sooner than Lizzie would have liked but, then again, these things happened. Grace had already brought such joy that, once Jack got used to the idea, both had shared the excitement of Anne's birth. And just look at the child now! The Virgin herself.

Mother Knapp had had nothing more to say when Ralph was born, then Little Elizabeth, and now Baby John. Was it another on the way that was causing this nausea? Lizzie wished she had an answer and stopped. She'd know one way or the other soon enough.

She must have been deep in thought for Jack reached over to squeeze her hand before extending the other side of the hymnal. She caught the glimmer in his eyes – oh! those wonderful deep eyes – before smiling back. Things would be all right.

The processional was beginning. Then the prayers, the first readings and it would be time for the pageant. Lizzie silently prayed Anne would be as gracious a Mary as her sister had last year. The little ones of course, as well-rehearsed as could be hoped, were expected to be a little – hmm, *exuberant.*

She did love these Christmas pageants.

. . .

Maggie pointed to half an empty pew in the loft and Bert and Hannah scooted in before her. The first row was filled. Those seats always went fast. She hoped the little ones could see enough from back here. Not chosen to participate, they had still looked forward to the festivities with glee. Even now, they perched up on the front tip of their seats, craning so as not to miss a moment of the action.

Maggie settled back in reverie to listen to the lovely notes of the organ, grateful for all her aunt had taught her about music.

While *Aunt Sarah* had been pooh-poohed from the start, *Felicity* had remained too much for Hannah's little tongue. In spite of Bert's early giggles as he pointed out that it was a man's name, *Fil* it had stayed. Now, she thought to herself, Fil seemed downright proud of the nickname. And, come to think of it, of the children, too. And herself as well though she was certainly no longer a child.

Maggie had quickly understood that Fil had many accomplished friends and suspected it was more than mere happenstance when her aunt suggested she apply to the

Larkin Company for a job. However it had come about, Maggie couldn't imagine a better choice. Mr. Larkin was loved and respected by all his employees who, herself hardly excepted, felt convinced of his concern and respect. The hours were long for a fifteen-year-old but she knew that was true for a woman of any age. And where else could one get the available medical and cultural extras provided by Mr. Larkin? No other factory was as generous to its workers.

She had started with the other girls in the stamping room, checking each bar of soap to be sure the name was on straight and that it could be easily read.

She'd been able to put aside just enough, after paying Aunt Felicity what she could, to buy Christmas presents for them all. She'd been proud of being able to give Hannah the rabbit fur muff she wanted so badly. And hadn't Bert been pleased with his set of toy soldiers? The suit didn't excite the boy, she knew, but he was growing quickly and needed it badly. Though he'd never admit it, Maggie believed he wore it quite proudly tonight. She hadn't been as sure about Felicity but Fil had positively beamed when she unwrapped the tortoise shell comb. She'd wear it tomorrow, Christmas Day.

Maggie thought of her parents and the home she'd lost when they died. The tree would have been larger and there would have been stacks of presents for them all underneath. Still, life here wasn't bad.

There was the music. Although Fil had told them the day they arrived that she gave piano lessons, Maggie knew now that she hadn't understood the gist of those casual words. Or of the deep reverence with which Felicity regarded her piano. That she had one of the first Steinways in Buffalo was of little importance for her aunt placed no value on possessions. It was special, a lesson quickly passed on to Maggie, only because of the music it might produce.

Now she knew that Felicity Joy's playing was not only considered among the most accomplished in the city but that nobody had yet been able to rival her skills as a teacher. Maggie had progressed rapidly under her tutelage, loving every moment of it. She knew she was already as accomplished as any of Felicity's other students.

Even better was the great love of the music, the men who wrote it, and the expressions it was meant to convey, which Felicity included as a basic part of each lesson.

She knew she wasn't alone in her enthusiasm for even nice Mr. Larkin occasionally provided concerts for the help.

The sounds of the new carol brought her back to the moment.

"O, little town of Bethlehem, how still we see thee lie – "

Ah, yes, now she spotted Fil marching assuredly down the long aisle with the rest of the choir. Even here, in the darkened church, her red hair made her stand out. She wasn't like other women. She knew it. And so, she remembered, did they.

Embarrassed at first for Felicity, she had come to appreciate the great happiness surrounding her aunt. *Felicity* and *Joy* indeed.

. . .

Maggie waited expectantly with Hannah and Bert inside the front door of the church for the choir members to change and come back upstairs.

The children were squeezed by the mass exodus, too small to see as row after row of coats scurried by. Taller, Maggie enjoyed studying the faces. Tonight especially everyone seemed in a joyous mood, exchanging wishes for the merriest Christmas ever as they hurried on their way.

Taken aback, she looked up at the two men across the vestibule from her. Those were the same two Bert had run into at the depot the day they had arrived! Such handsome gentlemen, and something so kind reflected in their faces, too. Not faces one would easily forget. Now she saw the woman beside them and then the young girl, just about Bert's age she'd guess. They looked like the kind of family who would be asked to participate in the pageant. Moments later two girls and a boy reached the top of the stairway. The younger two looked unfamiliar but Maggie was almost positive that it was the older who had played the Virgin Mary. A little hard to recognize positively for she had worn a shawl over her head but, yes, she was sure it was the same girl. Now the mother excused herself as she heard the father congratulate all three children on their stellar performances.

The two young ones bubbled at the attention while Maggie watched the *Mary* react quite demurely to their praise. The men turned in unison as the returning woman reached the top of the stairs. The man who had spoken to Bert reached for the baby now in her arms, lifting it easily to his shoulder. They turned without a further word and left.

Fil and two other women reached the vestibule, deep in laughter over what Maggie could only surmise was some mishap that had occurred during the service.

Fil caught sight of the threesome and turned to take Hannah and Bert's hands before whisking all three out the door.

"How are you all feeling?" Fil was eager to know.

"Just fine," the three assured her.

"Sleepy?"

"Not too –, no, not really."

"Then let's take the long way home, shall we? We'll circle through town. Perhaps some of the stores will still have lights on their Christmas displays. If not, I doubt if you've been out too many times to enjoy the lovely gas lights on a dark evening."

After a cold beginning to December, the weather had turned surprisingly mild. Christmas Eve in fact had seemed destined to be a day of showers but now the rain had stopped and the warm weather offered a nice chance for a good walk. The lights, all agreed, were indeed beautiful especially, Bertie pointed out, when they were reflected in the large puddles standing almost everywhere.

Fil adored this child. Who else could find gold in a puddle of rain?

A group of carolers, preceded by their harmony, turned the corner and approached the foursome who stopped to listen.

"Shall we sing along?"

"Oh! Do you think we should?"

"Oh, yes, Fil. Can we?"

The quartet continued caroling as they proceeded through Buffalo's downtown.

Did Bert stumble or was it Felicity Joy who took the first steps?

Nobody really ever knew, then or in the years to come.

What none would forget, however, was the dance that followed. Swinging gaily on the lighted lamp posts, singing loudly, the aunt and her three charges pirouetted through the streets and, eventually, on to home where four very tired people were asleep as soon as heads hit pillows.

"And peace to men on earth."

VII
Spring and Summer 1878

Lizzie lost her baby as the last winds of winter hurled their fury through the streets of Buffalo.

At the same time Jack was growing more and more involved with the Larkin Company, turning into a man Lizzie hardly recognized. He was eager to talk, of course he was, as long as it involved the day-to-day problems of the Larkin Company, the irritations he found at the Larkin Company, future expansion planned for the Larkin Company or, on rarer occasions, his own ideas of the direction he'd like to see the business take as the new buildings now occupying the land John Larkin had purchased just last year were filled to capacity, the demand for their fine product continuing to increase.

He gave her what he could, both time and effort, knowing it wasn't enough, ultimately working even harder so that they might afford a girl to help in the kitchen and, he hoped, with the children as well.

While stressing it would definitely be a sacrifice, Jack had made up his mind and she'd been too weak to protest. From the start Ingrid was a whirlwind with more energy, Lizzie was certain, than she had ever possessed.

The children loved her, behaved well with her, and, lately, had even begun running to this young immigrant girl with their tears or jokes.

· · ·

In the summer of 1878, Maggie was offered a transfer to the wrapping department. Watching the soap bars being stamped was certainly an interesting way to earn a salary but wouldn't it be quieter in wrapping? Maggie accepted it as a definite first step up.

Everett Hopkins was Maggie's immediate supervisor in the wrapping department. She liked the older man at once. He seemed concerned with her welfare, easily explained her new responsibilities and introduced her to the girls in the line with whom she would be working.

She was placed next to a golden-haired young girl, a good half-head taller than herself with a lilt of a brogue, who introduced herself at once as Janie McFarland. Janie had come to Philadelphia as a young child, sailing from Ireland with her parents. Her mother had died and her father run off after bringing her to Buffalo.

The moment she saw that Janie also enjoyed the scents of glycerine and oatmeal soaps but turned up her nose in disgust at the Jet harness soap Maggie knew they'd be friends. Yes!

Janie had a simple furnished room over the corner butcher shop, clean and certainly livable, but terribly hot, especially during the torrid nights that seized Buffalo that August. Frequently the two girls would make plans to meet once supper was over to take advantage of the breezes in Delaware Park.

Jane and Maggie had of course discussed Everett Hopkins with some giggles, Jane adding her typically quirky suggestions. Still, both also admitted liking the man. If they'd work hard for their own sake, they'd do so even more for his approval.

And, while they remained oblivious to the attention their industry was attracting, others were taking full note and giving Jane and Maggie their due. And Everett Hopkins received credit for having made such a wise personnel choice, accolades that left him beaming.

VIII

Summer 1879

By Maggie's seventeenth year, 1879, life had settled into a satisfactory routine. Bert regularly proved the value of their decision to send him to school by getting top reports in every department. Hannah eagerly looked forward to summer's end when she would be going to first grade, an adventure so exciting she was already X-ing off the days on Fil's big lesson-scheduling calendar in the kitchen.

Fil continued her busy routine, teaching almost every day and hosting small parties during many evenings. Though the feelings had begun almost begrudgingly, now she doted on her three charges. It was obvious she enjoyed the children's company as much as they adored their eccentric aunt.

Life was relaxed and happy with one exception. It had been made clear on their first day at Aunt Felicity's that none of the children were to appear when her guests were present. Now it appeared even that rule could be broken for Fil invited Maggie and her friend Janie to attend her next soiree, laughing, "If you two girls can learn to pronounce *soiree* before then."

"Oh, Fil! Do you really mean it? You'd let us come to your party?"

They were not to attend as guests, Fil wasted no time making that clear to the girls. They'd be expected to pass food and refill glasses. Jane was personable and agreeable, certainly acceptable, while Fil had decided it was time for Maggie to circulate among the kind of people her aunt expected her to know.

The soiree was a merry experience for both girls. Fil trained them well so they would understand what she expected and they did not disappoint. Quiet and polite they were able to serve the guests without attracting undue attention for all knew that Fil was, and expected to remain, the center of attraction.

As the last finger sandwich was taken off Jane's tray and Maggie double-checked that each glass remained at least half filled, the girls met behind the closed kitchen door. They'd been kept so busy there'd hardly been time to exchange a word, much less share any of the thoughts that were charging through their minds.

"Oh, Jane, did you see that tall bearded man in the deep brown coat?"

"The one with the dark green four-in-hand?"

"Then you noticed him, too?"

"Not as much as your glancing so frequently at him."

"Was I really that obvious? Oh, Janie, I'll die of embarrassment. Do you think he noticed?"

"No, silly, I think your secret is quite safe. Only tell me. Who is he?"

"I don't know."

"Why – What? I don't understand."

"I have no idea who he is. A man I ran into at the train station – well, Bertie actually – and then saw again at church, Christmas Eve a year and a half ago. Can you imagine? And yet there's something about him."

"Did you smile at him?"

"I couldn't do that. What would he think of me?"

"But you do want him to notice you, don't you?"

"Yes. No. Oh, Janie, I don't know."

"Well, I do. Hmm, I imagine it's time to check those glasses anyway, before Fil starts her recital. Why don't you make a quick survey – only not too quick when you approach your mysterious stranger. Now get out there."

Shyly Maggie left the confines of the kitchen, slowly circling through the parlor to check on the contents of each guest's glass. She was able to approach her stranger, standing so close she could feel his presence as he continued to talk to the gentleman beside him. She stood quietly for moments, just waiting, unnoticed, before she returned to the kitchen.

· · ·

Summer was also a time of evenings in the park with Bert and Hannah, picnics along the Niagara River, ice cream socials, church outings and concerts.

Still in the Larkin wrapping department, both Jane and Maggie had been promoted to overseeing a division of the newer young ladies. They enjoyed teaching each newcomer, remembering only too well the initial confusion and their gratitude for the patience of Mr. Hopkins.

Everett Hopkins continued, too. On rare occasions he'd join the girls as their lunch was ending or, infrequently, stop one in the hallway to inquire of her welfare. Were they happy with their work? Was there anything he could do to make it easier? Or, perhaps, even more enjoyable?

Jane and Maggie didn't joke about him any more, quite fascinated to find themselves worthy of the interest of such a kind older man.

· · ·

Maggie regularly took her brother and sister to Sunday morning and Wednesday night services at St. Paul's, going at first because of Felicity's involvement in the choir. She soon found herself growing familiar with the structured service and, with that familiarity, welcoming a newfound sense of comfort.

Jane belonged to quite a different kind of church, a separation each respected. It was a separation not strictly enforced, however, particularly when either church offered an especially enticing social. Thus when Janie excitedly approached her with plans of a big – and, Maggie, I do mean big – Sabbath School picnic out along the Lake Erie shore the latter hardly needed further enticements of games and swimming, as much food as any would want to eat, music, and so very much to do. And of course she must bring Bert and Hannah. Jane knew there'd be many for them to play with, too.

Who knew, Maggie thought secretly, perhaps there would be dancing. And just maybe a handsome young man to dance with her as well.

Maggie was well aware of the changes taking place within as much as of her expanding interests in the world around her. Now she noticed the proud look in the eyes of a man with an attractive girl on his arm, couples strolling arm-in-arm along the boulevards. The whispers. The laughter. Often no words were exchanged. A look, a smile. That was all. She dreamed nightly that might someday be hers.

For now, however, it was enough to concentrate on the outing Jane offered.

They met at the church to climb aboard big hay wagons for the ride to the beach. Bertie at ten pretended the horses no longer interested him but Jane acknowledged his bulging eyes with a nudge to Maggie as they approached the hay wagon. He eagerly climbed aboard to get a seat as near the front as possible.

Hannah, on the other hand, found the huge snorting animals intimidating. She reached for her sister's hem and snuggled up close throughout the long ride out of town.

No matter how well Jane had prepared them, everything they encountered at the beach seemed even larger and grander. There were more people to begin with. More games and more cheering, more prizes, more laughter, more – well, so very much more – all rolled into one.

Bert and Hannah wandered off with newfound friends as the afternoon drew to a close. Jane and Maggie walked slowly, still savoring each moment, across the fairway and back toward the tables where huge pitchers of fresh lemonade waited only their request. After the first few hours, the girls had, by mutual pact, limited their consumption to one glass per visit. How wonderful, however, to know they could have all they wanted whenever they desired. They had circled the game areas and walked along the sandy beach and so now felt it respectable to return for just one more glass.

They had almost reached the food pavilion, chattering excitedly as they strolled along, when each became aware of a stunned silence. The stillness crashed like a wave across the gathered crowd.

A sudden scream sent shivers down their spines. They turned to each other mystified. Now murmurs were rising as new sound came uneasily across the field.

"What happened?"

"What happened?"

"What's that?"

"Help! Help us, please."

"Is somebody hurt?"

"She was in the water."

"She's drowned."

"Oh, my God."

"It's a little girl."

Of all the little girls present that afternoon, why did both Jane and Maggie race as fast as their long skirts would allow across the field and down to the beach where a crowd was rapidly gathering, all the time knowing whose little girl it was? Nobody made an effort to stop them as they pushed through.

Bert saw them coming, looked up from where he was kneeling and sobbed. They saw Hannah lying on the sand beside him. She looked so beautiful, so relaxed, just a tiny bit of a smile twisting the corner of her mouth. Eyes closed, serenely asleep.

No; too quiet. Too peaceful. Not the time to be asleep.

Oh, no! My God, no! No!

Maggie wasn't even aware the shrieking came from her lips.

. . .

Bert returned to school where he continued to excel. Fil still gave her parties, only less frequently, as if the spark had gone out of those, too.

By the time Maggie resumed her position in the soap-wrapping department the incident seemed forgotten.

In time the flowers stopped growing; the leaves, first bright and glowing, turned brown and fell, until at last the snows of Buffalo covered the little grave of six-year-old Hannah.

IX

September and October 1879

Lizzie's life had taken a turn and, were anyone to ask, it definitely had not been for the better. She had long ago recovered her health only to reenter a world where it wasn't needed. Any more than, she felt, was she.

The children seemed to be positively prospering under the tutelage of Ingrid who managed to have time for each one as well as to manage the kitchen.

Jack had risen quickly as the Larkin Company prospered and now enjoyed an income that permitted a more comfortable life. To Lizzie, however, it seemed merely that his money was doing everything possible to make her superfluous.

She had grown up in her mother's home and knew how a woman of leisure was expected to behave. She was well acquainted with the card parties, the ever-open novels, the teas, and all that went with being a woman of comfortable position. She had believed she was giving that up on marrying Jack and, truthfully, had done so happily.

Her mother had never seemed particularly fulfilled, nor rewarded. In fact, though not one to admit it, Lizzie had always considered her life one of waste. At the end of her time, what had she done? What had been the purpose? There were times when Lizzie did envy the idleness that must fill the minds as well as their days of such women, when she couldn't help but recognize their futile lives seemed satisfactory to them while she grew only more disillusioned with her lot.

Worse, that feeling was accompanied by a bewildering confusion for she had no idea what direction she should take.

She attended church regularly. The children always

participated in Sunday classes, from the days when the youngest terrorized the nursery till now when Grace and Anne were enthusiastically memorizing great sections of the Old Testament.

She never particularly cared for the women's groups, had joined one when they first married, and continued to do what she felt necessary but never with enthusiasm and certainly not as a volunteer.

Thus it came as a major surprise when Mrs. H. S. Bandfield came calling that Wednesday afternoon. Might she take a few of Mrs. Knapp's moments to visit? And, yes, she had come for a very special purpose, bringing a request she hoped Lizzie would entertain seriously before making a decision.

"Why, Mrs. Bandfield, I'd be most pleased to hear whatever you have to say. But first, may I ask our girl to prepare some tea?"

"Thank you, Mrs. Knapp. I'd like that very much."

. . .

"Oh, Jack, Jack! You won't believe what happened to me today."

"Why, Lizzie, I don't believe I've seen you this excited since . . . well, to be honest, I can't remember when. It does my heart good to see that smile on your face. And what enthusiasm! My girl, whatever has happened?"

"Mrs. Bandfield came to call–"

"If that's the same Mrs. Bandfield we know from church, I feel quite certain that is not the reason for your present delirium. What on earth can she have to do with it?"

"Jack, she asked if I would be the speaker for their annual tea next month."

"You? I don't believe I knew you were a speaker. A talker? Yes, of course." His happy eyes twinkled at his jest. "But a speaker?"

"Do you think I can do it? Oh, I do so want to try."

"And what shall you be speaking about? Or has Mrs. Bandfield arranged that as well?"

"Do be kind. Though, actually, she did have a topic in

mind."

"Don't keep me in suspense then. About what shall my wife be elucidating the good Episcopal women?"

"Temperance."

"*Temperance*, Lizzie? Are you planning to get that sedate bunch of old biddies out on the streets smashing the windows of our local saloons?"

"Good heavens, no. You know better than that. I know you aren't opposed to drinking any more than I but everyone's talking now about the WCTU and she thought a history of the group with . . . ahem . . . a few details about the evils of liquor would be quite appropriate for the ladies. And they aren't all old biddies. At least I hope not. I trust there'll be some younger ones there –"

"Like you, Lizzie?"

"Precisely. Like me."

· · ·

Lizzie had Jack to thank for what happened next for he realized that his mother lived in the community right next to Fredonia where the women had actually begun their crusade. Would Lizzie consider asking for the older woman's help?

She would, and she did.

For once, a letter from her mother-in-law became an object of anticipation. When it finally arrived, Lizzie knew at once that Jack's suggestion and her wait had both paid off handsomely.

It was Esther McNeil, an actual acquaintance of the senior Knapp and her brother Rufus, who had been instrumental in its start, taking her place as first president of the local, as well as the county, organizations. Mother Knapp had been delighted to call on her friend for further information.

Invited by the Baptist preacher in Fredonia, Lester Williams, over two hundred women responded to the call, giving themselves the official name of "The Women's Christian Temperance Union" before heading out to march against the local sellers of intoxicating liquors.

Mother Knapp also sent a pamphlet which covered in

gruesome detail the sins of the drunkard and the concomitant practices which accompanied such evilness: the poverty, and crime, and of course the dangers of premature death. It further told of the families left without a breadwinner as well as of the abandoned inebriates, many vicious, all definitely dissipated. It stressed the evils of those who continued to oppose all-out abolition, of those who argued that absolute abstinence was not required in most circumstances and among most good people. And at last it told of the reformed, their movements and their progress.

. . .

"So how, dear wife, did the meeting go? Tell me you were a success. You were, weren't you?"

"I was indeed! It was wonderful. I was so nervous at first. Indeed I believe my hands shook as I walked to the dais but, once I started my talk, I forgot all else but how important everything I had to say really was. And, Jack, you wouldn't believe how many came out today. I heard talk that there might have been over a hundred. Oh, what a day!"

"I'm sure we're all happy for you, Liz, eager to share your joy and your success. You'll have to tell the children all about it over dinner."

"The children? You won't be home tonight?"

"Sorry. Did I not mention it? I have a meeting with Larkin and some of the others from the company. Guess it should be a time of celebration for you, Lizzie, but I do have to get ready. Still, I know the children will be happy to hear your news."

"Yes, Jack. Of course."

She turned and began to walk away.

"Don't be like that, Liz. Come, give me a kiss before I go. That's a good girl. And oh, Liz, do tell me what's next for my promising speaker?"

"I almost forgot, what with your talking of going out."

"Then there is more?"

"There is. Oh, Jack, I must have impressed somebody, or some of the right people, for they asked me to be president of the group next year."

"*President?* My, my, we do rise quickly, don't we?"

"Don't tease. You wouldn't mind, would you? I truly don't believe I would be neglecting you, or the children, by taking on this responsibility and it would, yes, it really would, mean so very much to me. Besides I won't be taking over until next fall. That's almost a year away."

"Well, do it. Certainly. If it means that much."

"Yes, Jack, it does. I don't think I could explain if I tried, and I know you don't have the time to listen even if I did, but something wonderful happened today. It was a new feeling. I felt so alive. I felt so . . . so elated, if you will, standing in front of all those women and able to watch as they leaned forward to catch my every word. I don't know what it was. I just know how happy it made me. And if I can find that again, or keep what I had today, why, then I'd like that very, very much." She paused to look at her husband. "Do you think that's wrong?"

"Do what you want, Lizzie. I'm sure we'll manage just fine."

. . .

Lizzie was moved immediately into the ladies' vacant vice-presidential position so that she might begin learning the inner workings of the organization. With few exceptions, and she found them to be minor, she admired the women with whom she shared the board. For the first time she began to hear of the interests and concerns of other women more like her than not.

The children responded to her new gaiety with a renewed gusto of their own as her busy days were filled with a happiness that permeated their lives. If Jack was aware of the pleasant change, it went unmentioned as his activities took him further from home and family.

X

September 18, 1880

Maggie always headed straight home once her day's work was over. Fil frequently had piano students until close to their supper hour, which meant that Bert had to wait quietly upstairs until called.

It wasn't that Bert minded being alone. By now the library clerks knew him by name and frequently held out the newest Horatio Alger, Jr., so that he might be the first to devour its pages. This year he had also discovered Uncle Remus, the silliness of the animal capers capturing his imagination. Mind being alone? He couldn't imagine that.

There was a change in the schedule today, however, for Fil's students had already been told that she would be unavailable for lessons. Fil was preparing for the ball!

Maggie cooked a simple supper for herself and her brother, redded up the kitchen and then eagerly rushed up the stairs to help Fil dress.

Tonight she silently cursed her clumsy fingers as she struggled with the myriad buttons that lined the back of Fil's gown from the bustle all the way up her neck. The buttoned shoes were even more of a problem but eventually they too were properly fastened. The woman seated herself at her lowboy to begin arranging her hair. Though Felicity proudly wore it down on most occasions, wanting everyone to notice her flaming curls, tonight it would be wrapped tightly. Maggie competently inserted the last few pins, each sparkling with a different stone, certain there could be no one to rival her. She dreamed of someday emulating her aunt, practicing her walk and her self-assured mannerisms when no one was around to snicker.

Once finished at home, Maggie had made tentative arrangements to meet Janie in the park and Bert now joined his sister for the trolley ride uptown.

There was a quick exchange of greetings before Janie expressed her boredom. Nothing, absolutely nothing, of interest was going on here. How about a walk down Delaware Avenue? In fact it was such a beautiful night they might just possibly make it all the way home, saving one trolley fare for another time. Bert, ready to expend some of his extra energy, happily seconded the motion and raced off, waltzing far ahead of the two girls.

They had gone only three blocks when Jane recognized one of the other girls who worked with them in the wrapping department.

"Flo!" The carriages passing momentarily drowned out her voice so the girls hurried to meet their new friend.

Florence White had started with the Larkin Factory in April, winning everyone over with her cheery disposition. Initially Janie and Maggie had found her constant optimism annoying but before long the two had grown to admire her. More and more they were making two a threesome.

The clip-clop of the horses' hooves on the brick street grew constant as they neared the magnificent Buffalo Club. The girls stopped to watch as each of the ornate carriages pulled to the entrance and halted long enough to deposit a gentleman in white tails and his lady, her long ball gown rustling as she descended.

"Did I tell you Fil was going to the ball tonight?"

"Really?" Flo asked. "You actually know somebody *in* there?"

She laughed. "Guess I hadn't thought about it that way but, yes. Well, so do you, Janie. You know Felicity, too."

Janie and Maggie filled their friend in on as much of the life of the exciting Felicity Joy as quickly came to mind. As they ogled the stately couples, Maggie added details of her dressing while the others listened attentively.

"Oh, goodness." Maggie suddenly fell quiet.

Janie looked at her friend and then stared as two white

horses, pulling a carriage resplendent in polished red and black paint, approached the stepping-stone. The brass hardware gleamed brightly as it caught the last rays of the crimson sunset. With a woman she didn't recognize were two men, including the stranger Maggie had first seen at the depot.

Bert returned at that moment with news of his own.

Happy for the interruption, they turned from the party and continued down the avenue.

. . .

Lizzie knew there had never been a more perfect evening for a ball.

She leaned her head on Jack's shoulder, letting the clip-clop of the horses entrance her as she looked up at the full moon silhouetted against the maple leaves of late summer. Soon, she thought with a tinge of regret, they'd be changing their colors – her mother had called it putting on their party dresses – and then, before anyone quite realized, the trees would be bare again. But not yet, not tonight.

She wished there had been some way to capture the look on Jack's face when she was dressed. So filled with pride and such longing. Dear God, she had prayed, let me have this memory to treasure for the rest of my life.

The driver maneuvered the carriage in front of the Buffalo Club where a liveried groom waited to help her out onto the stepping-stone, and then down, careful now, to the solidness of the ground. Jack jumped down next to her, Charlie the last to alight.

The three climbed the stairs and entered the grand hall where a large crowd was already milling about.

Lizzie gulped as she gazed at the gathering. The men looked so resplendent in their white. Such a great improvement, she thought scanning a few of the men she recognized; too bad everyone couldn't dress all the time.

She wanted to squint, to make the cavalcade of colored dresses blur until she was reminded of the lower summer garden. If the men glowed, the women positively shimmered.

She felt confident she could hold her own with the best of them. It had been worth sacrificing those lunches. Goodness! For this she might be willing never to eat again.

Greetings were exchanged, introductions made where necessary as her dance card was filled. She wouldn't be sitting for a moment before the midnight buffet. So be it. Tomorrow there'd be time for fatigue, and time for sitting.

Jack caught her eye and smiled appreciatively.

The three became aware of the sudden hush and turned together to see the figure who had just entered. Lizzie was sure she had never seen a woman so beautiful. And this one, though apparently alone, seemed fully confident of her charms. Her entire head glimmered with the jewels positioned in the tight red twists that framed her lovely face. Her low cut silk set off a figure perfect in fullness.

"Oh, Jack! Just look at her!" Lizzie caught just a hint of the glimmer in Charlie's eye as she turned to her husband. "Who is that woman?"

"That, my dear, is Miss Felicity Joy herself."

"Oh, no! It can't be. And at a function such as this? But I thought –"

"She turns heads and she obviously creates talk, and granted she isn't like anyone else, but she is also renowned as a fine teacher of music."

"But I have heard that she rides bareback through the streets of Buffalo and that sometimes she is seen wearing –"

"Yes, and I've heard tell she has even been observed smoking a –"

"Oh, Jack, not really!"

"But for all that, Lizzie, Miss Joy is respected for her talents. I'm told some of the finest families send their children to her."

Lizzie stood spellbound as the stunning creature crossed the main hall to join a group of gentlemen eager to welcome her to their coterie.

. . .

Looking back on the evening, Lizzie knew it had turned

out even better than her best anticipations. Memories would erase the hurting feet, ultimately blistered, suffered for her vanity as she had convinced herself they could as willingly be squeezed a size smaller as was her waist.

Jack had joined her after the first set of dances. Was she hot? No, nor tired. Not yet, she smiled happily.

Would she care for a bit of punch?

Oh, Jack, it isn't, is it?

Now, Lizzie, he had consoled with a twinkle in his eye. I know the stand you took on drinking but just look around. Do you see any of those women who praised your position refusing a cup of punch this evening? We're not talking drunkards here, or the behavior found in lower class saloons. This is a party and it's meant to be festive. But of course I wouldn't force anything on you.

She glimpsed Charlie out of the corner of her eye at just that moment. Even her straight-laced brother-in-law had a cup of punch in his hand and seemed to be fully enjoying himself, engulfed in conversation with two beautiful young sisters whom Lizzie had recently met.

Lizzie was pleased to realize Jack had eyes for no one but her. He danced with her whenever he could cut in on the partner named on her dance card, solicitously brought her food and refilled her cup whenever there was a break in the music. Once they had even stolen out onto the balcony, standing alone to overlook the quiet city at their feet as the orchestra enthusiastically continued its waltzes. The moon, unobstructed now by any trees, seemed to hang in the sky for them alone. And would you just look at the stars? She eagerly picked out a few of the recognizable constellations and wished she had taken the time to learn more.

As far as Lizzie was concerned the party never ended. Jack held her tightly in the carriage, rubbing her shoulder in the manner he knew she preferred, occasionally kissing her hair where, tiara now safely in her lap, it fell gently down her back.

She had almost forgotten how much she enjoyed the feel of his body against hers, falling asleep at last tightly wrapped in his arms.

She prayed she would never forget a night as special as this.

XI

Monday, October 25, 1880

"How silly," Lizzie thought. "People install carpets, perhaps even a new davenport, but me?"

She adjusted the belt on her new dress, carefully clasped the pearls at her neck and clipped the matching earrings to her ears. She carefully pinned her hat in place, pleased that Jack, without even the smallest complaint, had agreed to the addition of the ostrich feathers.

He'd changed, too. She regretted not seeing more of him but, still, not having to worry about where the next meal, much less her quite extravagant outfit, was coming from certainly took a lot of worry out of her life.

She twirled completely, smoothed her skirt and felt ready for the Episcopal women. They could install her as they pleased.

She appreciated the warm October sunshine and the brilliantly colored leaves as the carriage took her down Delaware Avenue to the church. Would God smite her for approaching with such smugness? She prayed not. But she knew she felt darned good.

. . .

Tradition called for a Communion service before the ladies met in the undercroft for their tea and coffeecake.

There'd be no business transacted today, she knew, just get through the eating bit and then all attention would center on her and her carefully chosen committee. She had given her projected office much thought during these past eleven months. Perhaps the ladies had been a little rash – she refused to consider it an act of desperation – in choosing, as it were, one from outside the inner circle. But she knew it had been an excellent decision on their part. She would do well.

Smiling at her vice-president, Lizzie slipped into a pew beside some of the older women. Her *biddy* attitudes hadn't changed, God knew, but she had found these women influential and judgmental enough that it behooved her to stay in their good graces. She discovered she really didn't mind at all.

She had just knelt in silent prayer when a flash of dizziness coursed through her. The room spun momentarily, and then stopped again.

A quick glance showed no one else had shared the experience.

She bowed her head again.

This time the spinning didn't stop. Before she knew what was happening, nausea seized her.

"Oh, no, it couldn't –"

Lizzie bolted upright, pressing herself back into the pew as she took a series of gulps.

"Well, it makes sense," she told herself. "Nerves." She shook her head trying to clear it. "Guess it just proves I'm not as invulnerable as I wanted to believe." She smiled weakly and stood as Father Bowman entered, bowed and crossed to the high altar.

Forcing herself to concentrate on the words of the service seemed to work. It ultimately ended, Lizzie feeling weak and confused but confident in knowing whatever it was had passed.

Just tea and cake and then her installation.

She joined the women hurrying down the front stairs.

. . .

"Ingrid told me I'd find you up here, Lizzie. What happened? Did something go wrong with the installation?"

"Go wrong? Oh, goodness no . . . unless you include practically throwing up right in the middle of the tea table."

"What on earth happened?"

"I wish I knew, Jack. I can't honestly remember ever feeling so wretched, so terribly sick."

"Could it have been something you ate this morning? A case of nerves, perhaps?"

"I've gone through all those possibilities. I can't believe it could have been nerves but I know I had nothing out of the ordinary at breakfast."

"But you are better now?"

"I think I am." She raised her head. "Though if I try to get up – and I should for I know I've alarmed the children – then it starts all over again."

"Don't even think of coming downstairs. A good night's sleep will take care of everything."

"Yes, let me rest. I'm sure I'll soon be feeling as good as new."

He kissed his wife gently before leaving the darkened room, silently pulling the door closed behind him.

XII

Winter and Spring 1881

Lizzie did not improve.

Doctor Clark was called for at last.

He found his patient in distressing condition. She had grown progressively weaker until leaving her bed became a real trial. Eating was disagreeable though she attempted to sample a bite or two of each item on the trays Ingrid brought three or four times a day. And yet, as the doctor pointed out, she really was not getting any thinner.

Might she, he harrumphed, be pregnant?

Pregnant? Impossible! Well, not impossible exactly, but with symptoms like this? She felt quite experienced in the conditions of pregnancy, had in fact suffered minor nausea with the first child or two. But certainly, Doctor, nothing like this. If this was what pregnancy felt like she was certain the human race would have ended within a generation. Two, at the very most.

He really couldn't imagine what else might be affecting Lizzie, he whispered to Jack once the men had descended the stairs to the parlor. Keep an eye on her and do, of course, call me if she worsens.

. . .

By early December Lizzie was back on her feet, the doctor having been proved right once again. Mornings remained a nightmare and on many days she wished she could avoid even the mention of food, much less its consumption, but she ate as she could and slowly regained her strength.

With regret, Lizzie resigned the presidency of the ladies'

guild without attending a single meeting as its directing officer.

. . .

The Episcopal women were forgotten as the house was decorated for Christmas. The children had lines to learn for their individual school programs while the younger ones were assured roles in the pageant at St. Paul's. She regretted not having a candidate for the Virgin this year, remembered her condition with a tinge of irony, and wondered just how many more Mary's after Bessie she was destined to produce.

Charlie remained so involved as chairman of Pennsylvania's Judiciary Committee that he was unable to join them for the Holidays. He regretted not sharing the special time, especially with the children, but would take Mother Knapp and Uncle Rufus to his home so they might experience a quiet day together.

Ingrid and the older girls helped with the preparation of food, ever careful not to deviate from Lizzie's recipes and detailed instructions.

The pain doubled her over as she stood to walk to the dinner table. She was as white as the proverbial ghost by the time the others turned, silently questioning why she was so slow in joining them.

Jack helped her upstairs and sent for the doctor. By the time he arrived a frightened Lizzie reported that she had begun bleeding. Not a lot, mind you, but still . . .

This time she was ordered to remain in bed.

. . .

Anticipating spring was a boon to them all. The sunny days raised spirits that fell again as sleet returned, seemingly relentless but finally, as the weeks slowly passed, ushering in the riotous colors of spring. The early flowers, the crocuses and daffodils, then the forsythia, followed soon after by the magnificent fruit blossoms and, her favorite, the scentful lilies-of-the-valley, now appeared everywhere.

Lizzie was allowed to sit by the opened window where

she could enjoy the fresh breezes and songs of the returning birds.

Her back ached terribly. She felt so huge that walking required major effort as every step signaled jolts of pain that surged through her well-fatigued body.

She pressed the doctor for a more definite explanation. What was happening? And why? Certainly she had never gone through anything like this before, of that she was absolutely positive.

"Perhaps not," he said, trying to soothe as best he could. "But we are, well, my dear . . . you know, a little older now."

As the period of her confinement neared its expected end, the baby shifted position until it pressed against her ribs. Tiny amounts of food caused a reaction similar to a gorging. And, no matter how hard she stretched, the child seemed to fill every inch she was able to make. Please, God, how much longer?

XIII

June 1881

It was not what Lizzie had expected.

She was crossing the parlor when the cramps hit. Why did she have to suffer terrible backaches now, too?

Jack found her curled in a ball, whimpering quietly.

"Is it time, dear?"

"No, not yet though I wish it were. I've had terrible cramps and now these excruciating backaches. What do you think they are?"

At that moment she was seized again in pain, her face contorting as she writhed.

"Your back again?"

"Yes."

"What can I do?"

"Please, just sit here with me. Having you near is comfort."

But the pain engulfed her again.

"That does it." Jack stood quickly, a look of determination flashing across his face. "Let me send for the midwife."

"Yes. Something. Somebody. Anything. But don't forget: she insists that the doctor come as well." She grimaced again and paused. "I never did understand that. I mean, she delivered all the others and never made such a demand. But that's what she said."

"I remember. I'll send for both right away."

. . .

Experience, even the presence of both the midwife and their family doctor, mattered little to Lizzie as the pains grew stronger and steadier. She felt her resentment welling as she behaved, and was treated, as a tyro. Weren't all birthing procedures the same? How humiliating to actually have them tie her arms to the bedposts!

Dear God, how much longer?

. . .

Much, as it turned out.

Lizzie was exhausted by the time the ordeal finally passed. She paid scant attention to the words of the midwife until she saw her broad smile and accepted the cleaned infant in her arms.

"Oh, Mrs. Knapp. Just look at 'im, will you? In all my times I have never seen such a perfect baby. And, mark you, I'm not just a'sayin' that 'cause of all the trouble you had. Just you look at 'im, such a sweet little boy you got there."

Lizzie looked down at the sleeping child. All their children had been exceptional, but yes, there was something special about this one. Just a touch of down across his head, little fingers perfectly formed, curled now in slumber. She had seen his eyes when he had first cried, a deep perfect blue. Special indeed.

She smiled groggily at Jack as he leaned over to kiss her.

"Good work there, Liz. How do you feel now?"

"So sleepy . . . tired . . . And, Jack, I'm so very happy."

As she handed the baby to his waiting father another cramp surged explosively through her body. The midwife and doctor had been cleaning their tools when she cried out. The startled question they silently exchanged did nothing to placate a now thoroughly frightened Jack.

Quickly unpacking the two experts hurried back to the mother's side. Lizzie was wide awake, and groaning.

"What is it? What's the matter?"

"What's happening?"

"Try to relax, Lizzie. We need to see what's going on."

Further examination was unnecessary for it was obvious that Lizzie was once again in labor. She was bleeding heavily by the time her second son was delivered.

Her attendants finished their work and felt it safe to leave when she slept at last, the midwife promising to return as soon as she had settled her own family. Did the others realize, she wondered, that this had all been going on for some thirty-four hours?

Jack sat with Lizzie, holding her hand as she dozed. He was hardly aware of the return of the midwife, or, later, her departure after the doctor had come to replace her. One of the babies cried for a while but Jack hardly heard it. He knew only that the woman had fussed a bit and then it had grown silent again.

In time each of the babies was brought to Lizzie for nourishment. Though she fed them, Jack wasn't sure she was enough awake to register what was going on.

It was two days before she blinked, opened her eyes, looked around at the doctor who stood patiently waiting beside her husband.

"You gave us quite a scare there, girl." Doctor Clark wiped her moist brow before checking her pulse. "Still a little high but I believe you'll be all right now. How do you feel?"

"Better. Weak. Tired." She began to smile before the other thought caused her face to reflect her perplexity. "My babies? Are they –?"

"Quite all right, my dear. Both seem to be in robust health, though . . . well . . ."

His manner alarmed her. "What do you mean? What's the matter?"

"Here. I'll let you see for yourself. Just promise you won't get excited."

Lizzie grew frightened as she waited for the doctor to bring the first child. What was she worrying for? He was as beautiful, even more so were that possible than when she had held him earlier. He opened his blue eyes, looked right into hers and reached for her finger, holding it tightly in his tiny grasp. What then?

The doctor took the little boy from her and handed him to Jack. He crossed to the cradle to pick up the second.

Lizzie's gasp was predictable, Jack had expected that, as

she reached for the second baby. Head covered in dark black curls, his face was deeply marred by purplish lines. His angry eyes sought hers accusingly as he began to howl.

Lizzie leaned down and kissed his forehead, stroking his head until he quieted. Then she reached for a breast. He suckled hungrily.

XIV

Autumn 1880 to Autumn 1881

Seeing the men and women dressed in their fanciest finery had had a scintillating and unexpectedly long-term effect on Maggie and her friends. Whereas before, the girls had talked abstractedly of the *someday* partners they most earnestly hoped for, now dashing men entered dreams which soon became a part of their everyday lives and conversations. Eighteen was, after all, not too early to be thinking of courtship and then, perhaps, the exciting prospect of marriage itself.

Meetings during breaks at the factory were more often than not comprised of whispers, silly sideways glances, and the tittering so common among nervous ladies of a certain young age.

Janie dreamed of a tall slender man with a curving mustache and mischievous eyes. Flo's imaginary suitors changed with the day. Only Maggie, who perhaps dreamed most ardently of all, was never quite able to picture the man she felt certain would one day enter her life. Did they all hope for exactly the same, she wondered, as she looked down line after line of earnest young women, all laboring to guarantee the very best of soaps for the Larkin Company?

Maggie had hours, however, when she would take leave of her friends, watching them traipse jokingly off in hopes of further adventure. She never regretted these times for they were the moments when Fil had granted her permission to use the parlor Steinway. Fil still corrected and encouraged though most of the time found it quite unnecessary. Maggie loved her music and, while she could never have explained it, found a comfort and peace through the piano that pulled her back over and over again.

It was at the keyboard where she was able to lose all cares and concerns common to a young lady of that period, much less the emotional burdens of one who had suffered three such dreadful losses. Lost in a reverie, Maggie could forget.

So it was that Maggie eagerly took advantage of one Saturday when the house sat silent to study a new piece her aunt had set aside for her. It meant, she knew, passing up the Thanksgiving Social at Janie's church. Flo had enthusiastically accompanied their friend and, while they had begged Maggie to join them, the two had long ago resigned themselves to understanding there were some things that meant more to her than camaraderie.

It was a good party. Flo found many dashing young men who seemed delighted with her company. Arthur brought punch while David carried back a napkin filled with frosted cookies. Jeffrey made jokes and Alan caught her eye in a secretive smile that captured her attention until, shyly, she turned away. Janie, watching her friend across the large Sabbath School room, hardly noticed the shy man nervously approaching her.

Vernon Miller was new to Buffalo, having arrived just five months before. He had studied to become a teacher and now proudly had three classes of his own at Buffalo's Central School. Attracted by his earnestness, Janie liked him at once. Flo, still surrounded by a pack of eager young swains, hardly noticed when her friend left with the stranger.

. . .

"Oh, Janie, no! Tell me what happened." She turned from the one girl to the other. "Flo, what's he like?"

"I hate to admit it, Maggie, but I was having such a good time I really paid no attention to Janie. It's all your own fault for not coming."

"I'm beginning to think you're right. All right now, Miss Jane. One cannot, does not, fall in love overnight. So just who is this man who has stolen your attentions, if not your mind? What does he look like? What does he do? Tell us about him. Everything."

"He's a teacher. He came to Buffalo to teach in the primary school. His family is from Erie and he expects he'll probably go back there once he gets more experience in his field. He's tall, well, taller than I, has brownish hair, brown – no, greenish eyes, if you must know, and freckles."

"Freckles!"

"The most adorable little freckles. He's smart, it's wonderful just to talk with him, and he's funny – I can't remember laughing so much, or feeling so relaxed right away with a stranger. Only of course he isn't a stranger."

"So, you're going to see him again?"

"Did you let him kiss you?"

"Of course. No, I mean . . . Oh, you two! No, he didn't kiss me and, yes, I'm going to see him again. We've already made plans to meet when I get out of work next Saturday."

. . .

By now Everett had become a popular addition to their group. He never singled out one girl or showed any favoritism except to Bert who found the older man congenial while Everett seemed downright flattered with the attentions of the growing boy.

When Vernon returned to Erie for the Christmas holidays, Jane once more joined her friends and, often now, Everett and Bert as well. The laughter was there but it wasn't the same at all and each knew it.

The carols were as sweet, the snowflakes as large, but Janie's heart had been taken far away. Four admired a carriage passing by. Janie wondered how Vernon would react had he been there beside her. Maggie and Flo ogled the canned fruits and vegetables being introduced at the grocers but only Janie placed them in the cupboard of her dreams. Yes, it was a nice time, just not the same and she, for one, would be happy to see the holidays end and her teacher return. Erie seemed every bit as distant as New York City. There, they said, the streets were being lit now by electricity. The only light she sought was in Vernon's eyes.

By the time he did return Maggie and Flo were more than

ready to pass their old friend back to her swain. Janie was much too besotted to be a good listener and, heaven knew, whatever she had to say was now reserved for Vernon.

. . .

Meanwhile growth was taking place so quickly at the Larkin Company that the factory was forced to run day and night, necessitating the hiring and training of many more employees. Word filtered down that yet another building might have to be erected, simply to keep up with demand.

Newspaper advertising had replaced the days of the door-to-door salesmen with mail now handling the bulk of the orders and the shipping of the various products.

Everett wasn't sure if the idea originated with him or if it had grown out of a mutual discussion of ways to promote the various soaps. Bert, a natural collector, might even have set things in motion. But it was Everett who was given credit and put in charge of the development of premiums: prizes or presents to be given free as added incentives to buy Larkin products.

Soon each order was shipped with a set of "chromo cards," large picture cards which the customer was encouraged to believe were worthy of collection. The idea became popular so rapidly that in a short time the same cards were also offered for sale.

. . .

Maggie and Flo were not surprised when Janie announced her engagement soon after Vernon's return.

The wedding took place in her pastor's study on June eighteenth. Janie wore the dress she had made, the girls agreeing it was as lovely as any they had seen in the fancy advertisements.

Bert, ex-officio brother, argued he could give the bride away without grinning, an offer politely refused by Pastor Johnsen. Everett stood beside Vernon as his best man.

Flo's mind swirled with thoughts of socks to mend and collars to turn and no more parties to attend and hoped that, if she married at all, that day of reckoning would be quite far off. She thoroughly enjoyed the attentions she was garnering from any number of attentive young men. She'd let as many as wished come a'calling. Time later for picking just one.

Maggie found herself thinking of Everett, remembering how at first she had made fun of the older man. She had found him stodgy then, stuffy even. And of a stoutness which belied any hopes of attraction.

It was his impeccable manners that had first attracted her. He treated her like a proper lady and she was happy to respond in kind. Strange, she thought now, just how gentle a face he had. Why hadn't that been more obvious at the beginning?

She pictured herself in her wedding dress, standing before a minister up there.

Her gown would surely be longer, floor length at least and with a flowing train of course. Nothing wrong with Janie's. It looked especially nice on her, suitable for the occasion. But Maggie's wedding – well, that would require everything but liveried footmen. Maybe them too. Dreams never hurt. She reached up to touch the gold chain around her neck, a birthday gift from Fil. One of these years that would be replaced for she must wear pearls on her wedding day. Pearls, a gift from her bridegroom, from Everett.

No!

What was she thinking? That would never do. He was kind, yes. Bert doted on him, yes. But he was an old man. It was romantic excitement she wanted. She would wait till she found it. She wasn't looking for comfort.

Friendship? She and her brother could both use a friend. Yes, she'd like that, especially now that Janie was married. Maggie resolved to keep Everett in their lives as long as he wished.

She feared he was reading her thoughts for at that moment Everett turned to Maggie, caught her eye, and winked. She smiled back and felt happy.

. . .

Flo and Maggie eagerly awaited Janie's return, determined

to hear the details of her honeymoon. They might have continued to pester their friend more doggedly had not the news from Washington overtaken all local concerns.

James Garfield, newly elected President of the United States, had been shot in a Washington train station. Only Everett could vote, wavering until the very end before choosing Garfield with difficulty over Hancock, a jaunty hero of the War but without political experience. His man had been in office only a few months when the shooting occurred. Would he, the country asked, be given the chance to realize the potential all hoped lay within him?

Daily news releases covered his medical progress and setbacks until the country came to a standstill, waiting through July to see which way things would be resolved.

By mid-August the question, and the country, still hung in the balance.

Janie felt the same pressures in her own life, saying nothing to her friends as July passed and they entered the hot weeks of August, while she waited for Vernon to weigh the pros and cons and come to his own decision. She knew he cared very much for her feelings but, at the same time, her friendships could not be the deciding factor in his future.

Once the decision was made, she yet hesitated to tell her friends. She knew she had promised them. But now there was Vernon.

. . .

Vernon departed at the end of August, going ahead to Erie to get a place for Janie and him to live. His description of the upstairs half of the little house he found excited them all. There was even a second sleeping room, a room for visitors if, she whispered blushingly, they came soon.

She would take the train to join her husband after church on September 18th.

Maggie and Flo reported for work on the morning of the nineteenth. Knowing Janie was going, they had felt themselves steeled for the effects of her absence. Now neither could dismiss the new emptiness she experienced.

The country grieved the death of President Garfield. The two friends hardly noticed.

XV

Autumn 1881

The twins were baptized on a humid Friday evening in August. The Bishop had finally given in to the wishes of Lizzie and, particularly, Jack and agreed to have the ceremony performed privately, without publicity or fuss.

While there had been much debate about what to name the two boys, their parents had finally settled on *James* and *Abram* to honor the president who still clung feebly to life after being attacked by his crazed assassin.

Since he had been born first, the fair-haired child became *James*. His brother, no less theirs but more difficult to accept, was christened *Abram*.

James, being such a pleasant child, easily captured the hearts of all who saw him. It seemed as if his happiness were downright contagious. Then there was Abram.

In the beginning Lizzie had insisted on caring for the babies herself but, when the demands finally became overwhelming, Jack advertised for yet another girl to take over the care of the twins. None stayed more than a week before departing, always with the sincerest apologies: Of course, she had come with experience and believed herself capable of caring for any child. And that little James, well, you know what a sweet little boy he is. But it's Abram. I'm sorry, Mr. Knapp, and you too, Mrs. Knapp, but that boy's a real devil. You'll find no one who can handle him.

Lizzie always argued back. The child's not yet four months old, still just a wee small babe, hardly a devil at all. But there was nothing that would make any of them stay.

Doctor Clark continued to check on them frequently as he had right from the beginning. There was no reason for the differences, certainly none he could discover. Just a difference in personalities. One sees it all the time. Just be patient, you and the mister, and we'll hope the little one outgrows it soon.

In truth he was more concerned about the missus. He had seen women die after birthings less difficult than hers. She was, he felt and he said so, lucky just to be alive. It wasn't her fault the babes were the way they were, any more than it was in her power to change things. Leave 'em to the nurse, ma'am, and don't worry, we'll find you one who'll stay. What you need is rest.

Finally, Jack heard about, interviewed, and hired Mrs. Backstrom on the spot. A strong solid woman – he guessed her to be in her late forties, perhaps early fifties – she entered the house, soothed Lizzie, and took both boys under her wing.

Lizzie slept well for the first time in months, slept for many hours without the least stirring and, better yet, with none of the dreams that had continued to alarm her.

The other children returned now to her nurturing arms, happy to want to believe things were at last getting back to the way things were supposed to be.

Whatever normalcy was, to whatever degree the Knapp home was returning to it, only Jack failed to change. He had found the challenges of the latest Larkin growth intoxicating, enjoying the late hours and the work.

He'd be home more if he could but it wasn't possible. Not now, at least.

XVI
Autumn 1881

Maggie was surprised how readily she was able to accept Janie's absence from her life. She and Flo had liked each other when they were a threesome and now enjoyed each other's company as a duo. Bert was always welcome to tag along which he chose to do at unpredictable times. Mr. Hopkins continued to keep a close eye on them, enjoying their company when he could.

Both girls now readily admitted to liking the older man and would often find a reason to include him in their plans for a concert in the park or, once the weather turned cooler, an inexpensive night at the theatre.

It was on one of the evenings when Maggie had turned down Felicity's invitation to attend her soiree that the accident occurred. She and Flo had decided to go instead to a new play at St. Stephen's Hall. At the last minute the girls persuaded Everett Hopkins to join them though, Flo noticed, that never required much persuading on Maggie's part.

While they always enjoyed going to the theatre, it was as much to watch the audience as the drama. Tonight, however, all three found themselves riveted to the action onstage. The memory of the breathtaking experience remained overwhelming, a feeling each seemed reluctant to relinquish.

In no hurry to part, all agreed to go to the fountain for a soda afterwards. They had taken the back booth, Maggie remembered, eagerly talking over every word, every nuance, and every step of the production. Other customers undoubtedly came, were waited on and served, and went their ways while the three continued their earnest conversation. It wasn't until the clerk, refilling their water glasses yet again, reminded them he'd be closing in minutes that they realized how much time had passed. They finished quickly and said their final good-byes outside the shop as the lights within were extinguished one by one. At last the three separated and headed each his own way toward home.

. . .

Maggie heard the bells of the fire carriages. Still reveling in her magical night, she barely registered the distress ahead as she continued her slow path homeward.

She turned onto the street where they lived, she and Bertie with Felicity Joy. No! What were all those carriages doing up there? How close they were to her aunt's! The soiree should have ended quite some time ago. Would Felicity be upset at the lateness of her arrival?

Just listen to all those snorting horses. Such confusion. What was going on? It had to be a fire. But where? My God, it was right next to Felicity's house!

Maggie began to run. No! It mustn't be. She just wasn't seeing straight. For what she thought she saw, though obviously it was a mistake, her eyes playing tricks on her, were flames shooting right from the rear of Felicity's house itself.

No! Bert! Where was Bert? And Felicity? Where had her aunt gone?

Yes, of course, that was it. Felicity would have taken Bert to a neighbor's, or maybe a friend's, someplace where he'd be safe, where he could go back to sleep without worry. It would be just like her aunt to think of that.

She vaguely became aware of men pulling her back, telling her she couldn't go there. Were they so silly they thought she would voluntarily enter a burning house? They were fighting her. She had to fight, to scratch, to protect herself. Why were they struggling so? One – he must have been stronger than the others – carried her across the street, and laid her down, covering her with a blanket. When had it begun to snow?

In time somebody, she remembered hearing the deep voice, noting its pleasant timbre that soothed in spite of her wanting to struggle, began talking to her. Her name? Where she lived?

Silly questions! Couldn't they wait? Aunt Fil would find her any minute now. Certainly once Bertie was settled someplace safe, she'd come back for Maggie.

. . .

The next thing Maggie remembered was the whiteness. She was lying in a white bed. There were white walls, white sheets, white even outside all those windows. Why was she here?

A woman dressed in white brought water. Was there a pill? Medicine, too? And what was it she had said to her? Nothing important. Sleep. Yes, sleep.

Maggie slept.

. . .

How had she gotten burned? She had seen a house in flames but she hadn't been in it. She remembered now: the theatre, Flo and Everett, the fountain, even her ice cream soda. Then, oh. Yes, now she remembered. The walk home. The orange sky up ahead. Then the flames.

Maggie slept again.

. . .

The next time she woke everything was different. There was no white beyond the foot of her bed. She could see a lantern burning at the far end of the ward but felt surrounded by the dark.

She hardly remembered crying out. The sound came from somewhere, certainly not her.

A nurse, the white again, hurried in, shoes scuffling on the hard floor, her kerosene lamp flickering as she came quickly toward the bed.

She soothingly massaged Maggie's forehead, mumbled something and hurried away again.

In a short time the lantern returned, this time bringing two other figures. The tall man was a stranger, but the smaller one – Bert!

"Oh, Maggie, Maggie. I've been so afraid for you. Are you

all right, Sis?"

The tall man stepped forward. He was silhouetted by the lantern behind him so that Maggie could make out no features.

"It's all right, Maggie. Don't worry about those things now. We want you up and out of here as good as new –"

"And as soon as possible. Oh, please, Sis. We've been so frightened."

"*We?* But where is Fil? Why isn't she with you? Where's Felicity, Bert? I thought she'd come with you. She did, didn't she? Where is she?

"Bert?"

. . .

The truth was, and had been, that Felicity had died, immediately as near as anyone could reckon, when the large stove in the kitchen exploded. Later, given time for reflection, Maggie imagined that she had set water on to boil, preparing to wash the dishes after the last of her guests had left, when something had gone wrong. Stoves were notorious for being unreliable.

Bert, sleeping upstairs, had awakened at the explosion and rushed down the stairway which led him to the front of the house. He had tried to reach his aunt, assuming rightly that she was stranded in the back, but had been pushed away by the ferocity of the heat and the flames. The first firemen had found him sitting on the curb, crying inconsolably. At last he had been able to tell them where and what, as near as he could suppose, had happened.

Felicity's body was recovered the following morning.

. . .

Another time. Another funeral. Another coffin, side by side with the first in Forest Lawn Cemetery. Maggie and Bert promised to come regularly, bringing flowers once spring came, two bouquets from now on instead of one.

. . .

"I'm sorry, Miss Trusler, but that's the way it is. We can give you till the end of the week to get your things out."

Maggie hadn't believed there could be any further shocks.

Now she was being told Aunt Felicity's home hadn't belonged to Aunt Felicity at all. She lived there at the will and whim of one of the gentlemen who frequented her parties. Maggie never heard a name and didn't ask.

Everything in their home apparently belonged to this unknown stranger. The Steinway she loved so? That had never been Felicity's. And the chinoiserie box which had to be her second most prized possession? A gift to her aunt, of course, but it too must stay with the house.

Maggie was told that the owner had expressed deep gratitude that the fire had been extinguished so quickly. The kitchen would have to be rebuilt from the ground up but it had been added on after the erection of the original house, very old homes having no reason to want the cooking area inside, and the smoke damage to the adjoining rooms could be eliminated with a good scrubbing. Most of the better possessions, the Steinway, the Chinese chest, even the dishes and beaded lamps, had been saved and would be returned to their owner.

. . .

Flo found a room near hers for Maggie and Bert. They moved in before the weekend had passed.

Worried for their welfare but knowing he could do little, Everett Hopkins remained silent once a little quiet checking supported Flo's claims that the place was safe and comparatively clean.

It would have to do.

. . .

Before 1881 ended, Bert turned twelve, old enough he knew to be out on his own.

This time Hopkins was able to help, securing him a clerking position with an up-and-coming company in Omaha.

Nebraska. And, yes, quite far away, but the job has opportunities with it, Maggie, and it's a good position for such a bright boy. You'll have to let him go.

. . .

Bert eagerly packed his bags, thanked his friend for his help and extracted a promise that the older man would protect Maggie, kissed her devotedly and waved from the train until he could no longer see his sister, Everett, or their friend Flo.

He thought again of the orphans from an earlier time who had taken this train, also going west.

He was grateful for the job that awaited him and eager to prove his mettle.

XVII

April 1882

The publication in 1882 of *Treasure Island* made Robert L. Stevenson, at least momentarily, the most important man in young Bert's life. Settled now in Omaha, he discovered he enjoyed the challenges of his job even more than he had liked his public schooling. He approached the end of his twelfth year with a growing understanding that it was the test, and its successful accomplishment, that gave life both its excitement and reward.

He valued discoveries made on the banks of the Missouri as he explored the growing city. This was the wild frontier and he savored its bite.

Maggie, meanwhile, returned to her work with a new gusto. Where Everett and Flo would have expected her to grieve, she instead appeared vigorous and happy. Too happy, they sadly agreed.

. . .

Everett always thought it was his idea. Flo was never too certain who thought of it first but both agreed that one had mentioned that perhaps Maggie might miss her music.

Of course! But, each argued, she had only a room now, and third floor up at that. Even if they could afford a piano, and each knew that that was out of the question, there was no place – physically – for one in Maggie's life.

Or was there? . . Could they? . .

"Flo, don't you dare say a word," Everett cautioned. As if she'd say anything even if she could, even if she knew what he was talking about. "Let me see what I can do."

. . .

So it happened that John Larkin agreed that as long as there was a piano in the auditorium at the factory, and acknowledging it was hardly ever used – admittedly a bad thing for both piano and all concerned – that he'd heartily accept Everett's suggestion to give Maggie unlimited access to their Steinway and that, if – or whenever – she wished, the company would be pleased to grant a stipend to cover the full cost of her lessons. If, of course, the young woman was truly as talented as Mr. Hopkins averred.

Except in the most fleeting of moments, Maggie had accepted the death of her music as serenely as that of her sister and her aunt. Losses seemed an inevitable part of her life. Music was just one more.

A chance to play again? And to study? And with the greatest the area had to offer? For that was exactly what John Larkin, by now accustomed to accepting nothing less than the very best, offered her before week's end.

Maggie must study privately with Peter Kubrick.

. . .

Maggie stood speechless as a beaming Everett relayed the news.

"*Doctor* Kubrick? But I thought you said piano."

"He is a pianist, Maggie. And a Doctor of Music as well. Mr. Larkin was told he's the greatest pianist residing in Buffalo. I'd think you'd be pleased."

"Pleased? I simply don't know what to say. You must thank Mr. Larkin. No, that would be rude, wouldn't it? I must thank him myself. But lessons? And a piano on which to practice? I never dreamed – I never thought – oh, dear, Everett, I don't even know what I do mean."

He laughed gently. "Don't worry, I do."

"But –"

"No, quiet for a moment. Please, Maggie. I know you'll thank Mr. Larkin in due time. The best gift you can give us here at the Factory is your music. You must play for them – quiet, now – once you feel ready. Nobody wants to rush you.

Now, would you like me to contact Dr. Kubrick to arrange your first lesson?"

Maggie immediately agreed. Everett reported back that the teacher would be waiting the following Monday at seven o'clock.

. . .

Knowing sleep was more important than ever, that she must be alert for her first lesson, Maggie spent a sleepless Sunday night, tossing and turning as fears and doubts continued to cascade through her troubled mind.

What will he expect of me? Will I be good enough for him? What if I make a fool of myself? What if he sees me as no more than a child of average talent? What if he refuses to accept me after our first lesson?

She sat up in bed. Would he know how badly she wanted to learn, *really* learn? Oh! What if he didn't like *her*?

She stretched out again, pulling the sheet up to her chin, turning yet again in search of a comfortable – a sleep-worthy – position.

The sheet flew down again as her eyes widened in the dark. Or what if I don't like him? Will he be nice to me? Will he be demanding? I don't have that many hours when I can practice. What if it isn't enough?

Maybe he's an old man.

Maggie was on her feet now.

Yes, a *doctor*, probably very old – teetery, perhaps. What if he should drop dead during one of the lessons?

She pulled the curtain back from her window. Will he speak English? *Herr Doktor* sounds so awfully foreign. A heavy accent most likely. What if I can't understand what he's telling me?

Oh, dear, whatever shall I do?

It was light before an exhausted Maggie slept – a little – at last.

. . .

Her hands were shaking as she approached Doctor

Kubrick's studio. As she waited in his anteroom, Maggie could see at once that, unlike Fil who had always wanted her students to feel comfortable, the Doktor had no interest in his students' feelings. This dark room couldn't have been less homelike.

Maggie's shudder was interrupted by the opening of a door. A well-groomed man, about thirty years her senior, said something over his shoulder, solidly shut the door behind him, and hurried past her and out without the least acknowledgment that anyone sat in the room.

Unnerved further, the gloom began to settle over her again when the studio door opened another time. Though silhouetted by the light behind him, he was obviously tall and quite slender with a halo of fuzzy hair surrounding his shadowed face.

"Miss Trusler? Come in please."

Maggie rose quickly to follow the man into the studio.

XVIII

Summer 1882

James and Abram spoke only in babble-talk as their first birthdays approached. It was obvious that the twins clearly understood each other, equally certain that James seldom liked what he deciphered of Abram's rages.

The older girls had immediately taken James into their hearts, proud of their beautiful baby brother. And just look how good he was! Abram . . . well, it was just that Abram had a temper. Though the doctor had long since ruled out any medical cause for his distressing behavior, Lizzie held firmly to the belief that he would eventually outgrow it as he was the fading markings on his face.

Meanwhile, she struggled with her own fears. Was the child because of a fault of hers? Had she done something wrong? She thought of her smugness when so easily elevated by the Episcopal churchwomen. She had seldom returned since her ignoble retreat. Was God punishing her for that? Or had it been because of her pride at the ball? Would a humble mien have made things better? But could it really be wrong to have felt so lovely, so beamingly proud of her figure, and of Jack? Could that have been the . . . the when?

Good God, what had she done to be punished so? How could she hope to make amends – how could He expect it? – when she didn't know what her fault had been?

. . .

To everyone's surprise, Mrs. Backstrom remained, quickly winning over even the recalcitrant Abram.

At a party for the boys' first birthday, a family affair

with ice cream and cake, Abram embarrassed all with his demands. James would be allowed no toys; every present must go to – and be opened by – his brother. James was given a red sweater while Abram got a blue one. By the end of the afternoon, Abram, proudly sporting his blue in spite of the June heat, had managed to rip his brother's to tatters. James never cried. His astonished family watched as he quietly rose and toddled silently from the nursery, the older girls hurrying after to comfort.

"God, Lizzie, how much more of this do you expect us to put up with?"

"Jack, please. You act as if you think it were something I could control."

"I'm not asking you to control that child. I don't think there's a soul on the face of the earth capable of that. And I don't know what's the matter with him, or what's to become of him for that matter. But, Lizzie, oh, God! No, don't cry now. Just listen. Please. James and Abram are one-year-old today. You have a beautiful little boy who needs your attention and fails to get it because he never asks. Do you have any idea how much your behavior has hurt the rest of the family? We – especially the girls and I – love him so very much. He's a sweet boy, so intelligent –"

"But Abram is certainly every bit as bright –"

"Stop defending that child, Elizabeth. You have six other children. Have you stopped seeing them at all?"

"You're being ridiculous."

"No, I'm not. Grace is growing up. She'll be thirteen next month. Boys are fighting to carry her books. And Anne isn't far behind. That girl's a real sweetheart. But she needs a mother. And Ralph –"

"Ralph is a very responsible ten-year-old. I've done nothing to wrong him. In fact, I so often catch myself hoping *you'll* notice him. He needs a father's presence, too, you know."

"This is getting us nowhere. I didn't mention the other children to extend a fight. God, Lizzie, it isn't my wish to fight at all."

"Good. Then let's not. We spend so little time together

any more. Let's not waste it spatting over things neither of us can control."

. . .

Jack decided it might take Lizzie's mind off the boy to have a party while he looked forward to entertaining the men with whom he worked. He had studied how other men managed to get ahead. Indeed, he believed a party would be good for all.

Though it was obviously too hot in the summer for formal entertaining, Lizzie happily conceded to his wishes to throw a picnic. Certainly their back yard was large enough. Before she'd lost interest, Lizzie had planted many gorgeous beds of flowers. In those earlier days she'd taken much delight in watching them prosper, happy to weed and trim, proud of the vases of cut arrangements she could add to the house. He'd hired the gardener when the twins were born, sure she could do no more, and she'd never gone back. In fact, now that he thought about it, it was as if she went out of her way to avoid those gardens.

He was disappointed, too, that, after initially being so excited about the party, she seemed to lose interest in that as well. Jack had shared her pleasure as they planned the menu together and talked deliciously over each name that would be added to, or rejected from, the growing guest list.

"If we keep this up, we'll need a tent."

"Oh, Jack, what a grand idea! Do you mean it? Could we?"

"It was meant as a joke, but, yes, why not? We'll rent a tent, and tables and chairs. Let's make it a formal picnic. What do you say to that?"

"I've never heard of such a thing. We'll have everybody talking. Oh, what fun!"

Jack couldn't recall seeing his wife so elated as the picnic plans became more concrete. She dreamed of the decorations she'd use on each of the tables, the dishes she could prepare. It had been so long since she had spent happy time in the kitchen.

And the children! Grace and Anne would love to help with the food. Lizzie recalled times spent with her mother and reflected how good it would be to pass those lessons along. And, yes, why not? Jack could hardly mind if they were there to greet the arriving guests. Ralph, too. Certainly he was old enough to help with the carriages. Elizabeth and John would want to watch. No trouble with that. Perhaps she might find some decorating chore that could involve the youngsters. And, yes, she did understand about sending the twins to Mother Knapp's. They were far too young to appreciate what was going on. Nothing to do with being ashamed, simply more convenient for all.

Jack insisted on sitting in when the dressmaker he selected arrived.

Lizzie had begged for her favorite, Mrs. Green, who knew her tastes as well as she did herself.

No. He had been adamant. I want you to shine for this party.

Lizzie detested the new woman from the start. She was bossy, ordering her to turn this way, and that, pointing up her flaws rather than diplomatically stressing the finer points. Lizzie objected to the colors of the samples before noticing that the woman was not seeking her approval at all.

"Why, I never! Jack, really, I must insist –"

The entire pantomime was being put on for Jack's benefit alone.

"Hush, hush, Lizzie. Listen. To be honest, Mrs. Green was tending to make you look frumpy –"

"You never said that before."

"Well, I do now. I want everyone looking at you, admiring you. I'm proud of my wife and I want them all to know it."

"But, Jack, this color is atrocious. I wouldn't want to be seen in it. And the style. Fashion be damned! I know what it will do to my figure."

"No, Lizzie, you're wrong. Just be a good girl now and go along with us. You'll see."

. . .

Lizzie failed to see. Or to understand why Jack insisted it would never do for her to lift a finger. Why, didn't she know he had never expected her to do any of the work? In fact he'd already hired the caterers and engaged the florist.

"Lizzie, I thought you were really looking forward to the party. You seemed so excited. What happened? Certainly you must realize that I never meant for you to tire yourself out with all those trifling details."

"But the children?"

"Now you are being unreasonable. Everybody knows children mustn't be seen at a party. For God's sakes, Lizzie, I don't know where you get some of your ideas."

. . .

Lizzie hardly ever smiled now, instead spending most of her waking hours in the nursery amusing the twins. Jack never noticed for, with the party plans in capable hands, he had turned his attentions back to the affairs at the Larkin Factory.

. . .

Those fortunate enough to make the guest list agreed, once they had stopped talking about who had been omitted, that a backyard picnic was a marvelous way indeed to break up the tedium of summer. Who'd have imagined a tent! And all those banks of flowers, did you ever?

Then talk inevitably turned to Lizzie. Hadn't that Mr. Knapp seemed so beamingly proud of his wife? And did you notice her dress? And the style of her hair? That must be what they're doing in New York. Some of the guests even hinted that perhaps it was the latest Parisienne fashion. Pity though she seemed so slim. Never smiled either, poor girl.

Yes, they whispered, she must be sick. Well, what can you expect, having all those children? Quite a burden for that husband of hers as well.

Though, come to think of it, have you ever seen a man more saintly?

XIX

October 1882

"I swear, with so many children, getting ready for anything always seems to take longer than I expect."

"Don't fuss so, Lizzie. They look just fine. And we still have a minute or two before the program begins."

Grace and Anne had preceded their parents into the pew. Ralph and Elizabeth tagged after with Ralph scurrying across to sit next to Uncle Charlie, John snuggling up on his other side.

St. Paul's hadn't often promoted Sunday afternoon musicales and this promised to be an especially good program. The church was packed by the time Mrs. Wiles stood to greet the audience, thanking them for coming out on such a lovely fall day, and then turning to announce the first performers.

. . .

"Janie! They told me you'd be here! But to come all the way from Erie! My God, look at you! You look fabulous."

"That's what I told her," an excited Flo chimed in. "Married life is obviously treating her just fine."

Maggie remained flabbergasted as she took a better look at the friend she hadn't seen for more than a year. "Did Vernon come with you?"

"Not this time, I'm afraid."

"So you can't stay?"

"For your playing, absolutely, and there'll be time to visit after. But I must catch the late train back tonight."

"I can't get over this. Yes, afterwards, of course. You'll have to tell me everything."

"And you, too, Maggie. I can't believe you're actually featured on the program today. A lot has changed since I left."

"Girls, girls. It's time to take our seats. We don't want to disturb our star before she plays."

"You're right, Everett, of course." The three left the performers now pacing in differing degrees of nervousness.

. . .

"I must say, Lizzie, that was a stellar afternoon. I'm so glad I was in here to accompany your fine family." Charlie winked at Grace. "Did you enjoy it, Jack?"

"You know music isn't my primary interest. Some of the singers seemed dreadfully off key –"

"Well, yes, dear, some of them were."

"And that chorus was unbelievable."

"Whatever do you mean? Though I suspect I shall be sorry for asking."

"Just that I thought I discerned twenty voices, all going their separate ways, one for each of the women standing up there."

"Jack, that's a dreadful thing to say!"

"Ah, come on, Lizzie. You know it was also an honest one."

"Say," Charlie cut in, "did either of you notice that pianist in the final trio?"

"Weren't they wonderful? Hearing playing like that made the whole afternoon worthwhile."

"Did indeed, but did she look familiar?"

"Can't say I noticed, Charlie."

"Nor I, I'm afraid. Are you telling us you've found a girl who can catch your eye, and in church at that?"

"I didn't mean it that way. Just that I recall seeing her someplace else, sometime before this."

"Sorry, I'm no help at all."

"Well, let's not worry about that. Time to round up the children."

"And do let me tell you both that I was especially proud of

each and every one of my nieces and nephews. They were all on their best behavior."

"I did perceive a little giggling during those choral numbers you mentioned, but –"

"Jack, I said they were angels, not deaf. Human is still all right, at least in my book."

Charlie squeezed all five youngsters before they turned and proceeded up the aisle.

. . .

"Maggie, you're so good!"

"Well, no, I'm not. But I did think it went well, didn't you?"

" *Well* doesn't do you justice. The music was so perfect that, for long stretches at a time, I just sat back and enjoyed, forgetting all together that it was my friend who was playing so magnificently."

Maggie laughed. "Let's give a little credit to the violinist and cellist. Aren't they superb?"

"Of course they are. It took all three of you, but, Maggie, I didn't come all the way from Erie to hear them. I came for you. And I will never, ever regret it."

Before Janie, or Flo for that matter, could add another word, they were cut off from their friend by a large group of well-wishers. They retreated to join Everett who stood at the back of the huge room, watching Maggie. How gracefully she accepted all the compliments being heaped on her.

At Everett's suggestion, for both realized it might be another year before Maggie caught up with her old friend, he and Flo left to walk over to the river, promising to return in time to accompany Janie back to the station.

. . .

Changing out of the requisite black, Maggie slipped into more colorful garb and hurried with her friend across the street to the park, taking the first bench that caught the late rays of the October sun.

The two began talking rapidly at once, caught themselves,

giggled with a hug, and began again.

Maggie won, but insisted Janie must go first to tell her about married life, about Vernon, about Erie. Why, oh, why, couldn't she write more often?

"To be honest, it's you who writes so seldom. Or so it seems."

"Oh, Janie, of course you're right. But there simply hasn't been time. Once I began taking lessons with Peter it meant using every spare moment I could find. I'm able to stay after work to practice, you know. Frequently I get so wrapped up in the music that I forget the time until the watchman or Everett, more often Everett, comes a-tapping on the door to tell me it's past midnight."

"Midnight! But how can you do your work and still practice such long hours? Don't you do anything else?"

"To tell the truth, my life these past months seems little more than a blur of practice and work. Everett teases that he's sure I'd never leave the factory at all if Mr. Larkin would let me set up a bed in the piano room."

"That's terrible! I mean, you are good – no, you're wonderful. Your playing today was worthy of all those accolades."

"Oh, do you think so, Janie? I wish I could believe that. I mean, truly believe it."

"How can you not? Didn't you listen to all those people talking to you? Good God, friend, couldn't you feel it?"

"Well . . . yes. Part of me at least. I've worked so hard with the other two and I know they believe we did as well as we possibly could this afternoon. And yes, I did hear all those fabulous compliments. To be honest . . . I don't know exactly how to describe how I felt, Janie. It. . . It just wasn't good enough."

"I can't say that makes any sense but I do know you made a whole room full – look, a church full – of people very happy. I hope, however, that you'll be allowed to rest now, stay away from that piano for a little while. Sounds like you could use some time to rejoin the human race."

"Sounds as though you've been talking to Everett and

Flo."

"They're both quite worried. I haven't been here to see the day-after-day part so maybe they're exaggerating the bad, but –"

"The *bad?* What on earth did they tell you?"

"Nothing like that. It's not like we've had hours to talk, you know. I just felt they believed you were pushing too hard."

"They may be right."

"Then I truly do not understand. You're a smart woman, Maggie. Certainly the one of us who always seemed most sensible. Surely you know better now than to get yourself in a situation that makes you miserable."

"I never said I was miserable, Janie. And I don't believe Everett and Flo would have told you that either.'

"But –"

"Then again, maybe they would."

Maggie wished with all her heart she could explain it better. She hadn't felt right talking to Flo and, well, she couldn't say anything to Everett. The lessons had been his idea and she would never want him to think her ungrateful.

Dr. Kubrick was younger than she'd anticipated. Tall and surprisingly good-looking in spite of hair graying where it wasn't receding. Feeling attracted to him at once, it had been his voice that impressed her most. A nice, gentle voice that had immediately put her at ease. He questioned her about her past experience, had her perform at various levels from the many music books in his study, and then pulled out four or five to assign sections for the following week. She liked the way he took command, steadily guiding her progression, and was surprised to realize that first lesson had lasted a full two hours.

What she remembered most of all, however, at that moment and for many, many times to come, was their final parting for Dr. Kubrick had walked with her to his front door, talking all the while, and then stopped to wish her well. As he did he reached up – Maggie felt quite unconsciously – and patted her on the shoulder. Like a kiss, another touch she could not remember, it thrilled with a deep burn that was not to be extinguished.

She had hurried enthusiastically to the piano at the Larkin Company as soon as her shift ended the following day. As her hands reached confidently for the keys, she remembered the many hours happily spent at her aunt's Steinway. Her fingers responded quickly to her touch. Music!

She had no idea how many hours she played, lost entirely in the joy of the experience.

Her assignments included a recapitulation of the basics Aunt Fil had always stressed. Now, though, there was even more to remember for Dr. Kubrick added much that was new to her.

On the third day Maggie spent three difficult hours practicing and found she needed many more. By the fifth she was optimistic again and happily reported to Everett that it was coming. He had laughed at her when she quietly added, "I hope."

. . .

Maggie's doubts seemed justified as her lessons progressed for Dr. Kubrick proved a most mercurial instructor. Complementary one moment, he would savagely criticize the next, frequently leaving Maggie in tears as soon as she escaped his studio.

How could she have played that poorly? Her posture, the pedaling, her hand positions, tempi, the rhythm, how could they all be wrong? And those wrong notes! She supposed she should be grateful he had deigned to schedule another lesson for the following week.

One week he would greet her with smiles, seemingly eager to be personable and kind. If her playing were not up to his expectations, he at least treated her shortcomings with patience. The next week, or the one after that, would lead to more tears. It wasn't just that her playing was terrible, though Maggie accepted that some of it must be; it was that so much of his criticism seemed useless nitpicking.

Would she never be able to satisfy this demanding man?

. . .

At first she had hesitated when one of the girls from work mentioned her cousin's string trio. At least it had been a trio until the pianist left to be married. Might Maggie be interested in meeting her cousin the violinist?

Playing as part of a group had captivated her from the beginning. She was complimented they felt her talented enough to join them.

. . .

On a Sunday afternoon late in September Maggie accompanied her musical friends to a master class where each of the string players had enrolled for a private session with Preston Bryan. Every performer, she surmised after watching the first two or three, paid for and was given a twenty-minute coaching session with the visiting pedagogue. Each soloist sat on stage with Dr. Bryan before a crowded auditorium of rapt listeners. She had seen the nervousness in her friends until the lessons began. Then she could actually feel them relax, their instruments held just slightly looser as each listened to every word coming from the stage.

The first performer had been a young violist. Obviously nervous and not, if one were to ask her opinion, terribly talented, the boy played through the first page of his music. She shuddered silently, parroting the terribly cutting words she knew would issue from Herr Doktor.

"That was very nice, Philip."

Maggie couldn't believe her ears. Nice? Hardly. It was excruciatingly dreadful. What kind of teacher would compliment such playing? What a waste of time this was. For her. For them all.

"Just let me hum those first few measures. Now listen carefully." As he hummed she saw that the boy had lost his initial nervousness and was giving the man his full attention. The boy, Philip, turned timidly to face the audience when asked to hum the same passage. He did it. The man tried again. This time the boy echoed him quite closely.

"Very good, Philip, very good. You don't speak in a monotone, right? Then don't play in one. Make the viola speak for you. Even better, let it sing. Now I want you to try it that way."

Maggie smiled at such silliness, then looked up with a start. The boy played the passage with panache. Teacher and boy worked this way until their time was up. She couldn't believe the difference in his playing at the end of those twenty minutes. Even better, he left the stage smiling, obviously eager to try more on his own. Why, Peter would have reduced him to tears. And she would have considered it justified.

.   .   .

Maggie tried to explain all this to Janie but ultimately gave up, changing the topic back to learn more of her friend's new life in Pennsylvania. It wasn't much longer until Flo and Everett joined them for the walk to the train depot.

The friends exchanged final hugs and stood waving, Everett between Maggie and Flo, until Janie's train was out of sight.

He suggested supper at the corner café, hoping to celebrate her well-deserved success.

"That's so like you. But it isn't a question of deserving. I have so far yet to go. I simply have to work harder."

She turned and walked briskly away before either could utter another word.

XX

October 1882

Jack and Lizzie found themselves in demand socially after their successful party. At first Lizzie had felt quite overwhelmed by each new name on the cards delivered to her as yet another of society's matrons stopped to call. Previously she would have disdained their idle days. Now, facing nothing better herself, she capitulated eagerly. She'd join their clubs, partake of their lectures and teas. Yes, she'd even learn to play their game of bridge.

It was, however, as a couple that the two were most in demand. Boxes at the opera, orchestra seats for the symphony, previews at the gallery. The financial demands stretched their purse to the point of family sacrifice. Priorities were changed as Jack assured them that the company would reward his efforts. He was certain to gain enough to offset these new demands. Praying silently it might be sooner rather than later, he never shared his growing fears of insolvency.

Lizzie never meant to be demanding. She wanted only what was best for Jack, but certainly that must include the latest fashions for the children as well as herself. And shouldn't they consider enrolling them in the private academy so they could hobnob with the children of their newly acquainted circle of friends? Nothing less than the very best for his family, Jack agreed.

It was a gamble that would pay off for, within a year, Jack was earning enough to actually afford the life style to which they had quickly grown accustomed.

. . .

How easy it had been, and how rapidly the change had occurred, not just for Jack, or Lizzie but for the children as well. They had put on the mantle of their newly acquired wealth as easily as an old sweater on a breezy fall day. The proper clubs, the right activities, the friends who were now theirs to choose or reject, all seemed to fall into their hands.

Jack walked a little taller as he eagerly approached each new day at the Larkin Company. Why, he marveled, hadn't he understood before, long ago in fact, how much the realization of financial security can put a real spring in one's step?

The children continued to meet his expectations, staying near the top in each of their academic classes. Only Abram remained a problem. Jack supposed he always would in spite of Lizzie's dreams that James's good influences might eventually rub off on the boy. But if that was their major problem . . . well, things were progressing swimmingly. Certainly better than Jack would have dreamed a few years before.

He'd grown up poor, the elder son of a young widow. His mother and her brothers worked hard to keep the old family farmstead. No more animals now, or just the few he knew she kept more for pets than for practical purposes but that was all right, too. They'd struggled as they'd grown up, he and his brother. Jack had had to teach summers to pay for his college tuition but had graduated with honors, an example Charlie felt necessary to emulate. Charlie was doing marvelous things in Pennsylvania. Somehow it had been an easy leap to politics. Now after six years in the State legislature, he was running for Lieutenant Governor of Pennsylvania. Jack wouldn't have felt surprised to see his name bandied about one of these years as a leading candidate for a national office.

Glimpsing his new suit as he passed the mirror, Jack smiled as he recalled his college days when he'd worn his one and only black suit until it had become so patched and, ultimately, so tight that he was forced to buy a replacement, cutting back on his barebones meals until the suit could be fully paid for. Mother had been fanatical about turning collars, even taking old scraps to sew him a vest. He had tried, as he gained steady employment, to convince her to allow him to purchase *store-bought* clothes. Then another box would arrive with a shirt he thought discarded, restitched and wearable, more or less, once again.

Now he was able to regularly send money back to help her. It was important for him to know that she was comfortable. That was the least he could do. But nobody, or nothing, would ever get her off the farm.

Jack had missed it too at first. The stillness is what he remembered. And all those familiar smells. He loved to return when the haying was taking place. Yes, he reflected, it had probably been at the split second when Lizzie sniffed deeply, smiled, and said she loved the fresh scent of cow manure that Jack knew she was going to be his bride. Amazing, too, that she had ever agreed to marry one so poor, so lowly, so country.

Her parents had been city folk. She had grown up wanting nothing but, once she'd gotten to know him, that seemed the furthest thing from her mind. If he'd worried at first, she had done everything in her power to assuage those concerns.

And now just look! He could offer her greater wealth than any her parents had known. Although they had always remained proper and treated Lizzie's choice with politeness, he was only too aware of their continued disapproval. He, not the distance, was the reason they refused to visit now. Well, he had finally showed them all, hadn't he?

As if on a speeding carousel, Jack's mind swirled through all he had given his family: clothing in the latest styles, the best schools, all the ornaments of a good life, servants, a beautifully furnished home. Ah, yes, the house! Mightn't it be time now for something even grander? The children were growing. Certainly they could use rooms of their own. And a proper nursery for the twins. Rooms, too, for the enlarged staff their expanding needs would demand.

The best homes, Jack knew, were being built along Delaware Avenue. Well, he'd just have to go have a look for himself. No need mentioning it to Lizzie. Not yet. No need getting her excited over nothing. Just let things go along until he could be sure.

He'd ask for appointments for the early part of next week.

XXI

Summer 1883

"You're crying! What's the matter?"

"Oh, Flo," she sobbed. "It hurts so."

"Your hands? Oh, Maggie, remember what the doctor told you. You need to rest."

"But you don't understand. I can't give it up."

"Nobody said you had to give up the piano."

"That's just it. It isn't the piano. It's him. If I can't play, I won't be able to see him. I know he doesn't care for me, not *that* way at least, but –"

"But you feel that strongly for him? Is that what you're saying?" She turned to face her tear-stained friend. "Maggie, do you love the man?"

"*Love?* No, I don't love him," she responded quickly. "At least I don't think I do. It's just that . . . well, I feel so good when I'm with him. I don't know what it is, Flo, but I can't stop. I just can't."

"Then you haven't talked to him about your hands? Or what the doctor told you?"

"How can I?"

"If he means this much to you, and I know your music does, do you think he'd consider letting you cut back?"

"Cut back? You mean – Oh, Flo! You're a genius! Of course! Why didn't I think of that?"

"Because, my little miss, you do tend to see everything in absolutes. Practice, or give up your music forever. Ridiculous! It's obvious, just –"

"Of course! Continue to practice, continue my lessons, just do less. Why, I think I could even get to enjoy a regimen like that! Perhaps even find time again for old friends."

"Don't get carried away. I know you too well for –"

"Oh, dear."

"Now what?"

"Do you think he'll agree?"

"Your teacher? Well, there's only one person who can answer that. Go talk to him. Tell him exactly how you feel."

. . .

Before she had the opportunity Maggie was invited to join her trio friends for another master class with Preston Bryan. She was delighted when he asked all three young women to stay after to visit over a cup of tea.

Before she realized she was doing it, Maggie found herself pouring out her frustrations to this stranger. "It's awful. I practice and practice and practice. And then, at my lesson, everything sounds just awful. And Dr. Kubrick is always so critical. I know he tries to teach but he makes it all so difficult. I can play a line or even just a couple of measures right and then he'll stop me because one note is wrong. I've gotten so I dread playing before him at all."

Bryan and the two string players sat silently, letting her continue as she explained the pains that had lately crippled her.

"Do you know, the other night I was cooking dinner and I looked at the fire burning in the stove and thought – oh, please don't think me bad, I thought that if I just put my hands in the flames, that would make all my problems go away."

"Maggie!"

"Of course I didn't. I wouldn't. Don't worry, Flo. The thought frightened me, that's the only reason I mention it."

"Miss Trusler, please."

Maggie sat quietly.

"I understand what you're going through. It isn't wrong, and it isn't your fault. Playing well takes years and years of practice. It isn't something you can expect to achieve overnight."

"But –"

"No *buts* now. Listen. Please. You've been blaming yourself because you can't be perfect after a relatively short time. You work hard, perhaps too hard, but you must be progressing as well. Most of all, though, you must learn to enjoy the trip."

"The *trip*?"

"It's obvious you want to be a good pianist. I suspect you'll settle for nothing less than being the world's greatest."

"Oh, no, Mr. Bryan, I never meant that."

"Well, none of us know how far you can go, do we? But, as I said, it's not the destination that should matter now. It's the journey, the steps you take on your way to whatever level you do reach. Can you understand what I'm saying? Enjoy your practice. Enjoy your lessons. But above all, enjoy playing the piano."

. . .

It was a determined Maggie who approached her next lesson. She was deliriously happy when she left two hours later. Was there anything this wonderful man couldn't understand?

Why, he knew stress could cause the crippling pains in her knuckles. She half expected an immediate cure as he had massaged them gently. He knew she was working too hard, pushing herself beyond reasonable expectation. He had never asked that of her.

She hesitated, fearful of contradicting, wondering how he could fail to realize she was driven only because he demanded so much.

"It's your problem, my dear, you who push the limits only you set. Of course we can cut back. Here now, let's put these studies away for the time being and leave just . . . let's see . . . these three for you to work on. That won't be too much, will it?"

She departed in ecstasy, ready now for the joy of the trip.

. . .

"Why, that miserable, no good . . . Oh!" Maggie hurled her books across his yard, stooping quickly to pick them up again, hoping she hadn't been seen before hurrying on down the block. How could anyone be so uncaring? so feeling?

Replaying the events of the last hour, she kicked a rock beside the sidewalk as hard as she could. Let her boots get scuffed! Who cared? Bah! What an ogre!

Peter had made her spend two entire hours on the Bach. Though she had practiced hard and felt well prepared, in the middle of the second page her fingers missed one chord.

"Don't worry about it." Did she only imagine he chortled? "I realize it's just because you aren't practicing as much."

"But I am! I've worked on this as hard as ever." She wanted to protest more but kept silent. Cutting back had meant fewer pieces to practice, not less time spent on the ones still assigned. She knew. If he didn't, no words of hers would help.

She daren't glance at the clock now and risk being caught at it but believed his criticisms had never come so fast: your fingers aren't round enough, sit up straighter, too much pedal, that's too loud now, you've forgotten the accent, no – the melody must have a steady volume as it passes from right hand to left, relax your hand when playing those rapid octaves, you're bending toward the piano as you get louder there, stay erect. Had even ten minutes passed since his harangue had begun? How could anyone be expected to remember it all?

Later – finally, it seemed to her – they had reached the fast movement. She was certain he could find no fault here.

"Oh, yes, those places where you're having so much trouble." He interrupted her playing again. "Indeed, those passages are extremely difficult."

She gritted her teeth and continued. The next mistake didn't surprise Maggie.

Dr. Kubrick seemed to positively purr. "This isn't causing too much stress now, is it?"

I'm being overly sensitive, she thought, beginning to calm down. I just misinterpreted. Though wouldn't anyone think it obvious the stress is caused by him, not Bach? Could he possibly be that self-absorbed? He either didn't hear one word I said last week, didn't comprehend it, doesn't give a damn – or just couldn't control himself and had to make a nasty . . .

But why should she put words in his mouth? Make excuses

for his inexcusable behavior? She was relieved she had two full weeks before their next lesson.

. . .

"I missed you last week."

"Why, thank you, Peter." She realized her error as the stern instructor harshly spoke. She had obviously misinterpreted his opening remark.

He had waited for her the previous week, he nervously explained, expecting her at her regular hour. No, she was positive he had told her two weeks. See *here,* and she had pointed to his notation in her assignment book.

He was unremittingly insufferable through their ensuing lesson.

Pleased with her unwitting repartee while doubting she could ever be that quick again, Maggie left smiling.

XXII

April and May 1883

It was a beaming Jack who surprised Lizzie on the morning of their fifteenth anniversary, presenting a large circular box he had kept half hidden behind his back as he entered the room.

"Why, it's a hat! It must be, but –"

"Don't guess, dear. Just open it."

"Yes, Mama. Oh, do hurry, please." The children crowded around, each hoping to be the first to glimpse whatever lay inside.

Oohs followed aahs while Lizzie gazed speechlessly at the lovely creation lying before her. She lifted the ruched hat from its box, careful not to muss the ice blue satin ribbons. A cluster of tiny forget-me-nots surrounded a handmade rose.

"Jack, I've never seen anything like it. Where did you –?"

She hurried to the mirror, adjusting the tatted lace to flatter her face just so. "Oh! It's magnificent. Isn't it, children? But, Jack, how could you have known?"

"Easy, my dear. I simply told your milliner that I wanted the very best she could design. Is it all right? I mean, goodness knows I'm not one to judge ladies' hats."

"*All right?* It's perfect. It's . . . I don't know. I'm breathless. Speechless."

"I hope you won't mind. I believe it's a copy."

"A *copy?*"

"Yes, I'm told the original was worn by Caroline Astor."

"The queen of New York society? And I'm wearing her hat? Why, but that's a marvelous gift. You know our friends will turn positively green with envy. They say the Astors have perfect taste in everything they do. Oh, but I will enjoy wearing this. Thank you, dear. And I do have a gift for you – a surprise, at least – but I'll keep it till we're alone later tonight."

"That may be very late, if you don't mind. I made reservations for us at The Velvet Room, even booked the private booth I know you prefer."

"Private? Well, I guess I'll just have to make many trips to the powder room for surely everyone must have a good look at my anniversary gift. Oh, Jack, I still can't believe it. I'm thunderstruck. Thank you so very much, my darling."

. . .

Surprise might not have been quite the right word, Lizzie reflected. She was doubly sure *present* was the last thing that would spring to Jack's mind when she confessed she was pregnant yet again. She had certainly believed the twins would be the end, what with facing her thirty-ninth birthday in the fall. She wasn't eager for more.

She loved her children. It wasn't hard to care for so many, God knew, not with all the help Jack kept hiring. All but the twins were enrolled in school now and seemed to be meeting their father's expectations of excellence. James had grown into a darling little boy, capturing people's hearts wherever he went. Abram – well, he was still difficult though his temper seemed controllable as long as he remained with either her or Mrs. Backstrom.

Jack finished the last of his pie and looked up in time to catch her shy smile.

"Your thought must have been a dandy. I don't believe I've seen you sparkle so in a very long time, Liz. Have I told you how positively radiant you look tonight?"

"Only about a hundred times. But please don't stop. I love to hear you say so. And, to tell the truth, I do feel especially lovely this evening." As she remembered the hat, her hand rose unconsciously to her neck and the diamond choker Jack had presented as she finished dressing. Her husband was full of the most sublime surprises!

"May I ask about your gift now, or was it your intention

to make me wait even longer?" It pleased him now to see the diamonds sparkling as much as her beautiful grey eyes. She was a good wife and he felt grateful for the preceding years. Oh, there'd been rough times. Those times, too, when she seemed so sad, so remote, so very far away. He never had learned how to reach her then and felt frustrated by his lack. Still, didn't the rest more than make up for it?

"No sense, I imagine, keeping the secret any longer. Not that things like this can be kept hidden." Sipping from her glass she raised her eyes to look directly into his.

How did he know?

"Oh, Lizzie, no. Not another baby."

Tears quickly replaced the sparkle.

"I'm sorry, dear. This has been such a lovely evening, such a perfect day in fact, that I didn't want to do anything to spoil it."

"No, I'm the one who should be sorry. For being insensitive. Of course, a baby. But how about you? How are you feeling?"

"Just fine. This time, I mean. So it will be all right?"

" *All right?* Of course, it's all right. My dear, I think this is cause for even more celebration. May I have the waiter bring us another bottle of champagne?"

"Do you think we should? I mean, I could get quite tipsy."

"Would you mind? We do have much to be grateful for."

"Champagne. Indeed, it's a grand idea. But do remember who suggested it, just in case I have a case of the giggles on the way upstairs once we get home."

"No problem. I suspect I'll be giggling right along with you."

. . .

"Why, Elizabeth, pregnant? I can't believe it! You? No, say it isn't true." She set down her cup and turned to the other woman. "I mean, really dear, after the last time, and well, everything."

"True, I know I was sick after the twins were born. Before

too," she laughed awkwardly. "But I've been feeling perfectly chipper this time, and Dr. Clark sees no reason for any difficulties now or ahead. I thought you'd be happy for us."

"But what's to say God won't punish you with another Mongoloid baby?"

"*Mongoloid? Punish?* What are you talking about?"

"Lizzie, it's what everyone's said all along. God punished you for some sin. That's why Abram was born the way he was."

"Rubbish! How can you, of all people, believe such nonsense? Abram isn't Mongoloid at all –"

"Call him whatever you wish, dear. But don't tell me he's a normal little boy."

"No. Unfortunately, you're right about that. Abram isn't normal and, while we certainly hope he'll get better as he gets older, he definitely isn't Mongoloid. Now, as for sinning –"

"Well, we all know that the people with Mon – all right, that *bad* babies have been cursed by God for the sins of their parents."

"That is utter nonsense and I can't believe you don't know better. As a matter of fact, I can't believe you'd say those things to my face."

"But the church says –"

"The church says no such thing. Go ask Father Schuster if you want. Ask the church. Ask any doctor. These things just happen."

"Well, I –"

"And if you want to know something, dear, you'd be a much better friend and a bigger help if you could offer a little more sympathy and understanding. The boy is not an easy one to rear."

Rising, Lizzie turned on her heels and walked briskly away, leaving her friend speechless and alone.

XXIII

September to December 1883

The months that followed were dizzying ones. The Larkin Company, in fact it had been Mr. Larkin himself, offered Maggie the opportunity to train as a clerk. Everett, recognizing almost at once the turmoil the decision placed on her, sought – and won – a similar, though slightly lower, position for Flo. The girls, rejoicing in their newfound, if rather slight, wealth, decided to join forces to rent a small apartment and soon found a suitable flat in a better neighborhood, not terribly far from the factory. Having two rooms now, instead of just one, and having that include a simple cookstove and a sink signified to the two that they were indeed rising in the world.

Janie corresponded regularly, particularly after learning she was pregnant and reluctantly capitulated to Vernon's wish that she stop work.

Bert, meanwhile, seemed very happy in Omaha. He wrote of his work with an excitement Maggie envied, seeming to find new opportunities at every turn as he delighted in the stimulation life *out West* offered. She found it difficult to remember that the letters she held had been written by one she still considered her baby brother, a lad only just past his fourteenth birthday.

· · ·

Thanks to the prodding and encouragement of both violinist and cellist, more and more opportunities to perform were opening up. None was prepared, however, when Dushan Vojnovich, one of Buffalo's foremost composers, offered to write a piece for the three. She and her friends were stunned by an accolade none could have imagined and a date to perform it publicly was quickly arranged.

Maggie eagerly arrived for their first rehearsal of the Vojnovich. Seats were positioned, music placed on stands, shifted just so, and the first movement begun.

She listened critically, trying to separate the musical lines while, at the same time, hearing the piece as it must have reverberated in the mind of its creator. She felt grateful for all Peter had taught her about the modern works of Rimsky-Korsakov and Mussorgsky for this was not easy music to her ears. Its resonance spilled over into areas she'd not dreamt of going. Listening now, she began to feel the charm and hear the rhythms, spellbound, growing unaware of the individual players as the group melded into one.

Maggie made it a point to never be late for a single rehearsal though it was frequently difficult as the demands of her job increased. She enjoyed working as a clerk, being able now to dress as a young lady in the required high-collared white blouse and long dark skirt. Direct salesmen were being eliminated as the factory, through advertisements, turned to the more profitable mail-order special offers while other enticements promoted godliness, cleanliness and self-improvement. She was given a direct role in requesting lists of "respectable citizens" from those already placing orders.

She liked dealing directly with people, writing and receiving letters from strangers in even stranger communities across the country. The names themselves carried a certain romance as she grew aware of the various postmarks. Eventually, she would request and be given the right to clip some of the more enticing, filling an album as spare time permitted. Chicago had recently finished a building ten stories high while New York touted the opening of its Brooklyn Bridge. Maggie marveled as a new world opened through the collection of these curious postal marks.

XXIV

October through December 1883

Taking advantage of the warm October afternoon, Lizzie took the twins to play in Delaware Park. She settled comfortably on a bench as Grace and Anne crossed over to walk along the lake. Lately they seemed quite interested in catching the eyes of certain young men who indeed appeared to be parading by more slowly and more often than they might have a year before. Struggling as always, and doing a darned good job of it if one were to ask her mother, Bessie tagged after the older Ralph, still young enough to permit a girl to join his circle of friends. John shadowed the older two, keeping his distance, hoping to be invited to join them.

The twins had wandered off to the grass to roll their ball. Still quite uncoordinated at two, Lizzie knew they'd soon become frustrated with their games and plead for her to come play. She glanced back at her older children.

"Get out of here! Scram! Get away from us! Go!!"

Turning to where the twins had been, she saw a man shooing Abram away. The boys stood staring in utter confusion as the man continued his shouting.

Lizzie hurried to the boys.

"Do you see that child? Tell him to get away from here!"

"Why, I'll do no such thing. These are my sons." She knelt with an arm around each, pulling them close as if that might shield them.

"Your sons? And you bring them to a public park to play?"

"We come here frequently. I think it's marvelous to have a park like this so close."

"Not if it's going to be filled with retards. Not," pointing directly at Abram, "if it's going to be filled with ruined ones like him."

"How dare you speak so?"

"How dare I? Lady, how dare I not? Aren't you afraid your other boy will catch it? I certainly don't want my children exposed to . . . to that." Grabbing a protesting toddler by the arm, the man and his child hurried toward Delaware Avenue, away from the park.

By now her older children, attracted by the ruckus, had come running. The twins, uncomprehending, began to cry. Lizzie scooped Abram into her arms as James ran to Grace.

They hurried home in silence.

. . .

Jack took to accompanying Lizzie to the park though the older children promised they were ready to fight should there be a recurrence. At first Lizzie had been reluctant to venture out at all until made to see that the boys – all the children, for that matter – needed to play in the fresh air and sun.

It had not happened again.

. . .

Clara was born the week after Thanksgiving. A beautiful little girl, the birth was an easy one. Her arrival made little difference to the family's routine.

. . .

Lizzie checked the new baby and returned to snuggle beside Jack as the snow continued falling softly outside. The candles glowed within as logs snapped in the fireplace.

"Do you feel this averaged up to our usual Christmas, Liz?"

"I thought it a perfect one. Did it seem less so to you?" She yawned contentedly.

"No. I found it just fine. Guess it's just more difficult for me to settle down so. Do you realize how long it's been since I've taken an entire day to spend with you and the family?"

"Oh, yes, Jack; yes, I do. And, for all your generosity, that was the greatest gift you could have given me. I thought it a wonderful Christmas."

"What did you think of the card Grace got? I'd never seen one before."

"The Christmas card? Do you think it really cost that young man three whole dollars?"

"That's what the girls said. I found Grace and the young *crack* – for that's what Annie was calling him – hanging over the gate last night after church. You know, that trick's got to be at least twenty years old! But, Lizzie, imagine me impersonating the *old man!* Did you ever? And yet there I was, appearing on the scene right when I surely wasn't wanted."

Lizzie chuckled as she pressed her head deeper onto his shoulder.

"I think I'd just better toddle right back to the old homestead where nobody'll stare if I still play the boy. Gettin' mighty old around here!"

"Jack! You old? My goodness, don't talk like that. Besides, dear," she drew the words out carefully, "if you're getting old, what does that make me?"

Her smile deepened as he whispered in her ear. They blew the candles out carefully and hoped the baby Clara would sleep on.

XXV

January 1884

Lizzie stood by the window, forlornly watching the heavy snows that continued to pelt the area. The gas lamps, kept lighted all day, were hardly visible through the swirling white. Jack poked the blazing fire one more time, added another log, and turned to his wife.

"Well, Lizzie, what shall it be?"

"Oh, must I always be the one to have to decide?"

"Whether we venture out or stay here by our cozy fire, I'll do whatever you wish."

"That makes it so difficult. We've had these tickets for ages . . . and you know I've been so looking forward to the New Year's Day Musicale. Especially after we were able to finagle an extra ticket for your brother. It was supposed to be – oh, such a special occasion for us all."

"That I understand. But Charlie won't be coming. This weather has brought even our trusty railroads to a standstill. I'm sure he'll get here in a day or two, as soon as the tracks are cleared, though that doesn't help with your decision now, does it?"

"Seems we have so few evenings to ourselves any more. But, at the same time . . ."

"Yes, at the same time –"

"I just hate to miss something quite special. I'm sure everyone will be talking about it later. Besides, you know me; I'll be pacing the carpet every moment wondering if we really have passed up the most gala of all gala performances. Then again, on the other hand . . ."

He walked over to stand beside his wife and kissed her tenderly on the back of her neck. She turned to embrace him.

A log sparked momentarily sending red shoots skyward.

"It is a lovely fire, Jack."

"Might be a shame to miss it, don't you think?"

"Hmm, hmm. And so terribly unpleasant outside. Yes, my mind's made up. I'll tell the staff that we'll be dining in after all. Shall I ask them to set our supper here?"

"Here?"

"Before the fire."

"Ah, my eternal romantic. Sounds marvelous to me. Have to confess I wasn't looking forward to changing into formal attire either."

"Your brother may miss a better evening than he knows."

"Well, one doesn't have to tell him everything. Right, dear?"

. . .

Maggie had been pleased with the overflow crowd in the auditorium. The snows had showed no signs of stopping and the players feared a small audience for this New Year's Day Gala. Certainly the audience beforehand spoke in murmurs of eager anticipation for what should be a moment of musical history for all of Buffalo. Even Mr. Larkin and, she assumed, his wife, were there, seated in a prominent box just to the left of the stage.

Dressed in formal attire the trio made a handsome first impression. They were greeted with lengthy applause and seemed eager to get the performance underway.

Always a touchy moment, Maggie relaxed as she heard the first chord strike as one. The first movement was launched.

Maggie joined the group's celebration at the reception that followed as the audience tried to outdo each other with words of praise.

The crowd dissipated slowly until the three were left, surrounded only by their friends and close acquaintances. Maggie went for a cup of punch and stopped. Why had it never occurred to her that Peter might come?

Shyly, eyes gleaming, she stared at him speechlessly. Was she such a tongue-tied young woman that, even now, she must make a spectacle of herself? She felt he was relishing her discomfort for he made no effort to speak. How long could such insufferable silence continue?

The violinist, most aware of their friend's discomfort, broke the impasse. Not sure what to do but feeling something had to be done, and quickly, she nodded to Maggie. "If we expect them to hold our reservation, we'd better get going." Undone as well, she now nodded in Peter's direction. "You too, if you'd like."

Maggie entered the lovely old inn with her musical friends. She glanced around, recognized no one else, and felt a deep stab: would Peter not come after all? He actually had not said he would – or would not. Perhaps the nod she had accepted as confirmation meant something totally different.

No, here he was now, rushing in as if having deliberately planned a late arrival. Untwining the muffler wrapped high around his neck, he hung coat and hat and joined the group.

The meal passed quickly, the food acclaimed and then forgotten, as the four talked on.

It was quite late when the violinist caught herself after a particularly funny story, glanced at the time, and said she really had to head home. Acknowledging she would regret it by sunrise, the cellist pleaded with Peter and Maggie to stay for just one more coffee. Better yet, could he buy them each a beer? Maggie was pleasantly surprised to hear Peter agree. Of course she'd stay. She'd worry about the morrow tomorrow.

The three talked on, enjoying the crackle of the fire in the corner as other customers rose and left.

"Time for me to wend my way home, too." The cellist tossed some bills on the table, stood quickly, took her wraps, said a final adieu and departed.

Maggie felt awkwardly alone with Peter.

"I think I should be going, too." Maggie pushed her drink away.

"No sense letting good beer go to waste. Might as well stay and we'll both finish our glasses."

She sat back down again.

Sitting across from him, aware of nothing else, Maggie

sensed an overwhelming magnetism and electricity between them.

Wasn't this all she had dreamed of? Weren't these her dreams come true?

She pinched herself and smiled, certain that her life from this moment on would always be connected to Peter.

. . .

Charlie was welcomed heartily when he appeared two days later. Yes, Mother was well and the farm going along all right. But what of this weather? Jack and Lizzie had a hard time believing his insistent statement that, for whatever snows still lingered in Buffalo, they were stacked much higher to the south. The train ride, in fact, might have seemed perilous had not the sun come out just before he departed, creating a blindingly beautiful wonderland all the way into the city.

They knew his visit would have to be shortened for the Pennsylvania government was set to resume the following Monday. Now that he was Lieutenant Governor, well . . . of course he had to be there.

. . .

Charlie began his journey back to Pennsylvania at the same time the older children returned to school. Without exception they liked their teachers and enjoyed the hours spent in the schoolroom. Johnny remained in kindergarten when he wasn't being *taught* at home by his older sister Bess. Grace and Annie continued to excel as they studied spelling, reading, arithmetic and physiology.

. . .

Jack had granted permission for fifteen-year-old Grace to host a taffy pull. For once Bess and of course Annie would be allowed to join their sister and her friends.

Jack tried to make it home early enough to offer moral support if nothing else, but work again kept him till the party was almost over. Having greeted the youngsters and marveled at the length of each team's taffy, he joined Lizzie in the darkened parlor.

"Has it been like this all evening?"

"Yes, Jack. Or more so. But I do believe they are having quite a wonderful time."

"Of course they are. Just listen to all that giggling! But when I stopped in the kitchen to say hello – what a bunch of awkward youngsters! The boys, that is. Brought back memories I think I'd just as soon forget."

"Don't ever feel that way, my dear. The silliness is just a normal part of growing up."

"Perhaps that's it as well. I don't like to be reminded just how grown up my little girls are becoming."

XXVI

September 1884

Lizzie slipped into the shadow of the porte cochere and watched until the carriage was out of sight. She had told the driver not to return. Over his protests, she had insisted the September day was such a lovely one that she eagerly looked forward to walking the few miles back home.

Home. *This* was home now. The Larkin factory continued to prosper which had meant another promotion for Jack. This time she could hardly protest. The twins would soon need more room, the older children were already begging for more space, and of course now the staff was increasing with every need, new or not yet realized. Besides, though he had still made the purchase without telling her, Jack had shared his news with enthusiasm once the deal was closed and, now, given her a key that she might explore for herself before the work was set to begin.

It was certainly a handsome house. She felt pride welling within as her eyes circled the porte cochere, the thick beds of myrtle and box elder that ran below the finely columned outer wall. The stairs were in fine repair, she noted as she climbed the four and reached for the door.

The key turned solidly in the lock. She liked its feel.

She stepped into the small reception hall and looked around. The room was paneled from floor to ceiling, handsomely woodworked with fine details throughout the rich mahogany. The closet to her left was small but, then again, this would only house the coats of visiting guests.

She stepped into the main hall and was surprised how impressive it was. The vestibule leading to the front door was off to her right, the staircase to the second floor winding gracefully before her, its lower steps sweeping in a semicircle like the skirt of a grande dame.

Off to her left lay the family coat closet, conveniently set into the paneling under the staircase, and then a narrowing hallway which she knew would lead to the back of the house, its cooking area with rooms for the staff.

She turned to her right.

A small room, brightly lighted from windows on both sides, stood before her. She liked the way the gas fireplace had been built kitty-corner. What a marvelous room for cards! Hadn't Jack expressed the very same thought?

Passing the staircase, she entered the library, gasping in pleasure at the wall of glass-fronted bookcases. At last she would have a place for her treasured volumes. And over there, before the window, yes, the grand piano would fit perfectly. Once, that is, she had managed to convince Jack one was no longer a luxury but an absolute necessity. The girls were begging for lessons. She regretted not encouraging them to begin when Miss Felicity Joy had been alive.

The dining room lay beyond the library. Twin chandeliers sparkled in the late afternoon sun. Jack had chosen well for there would be plenty of room here for them all, even – God forbid – should there be still more children. She could picture her family, Jack's brother, perhaps even his mother and Uncle Rufus, sharing a happy holiday there together.

Yes, Christmas! They'd be in and settled by then. Where would they put the tree?

She hurried back through the library into the great hallway. The tree could be set in the sweep of the staircase. How convenient for setting the star on the top! No, she quickly decided. It might fit, especially if they selected a skinny tree, but why make passage to the rear of the house difficult? This house was certainly large enough for a good-sized tree someplace else.

It would engulf the card room, that was for certain. And she wouldn't want it placed anywhere near a fireplace. So far she had seen one in every room, a pleasing sign for Lizzie loved the warmth and color of fires throughout Buffalo's cold dark winters.

Her eyes circled the edges of the library. All right, it meant going in front of some of her precious bookcases but, for a week or two, she could accept that. Goodness knew, there wasn't time to read once the holiday festivities began anyway.

She paced off the length of the dining room as she passed through again, noting with pleasure that it measured a good twenty feet. How marvelous that the pantry ran the same distance immediately behind it. Her parents had given her lovely linens and sets of china, silver pieces, of course the candelabra, and the assorted sets of cut glass and crystal stemware. While it seemed each house had provided a little more room for their storage, much had always remained packed in crates in the attic in one house, the basement of another. Now, if she was a proper guesser at all, Lizzie felt sure that every piece could be unpacked and displayed behind the glass doors.

There had been one sink in the pantry. Here in the kitchen were two more under a wide window open to a huge yard in the back. The cook stove sat in the far corner, room for the cut wood beside it. She'd have Jack order a gas range at once. She opened each cupboard with curiosity and growing delight. How, in Heaven's name, would they fill them all? She had almost forgotten the convenience modern wives found in the canned vegetables and fruits now readily available. Though their novelty had made them popular at once, the flavors had improved to the point that she didn't object as much as she once had to having them served. Peas and beans were totally different animals, she had to admit, though corn tasted remarkably like the fresh vegetable and beets were quite acceptable. Fruits, however, were something else again. Pears and peaches bore no resemblance to their fresh cousins but, once the taste was acquired, each was quite delicious in its own right. And this thing imaginatively labeled fruit cocktail had certainly caught on quickly in her household. The children didn't seem able to get enough of it. Though couldn't someone realize how important it was for family peace to include more than one, or even two, cherries in each can?

She took the servants' back staircase to the second floor, watching her feet carefully on the narrow winding steps.

Opening the door she stepped into the upstairs hallway, pleasingly noting that it was almost as large as the one downstairs. The staircase arc continued so that the area to the right was banistered and open to the floor below. Further to her right she saw what had to be the master bedroom. The flowered paper, tinted in muted shades of pink with ribbons of green, would have been her choice exactly. Oh, this was a wonderful room! Windows ran down the side that would be over the porte cochere with a lovely marble-faced fireplace in the center. A window at the far left looked out on the street. She walked to her right, curious about the drapes pulled at that end of the room. They opened easily, dust motes swirling as the sun hit them, exposing even more of the property behind the house, a large barn for the carriages and horses, good-sized gardens, and, finally, thick woods far in the back. She wished only that the builders had made the closets a little larger. There were two, of course, but the two together wouldn't hold a tiny fraction of her dresses and there would have to be room for Jack.

The bathroom was large and comfortably bright. She completed her tour of the second floor, passing more quickly through the other four bedrooms and two baths. Grace and Anne would each want a room; she'd let them decide which girl took which as long as they shared the second bath. Ralph could go there in the smaller room with the last reserved for Jack. He had especially asked that room be set aside for a study. Lizzie felt he'd like the view of the woods when he was able to take a break, put his papers down, stretch and admire the scenery he had worked so hard to give his family. Each bedroom also had its own fireplace. Just wait till she told the children!

She opened the door now to the third floor and climbed the straight steps, happily anticipating the brightness that made her advance so easy.

The hall here was no larger than necessary though lighted by windows to the east and the west. The large room in the corner would make a perfect nursery for the twins and baby Clara with adjoining rooms, small but pleasant enough, for Ingrid and Mrs. Backstrom. There was a large bathroom and rooms she imagined Bessie, ten, and John, eight, would demand for their own. She had anticipated yet another bedroom in the far corner and was positively delighted to see that it had been outfitted instead as a storeroom, a pole extending its full length, perfect for all her gowns with enough room for Jack's out-of-season suits. Drawers had been built along the inner wall. She'd bet they'd be filled before too many seasons passed by.

Retracing her steps, Lizzie stopped in the upper hall for a last glance before starting back down to the main floor. Her bedroom was indeed as lovely as her first impression.

She sank down on the top stair where she could see all the bedroom doors at eye level and also the hall and entries to the library there and the card room over there below her. Indeed this would be a very fine house.

She watched the lengthening shadows as she sat anticipating the children's excitement when they were set free to explore their gigantic new home.

Still seated on the step, Lizzie thought back to her earliest days with Jack, the excitement she'd felt at her very first home. Nobody then to help out. And her with meals to plan and prepare, cleaning to do, his mending and upkeep, and trying to pleasure him, and then, before she knew it, the children had started coming.

She smiled, picturing Jack standing nearby, towel in hand, eager to dry as soon as each piece was rinsed. They'd had so little back then – just, really, more children than she'd been prepared for (or, she imagined, than he'd expected) but hadn't each day been a marvelous adventure? She'd not always known how much she'd be able to buy to put on the table, that was sure. And yet, hadn't it somehow always worked out? And that first home. How meager it seemed now, no more than four rooms but how wealthy they'd felt glorying in that.

She saw him beside her – in front of the fire in the winter

or on the front stoop when the days grew too hot, enjoying a refreshing glass of cool lemonade. He'd talk excitedly of his work then, sharing his dreams. She remembered as if it were yesterday his goals, the frustrations, people he had trusted who later betrayed him, those who rewarded him. The simple start – and now . . . now, everything growing so fast. Who could keep up?

Of course it tired him, too. He had neither the time nor the energy to share all that went on at Larkin now. It was enough, she supposed, that he gave her the house, the children, and of course the help, their numbers increasing even faster than the children, or the rooms.

If only they could turn back to the way things had been.

Such sweet days then.

Now. Now it was money. And bigger, as if that made it better. And no time for his family and out almost every night and short with her when he wasn't. Of course, she knew he was overworked and the pressure of a company growing so fast couldn't be turned off when he walked away from Mr. Larkin at six o'clock and he needed more time and perhaps she wouldn't understand the details. Maybe if he tried . . . But Jack's patience was short these days, and he really didn't want to take the time.

Did he, she wondered, ever question what it was she was supposed to be doing to fill those hours? Now that he had hired so many women to do the woman's work for her?

The children had their own lives as they grew. Friends and studies, games, activities but always Ingrid there to accompany them. Now a second nurse for the younger ones.

Although Jack knew she suffered these times of sadness and feelings of utter uselessness, he was too busy working to be directly affected beyond frequently expressing the desire that she snap out of it soon.

Snap out of it! Lizzie would have been delighted to do just that. She didn't like those dark moods any more than anyone else. Too many of her days had already been wasted in shuttered rooms as the nonstop tears fell. Lately too, she occasionally admitted, her dark times had become so bleak that they frightened even her. It was one thing to have a mood, even a bad day. That was expected of women. But it was quite something else altogether when those days became weeks, when she couldn't find a way out of the darkness.

. . .

Lizzie had no idea how long she sat at the head of the staircase but now noticed with a start that the shadows had crossed the hall and begun to climb the stairs towards her. The sun would set soon. Certainly a lady of her stature must not walk the streets of Buffalo alone after dark.

Descending the grand staircase, she took one last look around, knew she'd remember only the hugeness of everything, pulled the door closed behind her, and started for home.

XXVII

February through November 1884

Although Everett noticed the change at once, he couldn't understand this puzzling preoccupation. He had to speak two or three times to Maggie before she even acknowledged his presence.

Back in their apartment Flo found Maggie to be a tangled mess of inefficiency. Whatever was going on seemed locked tightly in her friend's head. Worse were the many hours she now spent in sought reclusion. If this was love, Flo knew she wanted no part of it.

Trouble was, Maggie didn't know what it was either.

How had dreams, which had taken so long to be realized, now been shattered? How could all she had believed in no longer even seem possible?

If there had been a fault, certainly it lay with him. She had done nothing. He'd never given her the chance for, since that one magical evening at the inn, she had heard nothing from Peter.

Oh, yes, the note. How could one forget that note? Saying nothing. Signifying nothing – that she could understand. Simply that "business matters" had made it impossible for him to continue her lessons at this time. Business? What could possibly matter except the glow, that special something, they had shared that night?

Could there have been something she might have done to steer the course differently? If only she knew what.

. . .

Everett hadn't expected good company when he invited

Maggie to accompany him to the band concert the following Sunday. He had patiently watched Maggie come out of whatever it was she had entered the winter before. He might still catch her glazed eyes, staring into a distance he couldn't discern. On other occasions he wished there was something he could give to erase the sadness he saw.

At first she had thrown herself into her music with such fervor that Everett believed it was actually worse than when she had been so miserable studying under that Doctor – Doctor Whatshisname. Nor did he fully understand why the lessons had been stopped so abruptly. Maggie refused to talk about it and he wasn't about to push.

He never had cared for the man. Nor would he try to hide his relief now that that portion of her life seemed over.

Yet she'd never played more beautifully, of that he was certain, especially now that her days had taken a more temperate turn. Each of her smiles radiated deep into his heart while her laughter was like the tinkle of audible sunshine.

Good God! How gross it sounded! Was he really that pathetic? Well, what if he was? Maggie was somebody special, certainly worthy of any feelings he might have. Not that she needed to know, of course. He'd be happy just having her close, listening to her laughter, watching the smiling young woman reemerging each day, just a little closer to the one he had grown to love.

Maggie felt her heart beating with the thump of the big bass drum, soaring with the trumpet and flutes. She looked up at Everett, smiled and wasn't at all surprised, or displeased, when he reached over to grasp her hand. She felt happy, way deep down inside, and was surprised what a simple feeling it was after all.

. . .

As the rays of summer shortened, Maggie experienced a growing resentment toward her music. Oh, to play was glorious, no question of that. To become submerged in something so magical – well, it was a magic. And Everett, God bless him, was patient with her, frequently sitting through what she imagined must have been dreadfully long hours of excruciating practice.

Her trio had been asked to put on a benefit performance in November. They – the violinist and cellist, close friends by now – were being asked to do an entire evening's worth of music. This would require consideration.

Deciding to add a violist and bassist, the five met at one of the neighboring taverns where they knew ladies were welcome. By the time they departed three hours later, their program was set. They'd play the Vojnovich, of course. That figured that to be the grandest of finales. The rest would be a combination of duets, trios, maybe even a solo or two. Rehearsals must begin at once.

At their first, the quiet violist, whom Maggie knew least of all, asked if she had ever considered playing the organ. She had laughed, perhaps too quickly for she hadn't meant to appear rude. But wasn't that about the same as asking him to give up the viola and play the double bass instead?

"I'd never get it under my chin," he had joked in reply. "And you know they tune in fourths, not fifths like the rest of us. But it wouldn't be that much different for you, Maggie . . . Oh, I'm not saying it would be easy. I know there are more keyboards and all those stops."

"And you'd even have to learn to play with your feet," the violinist who had overheard chimed in. "But I think he has a point. I bet you could do it."

"But why would I want to?"

The two replied in unison. "Because it's there."

. . .

Everett was less pleased when Maggie relayed this latest decision. He wouldn't complain, of course, didn't even want her to know how he felt. He had no right to interfere – and so encouraged her with an enthusiasm he couldn't feel.

Maggie read the depth of his disappointment immediately. She would do nothing to hurt him. Only just this one time, such a fascinating challenge. I've got to try. He assured her he understood. She could hope he meant it.

. . .

Her organ instruction began at once, nearly overwhelming Maggie with all the new technical information she was expected to retain. Piano seemed simple compared to the complex mammoth before her. It wasn't long, however, before she was finding the same comparisons in the sound. Once, someone had disparagingly referred to the piano as no more than another member of the percussion family. A piano like a drum? Hardly, she had argued while understanding the point. Now she was forced to make the comparison again. It wasn't that one was better than the other. It was – well, it was just that an organ demanded much more. In turn, it came closer to becoming one with its player. Maggie found that exciting. She was grateful too for the excellent teacher who brought out the best in both organ and organist.

And Everett continued to patiently wait, relieved that the Larkin Factory had no organ to offer Maggie. Let her think what she wanted, he didn't believe her music was the only reason for the contentedness which settled over her.

. . .

Maggie hung her cape on a hook in the dressing room, allowing Everett to see for the first time the gown she and Flo had selected. He felt her eyes searching his, seeking reassurance that he approved. Yet he couldn't take his eyes off her.

The green taffeta shimmered as she moved, making a sound he knew could come from nothing else. Her dark velvet vest was cut low in the modern fashion revealing pure white skin with just a hint of the cleft of her breasts. Short sleeves puffed over her shoulders. Her hair was tied back with a velvet ribbon, red curls cascading almost to her shoulders. He loved Maggie for the uniquely warm person she had always been. He wondered now if that love had blinded him to her beauty.

Catching sight of her, her four partners rushed in, each trying to out-compliment the other until even she recognized the comedy in the situation.

. . .

No musician ever plays perfectly. There is always the passage that could be tweaked this way or improved upon that. Still, all five knew without being told that this was not a night for what-might-have-beens. In tune with their instruments as well as each other, each recognized the brilliant performance. Backstage, after an embarrassing number of curtain calls, they had shrieked and hugged one another in total ecstasy.

. . .

Everett saw them still embracing and laughing with joy. He stepped to the side stairs, happily willing to let them share this moment among themselves.

A figure pushed past him, a young man who scurried up the stairs to the level of the stage. Whatever he said was lost in the din of the moment. Then one of them glanced over and saw him.

"Yes?"

"I've flowers here. Flowers for a . . ." the boy looked down at the card accompanying the lavish bouquet of roses. "Miss Trusler? Miss Margaret Trusler?"

Maggie blushed as she stepped forward to accept his offering. The joy in her expectancy was wonderful to behold. Why hadn't he thought of flowers?

Everett watched as Maggie set the flowers down to open the card. She lifted it from the envelope, turned it over and read the brief note. What was it to turn her joy so quickly to sadness? She checked herself quickly, smiled again and looked around, seeing Everett for the first time.

He hurried to meet her then. She accepted his compliments as easily as his embrace, comfortable in knowing both were genuine.

She turned now to where the roses lay on the dressing room table.

"Look at these, Everett. Did you ever see flowers so beautiful? And you'll never guess who they're from."

"No, I don't imagine I will." He hesitated. Her reaction had been so strange he wondered if he wanted to hear the answer.

"Bert sent them. Can you imagine? All the way from Omaha."

How just like Bert to think of something that grand! Fifteen now, Everett reckoned, and already quite wise in the ways of the world. Probably every bit as amazing as his sister.

The gaslights in the theater had been extinguished by the time Everett and Maggie said a final round of good-byes and hurried out the stage door into the November night.

XXVIII

November 1884

Charlie smiled at Jack and Lizzie as the gaslights dimmed for the evening's musicale. Seemed like every time he came to visit they were whisking him off to one performance or another. He hadn't heard the last of all he had missed last New Year's Day. The whole city was still talking about that one.

Funny, he reflected; he knew Lizzie and Jack held coveted tickets but he had never been able to get a straight answer from either. He'd long ago stopped asking but, thinking of it now, had only an impression of a funny little smile shared between the two. He assumed the music must have been very grand. Something certainly had.

There was that girl again! He watched her cross the stage to take her place at the piano. Bless Lizzie for getting great seats. He had an unobstructed view of the piano, or at least the pianist. And wasn't she a stunner! Something about her always made her stand out. The taffeta, shimmering under the lights, radiated a beauty that could only be matched by the flawless skin above her bodice. Such a perfectly shaped face! Her smile was angelic, the nose slightly upturned. What color were her eyes? Brown? Hazel perhaps? He couldn't imagine blue. Green! Yes, of course! With her complexion how could she have anything but green eyes?

He was grateful it was the pianist who attracted him for the others took turns on and off stage as the evening progressed. There was one duo, violin and viola, played without accompaniment but, for the rest of the program, her presence was essential. A most enjoyable evening of music. Yes, he could honestly say he hadn't enjoyed one more.

Charlie begged the patience of his brother and sister-in-law. Would they mind waiting, just a minute or two, so he could slip backstage to congratulate the musicians? Surprised, Jack assured him it would cause no trouble. He in fact meant to speak to a number of the Larkin managers also present. The men, looking at each other, missed Lizzie's all-knowing grin.

Charlie was swept along backstage in a swell of well-wishers. What, for that matter, did he intend to say? That she was beautiful? Hardly! That she played beautifully? Hardly news to one as talented as she.

He slipped off to one side to let the throng pass, watching as she and the other four gracefully received their well-deserved praises. She was even lovelier up close. He longed to gaze into those eyes – then he'd know what color they were – hoping he wouldn't get tongue-tied when his moment did come.

The crowd was beginning to diminish. Any minute now. He saw the young man carrying the bouquet even before he climbed the stage stairs, observed him wait patiently until one of the others became aware of his standing there. The question. Checking the card, reading her name. Charlie knew it well: Margaret Trusler. And she receiving them with grace. Charlie saw her lay them on the dressing room table just inside the doorway and reach for the card that was attached. He wished they might be from him.

But what was this? He read hope, expectancy, a sudden happiness in her demeanor, and saw it dashed immediately as the words on the card registered. Was that a tear she wiped away? She recovered quickly, turning to acknowledge the presence of an older man Charlie had not noticed before. Nothing to distinguish him from any of the others.

Now he came to her, exchanging hugs. A father? He was old enough but, no, it didn't quite fit. Probably too old for a brother. Their relationship seemed enviably close, two very comfortable in each other's company.

Charlie watched until the stage was nearly deserted. He'd feel foolish approaching this angel now. Worse, something cautioned he might be intruding.

He turned to reenter the darkening auditorium to join Lizzie and Jack.

XXIX

January 1885

"Lizzie. Lizzie! Where are you, Lizzie?" Jack positively burst through the front door.

His wife dutifully laid her pen down. At this rate those Christmas thank yous would never get finished. "What on earth is going on?"

"You won't believe it. Such news! Mr. Larkin gave us – can you imagine that, Liz, *us* – tickets for Laslo Lasowski's recital next week."

"Lasowski? But that's been sold out for ages. You know how hard I tried to get tickets, especially once we knew Charlie would be with us."

"That's just it. Here they are. Delivered, as it were, on a silver platter. And of all people, he picked us to offer them to. Lizzie, I swear, we must be doing something right."

"But . . . how . . . why? I don't understand, Jack. Did he know how badly you wanted them?"

"No. See? That's just the thing. I never said a word. Can't recall even discussing the pianist with anyone at work. This was just out of the blue. But, Lizzie, isn't it grand?"

She jumped up to embrace him. Oh, to actually be in the auditorium when the great Lasowski performed! His reputation, not to mention his antics, was legendary. Probably no figure living in the year 1885, certainly no man of music, was more revered than Laslo Lasowski. Occasionally people might still speak of the magnetism of Franz Liszt, the hysterical ladies throwing their jewels onstage, and certainly no one in her circle would pass up a chance to see, to hear, the magnificent Paderewski, but even he paled beside Lasowski.

"What's all the commotion – Whoops! Sorry, you two, am I breaking up something I shouldn't?" Curious about the uproar Charlie had put out his pipe and come to find its cause.

"Simply an answer to dreams come true," Lizzie responded honestly. "You know how badly I've wanted to see Lasowski play. And in comes Jack with four tickets in his pocket, given to him no less, simply for being an outstanding employee at the Larkin factory."

"Or something like that," Jack laughed.

"Four? But –"

"Have no fear, dear brother. Buffalo holds more than its share of attractive young women. I'm sure our Liz will have no trouble finding pleasurable company for you."

"Lasowski? And an attractive woman as well? That's a hard offer to refuse."

"*Refuse?* But you mustn't. You know we've been counting on your staying another week."

"I do know, dear Lizzie, as you must know there is nothing that would give me greater pleasure. Only I do have a business to run before the state legislature opens next Monday. Even lieutenant governors have something to do occasionally. And I've certainly got to convince my constituents I'm worthy of re-election."

"You?"

"Don't laugh, Jack. In fact, some consider it quite respectable these days and, to be candid, I do believe I enjoy serving the people in such a high capacity. If nothing else, I know because of me there's one less scoundrel sitting in an office in Harrisburg."

"I'm sure you're a very conscientious politician, Charlie. In fact, I wish we could persuade you to run in New York State. But I am disappointed – we both are – to hear you'll be leaving so soon. And you know how the children adore you."

He planted a kiss on Lizzie's cheek. "I promise I'll return as soon as I can."

Lizzie turned to her husband. "But what shall we do with

the extra tickets? I hardly think it proper to give them back to Mr. Larkin. And yet we certainly can't let them go to waste."

"May I offer my suggestion?"

"Yours? Of course, Charlie. What do you have in mind?"

"Remember that beautiful young pianist at the concert last November?"

"Well, I hardly spent as much time watching her as I gather you did. I'm not sure I'd even recognize her if I saw her again. Beautiful playing, though, as I recall."

"What about her?" Lizzie inquired.

"If it's all right – with your permission – I'd like to send the tickets, my two, to her. I don't imagine she was able to secure seats, not if you weren't, and at those prices," for he had glanced at the ducats still held in Jack's outreached hand, "I don't imagine many young women would find them affordable."

"Give them away? Just like that? And to a stranger? Oh, Charlie!"

"Liz, let him be. We offered – no, I gave them to Charlie. Let him use them as he wishes."

. . .

"You did what?" Flo threw her bag heavily on the table and turned back to face Maggie. "I can't believe what I'm hearing. You and that Peter? After all this time? Oh, Maggie, why? Why on earth would you invite him to such an important recital?"

"I thought of Everett, Flo. He goes with me to all these musical things but I don't believe he truly enjoys them. I think he just goes along for my sake."

"Well, of course, silly. We all know that."

"So it just didn't make sense . . . It would mean nothing to Everett, and Peter . . ."

"Peter what?"

"He was positively delighted. And the dress circle to boot! Oh, Flo, I can't begin to explain how marvelous it feels to have something to offer he couldn't get for himself."

"Then you still care for him? I mean, it's been ages. Do you still think of him?"

"Too much, if you want the honest truth. Less, fortunately, than I once did and I do treasure the times spent with Everett. Really. I find he's becoming quite precious to me. But Lasowski! And Peter."

"What can I say?"

"Nothing, Flo, absolutely nothing. Please. No, I'll take that back. Wish me luck."

"I think you're going to need it."

XXX

January 1885

"Beastly night, I agree wholeheartedly. But I'm very glad we were there to witness Lasowski play."

"My Lord, but wasn't that a performance?"

"Say something like that, Lizzie, and I'm not sure if you are talking about the audience, our pianist, or his playing. Struck me at times quite like a three-ring circus."

"Indeed. I've never seen the hall so packed. There couldn't have been an inch of standing room left."

"Nor should there have been. And what an audience! Cheering until I don't wonder if they'll all be hoarse by now."

"And such thunderous applause."

"Well deserved, if I say so. And didn't he make it all seem effortless?"

"Simpleness in the face of so much flamboyance. Shall I heat us some warm milk before we go up to bed?"

"If you don't mind, Liz, I think I'd prefer a dram of brandy. Care to join me?"

"How absolutely decadent! Don't mind if I do, dear. Do you think all those stories about him, his personal life I mean, are true?"

"Why not? Private railway cars, his own grand piano in a salon on wheels, a tuner at his beck and call, his private physician, and God knows what other attendants. Why not indeed? He looks like a king so why shouldn't he act like one?"

"I did notice quite a regal manner about him. Not that that shock of white hair hurt either. Speaking of manners, did you recognize the couple next to us?"

"Not particularly. Should I have?"

"I had hoped so." Lizzie accepted the drink with a nod. "Those were Charlie's seats so I assume the young woman was his pianist though I have no idea who the man with her was."

"I did notice she seemed fully captivated by his charms, though what they might have been quite escaped me."

"Isn't that funny? I had exactly the same impression. He certainly didn't strike me as particularly interesting either."

"Quite boorish."

"Well, I'm not sure I'd go that far."

"I would. You didn't see her after the recital ended."

"I didn't know you did either."

"Remember? I stayed behind hoping to get a chance to thank the Larkins for their generosity. I never caught up with my employer but did see a strange little pantomime, so odd in fact I hung around, waiting to see how it played out."

"So that's why it took you so long to get our coats."

"I'm afraid so."

"Then tell me, Jack, what it was you observed."

"As soon as the music was over, even before the last of the curtain calls was finished, our stranger rushed off, leaving the girl – Charlie's pianist if you will – quite alone. I don't believe he offered any explanation. I certainly didn't hear one and would judge from the stunned look on her face that she didn't either."

"So what happened?"

"Very little. She sat, and she sat, waiting and waiting. As the crowds began to thin, I could see her looking every which way, obviously hoping to locate her escort."

"Do you think she was afraid of being left behind?"

"Not likely, though I sensed a growing irritation."

"I should think so."

"But, even more, . . . Hmm, how should I describe it? Just confusion, I imagine, not knowing what was happening, or why."

"How terrible for her. The man, the one who'd been with her, he did come back though, didn't he?"

"Yes, he did. Though it was quite some time later – well, you know how long I kept you waiting."

"Did he offer an explanation? Could you hear?"

"I wasn't going to let that escape, not after spending all that time. And you'll never believe where he'd been."

"Probably not, dear. So tell me, please."

"He'd gone backstage to meet Laslo Lasowski."

"Lasowski? But why didn't he take the girl with him? If we're right, she's a pianist, and a good one, too. Why would he leave her to go by himself?"

"I've been mulling that over all the way home. Perhaps some mysteries aren't meant to be solved. Ready for bed, my dear?"

She took the snifters and ashtray to the kitchen while Jack extinguished the lights. They were halfway up the staircase when Lizzie turned back to her husband.

"That's a very disturbing story you told."

"It certainly seemed so to me. And you know what else?"

"You mean there's more?"

"Only the tickets."

"Tickets?"

"Yes, you haven't forgotten, have you? Charlie sent them – anonymously, I believe – but he sent them to the girl."

She let the thought settle. "Yes. He did, didn't he?"

XXXI

March 1885

The day began in a fashion fairly typical for March in western New York. Yesterday's heavy snows, up to thirteen inches people were muttering, had subsided late the previous afternoon in time for a stunning sunset to color the skies with a brilliant purple. Its rays across the fresh white-fallen snow created a picture recalled for weeks to come. Especially when they woke the next morning to the unmistakable sound of pelting rain.

The children who had counted on a final day of sledding now stood morosely, noses pressed to window panes as the droplets raced each other to the sill.

Amid general complaints and mumblings, one young boy played contentedly in the nursery beneath the eaves.

Ever since breakfast had been taken away and he properly cleaned and dressed, three-year-old Abram had been totally engrossed with a set of old dominoes. The dots of course were meaningless to the child but oh! what a challenge involved in setting them up, creating imaginary towers, and buildings, then paths that in time developed into wide avenues. Then it became possible for a cart, two or three dominoes high, to charge through those streets, pulled by an imaginary charger of unbelievable strength and speed.

Circling around the obstacle at the end and back to the beginning the small cart raced. Perhaps two could be constructed, similar in nature, and made to compete, right hand against the left. That competition dulled quickly as the child turned his interest back to the vehicle. If it could be a sturdy three layers high, then why not build even higher walls for it to race through?

Blocks from a nursery basket in the corner were added for height. Towers, walls, ultimately a childish obstacle course took form.

Shortly, Abram realized that the walls could be made even higher by the simple device of standing each domino on its side. Now barricades stretched in ever more imaginative curves and patterns across the floor.

If the dominoes remained standing on side, then why not try placing them on their ends? The child's unsteady hands realized the danger in this wobblier venture but warmed to the challenge. Walls soon stretched along the floor.

He heard a sound across the room, glanced up to investigate, saw nothing, but, shifting his legs as he turned back, knocked over almost six inches of the high wall. He was quick enough to see that, while his foot had hit most of the dominoes, knocking them down, two had fallen into two neighboring blocks, causing their fall in turn.

He dismantled the latest wall to experiment. Indeed! If two or three dominoes were placed in a row, like a group of soldiers standing in line, then he had only to fire at the first and it, falling, took the second, the second the third, and so on. It seemed to the child that the possibilities for this game were limited only by the number of dominoes at hand.

So grateful were the grownups downstairs to observe one child not grumbling as the rains continued, that an immediate search was begun for other sets of dominoes.

Abram returned to the still-quiet nursery with his arms full of game boxes.

When served, he ate lunch with disinterest, eager to return to his challenge.

He was proving quite adept at creating long lines of "soldiers" and watching them fall. And since he was playing quietly and not disturbing the others, he was left pretty much alone. Mrs. Backstrom, tending to her duties of minding the twins, checked regularly as was her wont, but finding the child so happily satisfied, remarked on this remarkable turn of events to any who would listen and returned to the more sullen twin downstairs. James was recovering from a late winter sore throat, seemed restless and hot, and required her attention.

Abram, not unrealistically, would have been pleased to garner any approval which came his way for such was seldom deserved. He had learned, however, that, while his temper brought as much attention as any child might want, it wasn't the kind that benefited him much. So, now that he had this magical project, he was satisfied to be left alone. It seemed proper to him, and Mrs. Backstrom hadn't objected, but his brothers and sisters might prove to be something else again. What if they wanted the dominoes returned? Worse, what if one, or more, should want to join in his play? Or show him those things they always termed *better*? No, Abram felt very happy being left alone.

While the solitude was satisfactory, shooting down rows of imaginary soldiers grew tiring. He was becoming aware of how long it took him to construct the row, and how quickly once begun they fell.

He tried making curves but more often than not the dominoes refused to fall in the same line and he was left with half-standing walls.

The curves now began to intrigue him for their own sake.

Soldiers and fallen men put out of mind, young Abram began to construct a long curving S from the many boxes of dominoes before him. When the snake shape was finished, he had enough blocks left over to encircle his original figure. Still more went out in a line and then curved around in the opposite direction. He had just about returned to the original circle and was ready to place his last block.

No. He stopped as he spotted one that must have been pushed out of sight during one of his soldier experiments. He jumped for it instinctively, his foot hitting the side of his latest, and last, construction.

It tumbled, noisily. Quickly. Some of the dominoes fell predictably. Some directions might have surprised Abram had he not ceased to be interested in the effects. He saw only the destruction of his latest efforts.

Abram was not a child of peace.

. . .

The commotion echoed quickly through the second story, and on down to the main floor of the Knapps' home. Each child stopped whatever he was doing, standing still in his tracks. James sniveled, swallowed hard, and regretted it at once. Mrs. Backstrom looked up and across the room, a shocked surprise crossing her face, at no one in particular.

Each sat, or stood, stunned. The question hung in the air though, of course, there wasn't one person, except possibly the baby Clara who had been awakened by the commotion and now began to sputter, her preface to tears, who couldn't guess at once the cause of the unearthly screeching and banging now taking place two stories above them.

. . .

Piece by piece, Abram had taken up each domino and hurled it with all his strength across the nursery. At first it had felt mildly satisfying just to pitch them as hard as his little arms could throw. Almost immediately, however, he had seen the sport in trying to hit various targets. Toys on the shelves fell, even pictures from the walls. Glass splintered and crashed to the floor.

He stopped. That had a pleasing sound, an effect he had liked.

But not enough.

He pitched the rest by handfuls. When that failed to satisfy the rage within, he overturned furniture, kicked the door after slamming it shut, and hurled the chair hard enough one of its legs fell askew.

He beat his hands against the table until he could feel the sensation no more. He tried kicking but found it no more pleasing. The child flung his body to the floor, screaming, finally lost in a world where none of it mattered.

XXXII

June 1885

"What in God's name are you doing up there? What if you fell?"

"Sorry, Flo. I knew you were busy in the other room and I just wanted to check for myself that this cupboard was bare."

"If you'd waited half a min, I'd have been willing to help you. Be sensible, Maggie. What if you'd gone and hurt yourself?"

"I suppose you're right. It's just that I feel so . . . so invincible, if you will. And so great!" Maggie grabbed her friend by the arms and swung her wide.

"Maybe I'm the one who should be worried about getting hurt!"

"Come on, Flo, let's just finish packing this box and I'll put the kettle on for tea. If you want my opinion, I think we've both earned it."

"Offer accepted, Miss Trusler. Whoops. Sorry, Maggie. It'll take a little getting used to, calling you Mrs. Hopkins. It all happened so fast."

"No need to apologize. I'm still getting used to it myself."

"But you are happy? I mean, you seem to be. It's just that it *was* so fast . . . and I know . . . I think I do, how you felt about Peter and . . . well, everything."

"Of course I'm happy. It did happen quickly but I feel it was right. We both know how Everett has felt for, well, I don't know how long. To be honest, I guess his very certainty overcame any doubts I had. As for Peter, that's one chapter of my life that's well worth closing. To be candid, I'm delighted now not to think about it – or him – ever again. Come on; let's find that tea. We haven't packed it too, have we?"

"No. The tea is right here. I had a feeling we might want it before we finished."

"I'm going to miss this apartment, Flo. It wasn't much but we did have good times here, didn't we? And you've become such a dear friend. You know I'll miss you."

"My goodness, it's not like I'm moving to the other side of the world. I'm looking forward to sharing a real house. Those girls from work were lucky to get it, if you ask me – and me every bit as lucky to be looking just when they needed an extra lodger. Why, I'll even have my own bedroom. That's more than you can say, Mrs. Hopkins. See? I did remember."

"I'm sure I saw a second cup somewhere. Yes, here 'tis."

"Come, sit over here at the table. You know I've heard next to nothing about your honeymoon. No, I didn't mean *that*. Tell me about Niagara Falls. Is it as beautiful as they say?"

"Actually it's even better. So big, and the noise from the water! You wouldn't believe it. And there's so much to see."

"To see? How long can it take to look at falling water?"

"That, too. There was something compelling about it. I kept feeling drawn back for one last look. Everett had a fine time teasing me about it but I couldn't help the way I felt. And then of course there was the Maid of the Mist."

"*Maid*? Who's that? You didn't tell me about any maid."

"It's just the name of a boat, silly. But it goes right into the Falls. Oh, Flo, you can't believe how high, or how powerful, they are until you're underneath them like that. You've absolutely got to go, to see for yourself."

Flustered, Flo hurried the dishes to the sink where they were rapidly washed, Maggie appearing in time to do the drying.

"You know, you haven't even talked about work, Maggie. I don't imagine Everett will want you to continue."

"That's still in the subject-to-be-discussed file, at least as far as I'm concerned. He does have this dreadful old-fashioned notion that wives should stay home and poke about the cinders, or whatever it is they do nowadays. However, I have no intention of leaving Larkin's."

"Well, I certainly don't want to cause a newlywed couple's first argument but that is quite a difference of opinion."

"We'll see."

"But once there are children . . . you do want babies, don't you, Maggie?"

"Of course I do. What married woman doesn't want a house filled with youngsters? And I know Everett is anxious to get started. I mean, I do want him to be around while the children are growing up. But until then, and that is still months, perhaps many months, away, I do want to keep my job. In fact . . ." She paused.

"Yes?"

"Well, I don't know if I should say anything . . ."

But of course she did, excitedly explaining the newest Larkin project as the two continued to pack. Already so closely attuned that neither knew the source of their new ideas, Everett had presented the idea and had it enthusiastically accepted. From now on, the Larkin salesmen would endeavor to sell only one box to each household every year.

"One box? How would that work?"

"Think about it, Flo. What if the Company put everything a housewife needed for her family in just one delivery – cleansing and washing soaps, perfumes, even the powders for sachets and teeth –"

"That's a combination I'd rather not think about."

But she understood. Still, Flo pressed, mightn't there be some disadvantage?

"Everett is going to check into it at their meeting this week. It's one of our questions, too. But, near as we can figure, it's probably the threat that it might prove too good an idea."

"Now you are talking in riddles. How can anything that increases business be *too* good?"

"Everett says the company is running at full capacity now. People are working around the clock and we've all heard talk of yet another expansion, more space, more equipment –"

"And more soap. And may we all live happily ever after!"

"Sudsing sillily away!"

"You tell me who the silly is. Come on; let's get back to work. We've got a couple more boxes to pack and, if you must know, I'd like to be out of here before dinnertime."

"A date? Oh, Flo! Really?"

"I'll not say another word, Miss Married Lady. But I bet your hubby would like to see you before dark as well."

"I'm on my way. Quick, let's finish the closet."

XXXIII

July 1885

Lizzie was happy in her new home, as happy as she could remember feeling for oh! so very long. The children had shared her initial excitement of the mansion-like expanse, watching gleefully as the workers readied it for their move, and then fitting quickly into their newly assigned quarters. Ingrid and Mrs. Backstrom, respecting each other without conceding friendship, had readily settled into their third floor rooms next to the nursery.

Summertime brought not only the end of school but, with it, more opportunity for all to explore the deep woods lying behind their home. Grace and Annie, reaching the stage of lovesick young maidens, preferred a particularly shady glen they had earlier staked out to exchange poetry and stories of their latest swains while Ralph had taken it upon himself to make their lives as miserable as possible. Bessie remained a fearless tomboy and happily joined the younger John in their explorations and constructions within the deepest sections of the woods.

Even Abram seemed to have accepted the move. There had been no repeats of his tantrum and, while never a congenial child, he hadn't caused more concern than his twin brother James or the baby Clara with whom he shared the nursery. Clara was toddling now and tended to be into everything. James had taken it upon himself to pick up both his own toys and those of his sister, happily trading the extra chore for the peace that replaced the otherwise constant fighting between his twin and the curious little girl.

July had begun auspiciously. Independence Day had been celebrated Saturday with a giant parade and late night fireworks. James and Abram had been allowed to go to the visiting circus during the afternoon and talked of little for the rest of the day but seeing a real live elephant. All except baby Clara were taken to the traveling carnival the following day, a weekend crammed full of more excitement than any of the children could remember. Ingrid, in spite of herself, appeared as excited as her charges as she accompanied them on the various rides while Mrs. Backstrom merely felt at her wits' end as she tried to keep up with both of the overly active and excited twins.

It was a difficult transition for everyone on Monday morning. While there was no school in the summertime, the normal schedule was enforced as Father woke and breakfasted at his usual hour in preparation for a full week's work.

Grace and Annie were taking turns swinging in the backyard while Ralph circled them teasingly, trying to catch a shoe as they swung through the air. Occasional giggles were the only traces remaining of Bessie and John who'd gone searching the woods for new bugs. Scolding James when she caught him at the screened window at the end of the hall – what was it outside that so entranced the boy? – Mrs. Backstrom watched until he returned to the nursery. Now she saw that Clara had moved to the third floor hallway, playing with some unwanted metal toys that had previously belonged to the twins. She could hear the boys playing quietly in the nursery.

Suddenly Abram swept past her so quickly she needed a second glance to identify which boy it was.

"Abram! Stop! Where are you going?"

"Out."

"Do stay close to the others until I come out with James and Clara." The child mumbled something and ran even faster down the remaining stairs. She heard the door slam on the second floor and assumed he had continued down the stairs and out into the yard. Her attention shifted back to the younger Clara playing peacefully at her knees.

He caught Clara's attention first. She looked up and, when she did, Mrs. Backstrom followed her glance to see James standing in the nursery doorway.

"James, what's the matter? What happened?"

The child wasn't sure whether he should tell, whether he should even be standing there. What would happen when Abram returned?

"James. I asked you a question. Tell me what's going on."

"I can't. I don't . . . It's not. . . It's just that –" Tears rolled down his cheeks.

"James, dear. Come here."

He ran to her open arms and snuggled in as deeply as he could. Mrs. Backstrom thought how marvelous it all was, how very worthwhile, when she could hold one as sweet as this, wrap him tightly in her arms. The satisfying feelings of mothering overcame her concern about the other child. She remembered now and pushed the boy away so she could see his eyes.

"I'm certain there is no cause for tearfulness, James" set off another torrent of wailing. "Oh, goodness, boy, whatever is the matter?"

Finally she was able to calm him and get the words out of his mouth. Disbelieving, she followed him back to their beds, smelling even before seeing the wetness which covered Abram's sheets. Had Abram wet his bed, she wanted to know. If so, and James had nodded yes with reluctance, well, why then was *he* crying?

"He'll hurt me for telling."

"Oh, goodness no, James. It was an accident. These things happen. Yes, even to four-year-old boys. Abram isn't bad, not for wetting his bed. Any more than you are for coming to tell me."

By the time the covers had been stripped and replaced, James, as if having already forgotten, was sitting near Clara playing with her and the tin animals. She giggled happily with the attentions of her older, and much admired, gentle brother.

. . .

Mrs. Backstrom casually mentioned it to Ingrid who felt

compelled to tell the older girls when they asked why the two women had been caught whispering so conspiratorially. By the time lunch had been served, and devoured, every child, except the oblivious Clara, knew precisely what had happened. Abram squirmed and then turned beet red before pushing back his chair and running out, slamming the screen door as he headed toward the woods, unaware and unhearing of Mrs. Backstrom's remonstrances to come back and remain seated until he was properly excused.

By mid-afternoon the episode had been generally forgotten. The children resumed their earlier play except for James who now preferred the company of Ralph and Bessie. At last he tired of their games and returned to the house, anxious to get back to the picture he had started to draw before lunch.

. . .

Jack was getting home later these days. Nothing Lizzie could do about it, just the demands of his more responsible position in the Larkin Company. With it staying light so much longer, she had adopted the habit of waiting to eat with him, frequently having their light supper served on the screen porch. By then the children were quietly occupied and, after he had said the proper good nights, the two were able to enjoy a quiet time together.

Lizzie sat back in the wooden lounge chair under her favorite cherry tree as she waited for the maid to bring her cup of tea. What treat would they serve this time? She especially loved the finger sandwiches the cook frequently prepared for the children's teas but was delighted today with the tiny iced cakes. Anything, she realized now, but the red, white, and blue everything they had been eating for the past two days!

Pangs of hunger rapidly disappearing, she lay back to watch the clouds through the heavily laden branches above her.

The scream had an unearthly quality to it. Awake immediately, it took longer to try to decipher the sound. Before she could, she heard a second scream. A child's cry this time. James? Or could it be Bessie? Then the girls' hysterical howling as they rounded the corner of the house and ran towards her.

"Grace! Annie! What happened? Girls, calm down. Tell me."

Their frantic sobs left both incoherent. As she attempted to comfort her older two, Lizzie became aware of the footsteps and voices, more crying, all around her. She thought she had imagined the worst – until she saw Mrs. Backstrom trotting across the lawn. She was on her feet long before the governess reached her side.

"Mrs. Backstrom! What in the name of God is going on? I have never heard such a commotion. Has there been a fight? Has one of the children been hurt?"

The woman collapsed at her feet. Seeing such behavior from one long considered emotionless, Lizzie stepped forward, then stopped as she realized she didn't know which way to turn. She knelt beside the prostrate woman.

"Mrs. Backstrom, you must tell us. Tell me. What has happened?"

"It's James." And the sobbing began again.

"Mother! Mother!" Lizzie looked up as Ralph raced round the corner of the house. Annie knelt to console Mrs. Backstrom as her mother rose to meet Ralph. Belying his tender age, the young man took his mother in his arms, gently soothing her as she grew even more upset.

"It's James, Mother. There has been a terrible accident."

"*Accident?* What happened? Where is he?"

"In the yard, Mother. At the side of the house."

"Is he . . . What?"

He cut her off as fast as he could speak. "James is dead, Mother."

. . .

The carriage sent for Jack arrived only moments after the doctor.

Dr. Clark met him coming up the drive. "I'm so dreadfully sorry, Jack. No. You don't really want to see him now."

"Nonsense. Where is my son?"

He followed quietly to where the boy lay in the grass at the side of the house, his body twisted, blood still seeping from his ears and nose.

A look up at the house told the story for the well-screened window in the nursery now gaped wide open. Jack looked down again at the twisted body of his child, then back to the window, his mind trying to make some sense of what he was seeing. Did he discern movement up there just now? God forbid!

And where were the others?

He hurried to where Lizzie attempted unsuccessfully to comfort Mrs. Backstrom who was also being soothed by Annie and Grace. Ralph had gone over to the edge of the woods to meet Bessie and John who, hearing the commotion, had retraced their path to the house. Ingrid, learning what had happened, had taken little Clara into the kitchen.

Abram? All were accounted for but Abram. Where was he?

Jack raced through the house, up the sweeping staircase to the second floor, opened the door and ran up into the third floor hallway, prepared to search the nursery for his missing son.

. . .

The boy sat in the middle of the floor, humming quietly to himself, as he played with the tin figures that had earlier occupied Clara and James.

XXXIV

July 1886

Lizzie was drawn by the happy squeals of the children. She reached the vestibule just in time to see Jack pull a cupped hand from his coat pocket. All could now see the tiny yellow and white kitten in his hand.

"Oh, isn't it darling!"

"Adorable."

"Let me hold it."

"No, *me*."

"Now, children, let's not fight over the poor little thing. It will become quite frightened, I'm sure, if this commotion continues. Here, Grace," she turned to her oldest, "why don't you take it to the kitchen and get a little warmed milk for your new pet."

Grace, followed closely by Annie, led the train of children into the kitchen.

"You don't mind, do you, Lizzie? I didn't think a kitten could be a bother. Between the children and the staff –"

"Oh, Jack. I wouldn't mind if it were. I'm positively delighted. To tell you the truth, I'm already looking forward to the children's bedtime simply so I can have a chance to play with it – did I hear you say it's a her? – to play with her myself. Let me see if I can find an old ball of yarn."

He hugged her quickly, content to see her bubbling in her own happiness, before turning to the closet to hang up his coat.

"Have a good day, dear?"

"I don't know about good, but certainly it's been a busy one. I was hardly able to get into the office at all."

"That doesn't sound like you, Jack. What's happened?"

"Oh, nothing like that. Everything is quite all right, chugging away nicely in fact. And," he turned to pour himself a Scotch, questioning his wife with his eyes, understanding her nod, and reaching for a second glass, "the way things are going, I imagine it's fair to say they'll be chugging even more before much longer."

"Now you're talking in riddles again. Thank you." She accepted the glass. "Do let's sit over here where we can enjoy the waning light. Good. Now please explain what you're alluding to."

"Hardly alluding, Lizzie, it's all fact. I've spent the day at Niagara Falls, going over the hydroelectric installations they're putting in there. Like it or not, I'm sure electricity will be the way of the future."

"Say what you may, I'm not convinced. I simply can't see any great advantage to heating and illuminating our home with electricity. Gas has always worked just fine."

"I imagine your ancestors were probably as adamant about giving up their candles."

"Touché, Jack. I know I'd miss the soft light of our lamps, and I think you would, too. But what will come will come."

"Indeed, my dear."

. . .

It seemed that waiting might be the solution when it came to Abram as well. Jack was growing increasingly critical of the boy and the attentions Lizzie gave him while she found herself constantly torn over the child and his demanding behavior.

Even dear Mrs. Backstrom had been openly hinting of her desire to return to the tending of younger children. "Babies in the nursery, ma'am. Boys, big boys like yours, are too much for an old woman like me to handle."

The opportunity came rapidly.

Unsure how Abram would react to losing his nurse, Lizzie was hardly prepared for his unconcealed delight. "What marvelous news," he had surprised her. "Then I'll have all my time just for you."

Assertive and loud, now he withdrew from the confrontations he'd forced with his siblings, content more often to play alone.

But hardly quietly. His friends were now invisible, his adventures imaginary. Spies lurked behind every tree, Indians ready to appear over each hill. Whoops and hollers marked the busy child's range as his games continued hour after hour. Then, once playtime was over, he would quietly return to the large house, seek out his mother, climb silently into her lap to be cuddled, thumb in mouth, until he fell asleep.

As he began to doze, Abram often asked questions Lizzie found unnerving. Where, she often wondered, did one so young find such ideas?

"What will happen when I die? Does it hurt? Where will I go?" He wanted to know if he'd be able to watch them all, from . . . well, from wherever. Could he come back if he wanted? He demanded her assurances that she would never die. What was she to say? What was it he expected? Yes, that she would stay with him forever, as if either one of them would ultimately have much to say about that. "When I grow up I'll take much better care of you than Father. We don't need him, not you and I. You'll see."

"Mrs. Knapp, you'd better come."

"What's happened, Ingrid?"

"It's Grace, ma'am. She's been hurt."

"Not another accident."

"No, ma'am; I'm sorry. Not that kind of hurt. It's her young man. She's upstairs in her room. I think you'd better go to her."

"Of course. Thank you for letting me know."

Lizzie could hear her oldest daughter sobbing even before she reached the door. She knocked quietly. She knocked again a little harder.

"It's Mother, Grace. May I come in?"

"Yes, of course. Just a minute."

Lizzie waited as the girl blew her nose. She heard her slow steps cross the floor. The knob turned and the door opened. She stood facing the tear-stained red-eyed young woman.

"Oh, Grace, what happened?"

The girl threw herself into her mother's arms and then let her lead her gently back to the bed. She flung herself down, burying her sobbing head in a pillow while her mother sat beside her.

"There, there, darling. Crying can't make it better. Is it something we can talk about?"

Grace looked up, sniffed loudly and nodded affirmatively.

Lizzie waited patiently.

"It's Paul, Mother."

"Paul? Did something happen to him? Oh, dear, I always thought he was such a fine young man."

"No, he's all right."

"Did you have a spat?"

"That's hardly the right word."

"You seem too young to have had a real fight."

"No, not that either."

Grace burst into another bout of tears, unable at first to staunch them.

"You know we went skating this afternoon."

Between episodes of choking tears, Grace managed to share the story with her astounded mother. Walking Grace home from their skating, Paul had confessed his desire to continue to court her, saying that she was by far the comeliest and most intelligent girl he knew. Lizzie could understand how such words would raise her daughter's hopes for she was aware of the depth of Grace's attachment to her young man. But, he had gone on, she must understand that she shouldn't expect anything further. *Further?* she had queried. You know, he had stammered, like love, or marriage. Her mind had raced with unanswered questions until he blurted out the final statement: I don't want *retards* for children.

Grace had reacted with astonishment. Abram was different, no one questioned that, but didn't Paul see that he was as intelligent as the others? Retard, indeed! How could he of all people, she had asked, so bright a young man, believe such drivel?

[155]

"But, Grace, we all do."

He had turned then and walked away, leaving the heart-stricken young girl standing alone on the curb.

XXXV

August 1886

The commotion began quietly as individual children rushed around the house, conferring with sisters and brothers and then speeding off to check with another. The murmurs grew with their anxiety.

Where was Annabelle, for such had they named the kitten? She enjoyed the outdoors and was frequently seen racing toward the woods. They imagined she found her own kind of play though nothing had ever been observed except once when Ralph saw her scratching on the trunk of a tree. Sometimes one or another would think they heard her sweet meow far above in the branches. But scour as they might, no cat was ever seen.

Trouble was, that while she liked being out, she had always returned in midafternoon for her saucer of milk. Today the saucer sat untouched until the milk began to curdle in the warm sun. As the children finished their supper they agreed something had to be wrong. Annabelle would never miss a meal for all the young Knapps were certain to save a morsel or two for her.

It would be dark within an hour. Clara, just three, looked to her older brothers and sisters, expecting their help and certain she would receive it. Ralph and John, ten and fourteen and brave beyond their years, offered at once to go into the woods, promising to be back before the shadows grew too long.

The lights were on in the house when they returned. Clara had only to see their faces to know they brought no news and began to wail in anguish.

"Here, Annabelle. Here, Annabelle." The children's calls

echoed through the trees.

Ingrid called the youngsters to their baths, herding the reluctant children upstairs in spite of their protestations.

"Here, Ingrid. Annie and I will take a lamp and go search for the cat."

"I'm sure Grace and I can find her. She probably just climbed a tree and can't get down. You get the others ready for bed. We'll bring her up when we get back."

Anne and Grace lighted lanterns and walked slowly into the dark woods, softly calling the name of their cat. Stopping frequently to listen and waiting for its reply, they became aware only of the strange sounds emanating from all sides of the trees.

Annie jumped. "Wha—?"

"Scared me, too. Listen." They waited in silence. "I think it's an owl."

"Didn't realize such familiar places could get so scary. Brrr, I've got shivers running down my back."

"Me, too. Let's hope we find Annabelle soon."

"Or give up until morning."

They walked on carefully, following the path which had always seemed so familiar.

"There! Look!"

"Where?"

"That tree. Right ahead. See it?"

"No, I don't see a thing . . . Oh, yes." She walked quickly towards the tree that held the gleaming eyes. "Here, kitty, kitty."

"Oh! Annie, stop. Don't come any closer."

Her sister caught up at once, both now standing beside the tree, the eyes shining back in the brightened light.

"What shall we do?"

"I don't know. Well, we can't leave her here, can we? What if one of the children should find it?"

"You're right, of course. I feel like I'm going to be sick."

"One disaster at a time, dear sister. Here, you hold my light while I see if I can get her down."

The stake had been honed to a razor-sharp point, skewering

the animal securely to the trunk. Anne tried unsuccessfully to avoid touching the stiff animal, gave one final heave and stumbled back, cat and stick securely in her hand.

. . .

Stepping off the well-worn path, the girls located a fallen branch, leaves obscuring it to its midpoint. They rapidly scooped out the dry leaves, grateful to find the expected recess beneath the limb, pushed the animal as far under as they could, and replaced the dry leaves.

They hoped nobody would ever have to see the cat again.

. . .

Lizzie was not told. She continued to console the younger children, frequently responding to their desires to traipse the woods behind the house, calling even again for Annabelle. The younger ones, especially Clara and John, included the cat in their bedtime prayers and steadfastly maintained that they knew she would come home as soon as she could. Yes, tomorrow must certainly be the day.

The girls had at last confided in their father. Now realizing something needed to be done and knowing he had no way of explaining that Annabelle was dead, Jack found himself wondering with an involuntary shudder if a puppy would have a better chance.

Thus it was that he arrived home the following Friday with a large retriever mix, a big black dog whom the children, once over their fear of a beast so enormous, named Blackie.

Seeing the children's delight, Lizzie quickly accepted the dog, relieved to discover he was as gentle as he was commandingly huge.

Annabelle seemed forgotten.

Grace and Anne vied with Ralph and Bessie for the opportunity to walk their new pet who diplomatically took turns sleeping at night with either John or little Clara. Only Abram showed no enthusiasm for the dog.

XXXVI

September 1886

The door echoed hollowly as it closed. How could a house seem so empty?

Jack and Lizzie had taken their eager daughters to the train station after the girls had said their good-byes to their younger siblings: Ralph, Bessie, John and Clara eagerly posturing for one more hug and kiss. Even Abram, to the girls' surprise, had put himself forth for their embraces, kissing each in turn on the cheek before running off to play.

After being shown the dining car and lounge, the girls had settled into their Pullman sleeping coach where they were encouraged to rest until time for dinner. The conductor, a bear of a man wreathed in genial smiles, assured the nervous parents that the girls would be well cared for. Going to college now, are they?

At last, feeling awkward as the good-byes dragged out, Grace and Annie encouraged their mother and father to leave them.

Noses pressed to the window of their compartment they waved to their parents until –mercifully – they disappeared from sight as the train pulled from the depot and resumed its course to the east.

XXXVII

Summer 1886 to January 1887

Maggie was frightened. Her experience with men had been limited. Lordy, why hadn't she realized that before? Her father's dying when she was but a girl, her little brother . . . but the rest of her world had been women: Aunt Fil on through to those with whom she worked at the Larkin Factory.

There was Peter but he was hardly an example, at least not of the good things she expected to find in a man. Had, in fact, expected to find in Everett.

Flo had asked her once, before Maggie married, if she was looking for another father in Everett. He was, after all, twenty-two years older. No, Maggie had responded quickly, surprised at the query. She would marry Everett because he was kind, considerate and understanding. And, perhaps also, because he was so insistent.

It wasn't that she regretted it. He was a good husband. She believed she was a good wife to him as well. It was just this baby-business. A year had passed and there was still no sign.

Everett accepted it well, at the beginning, even joking about having to try harder. He was such a gentle, loving man she hadn't minded that at all. Only as time passed love, *that* love, had become a burden.

And now, here he was, crying in the pillow next to hers, Maggie wanting to comfort him but not knowing what to say or what to do. It didn't have to be his fault; couldn't he accept that?

She rolled over to try to sleep, feeling as much a failure as did he.

. . .

In time Everett became more resigned to his heirless state. Maggie was all he expected in a wife – except for the childlessness, of course – and, if he didn't fully realize the pain his was causing her, he did appreciate the woman sharing his life.

She didn't suppose it had been a complete surprise then when he once again brought up the subject of her working. Although it hadn't been mentioned in months, since before last Christmas in fact, Maggie knew it bore heavily on Everett's mind. A wife didn't belong in a factory if her husband could afford better.

By the summer of 1886 Everett was adamant. The workmen in Chicago had only been demonstrating for an eight-hour workday till some fool exploded that bomb. By the time the ensuing riot was quelled, seven police and four of the workers lay dead.

It wasn't, Everett hastened to assure Maggie, that he feared such a thing here. Larkin was a good master and he saw little dissatisfaction at the factory. Still, these things did give people ideas. He simply wanted her as far away as possible from any danger.

Many of those with whom she had begun work had either been transferred or had left. She knew, too, that her biggest reward came from the discussions she shared with Everett. Their idea of adding premiums to the combination box had been accepted and was making rich men out of many.

Recognizing she would always be a valuable helpmate able to share every aspect of her husband's work, Maggie at last resigned. She knew she would not be cutting all ties with the Larkin Company.

. . .

Maggie was a happy housewife. She cleaned their small home from top to bottom – and then began again. She bought the latest books of recipes and tried to improve her cooking though Everett insisted he vastly preferred the simpler dishes she had made before. She followed the latest trends in dress, learning to sew many of the fashions for herself. She knit. She worked needlepoint. Cross-stitch. She taught herself tatting. She smocked dress after dress for Janie's two little girls and wrote her friend innumerable letters. She took long walks for exercise whenever the weather cooperated.

And eagerly waited every day for Everett to come home again. She listened while he told her – she insisting on every detail, asking frequent questions if his descriptions lacked the particulars she thirsted for – everything that had transpired.

She perked up her ears especially keenly when he told her of the latest Larkin premium idea.

"Darned, Maggie, if they aren't going to start offering silver pieces now."

"What happened to the chromo cards? I thought everyone enjoyed those."

"They did – of course they did. But the cards, even selling for six cents when not given away, are nothing compared to a piece of silver. See, here. I brought you these."

"Oh, Everett, they're lovely! Forgive me," she turned one over in her hand, "but by Gorham! Now I truly am impressed."

"Solid silver, too. Can you imagine?"

"No." She looked at the spoon again. "Well, yes, I can. I can imagine just about anything. After all, this is the same company that offered oatmeal soaps with the labels in French. *Notre Ontroduction* no less! Certainly you haven't forgotten that one. Or our *parfumeurs* and that terrible stuff called Madame . . .Whatever."

"But it sold, Maggie, don't you forget that. And so did the soap."

"I couldn't forget, my dear. It puts food on our table, and very nicely, too, I might add. Just makes me wonder what they can possibly come up with after this. I can't begin to imagine."

"I think I can, for I have heard talk of what they are calling the Mammoth Christmas Box."

"*Christmas Box!* How could anything be more mammoth than the combination box? Everett, we'll need a larger house just to hold all our soap. It was a hundred cakes last year!"

"And don't forget the perfumes –"

"Those I refused to keep, loyal wife or not."

"The cold cream, tooth powder –"

"Right, even that Napoleon Shaving Stick. Everett, our cupboards are full!"

"Then I'm afraid you'll have to make room for more."

"What more can they possibly offer? What more can they make?"

"Not soaps, not this time. But gifts. Baby toys, hair pins, glove buttoners, handkerchiefs, collar buttons, even, if I recall correctly, a tack hammer."

"A hammer! What on earth does soap have to do with a hammer?"

"I have no idea, dear Maggie. I'm sure the Larkin Company doesn't either. But it sells. Now, let me help with the supper. Just as soon as you tell me about your day."

Hard as she tried, there never seemed much to relate.

. . .

Christmas was a happy time – and a relief. Maggie spent many hours decorating their home, baking cookies and other sweets, planning a special dinner, and making ornaments and gifts for friends.

They celebrated their second Christmas together happily, and quietly.

. . .

It was on a Sunday morning early in January when the rector at St. Paul's made the announcement. A search would be starting soon to replace the organist and choirmaster who was forced to retire for medical reasons. Maggie's fingers involuntarily itched just thinking of the opportunity. She had continued her lessons and grown quite proficient, if she could be so immodest as to say so, thanks to a large extent to her being permitted to practice on the great organ at St. Paul's itself. Certainly somebody there had to know of her interests, her abilities.

"Pouting won't do any good, Maggie. You know the very idea is unthinkable." She turned as Everett helped her into her coat.

"I don't doubt that you're right." They had reached the line waiting to be greeted before leaving the church. She suddenly spun back to face her husband. "But why should it be? Why?"

"What's come over you, Maggie? Be reasonable."

"Why should I be, Everett?"

"Because you're a woman, that's why."

"Of course I am. But I'm also an organist. And a good one at that, if I may say so."

"But, my dear . . . In a church? Here? A woman up *there?* They wouldn't consider it for a moment."

Her head shot up in glaring disbelief. This was the end of the nineteenth century. Women were no longer expected to be kept unseen. Not even here at the cathedral. Why, look at all the years Fil had been a devoted member of its choir. Never, Maggie reflected now, was there a woman more noticed, more noticeable. Obviously no one had objected to her being there. So why now?

"No, I refuse to accept that. The congregation can't even see who's playing during the service."

"I'll grant you that, dear, but the announcement was for a choirmaster as well. St. Paul's has always combined the two positions."

"I can't say I've had much experience with singers but I certainly know my music. And, as for working in a group, why –"

She stopped, suddenly embarrassed as she grew aware of the many people around her. She hoped her words had gone unnoticed.

Smiling, she half-curtsied and extended her hand to the waiting priest.

Father Schuster continued his courtesies in the dwindling line. Words for Mr. And Mrs. Larkin stretched into paragraphs for no one was a larger supporter of the cathedral's projects.

"May I stop round to visit tomorrow, Father?" the

distinguished gentleman interrupted. "Mid-afternoon perhaps?"

"Of course, John. Any time. You know my door is always open for the Larkins."

. . .

It was to Maggie Hopkins' great surprise and much greater delight that she was hired as organist and choirmaster at St. Paul's Cathedral in early February. If there were any objections, neither she nor Everett was made privy to them.

XXXVIII

March 1887

Never had she seen such splendor. Still overwhelmed Maggie also experienced a tinge of sadness as she realized how much Fil would have enjoyed sharing this spectacle. Her aunt had won a certain degree of fame for giving elaborate parties but never anything to rival this.

Everett was seated quite far down the long table, animatedly talking to the buxom woman on his right. Maggie watched her lift her head and turn to smile at him as she laughed, the sound failing to carry through all the conversations in between. She was relieved the men seated on either side of her were occupied with their other dinner partners for she wanted nothing more just now than to silently drink in the scene before her.

She'd had her doubts when Everett first proposed membership in this thing called Shakespeare Club. What did she, or he for that matter, know about Shakespeare? And why a club? And why now?

The answer to the second, Everett reproved, was simple. "Because they asked us, dear. As for your other *why* perhaps I should counter 'Why not?'

"From what I can gather, the people are quite a nice bunch. They did choose us, after all, so they can hardly be all bad. And I know you do relish dressing up – perhaps even an occasion for a new ball gown or two."

"Then –?"

"Forgive me; perhaps I didn't mention it. These are dinner meetings, formal attire required, and there's nothing I'd like better than to see you fitted for a new costume. And a hat, I know how you enjoy those. The bigger the better, if I know my gal. Tell you what, Mag; let's just give it a try. If you don't like it – who knows? Perhaps I'll be first to beg off – well, anyway, we don't have to feel committed for any longer than we like."

Maggie frequently questioned who was being committed to what as the day of their first meeting approached.

She knew with certainty she felt intimidated as she walked up the stairs of the Niagara Club on Everett's arm. Who were all these lovely women? Their splendid dresses rustled with the colors of the rainbow. And the hats! She couldn't help but wonder if there would be any ostriches left for weren't all their feathers preening before her now? And diamonds! She had hers, too; no self-respecting woman would wear any less. But still.

Two women greeted her as she entered, welcoming her warmly as they offered to show her to the combination cloak and ladies' powder room. What a relief, Maggie smiled; these two at least seem very nice. Perhaps they only look stuffy.

Many of her performances were recalled now as introductions were made and she modestly acknowledged their praise. More than a few were also acquainted with her work at St. Paul's. How marvelous that a woman was considered capable for the position, they echoed. And have you ever heard the choir sound as good as it does now? My dears, you must come and hear what wonderful changes Mrs. Hopkins has made. More than a few kindly mentioned anticipating the great services at Easter.

They had been happy to introduce their husbands, faces and names turning into an indecipherable blur before the night's hosts and hostesses called them for dinner.

Now she sat, silently, thinking of Fil while trying to assimilate all that stretched before her. The single table had to be close to sixty feet long. Maggie counted quickly, estimating approximately forty-four men and women seated around it.

A dozen, no sixteen, silver candelabras held tall flickering white tapers as flowers of varying shades of reds and pinks were interspersed with ivy throughout its length. One huge arrangement at the table's center threatened to overwhelm them all.

Maggie had initially been dismayed on learning that seating was by place card and realized she would be separated from her husband but the gentlemen on either side proved congenial, welcoming her warmly and including her in their jests.

The soup bowls had been cleared and six waitresses dressed in identical black uniforms were now presenting dinner.

"Hmm? Oh! I am sorry. I'm afraid I didn't hear what you said. I guess I am quite overwhelmed with all this . . . this. I never dreamt such a thing could be happening in Buffalo."

"I understand entirely, my dear. I can remember when Fannie and I joined. Shall I tell you a little secret?"

She laughed. "Yes, do."

"I had never even owned formalwear before we were admitted to this club. I remember my terror that first night. I felt it was such a charade, my being here at all. Certainly someone would find me out. Why, I half expected to get the boot before the dessert plates had been cleared."

"You? Oh, no! Not really!"

"It's a jolly good thing there are more of my kind here than the other."

"Now you're speaking in riddles. I'm afraid I don't understand what you mean."

"Doesn't this select group look like representatives of good Buffalo's upper, *upper* crust? That was certainly my initial impression."

"You mean they aren't? To be perfectly honest, I have been wondering why we were invited. Everett has a good position, I don't mean that, but he doesn't hobnob with people like you." She laughed gently. "Oh, dear, that came out wrong, didn't it? I do apologize. It sounded quite dreadful. I only meant that, while Everett has a good position with the Larkin Company, we are hardly wealthy people, not by any stretch of the imagination. And what am I but a pianist who's become the organist at St. Paul's? Nothing I'm ashamed of, please don't get me wrong, but not exactly the likes of you."

"Of me? That's it! That's what I mean. *The likes of me!* Margaret – may I call you by your Christian name?"

"Of course, though I do prefer Maggie. And you're? You'll have to forgive me. I usually do quite well with names but tonight . . ."

"A veritable Niagara, to be sure. Nothing to apologize for, Maggie. Anyway, as I was saying, I fear it's you who may be here under false pretenses. Upper crust? Hardly. I'm a teacher at the local Academy. Could I perhaps have had one or more of your children in my classes?"

The rising pink in her cheeks and a quick shake of her head caused an immediate apology.

"I'm sorry, I didn't mean to pry. Let's get back to an easier topic – me!"

She laughed, comfortable with his openness. She was enjoying this encounter.

"The woman down there, in the pale yellow, is librarian at the main library. Name's Ardith Minor," he continued rapidly. "Joe's a doctor but the man two down is a cobbler. And at the far end of the table –"

"The distinguished gentleman wreathed in that lovely halo of white hair?"

"That's the one. He's our Presbyterian minister. Nothing fancy after all. Just a bunch of people who enjoy meeting and hope to better themselves, maybe even learning a bit about the Bard along the way."

"Nobody really explained the programs to me. Is it all to be Shakespeare?"

"Do I detect a look of fright? Really, it's not that bad. We study, we read, and, horrors! we also critique. But it's friends among friends. And all Shakespeare? Oh, no. Tonight for example, Ella May has promised to read from her latest book of poetry. Though that," he leaned closer to Maggie conspiratorially, "just might be worse than Shakespeare!"

She laughed again before turning to the hot dinner placed before her. A salad course followed; then coffee was poured as the guests waited for dessert. She refused a cigarette when the tray was passed and rose when she saw the other women doing the same and followed them back to the ladies' parlor.

"Don't look so surprised, my dear." A lovely older woman dressed in purple lace tugged at her arm as she spoke. "Your face gave you away. It's barbaric, and definitely out of date, but decreed by whoever does such things that we women must repair back here to ahem! powder our noses or whatever we feel needs attending to."

"Is there a reason?"

"For us? Hardly. But it gives the men a chance to talk together and smoke those smelly cigars over a glass of brandy. Bear with us. We'll be going upstairs soon."

"And that's for –"

"Why, for the program. If you've never heard Ella May read her poetry, you're in for quite a treat."

. . .

She'd have to wait to compare notes until she and Everett were alone in the carriage going home. She anxiously wanted his opinion. Was this strange woman, ranting on and gesticulating wildly, as talented as some seemed to suggest? Or had her dinner partner been more accurate when he had suggested it rivaled medieval torture? She had tried, really she had, but if there was meaning to be gotten from the words, much less the gestures, it continued to escape her.

Applause cut into her reverie. She and Everett rose with the others, congratulated the beaming poetess, thanked their hosts, bid hearty and genuinely happy good nights to all, and rushed into the evening's brisk air, full of impressions eager to be shared.

XXXIX

Spring 1887

"God, Lizzie, whatever is the matter with you? Any other woman would give her eyeteeth to be in your position. I want you over here . . . right now . . . Look at these plans!"

Lizzie slowly crossed the room to where Jack had spread the architect's drawings.

"It'll be one of the grandest houses in Buffalo," he continued, turning to look her square in the eye. "You should be thanking your lucky stars that you have a husband like me, instead of standing there sulking like one of the children."

"It's just that I had no idea. I thought you were happy in this house. Surely the children and I have been."

"The children will be happy anywhere."

"But what of Grace and Anne?"

"What of them?"

"This is the home they know, the one they'll remember. Do you expect them to return to a strange place?"

"Why not? Any place is a *strange place* at first. I'm sure once they see the plans, all will be well."

"And will they be allowed a choice in the decorating of their rooms?"

"Room. They won't be home that often. The architect and I figured that we could save space by doubling them up."

"Well then, will they be allowed any say at all in the matter?"

"Lizzie, be reasonable. They're away at college. How many more times do you think they'll ever want to call any place we are *home?* Perhaps we can allow them to choose a color scheme, if you think they can agree on one, and if the decorators don't object."

"So once again am I to be denied any decision-making in the process?"

"Damn it! I expected gratitude, not these immature objections, gratitude indeed that such an onerous burden had been lifted from your shoulders."

Perhaps, she thought bitterly, these frequent moves would – nay, might – be acceptable if he only would permit her some input. Was she really so wrong to want to choose colors she liked? To shop for furniture which pleased her? Or, at the very least, was comfortable? Draperies, carpeting, even the paper on the walls. All appeared as if by some dastardly hand of magic before her astonished, and despairing, eyes.

Lizzie watched morosely as the FOR SALE sign was hammered into the front yard of the house she had come to love as home.

She wept quietly . . . and often.

. . .

Though Jack immediately took credit, Lizzie suspected the new site was only accidentally no further from the Academy where the children were enrolled. Four-year-old Clara would remain at home in Ingrid's care while Abram was prepared for first grade.

Lizzie accompanied him to meet his teacher and was happy to be greeted by an attractive young woman who introduced herself as Sarah Andersen. She was also pleased, as she looked around the classroom at other new students, some showing definite signs of strong trepidation, to have Abram eagerly pull away from her hand to explore this new facility. It gave her a moment to seek out other eyes. How young some of these women seemed! Many had to be first-timers. One young woman, barely into her twenties, held a tugging youngster by one hand while obviously swollen with another.

How contented Abram seemed here. Her early fears were replaced with a buoyant joy that lifted her spirits as she walked away from the Academy, youngest son in tow.

"Yes, Mother, that was a lovely place. I imagine the

children who attend will be very happy indeed."
   She didn't dwell on the odd remark.

XL

September 1887

Now that J. D. Larkin & Co. had released the last of its
salesmen, all selling would have to come from advertising or
the mailings that continued to increase as satisfied customers
sent in friends' names with hopes of further Larkin rewards.
More people were being hired all the time, Jack explained
that too, but with it all, Lizzie must understand, came more
responsibility. The bigger the train the harder the engine
had to struggle. While Jack made no pretense of being head
engine, he did like to think he was close to the front of this
magnificent machine.

Groundbreaking took place the day before school was set
to begin.

The next morning Ralph, already fifteen, and Bessie and
John, thirteen and eleven, had set out toward school long
before Lizzie was prepared to leave with Abram. The child
seemed pleased as he was dressed in a new suit. It was a great
treat for Mama to be taking him on an outing alone.

. . .

"No!" he shrieked. "I won't be left here. I won't stay.
Mama, I want to be with you."

At Miss Andersen's insistence, Lizzie reluctantly left the
angry child. The sound of his familiar tantrums echoed as she
hurried down the otherwise-still hallway and out the front
door of the Academy.

She did not expect him to arrive home in a carriage. Nor to
find Miss Andersen standing at the front door.

"I'm sorry, Mrs. Knapp. Abram was terribly unruly but,

in all honesty, really looks worse than he is. I just wanted to accompany him so you'd understand. I have spoken to our headmaster and we feel certain things can be worked out quickly. After all you and Mr. Knapp have done for the school, I'm sure this problem can be resolved. I say now, has the boy ever been left alone before?"

Abram clung to Lizzie's skirt as the schoolmarm finished speaking, eyed the boy with disdain, turned and walked down the stairs and back to where her carriage waited at the curb.

. . .

"Jack, I'm at my wit's end. We all are. Nobody knows what to do with the boy."

"By *boy* may I assume you are speaking of Abram?"

"Of course I am."

"Then what is the matter? We are into the second week of school and, last I heard, there have been no further reports of trouble."

"Well, there have been no further reports, either good or bad. I simply have to hope – and pray, I might add – that he is adjusting. No, at this point I am more concerned with what I see."

"Which is?"

"Look at your son, Jack. He doesn't respond when one speaks to him. He won't play. He takes no interest in being inside, or out. And Ingrid tells me he hasn't finished a meal in days, not in fact since school began."

"Well, I hardly think the latter is cause for concern. The boy will eat when he's hungry. They always do."

"But this is different, Jack. He seems to have lost interest in everything."

"I doubt if that will last either. Boys are born to be boys after all. He is attending school, you're sure of that?"

"Yes. I've even stooped to having the older children check to be sure he enters the classroom. I'm certain, once inside, Miss Andersen will detain him until the day is over."

"Then, dear, I fail to see the problem."

. . .

"I am so sorry, Mr. Knapp." Sarah Andersen greeted Abram's parents. "Mrs. Knapp." She nodded in her direction. "Please, won't you have a seat?"

Lizzie glanced at her husband who sat stone-faced as he waited for the teacher to continue.

"I just want you to know I have dealt with aggressive students before. Some have seemed terribly immature when the term began. A few, I'm afraid, have been recommended to be held back a year."

"Our son?" Jack's voice rose as he became more adamant. "Are you telling us he's slow? I won't believe it. If you suggest holding him back, I'll ask the Board to review your credentials immediately."

"Threats won't affect me, Mr. Knapp, or, if you want to know, my position. But to answer your question, no, I am not suggesting the boy be held back. Abram, in fact, is one of the brightest children I have ever had in class."

"Surely you're not suggesting he be moved to the second grade. He is, after all, just a child."

"Oh, no. You mistake my meaning. Abram is definitely not ready for the second grade." She paused. "I said he was bright, Mr. Knapp, and he is that. I'm sure he could be a quick learner, could rise and could probably stay at the top of his classes throughout the Academy. But it's his behavior."

"Behavior? Pardon me, Ma'am, but I believed that was what we paid you for."

"Yes, Mr. Knapp. I understand. I am expected to be disciplinarian as well as tutor to my charges, and I can tell you I do my very best. Because first grade is always a difficult time of transition, I have been given extra training precisely to work with children of this age."

"Miss Andersen, we have hired you to prepare our son for higher education. Yet here you are now, telling us you can't deal with an unruly six-year-old, if I accurately catch your drift. Am I, or am I not, correct?"

"He's just – well," she glanced at Lizzie who smiled involuntarily. Misinterpreting the smile as encouragement, she continued. "He simply will not behave. In fact, I can honestly say that he has disrupted my class every single day since the term began."

"I want precise examples, Miss Andersen. *Disruption. Misbehavior.* These terms mean little. Why, for all I know, I may have been labeled equally so at his age."

Lizzie knew Jack would never stand up for the boy. He was fighting for his honor now, not that of his son.

"Abram is exceptionally active. Impulsive. He fidgets constantly. Has to have something in his hand to turn, or to tear, or to . . .well, do something with. He won't – or can't – pay attention. Examples? All right. I have a story time each morning. All the children gather around me, sitting cross-legged on the floor to listen as I read to them. They all enjoy it. All, that is, but Abram. I suspect he might be bored – although, goodness knows, I have found nothing else to keep him still. And, Mr. Knapp, I have tried. Really, Mrs. Knapp, I have."

"During this time Abram twists his hair while all the other children listen eagerly. Then he sucks his shirt, or a piece of chalk if he can reach one. By the time I am on the second page he has grown so restless he begins to bother the children near him."

"*Bother?* Explain yourself."

"Reaching out. Pinching. Hitting. Even kicking if one should continue to ignore him. More often than not, all attention is soon turned on him."

"Miss Andersen, be reasonable. There is more to class than reading stories."

"Yes, of course. I didn't mean that. But you did ask for an example. Let me give another. I can honestly report he gets along with absolutely no one in the room."

"You mean he has no friends?" His worried mother leaned forward to accent her concern.

"I'm afraid not. He has such a hot temper that many are already afraid of him. It's a strange thing but, if I were to try to describe his behavior, I'd say he is as immature in his actions as he is advanced in his abilities. Can you honestly tell me he has shown no indication of any of these traits at home?"

Lizzie looked to Jack for assistance, realized none was

forthcoming, and turned back to face the teacher.

"Yes, in fact everything you say is true."

"Lizzie! How can you?"

"Because what Miss Andersen says is the truth, Jack. If only you were home more, then you'd see it, too. Abram is impossible. He doesn't sit still. He pays little, if any, attention to anyone. Ingrid has told us the same thing for years now."

"What does she know?"

"I'm sorry, Jack. I assumed – hoped perhaps, school would be the answer."

"My guess would be that the classroom experience has only magnified the problems which already existed, Mrs. Knapp."

"What does that mean?"

"Here, you see, Mr. Knapp, a child is expected to pay attention. And of course behave in an appropriate manner. There is no other way to control a classroom of six-year-olds."

"Well then, Miss Andersen." Jack rose quickly. "I expect you to teach Abram to behave. You set the rules, let him know what they are, and enforce them. It's as simple as that. It's what we pay you for." He grabbed his wife by the arm, pulling her to her feet. "Come, Lizzie, we've wasted enough time here."

XLI

December – January 1888

There were no further reports on Abram from the Academy. While fearing tomorrow's news, Lizzie appreciated the relief each day's quiet brought.

The Holidays came and passed joylessly. For a while Lizzie had been able to fill the idle hours, carefully repacking all the heirlooms she had so carefully set behind the glass doors in the pantry. She no longer cared where the servants put them next.

Grace and Anne had arrived home, full of themselves and the experiences of life at Vassar. Vacations now over Lizzie felt a new emptiness as she watched their train chug slowly out of the station. Ralph and Bessie stood, arms around her waist, until it disappeared from sight, fearing the little death they saw taking place within their mother.

. . .

"Do you think she might? I don't know, it sounds like a wild idea to me."

"Can't hurt to ask, can it?"

"But what would Papa say?"

"Dear Bess, let's first find out what Mama will say."

Lizzie perked up her ears at the mention of her name. "What Mama will say about what?"

Ralph stooped to scratch Blackie's ears before continuing.

"We know how unhappy you've been. I'm sorry, it isn't a secret. Anyway . . ." He began to stammer.

"Well," Bessie cut him off. "We just wanted to suggest that perhaps you'd be happier if you found something to do outside the house."

"Outside? Like . . . oh, no! I've had my fill of charitable work and church organizations."

"Oh, Mother, we both realize that. What we were thinking of was more like the Women's Temperance Union –"

"Or the Red Cross –"

"Working for the women's suffrage perhaps. There are a lot of things you could do."

"And I've thought of every one. I appreciate your concern, I really do, but I just can't interest myself in woman's work. They all seem such fussy biddies. I'm sorry."

"No," Bessie cut in quickly, "I'm old enough already to know exactly what you mean. But mightn't there be something else?"

"Could you get a job?"

"Oh, Ralph! Can you imagine your father if I did something like that?" She paused. "Doing what? Working in his factory?"

"Of course not, Mama. But there are respectable positions available, you know."

"Such as?"

The two youngsters answered in unison. "The Public Library."

"The Library?"

"Yes! They've just posted an advertisement for an assistant to the librarian. Wouldn't you like to be something like that?"

"Yes, I would in fact. You know, I really would. Let me think about it . . . yes . . . but shhh now. Promise you'll not say a word to your father."

By the time Jack learned of his wife's undertaking she was already happily ensconced behind the files of the Buffalo Public Library.

XLII

March 1888

The head librarian and her second assistant were flabbergasted when Lizzie struggled to work Monday morning, March twelfth. Snow had been falling steadily since the day before, mounds rising quicker than road crews could cart it away. There was already talk that the snows would bring the city to a halt. This came as startling news to Lizzie. She couldn't imagine J. D. Larkin & Co. coming to a stop for anything. Was such a thing even possible? she asked, shaking mounds of snow from her head and shoulders as she removed her cape.

It was, both assured her. In fact, they continued, there was absolutely no reason for her to be out and about. Weren't the snows enough to make her want to stay at home?

She laughed easily, for these were friends by now, explaining that she was much happier here than roaming around a house which still seemed strange. It occurred to her that she was more familiar with the library stacks than with the contents of her rooms at home.

The women completed their filing and paper work while waiting for any customer brave enough to appear. When none had come by eleven, Ardith, for the head librarian was Ardith Minor, sent her other assistant, Jo, home. Knowing she was welcome to depart, Lizzie elected to stay.

It was only as they were finishing their soup and hot tea that Ardith mentioned Shakespeare Club to Lizzie.

"A what club?"

The other woman felt encouraged to describe the organization and its proceedings to the unbelieving newcomer.

Lizzie thought it sounded wonderful, challenging yet full of warm, nice people. She would enjoy spending an evening that way.

But there was Jack. The moment she thought of him, she turned to her friend to offer both an apology and her regret. No, she didn't imagine Jack would be interested in joining any club, much less one with literary goals, and certainly never one who accepted members like . . . well, such as the head librarian herself. Jack, hoping to follow his brother, had already set his ambitions toward the state level. Mingle with a bunch of preachers, teachers and librarians?

Ardith laughed uncomfortably. Not every member was married. Nor did every married member bring a spouse. No, Ardith continued, this was open to all those eager to learn, to improve themselves, though, needless to say, the socialization was appreciated as well.

Lizzie didn't refuse outright.

. . .

The snows ended Wednesday night. Townsfolk heralded the moon. By Sunday afternoon the thermometer had risen into the high fifties and the streets, impassable before, were now equally bad as the slush once more brought the traffic to a stop.

Throughout the east four hundred died before the storm ended.

. . .

Lizzie wondered bitterly why she should have been surprised that she anticipated every objection Jack offered. She knew the man so well while, she reflected, he knew her not at all.

It was not a club that offered him any advantage. It sounded boring, its members trite and dull. As for dressing, well, he had his Niagara Club. What else did he need?

. . .

Perhaps it was meant as compensation to Lizzie, a way of

saying that he realized he had disappointed his wife. Maybe there was no relationship between his acts at all.

. . .

Jack's bringing the rabbit home met unanimous approval. It should have been an Easter gift, he assured them, but with the weather this year, it seemed better to take one when it came available. Leave the Easter bunnies for others. A hutch was quickly and enthusiastically erected.

It was Blackie, however, to whom the children remained most devoted while the beloved dog returned their love tenfold. He came scampering when called. He cuddled when it proved helpful. He slept with whomever felt lonely or afraid. And, when possible, he remained steadfastly at Lizzie's side.

It was especially painful therefore when Lizzie heard reports of his snapping – even, on rare occasions, growling and, once, worse, threatening to bite. She was sure it just had to be the children's wild imagination. He was a good dog, the best she had ever had.

Now Lizzie stood above the rabbit's cage, utterly taken with the soft gray animal, bewitched as she watched its twitching nose as it looked up with the softest eyes. Jack had made a good decision in choosing the family's newest pet.

. . .

Ralph claimed he saw Abram poking the big stick at Blackie while the dog was in his cage.

Bessie said Abram would offer a bone and then snatch it away when the dog was tied and helpless.

John insisted his younger brother had kicked the poor pet on at least one occasion.

Clara wouldn't testify against him but pouted until everyone noticed and then sulked away, turning once to sneer at the angry boy.

Lizzie and Jack, who did talk it over, wished only that they could know for sure.

. . .

Jack had had to return to the Academy once that spring. A round of visits rapidly followed until he too was forced to accept the ultimatum to which Lizzie had long ago become resigned. They could withdraw their financial backing if that was their desire. The school had no control over that. But didn't they want to consider what might be best for Ralph and Bessie and John, too? Ralph would be graduating in just over a year. Did it make sense to move the boy to another school now? And, nobody needed to remind them, Clara would be starting first grade in the fall of 1889.

Not, the official assured the Knapps, that this was to be interpreted as any kind of a threat. Their three children were excellent students, all of them a credit to the school and welcomed there. At the same time certainly they recognized there were many well-qualified youngsters in Buffalo. Some, in fact, had been on the Academy's waiting list for one, going on two years.

Lizzie always avoided Jack when he was angry.

The private tutor had already been hired before Jack casually mentioned his decision to Lizzie one night as they were preparing for bed.

. . .

Now life in the Knapps' household seemed stuck in its routine. Ingrid welcomed the students home each day after school while their mother waited not far away, anxious to share the peaks of the day. Abram remained cloistered in his room where many hours were spent with the tutor, a brilliant thug-like fellow who enforced peace and resisted any questions, complaints or compliments.

The children were fed promptly at five-thirty, ate in the kitchen chatting among themselves and with the help, and were then released to their lessons or, once those were finished satisfactorily, to practice, for each child was expected to learn music as well as the basics and the classics.

Though Jack seldom joined her at the table now, Lizzie rigidly stuck to her "dinner hour", ultimately eating quietly, and alone.

Word, rapid murmurings, spread quickly through the second and third stories of the house. Mama had not taken dinner tonight. Bessie sneaked down the stairs to spy at her mother's bedroom door and raced back up to report the unlikely. Not only was she not putting on her nightclothes, she believed Mama was dressing up.

Impossible, the boys retorted. Clara tittered.

They raced to the banister in time to see their mother walking proudly down the grand staircase. She was wearing her newest gown, the ostrich feathers on her hat nodding under the gaslights of the many-tiered chandelier as she descended. As she reached for her fur cape, they caught the sparkle of her diamonds. Yes, they murmured, surely she was wearing the earrings her mother had given her. And look! That had to be Grandmother's diamond ring. Nobody now, not even Papa, could afford one that size. She checked her diamond watch before stepping into the vestibule.

Mama! Mama! The children clamored down the staircase, eager to discover what was going on. Where's Papa? And where are you going?

"I'm going to Shakespeare Club."

XLIII

May 1888

"Good meeting tonight, wasn't it?" Maggie nodded in appreciation as Everett helped her into the waiting carriage.

"I'm enjoying Shakespeare Club more and more. Think it just takes some getting used to."

"It is hard to believe we're already into our second year, isn't it? What did you think of our new member?"

"Who? Oh, that woman?"

"Come now," she laughed, "don't tell me you didn't notice her. Dripping in diamonds and ostrich feathers, and have you ever seen a dress any more magnificent? Very pretty, too."

"Oh, I noticed her all right. Man would have to be blind and deaf not to. But I liked her. Did you have a chance to talk with her?"

"I did indeed, and agree completely. First impressions aren't always the lasting ones. I learned that many, many years ago. I liked her, too. Had to admire her pluck as well."

"*Pluck?*"

"Yes. From what she told us, I gather she had tried repeatedly to convince her husband to join. Once she realized he wasn't going to budge, she made up her mind to come alone. I like that."

"Just so it doesn't give you any notions."

"Hardly. That's one thing, my dear, you'll never have to worry about."

"Hmm. My gracious, Maggie! What will the driver say?"

"Who cares? Be a darling now and come, kiss me again."

. . .

"Oh, Mrs. Hopkins! I didn't hear you come in."

"Good morning, Mr. Tremaine. Mr. Gordon not in today?"

"No, ma'am. Says the gout's too bad, what with this cold, rainy weather."

"It certainly has been unpleasant, hasn't it? I know I'm tired of it, too. I am sorry to hear about Mr. Gordon. How are you?"

"Well as can be 'spected, I 'magine. Figure on practicing this morning, do ya?"

"If I'm going to play well for Ascension Day, I'd better put in some time now. The choir will be in this evening for their last rehearsal before tomorrow's service. I see you're sprucing up for that as well."

"Just the bigger things today, ma'am. I'll catch the dusting and final work tomorrow morning. Don't mean to disturb you; I'll be finished in a quarter of an hour or so."

"You won't bother me. Go ahead and do whatever's needed."

"Thank you, ma'am." The janitor returned to his work as Maggie walked down the aisle of St. Paul's Cathedral. It seemed so big, forbidding really, when it was empty. Yet, once the organ was heated and she had begun to play, the sound filled every nook and cranny, bringing her a comfort she found impossible to describe. Enough, she reminded, just to accept, and enjoy.

Organ music, Maggie had long ago discovered, was far richer and deeper than anything that could be wrung from a piano keyboard. She could lose herself in newfound depths and feared quite often she did just that. Stops pulled all the way out, she felt the vibrations as the music coursed through her slender body.

A crowd was expected for tomorrow's noonday service, the choir swollen with a number of paid soloists for the occasion. It was a practice with which she adamantly disagreed. She played, and they sang, to something greater than their sum. She could neither understand nor sympathize with those choir members who would not participate until silver lined their palms.

Well, that was neither here nor there now, was it? She looked forward to the evening rehearsal and then the service tomorrow. She'd duck in again in the morning, just to quickly run through some of the less familiar music. No sense losing her edge before the service actually began.

. . .

"Funny," Maggie thought as the trolley moved slowly downtown through the crowded streets of Buffalo, "yesterday I was telling Mr. Tremaine how tired I was of the miserable weather and what happens? Today it's sunny and warm; in fact, it's almost too hot."

She felt the explosion at the same moment she heard it. By the time the trolley reached the next corner she could see flames erupting from Dr. Pierce's Hotel. Already the fire equipment was beginning to arrive – as, she noticed, were crowds of onlookers.

Another explosion, even larger. St. Paul's!

The crowd surged forward, pulling her along in their excitement. She stopped the moment she could see the church. The front doors, four-inch-thick solid walnut, had been blown into the middle of the street while thick smoked billowed from the shattered windows.

She spotted Mr. Tremaine, standing shakily at one side and rushed to the old janitor. He seemed all right, smudged a bit and frightened to the core. Looking up, he acknowledged the familiar face with a sign of relief.

"I was just about through, Mrs. Hopkins. Dusting off the back pews before getting ready to leave. It happened so fast. I ought to be down on my knees thanking the good Lord I was spared. Wouldn't have been if I hadn't been so close to the door either. Don't know what happened, do you?"

She shook her head weakly.

The organ! Her music!

Maggie turned and raced for the church, entering the gaping hole where the doors had so recently stood. She got no further than the narthex, far enough to witness the line of flames snaking down the center aisle toward the altar, before the smoke drove her back. She glanced up one last time at the roof timbers. Wood, all of it wood. What chance did it have?

She was still there as the fire burnt itself out, still there to stare silently at the smoking ruin with nothing left but the sandstone walls and steeples. Still there when the first choir members appeared for the service that wouldn't be.

Maggie realized her fear of fire would prevent her entering the building again. But she was standing there still when all stopped in amazement to listen as the church bells rang. Noon!

Hurrying over she saw the exhausted fireman slowly let himself back down the winding staircase to the ground, smiling weakly as his companions rushed to meet him with hearty congratulations.

When there was nothing more to do, Maggie turned from the empty shell and walked toward home.

XLIV

May 10, 1888

"That is you, isn't it?"

As she closed the door behind her, Maggie could hear Everett's book drop to the table and his rapid footsteps approach.

"I'm glad you're home, my darling. I've been so worried about you."

"Worried? Then you know about the fire?"

"Of course. I hurried over as soon as I heard. What a terrible, terrible disaster."

She kissed her husband's cheek before continuing. "Such a beautiful building, and almost new, too."

"*New?* Well, hardly, though I can remember when it was built. Whole town was talking about the expense. Cost close to $130,000 as I recall. Believe, if memory serves, they even brought in an architect from New York."

"You're right – but so am I. To me, thirty-three years is no time at all, not much older than I. And worth every penny, if you want my opinion. Did you hear anything about what might have caused it?"

"Darnedest thing. Gas pressure built up in the lines under the street till, with nowhere to go, it simply exploded. They're saying now it caused over forty fires before the danger passed."

She shook her head trying to digest this bit of astounding news. "But why would you worry about me?"

"While I was standing there, dumbly staring I suppose at the smoking ashes, one of your choir people saw me and came over. When I asked if she'd seen you, she replied in the affirmative, going on to say that the last she had seen you were walking into the building itself. When nobody could find you later well . . . forgive me for sounding foolish, but – oh, Maggie, thank the good Lord you've come back to me safely."

"And I'm equally happy to be here – and safe and sound as well. Your chorister was correct, as far as she went. I wanted so badly to check the damage, to find out if my music had been lost. I entered the narthex but, as soon as I saw flames snaking along in front of the altar, I turned and fled. Oh, Everett, it was terrible!"

"Such a lovely church."

"That too, although that isn't what I meant. Seeing those flames brought back the night Fil died. I felt as if I were in it all over again, trying so desperately to reach her, knowing I couldn't. Oh, Everett, hold me. Yes, even tighter." She pulled away wildly. "Oh my God! If I close my eyes it's all there, all over again. The fire. And Fil."

He covered her trembling body with his arms, holding her until her sobbing was tamed once more.

. . .

They learned later that the vestry had called an emergency meeting on the very evening of the fire to unanimously agree that rebuilding must begin immediately. Maggie's healing continued apace as well.

As feared, her music had been destroyed when the flames swept across the altar and into the choir area, ultimately razing the organ and all its contents. Only the massive pipes still stood as reminders of the glory now past.

XLV

July 1888

Tickets clasped in his hand Everett burst into the house on a sunny June afternoon. He searched rapidly for his wife.

"Maggie, would you like to come with me to Chautauqua?"

"Chautauqua? But . . . Where? . . .When? Oh, yes, Everett, I'd love to go. I've read so much about the place. Truly, I would like to see it. And you're saying we can? Just tell me when. I promise I'll be ready . . . and waiting."

Maggie knew that the facility had attracted reputable instructors since it was started as a retreat for Sabbath School teachers. In time, as church studies were pushed aside for more secular instruction, the site on the shores of Lake Chautauqua grew progressively popular as a vacation destination in its own right. Music was added. Then art. Wood cottages replaced the earlier tents as steamers regularly plied the waters of the lake, bringing more and more visitors to its shore.

They set out three days later.

. . .

Maggie regretted the briefness of the hour-long train ride to Dunkirk for the views of the deep woods and the prospering farms along Lake Erie entranced her. They transferred there to a second train which took them over the hills and down into the Chautauqua valley. Maggie couldn't contain her excitement as the train crested the last hill, affording its passengers a crystal view of the many steamboats carrying passengers across the sparkling waters.

The grounds were laid out beautifully, designed so that

strollers might catch glimpses of the lake from every turn. The cottages, already renowned for their "gingerbread" style, seemed to belong here in the wooded glens.

Their room was regrettably in the back of the house where the only view was of the house on the street behind. The bathroom at the end of the hall was comfortably clean and the bed squeakless.

Lectures were attended. Food and fellowship, meant to be enjoyed, increased the pleasures they continued to discover.

Returning one day from the lakeshore where they had been watching the boats and swimmers, they passed a bulletin board advertising the evening's activities.

"Oh, Everett, look!"

"I knew we'd find something for you, Maggie."

"For *me?* Why, this whole experience has been special for me!"

"I realize that, but can you deny that this is the frosting on the cake?"

"No, of course not, and you're truly a dear to realize it."

"Forget those master classes you took? Not likely."

"I wonder if you remember then how much encouragement Preston Bryan's words gave me – oh! it seems like a different age entirely, how he took me from gloom into the discovery of the joys that music can, no, *should*, hold for us all."

"Perhaps I'll have a chance now to thank the man."

"Do you suppose he'd even remember me? That was ages ago."

"I don't believe anyone could forget you, dear Maggie."

"And do you know, for all the help he gave others, I don't believe any of us ever heard him play, certainly not an entire recital as the one scheduled for this evening. Oh, it shall be hard to wait till then."

"Then come, let's try to get your mind on other things. And, now that I think about it, that shouldn't be hard at all. Do you realize we brought the new camera and haven't shot a single photograph?"

"Oh, Everett, you're right! The Kodak box! I can't imagine a more perfect place to try it. You sit. No, I insist. Over there by the fountain. Please. Let me run back and get our camera."

"Margaret, you make me feel seventy years old."

"I didn't mean that . . . Oh! You know it, don't you? I'm just so excited that I don't think I could walk back if I had to. And I'd hate to scandalize you being seen running like a little tomboy."

"Go, Maggie. Go, and enjoy."

. . .

The hall filled rapidly. The two had been wise to come over immediately from their early meal, thus securing seats near the front for an unobstructed view of the pianist.

Here he was now! Anticipating a night of greatness Maggie realized later how shallow those words lay in comparison to the miracle that followed. The notes, so soft and tender, flowed easily. The fast passages, many of which she knew almost as well, were played to perfection.

Encores were requested by the stampede of applause, and willingly granted.

Now, watching the crowd disperse, Everett turned to his wife. "Want to see if we can get backstage, give you a chance to say hello?"

"You'll find this strange but I'd rather just leave. What could I say? Besides, I don't want the magic to wear off. Would you mind if we just walked for a while?"

"Of course not. No better time than under such a huge full moon. Let's circle back to see how the fountain looks at night. Afterwards, if you want we can walk along the lakefront as long as you wish."

"You always understand. That must be why I love you so."

"Here then, let me help pull your wrap around your shoulders. The lake air is certainly cooler than our nights in Buffalo."

They were halfway across the main street, the fountain coming into sight, Maggie deeply lost in her reverie, when she happened to glance up at Everett, responding to a remark just made.

Her eyes caught his but turned immediately back in the direction they were walking. A tall figure passed in front of them and hurried along the same path they followed, distance increasing as he strode purposely to the corner and turned out of sight.

The glow of the concert disappeared as fast as a bubble's burst.

"Everett," she said once she had recovered, "I do believe you are right. It's chillier here than I thought. Would you mind if we returned to our room?"

XLVI

Autumn 1888

Maggie dreamed not of the wonderful music she had heard. She dreamed of him. She consciously tried to pull her thoughts back to the marvelous experience the evening had brought but he intruded into every vision.

Home again, where she expected life to return to its normalcy, that singular fleeting apparition continued to overwhelm her. It wasn't a daydream, for she continued to push the image out of her mind almost as quickly as it appeared. At times the struggle grew so difficult she was tempted to give in, to savor those old memories, let them live again.

Had it even been he? Perhaps it was merely a stranger who bore a curious resemblance.

Yes, that was it. Simply a stranger, mistaken for the ghost.

Now she forced her mind into the past, trying to remember. What color was his hair? She recalled the balding spot he vainly tried to conceal but remembered nothing else. How could she remember so little about the man who had once held her entire life in his fingers?

Well, let him be gone. She thought of all she had gained since those terribly unhappy days. And felt grateful.

But why . . . why, after so many years? Good years, too. Why now?

One stranger. One glance.

She was left with just one memory that refused to go away.

· · ·

What was he doing these days? Did he perhaps still think occasionally of her? Would he even know her?

Had he married? She remembered that he had spoken often of such a desire. What was there now to hold him back? What, for that matter, had there been then?

Had his teaching manners improved? No regrets there, Maggie was absolutely positive about that. Just look how quickly she had progressed once she was no longer his pupil. Found herself and her music as well.

But how, she cursed the memory, could you be so warm one week and then turn on me the next? You left me painfully confused.

She allowed herself a moment to reflect what might have been his real motive in ending their lessons, recalling too acutely the devastation she had felt at the time.

Do you have any idea how often I think of you?

. . .

Fall returned as the leaves reddened and finally dropped from the trees. Accepting her now as all the family he was likely to have, Everett grew increasingly tender with the jewel who continued to fill his heart.

After a while Maggie was able to curl up in her husband's arms and know peace once more, hardly remembering – or fearing – the rude intrusion into her well-organized life.

She thanked God again for such a good man as she blew out the lamp beside the bed, laid her book aside, and stretched a foot out to connect with the sleeping Everett.

XLVII

November 1888

"Jack, there's no reason to raise your voice. I wholeheartedly agree. All I said was that it isn't that easy. The boy is seven years old and, thanks to the tutor we engaged for him, he's reading at near adult level. There simply is no way to prevent his seeing the tabloids."

"But all this killer talk. He dwells far too much on death as it is. Now, with the papers writing of little but this demon London has named Jack the Ripper, I don't believe I've heard the boy utter a sentence all week that wasn't somehow connected to those gruesome deaths. Why, I try to avoid the details myself – as I trust you do too, Lizzie – but the child is positively fixated on them. And the more explicit, the more he hangs on every word. Is there nothing we can do?"

"I suppose we could see that no papers reach the house, at least until this latest spate of killings is over. Do you suppose that might help? Abram really doesn't go out that often."

"It's worth a try. Personally, I hope they catch the fiend soon." Jack set the paper down.

"I imagine they will. It says right here Queen Victoria herself rang up the police. Now if she's checking on their progress, what more could anyone do?"

"It's just that they were such brutal slaughters."

"Sounds like my husband is keeping a pretty close watch on the papers himself."

"I confess it does intrigue me, Lizzie. Besides, somebody has got to know what's in the head of that young son of ours."

"I don't feel any of the other children are particularly affected."

"They know about it of course but I don't think they think about that any more than they do the rebuilding of St. Paul's."

. . .

Two days later, dinner finished, Jack and Lizzie repaired to the library where he refilled their glasses with a nightcap of whisky. Lizzie thought of the pleasure his being home for dinner brought her and uttered a silent prayer that nothing might disturb this happy evening.

No sooner had she finished than a scream pierced the silence.

Jack bounded up the staircase faster than Lizzie's feet could fly. Ralph and John raced down from the third floor at the same time. Bess, having slipped off her shoes and stockings to study more comfortably, was the last to arrive. All saw Clara cowering in the far corner of the hall, tears streaming down her crimson cheeks.

"Mama! Papa! Make him stop! Make him stop it!"

Jack pulled the boy away from his sister, wishing he had some way of removing the smirk now crossing his face. Holding him securely by the back of his collar, he turned to his youngest daughter. Lizzie was already kneeling, wiping her tears and trying to comfort the child. As soon as she was able, Clara stood, relieved to be freed and walked gratefully to her room, still clinging to Lizzie.

Jack turned to the boy. "Tell me exactly what happened."

"Ahhhh, I was only teasing her; that's all. Clara's such a crybaby."

"Clara's a little girl, Abram. There is no reason on the face of this wide earth for you to make her cry. I want to know what happened."

"Nothing, Papa. I was just telling her, well, telling her about the London killer."

"You mean Jack the Ripper?"

"That's the one."

"And what exactly were you telling her?"

He fidgeted but stood quietly, defiantly facing his father.

Lizzie raced from Clara's room. Seeing Bessie who by now had re-dressed, she implored her to please go comfort her sister. Regretting the scene she anticipated missing, the fourteen-year-old turned to do her mother's bidding.

Lizzie looked with disgust at her son and then turned to her husband who still had a firm grip on Abram.

"Clara told me what happened. It must have been perfectly dreadful for her."

"Well, what did occur? Doesn't look like we'll get it out of the boy."

He melted at her look of derision. "Mama, Mama, I meant no harm. Truly I didn't. It was all in fun."

"I certainly see nothing *fun* and I assure you Clara didn't either in the things you said to her. Honestly, Abram! She's five years old, hardly more than a baby herself. And you filling her with all those dreadful descriptions of the girls he ... he ..."

"Ripped, Mother. That's why they call him The Ripper. Around the neck," his hand followed his descriptions, "then down the middle, rips open, tummy falling out. Slice. Slice."

"Ooooh," John uttered involuntarily.

"Enough! Boys, back upstairs to your rooms. And, Abram, I'll see you in yours. It's the only place you'll be for quite some time."

The child began to cry piteously. "Mama, I'm sorry. Don't hate me. Please."

XLVIII

June 1889

In spite of the grumbling that inevitably accompanied anything new, St. Paul's was rebuilt in record time. The exterior of the lofty cathedral was redone to look as it had before. The interior, however, was changed drastically by local architects called in for the redesign.

Within a year of the disastrous fire, the new building was rededicated, Maggie happily – and popularly – back behind the pedals and keyboards of the refurbished organ.

People squeezed into the pews so that more might sit as the hour for the rededication neared. Many, trusting God would never allow His building to burn a second time, overlooked the warnings of the fire marshal and elected to sit in the aisles while a lucky few crowded onto the stairs which led up to the bell tower. The bells remained the same, those that had been rung the year before by the exhausted fireman.

Everett sat unassumedly, unnoticed, toward the back of the sanctuary. He wanted to hear the full scope of the music, the organ and the enlarged choir as well. He also wanted to gauge the reactions of those who sat around him.

There was no doubt, he knew almost as soon as the service began, that this would be a moment long cherished among the annals of local church music. He wished he could telegraph his message to Maggie, regretting the hours that would have to pass before he could speak to her in private. He wanted so to tell her now how gloriously she played, how the choir, following her every lead, sounded better than ever, and, perhaps most important, at least from Maggie's point of view, how happy the congregation was as they inaugurated their new life.

Maggie, you're positively marvelous!

. . .

"Everett, don't go. Please. Just let me do these few more stitches. Then I want to ask what you think."

He returned to where his wife sat to catch the late afternoon sun. He watched her needle expertly bobbing up and down before she turned the garment inside out to make a final knot. He admired the way she could cut a thread with a quick motion of her teeth, a talent which would forever remain a mystery to him.

"You aren't using your sewing machine? I thought it was the answer for making all these clothes."

"Most. And, to be honest, I do wonder if it wouldn't have straighter seams, perhaps even look better, if I were using the Singer. But it's to be special, a peignoir and robe for Flo's trousseau, and I knew it wouldn't be the same if I ran it up on the machine. Besides, look – see these rows of smocking? They can only be done by hand."

He looked at the garment she held up. She had given so much time and love to this set and he marveled now at the lovely piece before him. Lace edged the neck, a bow falling just beneath a tiny floral rose, the smocking across the bodice and then a plain skirt with sleeves and the wide hem made of the finest Chantilly lace Maggie had been able to buy. He had already been invited to inspect the matching robe with the heart-shaped buttons running down the front and its longer sleeves, those made of solid cotton with lace again at the wrists.

Why, he thought with a tinge of sadness, hadn't Maggie had something this lovely for her wedding? She reminded him that their speed had precluded wedding presents of any kind. He knew he'd gotten the better of the deal once she kissed him smartly and said that she wouldn't change anything about the way they'd been married. Neither, he knew, would he.

. . .

Flo's wedding was lovely. Only Maggie knew where

the tucks and hems in her homemade dress had not turned out precisely as the bride had hoped. With her last-minute help, it looked perfect now. And so, Maggie reflected, did her beaming friend.

She and Everett enjoyed their time with Janie and Vernon, happy that the years apart had not brought a chasm into their friendship. Hadn't Everett joked almost immediately that the two women seemed to have picked up right where they had left off years before?

Janie brought photographs to proudly show off her handsome young girls. She waited till Vernon and Everett had gone for a walk before pulling them from her purse, letting the two women squeal appropriately before Maggie quietly thanked her for her sensitive judgment. There was still a recognizable hurt in her husband's eyes whenever she saw him looking enviously at another's children.

XLIX

January to June 1890

Everett hung up his dishtowel as Maggie put away the last of the pans. He'd been whistling as he'd helped and now switched to song, Maggie eagerly joining in a second chorus of "Just A Song At Twilight." Laughing at their erratic harmony on the final refrain, she closed the cupboard door and turned unexpectedly into his waiting arms, accepting a long and lingering kiss.

"Enough already; love may be sweet but I believe the banquet is over."

"True enough, little darling, though with the recent Larkin success we might go on celebrating forever. Did I tell you that last year the company sold more than 91,000 Combination Boxes?"

"Only about a hundred times." She laughed in mock exasperation.

"Then I must also have told you that was the fourth straight year that product has been a success."

Maggie mouthed "fourth straight year" as he arrived at that passage.

"Why, they figure the company's made over half a million dollars."

He stopped her charade on "half a million dollars" with a long kiss.

"There's still a little red in the western sky. Shall we take advantage of the break in the weather and go for a walk around the block?"

"What a lovely idea! I'd relish getting out for a spell. Who knows? Perhaps I'll be able to talk you into two blocks!"

"You, dear Maggie, could talk me into just about

anything."

. . .

"Oh! I did it again."

Jack glanced up from where he sat reading the Sunday paper, expecting some clue as to what had upset his wife. He watched her make a quick scribble and then resume her writing. "Am I to be elucidated about that little outrage, or do you intend keeping it a mystery?"

Lizzie reacted in surprise. "I had no idea I had spoken aloud. Forgive me, particularly if I interrupted your reading."

"Nothing important. Just curious what caused such an outburst."

She smiled. "It's silly of me. I was just starting a letter to Grace and dated it 1889. It's hard to believe we're entering another decade. I'm wishing Grace much happiness on her birthday. You'll want to add a note too, won't you? Imagine our baby turning twenty-one. Seemed so strange at the Christmas pageant last month. I can remember when Grace was the Mary, then Anne the following year. Now Elizabeth is practically grown up, too. I expect they'll ask Clara for this coming Christmas – you do think so, don't you? – and then . . .well, then no more Knapps to be in the pageant until a new generation comes along."

"Good God, Lizzie. You don't expect that to happen any time soon, do you?"

"I certainly hope not, though of course both girls will be graduating in June. Then who knows? And now here's Ralph hardly able to wait till we send him off this fall. He's quite set on Haverford, hardly my first choice but it seems to be what he wants."

He looked up in time to catch her in a quizzical smile.

She smiled shyly at being caught. "I was just thinking how we used to wonder if we had too many children, wondering sometimes if they were ever going to stop coming, but now, well . . ."

"No, Lizzie, don't say that."

"Hmm? Oh, good heavens no, Jack. Enough is enough.

It's bad enough just turning forty-five. No, our child-bearing days are over."`

Jack harrumphed, picked up his paper and left the library without a further word.

. . .

"Damn it, boy. I'm talking to you. I expect an answer and I expect it now. Sit up. Your manners have become atrocious. Why should I bother to come home to eat – 'with my family' as you so delicately put it, Lizzie –" he turned back to the stone-faced boy, "when I have to put up with this? You're a disgrace to our family."

"Jack!"

"Silence, Lizzie. Let me speak." He gulped from his wine goblet before continuing. "Just look at him. Slumped over the table, stuffing the food into his mouth, hands dirty, hair unbrushed, even his shirttails sticking out from his trousers. His behavior is reprehensible."

Abram started to say something, knew better than to continue with a mouth filled with turkey and mashed potatoes, and lowered his gaze as Jack threw his napkin down and strode from the room. Abram waited a moment, perhaps hoping for a rupture in the overwhelming silence that engulfed the rest of his family. When it was not forthcoming, he filled his mouth with the remaining vegetables on his plate, grabbed a roll and fled.

Lizzie knew where he was going. Abram had constructed a rough but admirably adequate hideout in the woods behind their house. He had shown it once to his mother, proud of his accomplishment while eliciting her promise to keep site and quarters a secret. Only she knew it had become a refuge, perhaps almost a second home, for the troubled boy.

. . .

"Uncle Charlie! Uncle Charlie! Anne, look! He's here!"

The two girls swooped across the manicured lawn to welcome their favorite relative. Lizzie and Jack stopped in their tracks waiting until the initial greeting was finished, happy the entire family had been able to attend the Vassar graduation ceremonies for Grace and Anne. Kudos were in order, and modestly received, for Grace as class president and valedictorian, Anne following immediately as vice-president and salutatorian.

Jack found it especially easy to override his prejudices and misgivings about women to accept the distinctions conferred upon his two eldest daughters.

As the festivities ebbed, Lizzie joined Jack in time to hear him ask the girls what they intended to do next. She hoped their plans included a return to Buffalo for she had missed them greatly. The company would be appreciated.

"Didn't he tell you?" Anne, always the noisier, interrupted.

"He? Who? What?" Lizzie's head was still swimming from the honors she had watched bestowed on her own flesh and blood.

"Uncle Charlie," Grace interjected. The two graduates stood quietly looking at their mother waiting for as answer to their not-too-sensible reply.

"Uncle Charlie what?"

The girls laughed as they gave her a hug. "Uncle Charlie asked us what we wanted for graduation presents."

"Of course," Anne chimed in, "we told him having him here for the ceremony was the most wonderful thing we could imagine."

"And of course he did come." Lizzie was already experiencing some doubts.

"But," added Grace, "he said that would never be enough for his oldest nieces. Mama, he insisted!"

"All right. I know Uncle Charlie. I can understand that. So what did you – or he – decide?"

"It wasn't us. Oh, Mama, I promise. It wasn't our idea."

"Good God, girls, tell me. What did he do?"

"He's sending us – both of us – to Europe."

Lizzie turned quickly to Charlie. He raised a finger to her lips before she could speak a syllable. "Lizzie, I know what you're going to say. Hear me out first. The girls are right. It wasn't their idea; it was mine. You must know how dearly I love these children. I would be pleased to give them such a trip, and am in fact already enjoying their excitement."

"But," Lizzie sputtered.

"No buts, please. The girls will be perfectly safe. Three, perhaps as many as five, of their classmates will be going along . . . plus they'll be chaperoned by one of the faculty here. No more objections, please. I'd send my own daughters had I been fortunate to have had any. Besides, if it gets us away from that beastly hot Rosedale Opera House and spares me any more French declamations, believe me, it'll be money well spent."

Grace and Anne shrieked happily as they embraced Charlie.

"Come, girls. It's time we were off in search of the rest of the family." He turned back momentarily. "Coming, Lizzie?"

She shrugged helplessly, flashed a wide smile and trotted to catch up to her daughters.

L

Winter 1890

The winter of 1890 was a harsh one in upstate New York, made particularly bitter as the vestiges of a global influenza epidemic reached the Eastern shores of the United States and quickly spread westward. Clara lost a second grade classmate. Ralph, happily ensconced at Haverford reported duly on the ravages as they swept through Philadelphia and then the campus. He and his new friends were spared.

It was late November when Lizzie took sick. Dr. Clark confirmed it was the dreaded illness and left orders that she be given complete rest. A nurse was sent to sponge her off after each fever attack and to wrap her in heavy blankets when the chills returned. Once diagnosed and confined to bed, she seemed to hold her own against the wracking illness. It was left to the rest of the family to maintain quiet and to listen with a minimum of distress to her hollow coughs.

At its worst, Bessie, unable to sleep because of her mother's noise, tiptoed out of her room for a glass of milk. She was surprised to find Abram huddled in a corner of the hallway, hardly visible, his boy's body shaking as his mother's distress continued.

"Abram, whatever are you doing here? Why are you up at this hour? You're not getting it too, are you?" The boy crept hungrily into his sister's outspread arms. It took her a moment to realize his sniffling was caused, not by sickness, but by inconsolable tears. "What is the matter, Brother?"

"I'm so afraid."

"Of what?"

He shook his head in denial.

"Abram, if you don't tell me, how can you expect me to

help?"

"You can't help me. Nobody can."

"That's a pretty sad way for someone to feel. No, don't pull away. Stay here and let me try to calm you. You must tell me – or somebody – what's upsetting you." The sobs grew louder. "Hush, Abram. You don't want to waken Mother now, do you?" For in truth her coughing had stopped and they presumed she rested again. He shook his head adamantly from side to side.

"Come on. I was going downstairs for a cup of milk. Let me heat some for you, too. Who knows? I may even know where cook keeps the cookies she made this afternoon."

Properly nourished, sharing the lighted kitchen with his older sister, Abram appeared to relax. Bessie happily observed the boy emit a wide yawn.

"I think you and I are both about ready for bed. Don't you agree?" He nodded affirmatively, winning a big grin in response. She rinsed the dirty cups and plates and extinguished the gaslights in the kitchen.

"Come on, little brother. Let's get some sleep before morning comes. Want to tell me now what was bothering you?"

"Mama isn't going to die, is she, Bessie?"

"Is that what had you crying, Abram? Oh, dear, let me give you another hug. I should have realized that would be your fear. I'm sorry I let you go on so long."

"Well, is she?"

"Abram, listen to me. Nobody can say for sure. Now don't let that lip start quivering again. Hear me out. This is a bad year for influenza. We all know that. But Mama isn't getting any worse and it's been a whole week since the doctor was first called. That's a very good sign. Do you know that? You go say your prayers, just like the rest of us do, and we'll see what tomorrow brings. As for me, I truly believe that one of these mornings, if not tomorrow then perhaps the day after, Mama will wake up feeling much better. Then we'll all know she's going to get well."

The boy nodded sleepily as he walked to his own bedroom. "Tomorrow, or the day after."

LI

March 1891

"Charlie! What a surprise!" Lizzie finished descending the staircase and crossed the hall to greet her waiting brother-in-law. "I couldn't believe it when they said you were at the door."She glanced down, aware now of the bags at his feet. "May I take it we're in for a visit?"

"I should have let you know I was coming. And I needn't stay. I'll understand completely if it's not a good time for you. Thing was, I was in Fredonia visiting Mother and Uncle Rufus and they were getting along so well there seemed no reason to hang around the farm . . . and, well, I'm not expected back in Pennsylvania till next Monday so . . . so, I decided it was worth an hour on that filthy train to see if there was a chance of catching up with you. And here I am!" He released her and stepped back for a better look. "So how are you? And Jack? And the children?"

"Goodness, come sit down. I'm feeling much better by now, thank you. You just caught me by surprise but it's always a treat to have you here. John and Clara should be home from school soon. And Abram's upstairs with his tutor but I expect them to finish within the hour.

"Oh, Charlie, everyone will be so pleased to have you here. Honestly, this family could do with a little bit of cheering up. I might even hazard a guess that your visit will prove a real godsend."

"Cheering up? Whatever is the matter?"

"To be honest, it's been dismal around here. I know you're aware of the problems we've had with Blackie. He was the dearest dog I ever knew, so sweet and so gentle with the children. Then – well, something happened. He began growling and snapping. We felt he had to be kept caged – except when the children were here to play with him.

"*Children* is hardly right any more either, is it? Ralph adored him and was his constant companion before he went to college. John loved to roughhouse with him – we never knew any trouble there. And he always slept in Clara's room. Abram, on the other hand, never had any interest in the dog."

They sat over tea while Lizzie told the story. The rabbit, making it to almost three years, had been found in Blackie's cage. John had discovered its remains when he went out to feed him the next morning. The dog's mouth was still covered with blood.

"Oh, Charlie, you can imagine how terrible that was for the children! And of course they all hurried out to see what the original commotion was about.

"Needless to say, after that Jack forbade us to keep the dog. Blackie was gone before noon. None of us has had the heart to ask what happened. It's been simply dreadful for us all."

"I am so sorry, Liz."

"And here I am, listening to you say you're sorry. I should be begging your pardon, keeping you waiting like this. Of course you're staying. I'm sure the guest room is ready but let me call the maid. Excuse me for just a minute."

Lizzie stopped at the door to turn back. "Charlie, I know I speak for us all when I say I'm very glad you're here."

LII
June 1891

"Everett, look at you!"

"Don't laugh, Maggie. The haberdasher swore it was in the latest style."

"And well it may be but certainly one I haven't seen before. Turn around. Oh, do, please."

Everett turned uncertainly as Maggie inspected the new outfit. Knickers rose above his wool stockings to a waisted jacket pleated down the front. His shoes were unlike any she had seen before.

"Did you – ahem – did that haberdasher explain what such a getup was supposed to be for?"

"For cycling, Maggie. I'm going to learn to ride the wheels!"

Spring had come and the world, feeling reborn in its new health, anticipated the outdoor days that lay ahead.

"And what's more –" he continued.

She fought hard to stifle a laugh. "There's more?"

"You bet there is. I've booked tickets on the new steamer to Chautauqua, the *C.W. Rinearson,* and just wait till you see it, Maggie, they say it's huge."

"So you're taking me all the way back to Chautauqua because of some big boat?"

"Let me finish – please. It's taken a lot of effort to put this all together, especially to keep it a secret . . . until now."

"I'm sorry, Everett. Do continue, please. I promise not to interrupt again."

"I've booked us on the train to Dunkirk and then a second one to Mayville where we'll board this new steamer to go on to hear a talk by that woman you keep talking about, Susan

B. Anthony."

She shrieked in excitement.

"And then – oh, yes, my dear, there's more –

"Afterwards we'll return to Fredonia where I've secured a room for two nights. On the second we are to attend the grand opening of the Fredonia Opera House." He leaned over to kiss her lips, effectively cutting off what proposed to be her next remark. "I heard some of the men at work talking about how special this would be and I knew – or at least I hope – that it will be enjoyable for you. I imagine it will prove to be even more than merely that for, in fact, I have learned your old trio will be among the featured artists."

He raised his hand before she could be permitted another squeal.

Settling a moment later, however, a look of puzzlement crossed her face. "It sounds perfectly marvelous, and I certainly mean no criticism, but where does this bicycling fit in?"

"Why, at Chautauqua. I'm told it's all the rage. And just think of how much easier it will be to get around the grounds."

"I'm already thinking of those beastly slopes."

His sudden silence surprised her. "Why, dear, what's the matter? Is it something I said?"

"Yes. No." He smiled at her obvious confusion. "Slopes."

"What?"

"You used the word *slopes*."

"Why, yes, I believe I did. Shouldn't I have?"

"Of course. It just reminded me of . . . well, of *slopes*. That's the word they were bandying around the factory. *Slippery slopes* I believe was the expression they used."

"Everett! Are you making any sense at all?"

"Sorry, my dear. It was a reference to the Larkin Company. You remember, I'm certain, what happened when John was gone."

"How could anyone forget that? The great silverware fiasco."

Elbert Hubbard had taken advantage of his brother-in-law's

absence the previous fall to substitute less expensive German ware for the six solid Gorham silver spoons promised to any who signed up three friends to purchase the Mammoth Sweet Home box. The ensuing publicity had caused a disastrous fall in sales.

"And once again my trusted husband to the rescue."

"I can't take all the credit –"

"Nor sadly was it given to you but, Everett, you know as well as I it was your suggestion to keep encouraging customers to enroll their friends that caused those sales to rebound."

"It was an immensely successful operation which, ultimately, my sweet, is all that matters. In fact, were it not for that turnaround we would certainly not be planning our getaway now."

LIII

June 1891

"There she is again." Charlie and Jack had just returned to their front row balcony seats in preparation for the second half of the grand gala at the Fredonia Opera House. Their mother was seated with Uncle Rufus and Lizzie immediately to their left. Now Charlie pointed none too inconspicuously to the attractive woman taking her place in the rows beneath them.

"Yes, I see the one you mean. But I'm afraid I can't help you. She doesn't look all that familiar to me."

"How strange! I'm sure I've met her someplace, sometime. More than once even. But who do we know in Fredonia?"

"She's certainly pretty enough – though, gathering by the looks she giving the gentleman with her, I don't imagine she's free."

"Pity, too. He looks old enough to be her father. Oh, well, pardon your silly brother but the glinting highlights in her hair are much more intriguing to my eyes than some of that so-called talent on stage."

The announcer silenced any further conversation between the two.

· · ·

Maggie rested her tired head on Everett's shoulder as the train swayed back toward Buffalo.

"I've had such a wonderful, wonderful week, darling. I can't imagine how I can ever thank you. Well, besides that, I mean."

He chuckled and pulled his arm tighter around her

shoulder. "It is nice when things work out as well as we hope, isn't it?"

"*As well?* It was absolutely perfect! My mind is still swirling with all that's happened. The beautiful weather for our stay at Chautauqua – and, yes, I promise next time I'll try the wheels, too – and that crazy, wild woman."

"Wild? But I thought you enjoyed her."

"Oh, I did, and I gather you did, too. But what a cantankerous character! I think she had an opinion on every topic imaginable. She certainly wasn't afraid to say what she thought either. Do you suppose I'll be like that when I get to be seventy?"

"Seventy-one. Good God, Maggie, I certainly hope not. I always thought women's suffrage made a lot of sense and I'd be all for seeing you given the right to vote but, if your Miss Anthony represents the typical female, well, I just may have to rescind my approval."

"Come now, certainly you know better than that. And what – she says, changing the subject quickly – did you think of that Opera House? I'm so pleased you thought to get us tickets. It was like old times hearing the trio again."

"It really is a little jewel, isn't it, Maggie? I know Buffalo has bigger and, perhaps, better but, for a small theater, I've never seen any space quite as lovely."

"I thought the choice of colors was splendid. The gold and the soft greens added just the perfect touch. There may be other theaters more lavish but I can't imagine one decorated in better taste. And of course the performances! Well, that goes without saying."

"I thought your old group sounded superb though, watching, I did wonder if you still miss the piano."

"Miss it? How can I since you were able to buy me my own? My Shaw is still my most prized possession – next to a certain husband of course. Admittedly, I have missed the camaraderie we developed – though, again, as they say, every time one door closes, another opens. I certainly wouldn't give up my work at church, or the organ for that matter."

"I know I asked you before but, in all the excitement, I

don't believe I ever got an answer. That was your old music teacher on the program, was it not?"

"You did ask, and I thought I answered. Yes, Peter Kubrick."

"You're the judge, not I, but I felt he did passably well. The audience certainly seemed pleased."

"Passably well, yes. I don't mean to sound overly negative but that audience was so worked up I believe it would have given a standing ovation to a barking dog."

"Maggie! Are you saying you found his performance poor?"

"No, not really. It's been so long since I've heard him play, and I've heard so many since who, honestly, are much better pianists, that I found it quite routine. Not disappointing, not surprising either. I'm glad Fredonia liked him."

"An odd chap though, isn't he? I found his lip-chewing quite distracting."

"To be sure, but tell me what you thought of the soprano soloist. I found her out-of-this-world."

. . .

"Jack, if you don't mind, it's been quite a tiring week for me, and I'd be content just resting until the train gets to Buffalo. I'm glad your mother invited us for the weekend – can you imagine such a fancy theater in that little town? And it was especially good to see Charlie again, and of course your mother and Rufus though, to be honest, five days on that farm is more than enough for me." She allowed herself the luxury of a loud sigh. "I'm sure the children are doing well. They probably haven't missed us at all. And, yes, I know I should be grateful for this little sojourn. But the farm . . . and your mother . . . and well, I'd just as soon not have to do anything but relax for a while. You don't really mind, do you?"

Jack returned to his paper as Lizzie picked up *The Picture of Dorian Gray*, silently thanking Ardith once more for recommending such a fascinating new novel.

. . .

"Bang, bang, bang!" Abram's shouts echoed through the house. Must everything he does be in threes, Lizzie wondered with a shudder. The boy ran into the room, ducked behind the chesterfield and began shooting at something just over Lizzie's right shoulder.

"Abram! How many times have I asked you to be quiet in the house? If you must play your games, please do it outside."

"But this isn't a game, Mother. They really are dead."

"*They?* Who? Who's dead? What in the world are you talking about now?"

"The bad man. *And* the good man."

"I swear, now you're talking in riddles. Would you please explain to me *what* good man, *what* bad man, and who is dead?"

"Both of them."

"Abram!"

"Wild Bill Hickok, just last month in Deadwood. They say he was playing poker and got shot down right at the table; can you imagine? And now the sheriff in Fort Sumner has killed Billy the Kid. I saw it in yesterday's paper. They caught up with him in New Mexico. Bang; gotcha! Bang; and you're dead!" He ducked for a silent moment. "Then there was the man they fried in the electric chair." His head peeked over the couch. "What do you suppose it's like to be dead, Mother?"

"I can't honestly say I know."

"But you were close to it last winter, weren't you?"

"I suppose I was. Certainly sicker than I hope to be again for a long, long time."

"You aren't going to die. You'll promise me that, won't you?"

"Where do you get such ideas? Really! Nobody's going to die."

"Well, I know they will in time. Probably Grandmother first, or maybe Uncle Rufus. Because they're both already so old. Then Father, of course. I know he's going to die sometime. But not you, Mother. You must stay here for me. Always. I promise I'll be here for you forever and ever. We'll be happy together. And we'll never die, not you and not me."

He kissed her forehead tenderly, then wheeled, and raised his forefingers and – "Bang, bang, bang You're dead. Gotcha." – galloped from the room.

LIV

August 1892

The summer of 1892 passed much too quickly. The older girls had become totally involved in their own lives, careers opening up as Buffalo prospered and a steady stream of enthusiastic beaus appeared. Ralph had chosen to stay on, helping with the developing chemistry department at Haverford, while Elizabeth, having elected to take her older sisters' place at Vassar, welcomed the months to prepare for school. Shopping downtown held ever more treasures as Rung Brothers opened their store to offer the finest in carpets and furniture. Even more enticing to the young women was Heinhold's with its well-stocked shelves of imported European wines, cheeses and other delicacies. Word of its opening quickly spread as the younger Buffalonians struggled to outdo each other in sampling their share of culinary treats.

. . .

"Whack! Whack! Whack!"

Lizzie laid her needlepoint down on the footstool, waiting for Clara's inevitable shriek.

"Whack. Whack, whack! Gotcha!"

"Mother!" The girl raced into the parlor.

"What is it this time?"

"It's Abram."

"Well, I guessed that much. Now what has he done?"

"He says he has a hatchet and is going to kill me with it."

The boy giggled with delight as he raced into the room. "Not a hatchet, dummy. It's an ax. And just you wait. One of these nights, when you're sound asleep, I'll come tiptoeing in, tiptoeing quietly right up to your bed, and . . . whack! Whack! Whack!"

She screamed again. Really, weren't those screams worse than any of Abram's threats?

"Obviously, you've found something else in the newspaper to awaken your imagination. I must have missed it. Perhaps it would be a blessing if we could all be forewarned. Do you want to sit down and tell us both what it is this time?"

Sticking his tongue out at his sister, an act not missed by their mother, Abram sat smugly on the edge of her stool.

"It's the Bordens. Or rather, it *was* the Bordens. She hacked them both to pieces."

"My goodness! What on earth are you talking about now?"

"Mother, really! It's in all the papers. Lizzie Borden killed her parents – or so they say though, of course, nobody can really know for sure."

"What a terrible thing." Lizzie shuddered involuntarily.

"Well, they weren't really both her parents either," the boy continued. "It was a stepmother who had married her father. Seems a fitting end for a stepmother, doesn't it?"

"Abram! That's no way to talk. What, pray tell, happened to the girl?"

"Not much so far. She's still alive, if that's what you mean. Won't confess to any of it. I imagine there'll be a trial. We'll see."

"Well, I'd very much appreciate it if you'd spare your sister your taunts *and* these little tales of gore." He sullenly turned away from her. "And, Abram –"

"Yes, Mother?"

"I want you to behave. No more trouble. Is that understood?"

"Of course, Mother."

. . .

"Ta-ra-ra Boom-de-ay! Ta-ra-ra Boom –" Everett's baritone stopped suddenly as he became aware of the giggling behind the kitchen door.

"Maggie! Don't mind saying you startled me. I had no idea you were home."

"As I can well imagine! But don't let me stop you. I always enjoy your singing, especially when it's such a cheerful song. The words for the chorus may lack a little imagination perhaps, but who cares? Come on, I'll join you for the final verse."

"No, that'll have to wait. I've got something much more important for you."

"For me? What?"

"It's a gift, Maggie."

"Why? It's not my birthday and our anniversary was two months ago."

"But it is almost your birthday, right? And, though I know you don't like to speak of age, I believe it is rather a special one at that."

"Thirty? What's so special about turning thirty?"

"Sounds more important to me than twenty-nine – or thirty-one."

"I'll grant you that. So stop teasing. What is it? Or must I wait till the very day to know?"

"Hardly. In fact, you'll be spending that special day on a train heading toward Omaha."

"Omaha! Oh, Everett, you didn't!"

"Matter of fact, I did. The tickets are over there in the pocket of my suit coat. And all, I am very proud to let you know, the plans have been made. We'll leave here August twelfth to spend a week with Bert."

"A whole week? What will he think when he hears that?"

"He already knows, and is perfectly delighted. To tell you the truth, it sounded to me as if he already had a month's worth of things for us to see and do once we get out there."

"Oh, Everett, it's been so long. I can't imagine a more wonderful gift. Thank you. You always were the most thoughtful man in the whole wide world."

"No use buttering me up yet, Maggie. There's more to come."

"More? How could there be?"

"I've also written to Janie and Vernon. They've invited us

to stop on our way home. So we shall. Two days in Erie with your first best friend."

He took advantage of her stunned silence to smile. "Now you may start buttering me up . . . whenever you're ready."

"Oh! You are such a dear. A dear, dear . . . dear."

. . .

Whatever Maggie had imagined Omaha to be, she knew the minute she and Everett stepped off the train that she had been mistaken. Her first impression was of the heat that overwhelmed them before they were even out of their car. The second was the howling wind that encircled them with a near invisible stream of sand, causing their eyes to tear and their skin to burn. And, whereas Maggie had anticipated a small cow town, the hugeness of the metropolitan downtown came as a further surprise. She had known that Buffalo was more than three times larger but had naively never imagined a city of a hundred thousand to exhibit – and proudly – so many signs of its newfound growth.

Bert had been waiting with a huge bouquet of local flowers. Although his gift had encumbered his embrace, Maggie stubbornly insisted on keeping every one of the squashed blooms as a special memento of her first arrival in the city that would ever after be known as Bert's.

There was no question that he was doing all right. Men acknowledged him as they passed on the streets, always with a friendliness that never belied the respect and admiration they felt.

Barriers of time were crossed in moments of joy as Bert excitedly spent the next days showing them the city and the outlying areas that had so fascinated him on his arrival. Maggie could see her brother was happy here. Still, she marveled at a territory not long tamed which frequently seemed as foreign to her as the moon.

Where were the trees? Where were the grassy lawns? And all the beautiful flowers she had come to treasure? Sand hills replaced the forested rolls of home, a strange beauty she tried very hard to understand.

Things blurred in a whirlwind of sights, laughter, more food than she thought possible to eat (much less enjoy!) and, always, more laughter.

How, all three wondered, could it so soon be time for Maggie and her husband to depart? Maggie had no trouble wheedling a promise from her brother that he would return to Buffalo, for 1893 promised to be as prosperous for all as '92.

In the meantime their suitcases were crammed even fuller by the last purchase they had made in Omaha: the proper, Bert had absolutely insisted, attire for their days at the beach with Vernon and Janie. Everett had initially been ashamed to model the getup: wide black and white horizontal stripes on a one-piece wool bathing suit that stopped just before his knees. He still hadn't decided which was more foolish: those horrendous stripes or the sight of his white legs sticking out beneath. Maggie shrieked from her dressing room. Her suit was a more modest two-piece garb though again ankles – good heavens, legs no less! – were exposed for everyone to see.

Their last hopes of modesty retained were dashed when they discovered Janie and Vernon regularly sported similar outfits for their days at the beach.

The weather was lovely for late August: sunshiny days, gentle breezes, and warm waters that encouraged swimming and the inevitable picnics. The foursome enjoyed their days together, happy to watch the little girls, Rosalie and Alice, involved with their playmates, eagerly discussing amid giggles the latest schemes for their returns to school in another two weeks.

· · ·

"Whatcha' reading, Bessie? I could hear your giggles across the hall."

"Uncle Charlie sent us another copy of his *Evening Mirror*."

"Marvelous! May I share it with you? I can't imagine how a small-town paper can get filled with such silly ads.

Never any news of course – but then, he doesn't send it for our elucidation, does he? So what goodies have you found so far?"

"Take your pick. I hardly know where to start. Want your manhood restored, John? For just a dollar, or six for five, you can get nerve seeds, guaranteed to restore any loss of brain power, lost manhood, nightly emissions, evil dreams, even lassitude or –"

They spoke the well known words in unison: "– or your money guaranteed fully refunded."

"Look at this one, Sis. 'Ladies Shirt Waists and Wrappers Just Opened.' Wouldn't you think some might prefer to keep their dresses closed?"

"Think I'd prefer the Royal Ruby Port Wine." Says it's particularly adapted for invalids, convalescents, and the aged. Guarantees to be economical for medicinal and family use. And just a dollar a quart, never sold – like the . . . ahem – cheap wine by the gallon. Golly, Johnny, why is our family still pushing soap?"

"Don't knock it when it keeps the food on the table and us in these fancy houses."

"Plus college and . . . yes, I know."

"You don't sound convinced, Bess. Is something wrong?"

"No. Of course not. It's just –"

"Well?"

"I don't know exactly. Here we sit making fun of all these silly ads. Seems like there's an elixir guaranteed to cure just about anything."

"Even if you know as well as I that most of them are downright fakes."

"I guess I was just wishing –" Her brother looked up at her expectantly. "I wish there was some magic syrup that would cure us. Does that make any sense?"

"Honestly? Not in the least."

"It's just that Mama seems sad so much of the time . . . and Papa is hardly ever home at all and then –"

"I know. It's rough on us all. Why do you think Ralph, and Grace and Anne before him, find so many reasons not to come back?"

"But –?"

"I don't imagine we'll be any better." John put his hand up to stop her. "I know. But it won't be that many more years till you and I are out of the nest, as they say. Leaving just Abram and Clara."

"She'll go to college, I'm certain of that, but what do you think will happen to him?"

"I don't, to be honest. Think about it, I mean. Guess if I were to, I'd have to say I can't imagine him anyplace – or doing anything – except living here for the rest of his life."

"Sad, isn't it?"

"Sad? or scary."

LV

To the summer of 1893

St. Paul's attendance was growing exponentially due in part to Maggie's skills as choirmaster and organist. She knew the look in her husband's eyes when he stopped to watch children at play but selfishly, as the years had passed, felt gratitude that their lives were not entwined with a family of their own. How much better to pursue the things that appealed to each of them! They'd be celebrating their eighth anniversary this summer. And, truly, could any couple be happier?

Mr. Larkin's brother-in-law had chosen the beginning of that year to noisily announce his resignation from the newly incorporated Larkin Soap Manufacturing Company. Rumors were that he intended to go off to Harvard to become a writer. Feelings within the company were that his going would be a relief to all who stayed behind. No more faux silver pieces! God knew he had been blessed with fertile powers of creativity and had certainly made his contributions but talk about being a thorn in everybody's side! Did any doubt that they would prosper once he was removed from the scene?

Much of the burden, especially in the early weeks of transition, seemed to fall on Everett's shoulders. He knew, and of course told Maggie too, of the bitter feelings that continued between boss and brother-in-law. Unaware of the details and not eager to pry, he left the personal issues to the men involved and concentrated on the work at hand.

· · ·

Maggie was bustling about the kitchen, preparing the lamb roast she knew to be Everett's favorite. Although she treasured her position at St. Paul's, it was always a welcome treat once choir practice finished on Thursday night to have two whole days to spend at home. Time too, if she delayed things just a little, for candlelight though these early May days were warming up and staying brighter longer.

How tired Everett must be, she thought as she heard his slow footsteps through the screened front door. Scurrying to meet him, she was shocked at his ashen face.

"Everett! Something's happened. Tell me what it is. No, come in and sit down. May I get you a glass of water? Or brandy perhaps? There now. Do tell me what has happened to you."

"Not I, Maggie. Or not just I. I'm afraid it will affect us all."

"What will? I don't understand. Tell me what's happened."

"There's been a major panic in the stock market. I'm afraid our money is gone. All that we had saved. Everything."

"But that can't be true. What could more secure than this country's economy? I can't imagine a safer place to put our savings. You don't really believe what you're saying. You don't, do you? Certainly whatever caused such a disruption in one day can be over as quickly the next. Tell me it's possible. That by Monday things could all be well again."

"No, Maggie. Not this time."

"But it could. Things could recover. Tell me there is that chance."

"I suppose there is. But, my dear, please don't count on it."

. . .

"I told you it would happen, Lizzie. First, the panic last month and now, the market has crashed. There's no easy way out."

"But what does it mean for *us*, Jack?"

Lizzie shuddered at the tone in her husband's voice as he attempted to explain. These had been hard months for him and she was determined to do nothing to cause further upset.

[231]

There'd been that whole ugly scene when Elbert Hubbard had announced his departure. Imagine, wanting to be a writer at this late date, and then going off to Harvard to do it. Funny, that he and Charlie had somehow become friends, much to the consternation of Jack who considered him a thorn in everybody's side.

Well, they'd gotten through that. Larkin was still upset and there was talk of lawsuits which she didn't understand but things seemed to be settling down, at least Jack was in a better temper, until this market panic last month. And now a crash.

Good Heavens! Would this market crash affect her eldest daughter? Perhaps the wedding might have to be a wee bit less lavish though Lizzie knew the money for Grace and her William was already safely tucked aside. What could be more important than the marriage of her firstborn daughter? She'd do all she could to see those plans progress exactly as they should.

And as for William – well, she couldn't imagine that people wouldn't have a need for an ambitious up-and-coming young attorney no matter what the stock market did.

· · ·

Jack's temper worsened as the effects of the crash spread. Losses throughout the country inevitably led to further declines in sales.

Now he avoided coming home because of the boy.

Twelve this year, too. Six more years and he could be out on his own. Sooner, Jack imagined, if they could find him a position. But who'd take him? And what could he do?

Then there was all that whack-whack-whack business. Lizzie Borden, my eye! So the jury had finally decided she didn't do it after all. Well, who'd ever believe that? But hadn't the decision delighted Abram? Giving him more ideas, was that it?

Whatever sacrifices he'd have to make, and he knew there'd be plenty before this was over, one that he wasn't going to do was his membership in the Niagara Club. Where else could he find refuge once the workday ended? It would always be better than going home.

. . .

"I declare, this summer can't possibly get any worse."

"Oh, Jack, don't say that. Please. You know it always brings bad luck."

"Well, my dear wife, if you can think of anything more that can conceivably go wrong, I'd certainly like to hear it. It was just two weeks ago yesterday that the market crashed and now here we are, coming back from Uncle Rufus's funeral. If it isn't one thing, it's another."

"Don't be so hard on Lizzie, Jack. I'm glad you two were able to get here for the funeral. I know how much it means to Mother."

"How do you think your mother is taking it all?"

"I wish we could know that for certain, Liz. She appears strong and his death couldn't have come as much of a surprise. Not at their ages."

"Did she talk to you at all, Jack, about wanting to sell the farm?"

"Sell? You can't be serious, Charlie. What nonsense!"

"I don't know where she could find anything better for the money. Especially now."

"Perhaps you can talk to her after Lizzie and I return to Buffalo. You are staying on for a few days – I heard that correctly, didn't I?"

"Yes. I want to see her settled. Get all these silly ideas out of her head. She was even speaking of selling off all the animals."

"What?"

"My feelings exactly. I did tell her I thought it best to sell the old cow. I don't think it wise to keep her over the winter but the heifer? That must stay of course."

"She's a stubborn old woman, Charlie, always has been. Still you always had a way with her that I lacked. I'm sure you'll be able to iron it out."

"You know I'll try."

"And do be sure to keep me abreast of all that's happening here."

"And, Charlie, you know we'll be looking forward to another visit."

"Of course." He laughed at his response before elucidating. "Yes, Jack, I'll keep you abreast of everything that goes on here. And yes, Lizzie, I look forward to visiting as soon as it's possible. Perhaps Thanksgiving or over the Christmas holidays."

"But that's over four months away! You mustn't wait that long."

"Let's see how things go. I do want to see all my favorite nephews and nieces and I imagine it's becoming more and more difficult to catch them at home."

The three continued to talk as they walked slowly back to the farmhouse.

LVI
April 1894

"Lizzie, I simply cannot understand that boy of yours."

"Ours, Jack. Ours."

"I'm talking about Abram."

"So am I, dear. But he is *our* boy, not mine alone."

"Of course. Though I admit there are certainly times – today especially – when I find myself wishing he weren't."

"Today? But I thought the wedding was lovely. Grace seemed to positively glow. And didn't William make a handsome groom?"

"Of course – but that's hardly what I'm talking about."

"I thought it an absolutely perfect wedding. In fact, I can't remember a ceremony where the couple seemed so relaxed and happy – not nervous at all. And I was hardly the only one to sense those feelings. Why –"

"Damn it, Lizzie, stop your prattling! The wedding was fine. But it's over. Our daughter –"

"Our firstborn –"

"Whatever." He opened the front door, entering before her. "That's hardly my point. Grace and William are married. I don't imagine it will be too long before Anne follows the same path."

"You –"

"Elizabeth, I am trying to speak."

"Sorry."

"Good. Now . . . I am trying to discuss Abram."

"Yes, dear. Well, why didn't you just say so?"

Lizzie had stopped in the vestibule to stare speechlessly at her husband who, having removed his hat and coat as they entered the house, had hurled them toward the nearest chair

[235]

in the library as he passed. With a certain feeling of satisfaction she had seen the hat miss its target by a good eighteen inches. Now she watched as his coat slowly slid off the chair onto the Persian carpet beneath.

"This has got to stop!"

Aware that the preceding scene had further kindled his rage, Lizzie decided her safest course was to remain still. The quiet stunned him, causing Jack to turn his gaze back to the spot where she still stood.

"Abram."

She remained silent, watching him expectantly.

"He can't leave Clara alone for one moment. Have you heard him? The taunts? The way he teases her to tears? God knows, I've tried to explain to the girl that it's just his way – nasty as it is. But it seems he can't be happy till he has stripped her of even a moment's peace. I don't know what to do."

Except for listening intently, Lizzie tried to emulate a stone-faced statue.

"I swear that boy'd treat friends the same way – if he had any." He paused to wait for her reply. "Lizzie, I asked you a question. What do you think?"

"I'm sure you're right, dear."

"Well then, what do you propose we do about it?"

"I'm very glad you have noticed, Jack. Beyond that, I honestly have no idea."

. . .

"More rumblings at work, Everett? You look particularly distressed. Here, give me your hat and coat and go warm up by the fire. Let me put the kettle on. Then I expect you to tell me all about it. Judging from your expression this day has more than one chill to it."

"Maggie, I swear, if you hadn't always been able to read my mind, you're getting better and better at it. Tea sounds welcome – and warming. Thank you. Let me freshen up and I'll tell you everything over a hot cup. Nothing that can't wait a few minutes."

The break created by Elbert Hubbard's resignation and its

subsequent disruption to John Larkin and his company had become common knowledge as the months passed. Hopes of a quick settlement to what had originally been viewed as a family squabble, a falling out between brothers-in-law, had been dashed as the bitterness and threats escalated into a tangled lawsuit. Hubbard demanded money Larkin had no means of paying as the country still smoldered through its deep depression. Encouraging signs of an economic turnaround were beginning to flicker but the men of business knew better than to bank on the maybes of a better tomorrow while John Larkin, judging himself unfairly backed into a corner by his tyrannical brother-in-law, struggled to extricate himself and to restore the company that bore his name to its previous position of prominence.

"Maggie, we've talked so much of Larkin and his dealings with Hubbard that I plumb forgot the other news!"

"There's more?"

"There is indeed. Though one wonders a bit if the old man might not be better off learning his lesson about involving his family in his work."

"Why? What else has he done? And who?"

"You'll never guess. No, I shan't make you. His wife – can you imagine?"

"*Frank?* What can she do?"

"You remember the fun she had writing the soap advertisements a while back?"

"Who could forget that? Our *perfumeurs* and the labels in French with all those flowery descriptions. Though, to give credit where it's due, the sophistication did appeal to the buyers. So she's done it again?"

"No, this is different. Here, I've got a copy in my pocket."

"They're picturing her in an ad!"

"But notice. Not for the soap itself."

"I see that. A 'Chautauqua Spring Rocking and Reclining Chair.' She certainly looks comfortable, quite elegant in fact. Yes, I think it should make that premium sell well. Can't say I'd mind one myself."

"Maggie, I swear. You find room in this house for one more

premium and I'll see that you get it. And no fair suggesting a larger place."

"Sorry. I only meant to tease. We certainly don't need another chair. And, trust me, I have no desire for more space. Our home is just perfect as it is for you and me." She kissed him on the forehead as she picked up their teacups. "Now, if you'll excuse me, I have a supper to see to."

LVII

July 1894

The steamer rocked gently as it crossed the azure lake. Gulls shrieked above. The cooling breezes were a boon to all, especially the two who were just coming from the stifling heat of a week on the inland farm.

"I thought Mother looked quite good, didn't you, Jack? She certainly seems to have recovered all her old spunk."

"It did my heart good to see her so active. Mentally, too. I'm so glad Charlie was able to talk her into keeping the house. I can't imagine her being happy any place but on the farm." He slipped his arm around her shoulder. "Must say, too, I was pleased with the way you acted, Lizzie."

The remark caused a look of surprise to flash across her face.

"Oh, come now, Lizzie. It's no surprise the old lady gets on your nerves. Always has, is how I see it. But Mother seemed grateful for your help and I know our visit meant a lot."

"You should know by now that I have always tried to do whatever I can for your mother. She's set in her ways, no question of that, but still your mother. It's just, I suppose, that farm living has never really been my cup of tea."

"It's over with now. I'm just trying to let you know how relieved I am that things – everything – worked out so well. Now tell me, what plans have you made for us at Chautauqua?"

"Plans? Why none. To be honest, it's such a marvelous treat just to be coming back here that I could be happy doing nothing beyond strolling the grounds. What are you looking forward to?"

"Obviously, the new Men's Club."

"That hardly surprises me."

"Don't be harsh, Lizzie. From what I've been told, it is absolutely the best place to make contacts, and you know they're important to us, both socially and in the business. But I'm also looking forward to sailing and swimming. Perhaps a little fishing. You won't mind, will you?"

"Of course not. I seriously doubt if either of us will lack for things to do. There! Look ahead. It's the tower of the Hotel Atheneum. I can see it from here."

. . .

"Everett, just look! There it is."

"By golly, so it is. Built so low I almost missed it. That big hotel certainly dwarfs it."

"Let's take a closer look. It certainly sounded immense."

"It had better be – for twenty-six thousand dollars."

Maggie and her husband hushed as they reached the edge of the new amphitheatre at Chautauqua and stared into its deep recess, then across the huge bowl to the far side where the choir loft rose.

"It's enormous," she gasped at last. "Can't imagine its ever being full of people."

Quietly they walked together to the bottom of the open bowl.

"I can hardly wait to come here for a concert." She started to turn to follow her husband, glanced up once more at the lovely Atheneum and stopped. "Everett, would you mind terribly if we crossed to the hotel before going to our room?"

"Of course not, dear. I hope in fact that one of these years we'll have the money to be able to stay there. I love the place as much as you. Come, why not sit a spell on the veranda?"

"Oh! Do you think we could?"

"Why not? With a hundred or more empty rockers on the porch, I can't imagine anyone would throw us out. Come; sit. There'll be time later to find our place and get ready for tonight's lecture."

. . .

"Forgive me, Jack. I must be getting absent-minded in my old age! For I had meant to ask you long before now who the distinguished looking man was you were talking to last night."

"Which one? My God, that sounds pompous, doesn't it? I assure you I didn't mean it that way."

"I hardly imagined you did. Isn't this a lovely lunch? I thought I was full but who could resist those marvelous desserts?"

"I noticed you had no trouble not resisting any of the three the waiter brought you, Lizzie."

"Or enjoying every bite. I hear they do that for every meal here at the Atheneum. If we stay much longer I'd be afraid to relax on the beautiful wicker furniture in our room."

"I'm happy you take too much pride in your figure for that. But we seem to have gotten off the subject. You were asking about a distinguished man, not the dessert."

She laughed. "Of course! I was referring to the younger one, in his mid-thirties, I'd guess."

"Oh, him. Quite the adventurer from what I hear. Big hunter, rancher for a while in the Dakota Territory, ran for mayor of New York City a while back. Lost, of course, which seems a pity. Name's Roosevelt, Theodore Roosevelt. He's Civil Service Commissioner in Washington now. The men with whom we were speaking seemed to feel he had a good future. I'll have to ask Charlie what he knows of him."

"I imagine quite a number of renowned people pass through. I know that Susan B. Anthony spoke a few years past. Sorry I missed her."

"Suffragettes, bah! That type'll get no sympathy from me."

"Interesting story though. The women last night said that the powers-that-be at Chautauqua – men, you might know – refused at first to let her speak here. So her initial visit to the area was an appearance at Lily Dale. When Chautauqua realized its mistake she was invited – twice."

"That name again! I keep hearing it over and over."

"Surely, you can't be referring to Miss Anthony."

"No. To Lily Dale."

"They say it isn't far away. I'd love to see it. Can I entice you to take a drive over the hill?"

"To a haunted village? Isn't that what they call it?"

"Why, Jack, you know better than that. It's a home, a refuge if you will, for spiritualists."

"Have you ever heard such nonsense? Ghosts and goblins. That's what I mean by haunted. Oh, I've heard the stories: flying guitars, paintings done by ghosts as the paint mysteriously leaves the cans and appears on the canvas, dead people speaking. Balderdash. You know it as well as I."

"I never said I disagreed, Jack. Whatever life there is after death seems to reside quite securely – and permanently – in heaven, or wherever it is they go. Our souls, I mean. I'm simply curious, that's all. We're so close and I really would like to see what it's like."

"Chautauqua's fine. Let's stay where we are, enjoy this little respite before we return to Buffalo. Enough is enough. Do I make myself clear?"

. . .

"I'm so glad you suggested we stop for a dish of ice cream. Our lunch was delicious but I was ready for a little sweet." Maggie wiped a drip on her chin before taking another lick.

"Perfect on a hot sunny day. While we're at it, I want to thank you again for suggesting we visit that new chapel. The Good Shepherd will be a lovely corner of solace."

"Odd, isn't it? They established Chautauqua for religion and already it's become so filled with secular activities that the individual denominations are establishing houses of their own, and now even this lovely little jewel of a chapel."

"Speaking of the secular, I noticed how quickly you picked up your ears when Lily Dale was mentioned last night."

"I can't help but be curious. What a strange place it must be."

"You don't believe in that hocus-pocus, do you, Maggie?"

"Of course not. Though I admit I have certainly thought

about it. If spirits could communicate with us, then I'm sure one, or both, of my parents would have had plenty to say to me before now. Or so, for that matter, would Hannah. Much less Fil. Golly! I could have a whole row of spirits lined up eagerly waiting to communicate. So how come all I hear is silence?

"Still, I've heard of people going to the readings there – they don't call them séances, you know – and I am curious. Very much."

"I'm a little curious, too. Can't picture it exactly. I don't think that you'll be hearing from your family there any more than anyplace else but, if you want to go take a look, I'll go with you."

"Oh, Everett, do you mean it?"

"Of course I do. Though perhaps you mistake my gist. No crystal balls for me, no ghosts hovering around. I won't go to a séance – whatever it's called. If you want to, go ahead. But I am curious to see the place. It isn't that far, you know. I could arrange a carriage for the morning, if you like."

"Yes, let's! Who knows? Perhaps we will run into the spirits. Or even see ghosts. Oh, Everett, dear, I can't wait!"

. . .

Ghosts and spirits, if such there were, stayed out of sight for Everett and Maggie's visit to Lily Dale. In fact the two discovered nothing sinister in their surroundings.

The smaller community lay along the eastern shore of a fittingly smaller lake. Victorian homes stood among the foundations of promises of more. Though seeming minuscule in design and ambition when compared to its more prosperous cousin Chautauqua, the Assembly welcomed the couple with an agreeable quietude. So few people were in evidence, in fact, that they later joked that after all perhaps it was peopled with ghosts and not much else.

While Everett went in search of a toilet, Maggie meandered down toward the lake, marveling at the lovely view, stopping then with a start as a Bach double invention wove through the trees. She turned, unwillingly thinking of Peter who had so often played the same piano piece, seeking its source. A crow cawed in a tall pine above her. When it quieted the music was gone. She turned in time to see Everett quickly walking toward her.

They roamed freely around the grounds, enjoying their outing.

They continued to admire the scenery as their carriage struggled up the hills and back down to the lake of Chautauqua, circling the northern end to return to the Institution.

LVIII

August through December 1894

"If I didn't know you better, Everett, I'd swear you were losing your mind."

"It's a long way down to the pavement, no denying that, but bicycling has become such a popular sport and, actually, once one gets the hang of it – it's all just a matter of balance, you know – then it's quite easy."

"To be honest, it does look like such fun I believe I might try –"

"Maggie!"

"I just might . . .if someone were to invent a machine just a little bit – well, actually, a lot – closer to the ground. Couldn't the front wheel be smaller, even the same as the one in back? I'd like to know my feet could touch ground whenever I wanted. Sitting way up on that huge wheel is just too scary for me."

"Then I'm safe for now. And, we can presume, so, too, are the streets of Buffalo."

"It must be nice not having all those ruts."

"We cyclers do have our good points. Buffalo would hardly lead the country in paved streets, and they do, if it weren't for our being known as the 'Wheelman's Paradise.'"

"I hadn't heard that title. Makes sense, though. I'd be willing to bet there must be thousands of you bicyclists out there – usually right in front of where I'm trying to go, too."

"*Thousands?* Why, last week I heard someone estimate Buffalo now has eighteen thousand cyclists on the roads. And, while I've no wish to see you join them, in all fairness I must tell you that our Club will probably vote before the end of summer to share rooms with the Women's Wheel and

Athletic Club."

"Of Buffalo?"

"Certainly. So maybe you'd better not get too set in your ways. Unless, somewhere in the future you plan to include the wheels."

"And risk injuring my hands or arms? I confess being organist is too important to me now. But don't count me out. Give me a while longer. Then we'll see."

"Well, I won't give you too many *while longers*. I'm not sure I want you racing around when I'm in my seventies."

"But you're not yet, my dear. Not yet."

. . .

"Of course I had a happy birthday, Ardith, though I'm not convinced turning fifty is anything to celebrate. Jack gave me a garnet bracelet and apologized that it couldn't be something more expensive, promised in fact he'd make it up once we pull out of this damnable depression. The children were lovely and, in fact, all came to dinner . . . at home."

"That sounds good."

"I'm just not prepared to have my children grow up. They're becoming so . . . well, so independent."

"Not needing Mama as much, is that what you mean?"

"Ardith, you know me far too well. But yes, you're exactly right. And I don't think my feelings have anything to do with turning fifty. Except we wouldn't have had the dinner last Tuesday if it hadn't been my birthday. Though now I fear the children – I must stop calling them that, mustn't I? – that they'll use my birthday get-together as a substitute for our usual Thanksgiving celebration. I've already heard talk from some about wanting to make other plans."

"But –?"

"But . . . well, I suppose I pictured that somehow they could go out on their own and still include me. I'd love to shop, or meet for lunch, spend more time with Grace and William, even be let in on Anne's secrets for I do imagine she'll be wanting to be engaged before too much longer. I guess," she sighed, "I just want to feel included."

"A perfectly sensible attitude, my dear," Ardith watched Lizzie nod in agreement, "and completely unreasonable."

"*What?*"

"Think back to when you and Jack were first married. You've told me about it, memories filled with a great deal of happiness, I believe: counting pennies to skimp by, your modest first home, and all the beginnings that life with another entails. Right?"

"Yes, of course. But what does that have to do with –? Oh, you are a wise one, aren't you? Of course. There comes a time when a young person needs to be out on one's own." Lizzie picked up a stack of waiting books and prepared to sort them before returning each to its place in the stacks. "Thanks, Ardith, I needed that." She started to move away, then turned back. "And as for turning fifty, I think I may find getting old to be quite enjoyable after all."

. . .

"I can't believe it, Everett. The depression, the market crash, they were less than two years ago. And you're telling me the recovery is so complete that business is better than ever?"

"It must be – or Larkin has lost his mind. And you know what I think the odds of that are. I've never met a keener businessman. No, Maggie, that man knows what he's doing all right."

"So they're going to expand again, is that what you're saying?"

"A little bit more than just that, I believe. When the Directors met after Easter they agreed to buy the old New York Central Railroad Station, tear it down, and erect a six story building in its place. To tell the truth, I don't imagine this will be the end of it either. Larkin loves to build. I've never seen him as happy as when he's planning his next building, contracting the work and then watching it take shape. That man is full of surprises. The way I see – "

"Oh!"

"What is it, my dear?"

"Speaking of surprises, here. This letter came for you this morning. Have to admit I'm dying to know what it's about."

"Patience, dear. I can tell you better if I open the envelope first. Here now, let's see what it says. Ah! The powers that be want me to give a talk for the coming season of Shakespeare Club."

"Oh, Everett, how exciting! When will they want you to do it?"

"Says here – yes, next November. That will give me all summer to prepare."

"What subject will you choose?"

A broad smile slowly crossed his face. "I'll have to give that a little consideration. It should be most enjoyable . . . and very, very interesting."

. . .

"Whew! I thought we'd never get out of there. I certainly didn't want to drag you away from your admirers but how long can such gushy compliments continue?"

"But it was all right, wasn't it?"

"*All right?* Everett, didn't you listen to one word any of the members said? Your talk has to be the hit of the season. In fact, if you want my totally unbiased opinion –"

"Oh, but I do, my dear, and I'm sure it will be –"

"I thought you were utterly fantastic. So many of the talks at Shakespeare Club are dry, downright dull as a matter of fact. I've watched a couple of those portly men nodding off in the back. And more than once, I assure you. But nobody slept through a word of yours."

"I imagine standing before them with a dagger in my hand might have that affect."

"That didn't hurt – oh, Everett, the whole thing was extraordinary. The humor kept them all on their toes. And you certainly knew your topic. I know you've enjoyed researching it these past months."

"Yes, the dastardly villains of Shakespeare. The subject was a good choice."

"I imagine everyone knew the obvious few: Lady Macbeth

and Iago, Shylock and Angelo. But you found so many others. And those quotes! Some members are probably now convinced you have every word of the Bard committed to memory."

"And you don't think I have?"

"Nothing you do, dear, would surprise me."

. . .

"Uncle Charlie! Oh, Mama, he's here!"

"Out of the way, Clara. I want to get the door."

"I was here first. Ouch! Mama, Mama, Abram hit me."

"Shush, you two. Can't you stop your squabbling for one day at least? It's Christmas Eve, time for peace . . . or at least a little quiet. Do you understand me?"

The reply came slowly and in unison. "Yes, Mama."

"Now, I want you to remember it. Today *and* tomorrow. Uncle Charlie has come all this way because he wants to be with his family. He wants smiling faces, and happy children. I'm sure he didn't fight this terrible rain just to be in a home full of quarreling youngsters."

"Well, is anybody going to open the door and let me in?"

Clara and Abram squealed as they raced to be the first to greet their uncle. Lizzie was just steps behind, ready to take his hat and coat once he transferred a large parcel to the hall table. The youngsters started to question its contents, caught Charlie's wink and grew quiet.

"Why, Abram, just look at you! You're almost a man, aren't you?"

The boy blushed at his uncle's words.

"And what, if it's not a secret, have you asked Santa Claus for?"

Abram stuttered at the unexpected attention. "*Santa?* But – Well, sir, I'm hoping for a copy of the newest book by H.G.Wells. It's called *The Time Machine* and, to be honest, sir, I can't wait to get my hands on it."

"Growing up indeed. I'm afraid I can't remember: how old are you now, boy?"

"Fourteen-and-a-half, sir."

"Fourteen and a half. Yes, quite grown up. I hope you're

getting along better –" He stopped abruptly sensing the warning in Lizzie's eyes. "And just look at my little girl. Though hardly *little* any more, are you, Clara?"

She smiled as she curtsied. "And I'm twelve-and-a-half, sir."

"And a very fair twelve-and-a-half, too. It's good to see you both. I promise we'll have more time to talk later but right now I want to visit with your mother. Would a cup of tea be possible, Lizzie? It was frightfully cold out there. And I want to hear all about the others. John's in college now, I know, and Bess about to graduate. I suppose she'll be wanting a trip to Europe, too. Don't frown, Lizzie, why shouldn't she? I can afford it and there's nothing that would please me more. Perhaps I should tuck it in a Christmas stocking. Ralph's at the company; I bet Jack's happy to have a son following in his footsteps. And you must tell me all about Anne's wedding plans. Will I have a chance to meet the young benedict? I want to see them all . . . I will, won't I? Grace, too, and William, of course . . . and that little rat of your grandson. I hear he's tottling already."

"My goodness, Charlie. Slow down! So many questions and no time for an answer! Yes, they have all promised to be here tomorrow morning. Christmas at home, presents under the tree, the whole ritual. Though they have asked – I know Grace was particularly concerned that you might not understand – they want to leave afterwards, to have their own tree at home."

"I can understand that. Might, if you didn't object too strongly, dear Lizzie, give me a chance to get Jack to give me a quick tour of the company. I hear it's expanding ever so rapidly."

"So much building going on. I simply don't know where it will all end. Seems like every time I turn around I'm hearing of a new one."

"I can remember when we used to say that about you, Lizzie. Oh, don't look so shocked. Come now; let's get that tea. I'll help. And you can fill me in on all that's been happening."

LIX

Fall 1896

Everett hurried down the steps from the polls, catching a deep breath in the brisk autumn air as he crossed over to where Maggie waited.

"I know better than to ask who you voted for, not that you'd tell me anyway. But who do you think will win? And will it really make much difference in how the country's run?"

"I could easily accept your skepticism on the latter point, Mag, but do hope McKinley is the victor. I like the spunk I see in that man. He's willing to fight for what he believes, even when it isn't popular. That's a quality Washington can use."

"I hope we won't have to wait too long to learn the outcome."

"Things seem to speed up everyday. Turn around once and Buffalo is claiming to have built the largest office building in the world. Turn around again and is there talk of anything except the hydroelectric plant in Niagara Falls?"

"I know what you mean though some of the newest things turn out to be the oldest: the Olympics in Greece, the gold rush in Alaska. It's hard sometimes to know where we fit in this ever-changing world."

"Gives us much to be thankful for, if one stops to think about it. A good home, good job, good friends. Not to forget the love of my life."

"You know how my mind works –"

"Convoluted, to say the least –"

"You mentioned good friends and that reminded me of all those people we've come to know through Shakespeare Club."

"And that, I imagine, further reminded you of the paper you're scheduled to give in February. Have you picked your subject yet?"

"It was hard to make up my mind. Then I decided to stick with the topic I know."

"Music? Surely you aren't going to play the organ!"

"This is a literary club, hardly the proper place for a recital. Actually I thought I'd like to do a paper on the music used in some of Shakespeare's plays. It was generally made up on the spot and forgotten by the next day so, while I can't be precise, I think I could give examples of the type that was performed then, what kind of instruments would have been used, the training expected – or certainly hoped for – in the musicians, those things."

"A stellar idea, my dear!"

"Speaking of ideas, do you think I should buy a new dress for the occasion? The gowns in the stores are quite unlike those of last season."

"Why, what have the fashion mavens done now?"

"Covered us up, that's what! Those revealing bosoms are out."

"Oh, dear." Everett clutched his breast in mock distress.

"Sorry, but collars are clasped right up to the chin. Still down to the floor but with wonderfully huge puffy sleeves and the tiniest waists you can imagine. I may fight the latter – or, should I say, it may fight with me – but it really is quite attractive – especially with a high crowned hat to match – with a few ostrich feathers of course."

"Good God, haven't you women made those poor birds extinct yet?"

"Of course not, silly. There must be millions and millions of them. Besides, it's very important to me that I not only give a stellar program but that I look as well as I possibly can, too. Funny, but I feel it's almost a sign of respect to our president."

"Mrs. Knapp? Yes, I believe I can understand what you're saying. She has done wonders for the club, hasn't she? I admit I was beginning to find it a little tiring, the same routine week after week after – yes, yet another week. But she's brought new life into it. A *joie de vivre,* if you will."

"I was surprised to learn her husband also works at the Larkin Company. You've never mentioned him. Do you know him?"

"I've seen him around, know who he is. But I doubt if we've exchanged a dozen words. Too bad. He must be some crackerjack to have a wife like that. Too bad he hasn't joined the club."

"I'll second that."

"I do admit I was quite surprised," he paused, "well, let's just say *surprised* that there are two beautiful women so literate and so well-educated in the city of Buffalo. Quite a lovely sense of humor, too."

. . .

"Lizzie, what a stellar year you've given the club as president. I can't remember as many good, really good, programs."

"Yes, they have been, haven't they? You're right. I can't think of one that disappointed though I especially liked Mrs. Hopkins' demonstration on the music of Shakespeare."

"This club can rise beyond mere sociability when it desires. I don't know of a single soul that hasn't commented most favorably on the changes you instigated."

"So much flattery, Ardith. Goodness! Being president meant a great deal to me. I needed it – and, honestly, also the recognition that's accompanied my hard work. It just went past so quickly, too fast."

"But surely it must be a relief to have that out of the way now."

"Relief? I'm not sure. I confess I really enjoyed the glory. And I wish even now that Mrs. Ashland had asked for a little advice, had figured my experience counted for something, when she was elected the new president."

"But –"

"No buts needed, Ardith. I know better. It never occurred to me to ask the past president when I took over. And I wouldn't have even if I had thought of it. I was much too brimming over with my own plans and ideas. The club will do fine without me. That's what hurts."

"You sound like you're thinking of bowing out. You wouldn't do that, would you?"

"Of course not. I have already been asked to prepare a play for the coming reading season."

"A play? Good for you! That could be quite a challenge. To make it interesting, I mean. Got to keep those old timers in the back row awake."

"I certainly intend to try. *Pericles* and I, that is."

"Oh, Lizzie, no! That's a dreadful play. Though I suppose, if anyone can rise to the challenge it would be you."

"Thank you, Ardith. And I don't think you'll be disappointed. Not this time either."

LX

Summer 1897

Jo set down the stack of books she'd been lugging as she approached the library's main desk where Ardith sat, deep in thought. She waited a silent moment, hoping impatiently for acknowledgment. Finally, she cleared her throat in an obvious gesture. Ardith looked up immediately.

"Not bothering you, am I?"

"Jo! I'm sorry. I was so engrossed with this order sheet I confess I wasn't even aware you were standing there. Can I help you with something?"

"No." She laughed at her own reply. "Not that I interrupted your study just for the fun of it. But it isn't work-related. It can keep . . . I guess, only I did want to talk to you before Lizzie came in."

"Lizzie? There's nothing wrong, is there?"

"No, I didn't mean that. Quite the contrary. I can't remember seeing her so happy in – oh, goodness – well, for ages."

"Yes, she is, isn't she? That's all right, isn't it?"

"Oh, Ardith, you know it is. It's just that . . . well . . ."

"Yes?"

"You know her moods as well as I. I wish she could always be happy. It's just that –"

"I believe I understand now. You're thinking of some of her 'highs' in the past, and –"

"And remembering how many of them led to those awful lows. You don't think that will happen this time, do you?"

"I hope not. No, to answer your question, I truly don't believe it will. She did a masterful job with Shakespeare Club – certainly you'd agree – and now, well, now she's so involved with – Hush! Here she comes!"

Lizzie swirled in to the anteroom of the great library, spotted her friends and eagerly hurried over.

"Good morning, one and all. I just love summer, am so glad it isn't fall – yet. Tho' soon enough will *be*, and we'll have to start trimming our Christmas tree."

Jo and Ardith exchanged confused glances.

"Lizzie, whatever has gotten into you?"

"Why, Ardith dear, and Jo, you too, I'm getting ready for the play I must do. *Pericles* they say it must be this time, so I've decided to do the whole program in rhyme!"

The two librarians whooped in laughter.

"The whole thing?"

"It's a terrible play, Lizzie. I couldn't believe it when I heard they offered it to you. It hasn't been done in ages –"

"Yes, I'm told it is difficult –"

"And not very good."

"True, Jo, and equally true, Ardith, though I confess I'm having a marvelous time with it."

"But rhyme? Why?"

"That seemed obvious, once I got into it. I figure if Shakespeare could endeavor to write it all in rhyming verse, I could do the same for my synopsis."

"I didn't know you were a poet, Lizzie."

"Poet? And who, pray tell, is there says I am – just because I do a few lines in iam—bic. Pentameter, that is – or not. Besides, all I have to do is present the plot."

"Lizzie, I really believed I had heard it all. You never cease to amaze me –"

"Or me. It's a great idea. And I think your program should be marvelous fun. How long do we have to wait?"

"Goodness, don't rush me. I've a little over six months and I'll need every day of it. The thing's set for January." She paused to look from one woman to the other. "You don't think anyone will mind, do you?"

"Mind? Lizzie, it's a wonderful idea."

"It's just that some of the older members seem so . . . well, stodgy, so set in their ways."

"You mean the ones who sleep through most of our programs? Lizzie, I guarantee nobody will be asleep for this. Do it."

"Absolutely. You must."

. . .

"There, see, I said you could do it."

"I know you did. But, Everett, I was terrified at first. I'd never have dared if you hadn't kept after me. And of course knowing Chautauqua was using the skating rink this summer for bicycle lessons – well, after you were good enough to arrange a week's stay again, how could I not try? Oh, I do so love it here."

"I know, my dear Maggie, though quite honestly I do not imagine I would take the time – or make the effort – were it not so pleasing for you."

"Whatever your reason, dear, I assume you know how grateful I am. Oh, just look! We've come back again to the Octagon House. I think it's the most marvelous design in the world – from the outside anyway. I can't imagine how they arranged the rooms inside. Too many nooks and crannies, wasted space, I'd suppose."

"You know, dear, Mrs. Shaw mentioned that a class on early American literature would be given here this afternoon. I'd like to attend. Would it interest you?"

"At two, I think she said. Yes, let's both go."

"Would you mind if I deserted you now for an hour or two? I've been reading about the new Men's Club and really am curious to see it. Now that I'm sure you're safely away from your bicycle.'

"Until tomorrow. Actually, I look forward to trying again – and I certainly hope to be safe enough by the end of the week to navigate some of the streets. Quite honestly, I'd love some time to myself. I think I'll stroll through the glen, then down along the lake. Perhaps see what's new at the bookstore, or maybe even find a rehearsal to sit in on. I could meet you for lunch, if you wished, though would just as soon pass that up. I'm eating so much here at breakfast and dinner that I fear I'll be waddling by the time we head home."

"I'll see you get twice as long at the cycling lesson tomorrow!"

"Oh, you!"

"Truly, Maggie, I'm glad we both have things to interest us – separately, and together. I'll meet you back here at two."

An hour later Maggie had completed her circuitous stroll, enjoyed a double-dipped ice cream in the plaza, and was now leafing through a booklet she had purchased at the booksellers. The store had been embarrassingly full of a large display of *Studies in the Psychology of Sex* by Somebody Havelock – or had it been Havelock Somebody? She supposed it was being discussed in lectures somewhere on the grounds – but what a strange subject for Chautauqua! – but had instead purchased a pamphlet on the celebrations for Queen Victoria's Diamond Jubilee. Now, eager for the details, she intended to find a shaded bench to wait until it was time to meet her husband.

"Oh, I'm sorry. I should have watched where I was – You!"

"Why, Margaret! And looking quite beautiful, too – even if a trifle preoccupied. My, God, how long has it been?"

"I have no idea, Peter. I can't remember the last time we saw each other," she lied. "How have you been?"

"Well. And doing quite well, too. That's what brings me here to Chautauqua."

"Really?"

"Yes. I've been asked to do a series of master classes and a recital next week. Will you be staying that long?"

"Afraid not. We plan to leave on Sunday."

"Pity. It would have pleased me to have you there. And how is – it was Everett, wasn't it?"

"Everett it is. And doing very well. Thank you for asking."

"And you, Margaret, are you doing very well as well?"

"As well as could –" How asinine it all sounded to her. How many more *wells* would be awkwardly added? If there were one near by, she'd gratefully jump in. "I'm fine, Peter. And late actually. I promised to meet Everett. It was good to see you again."

"Take care, Margaret." She scurried off so rapidly Peter had no way of knowing if his final words had been received.

. . .

"I know you were busy, Lizzie, but I am sorry you couldn't come with us last Saturday."

"To Lily Dale? I couldn't believe it when you told me you were planning to go, Jo. And you too, Ardith. Weren't you afraid of what might happen?"

"It isn't ghostly at all. In fact, it's quite a lovely little spot. Serene. Pretty lake. Even a few swans around."

"But the spirits?"

"Spiritualists, Lizzie. There is a difference."

"Did you go to one? Weren't you afraid?"

"Of course not."

"Jo may not have been but, yes, I confess I was at first. A little. But there isn't anything frightening about it. You absolutely must come with us next time."

"Did you have your fortune told? Talk to dead people? What was that like?"

"Funny, now that I think about it. *Dead*, yes, but so far removed from anyone I knew, really knew, a great aunt or whatever –"

"Mine was a grandfather who died shortly after I was born. I never knew him, certainly had no memory of the man. But growing up in the family home, I was always surrounded with the things that had most interested him. And my medium hit it all right on the head!"

"What if one told you bad things? I'm not sure I would want to know my future."

"They won't tell you if what they see is ominous. Besides, for the most part it's very general: you have an important decision to make, you will be feeling better, something good is coming your way, that sort of thing."

"You should have come, Lizzie. I bet they would have told you what a success your presentation of *Pericles* is going to be."

"I hope so. I had no idea how time-consuming my *little project* would turn out to be."

"So how's it coming?"

"If you're sorry you asked, don't me please blame.

'Pericles' you know was writ in Shakespeare's name.

It's the only play he writ in rhyme.

And we've got to read it. It's got to be time.

If Shakespeare can do it, I thought as I sat,

Why heavens! So can we. It's as simple as that.

There are coffins, and daughters, wives dead – or alive?

Pirates and prostitutes. Will Marina's virginity survive?"

"Oh, Lizzie! You're going to be great."

"Well," chimed in Jo, "I for one can hardly wait."

"But there's more," Lizzie said. "I erred! *Pericles* is not in rhyme –"

"Really? Oh, no! "

"What will you do?"

"Turns out only Gower's intros are in verse sublime.

His, the words to explain the action.

Still, I'm going to be rhymer for my satisfaction."

. . .

"Can I get you anything?"

"Thanks, dear, but no. Can you join me? The paper has two sections today and I know you haven't had a chance to look it over either. Unless you have some great interest in the famine in India, I'll take the first section and give you –"

"What's this?"

"What's what?"

"It's pictures." Everett had risen and stood now behind her shoulder. "They call it a comic strip!"

"Really? May I see? Hmm, *Kat-zen-jammer Kids*."

"Hey, I get it first. You gave it to me, right? Go back to your starving Indians."

"Why, Maggie, did you know Brahms had died?"

"Did you see this ad?"

"Oh, hush. Let me read."

"I'll be quiet if you will, my dear."

The room brimmed with the silence of the two curious readers. At last, Everett set down the first section and looked up to see Maggie impatiently waiting for him to finish.

"What a look! My goodness, you must have uncovered a real gem. What is it, Maggie?"

"May I read it to you? It isn't too long . . . and really, it's quite lovely."

"Of course, dear. Go on."

"Seems a little girl wrote to the New York *Sun* with a question we are hearing more and more these days. This is their answer, quite touching, I think." She adjusted her glasses and began to read. " 'Virginia, your little friends are wrong. They have been affected by the skepticism of a skeptical age. They do not believe . . .' "

LXI

December and January 1898

"One last sip please, Jack. Then I'll be ready for bed. It's been a long day for everyone." Charlie nodded as he accepted the half-filled glass from his brother.

"Certainly one of the happiest Christmases I can remember. Having their uncle here is always a treat for the youngsters."

"Who, I hardly need point out, are hardly youngsters anymore. Clara's turning into a beautiful young lady, looking more like her mother every day."

"Ah, yes. Lizzie was a beauty once, wasn't she?"

"*Once?* Still is, if you ask me. Matter of fact I had meant to tell you how good she really does look. Whatever you're doing for her is obviously working well."

"I? Hardly. Putting up with one fool project after another, that's all. Not that that's always easy either. I thought I'd lose my mind when she became president of that ridiculous Shakespeare Club but, believe me, that was nothing compared to this Pericles project."

" *Pericles project?* Sounds mysterious."

"If she hasn't foisted her ideas off on you yet, it's only because you haven't been here long enough. I doubt you'll escape. Nobody else seems to."

"Escape? From what?"

"Her fool poetry. My God! You'd think she was a budding writer or something. The good part is she gives the program next month. Then maybe – just maybe – we can have a little peace."

"And a major anniversary, if I can count correctly."

"Thirty years, can you believe it?" Jack turned toward the noise on the stairway. "Here comes our poetess now. I'll let

[262]

her explain her latest project."

"Excuse me, you two. I didn't mean to be upstairs so long. Can I get either of you a cup of coffee? Or an extra piece of mincemeat pie? I saw cook putting some away."

"No thanks. I couldn't eat another bite. Matter of fact I was telling Jack that I was ready to head upstairs once I finished this last smidgen of brandy. Then he started telling me about your latest undertaking, something to do with Pericles, I believe. Care to tell me about it?"

"It can wait till morning if you'd rather."

"No, please. It won't take that long, will it?"

"I promise to be brief for I'm tired, too. Simply stated, I was asked to present the background on *Pericles* for two of the Shakespeare Club reading sessions next month. Since the play is so wrapped up in rhyme, I decided to do my explanations and scene cuts the same way." She paused to look at her husband. "Jack, I'm afraid, finds my poetry simplistic to the point of embarrassment. I hope the members don't agree. In any case, I know I've had marvelous fun putting it together."

"Sounds pretty ingenious to me, Liz. Would it be asking too much to hear a sample?"

"I'd be tickled pink. Jack?"

"Go on," he replied somewhat gruffly.

"Though the plays are read over two nights, Charlie, cuts are still needed to keep the readings within the expected time constraints. Generally about forty-five minutes an evening is all the audience will tolerate. Then, when a scene is cut, the narrator – me, in this case – is expected to briefly explain what's going on. Here's what I've written to explain the third scene of Act Two:

> Marina, daughter of the sea, is brought by Pericle
> To the island of Tarsus, for he did believe,
> That it was safe there for his daughter dear,
> Since on his travels he's been kind to the people here.
> So Marina, daughter of the sea, need not fear,
> He left her with the governor without a single tear.
> The governor and his wife agreed to volunteer

While Pericles took his leave to pursue a kingly
career.

"Hardly great art, agreed, but fun, don't you think,
Charlie?"

"I'm impressed. And I bet your club friends will be, too."

"Oh, I do hope so."

"And when is this to be presented?"

"The second and third Tuesdays in January. It's getting
close."

"I'm sorry I can't be around to hear it all, Lizzie, and to
watch the faces of your audience. I think you'll have a real
success."

"You're a love. Thanks. And good night to you both. We'll
talk more in the morning."

"Good night, Lizzie."

"Good night, Lizzie."

The two brothers watched her leave the room, cross the
hall and climb the staircase till her flowing skirt was no longer
in sight.

"She's having a good time, Jack. Don't be so hard on
her."

"Harrumph. Here, one more tot of brandy and then we'll
both be ready for bed."

. . .

"Everett, I swear I don't know what in God's name is
happening to you."

"Why, Maggie! I'm not used to hearing you talk like
that."

"And I am not used to your behaving as you've been."

"A short temper doesn't become you, dear. I think, before
you start complaining about me, you might do well to examine
your own behavior."

"My behavior? Everett, I am not the one who has grown so
preoccupied. Why, days go by and you hardly say ten words
to me. It doesn't seem that long ago that you were hurrying
home to share your latest news."

"Oh? Well, yes, I suppose we did talk more then. But you weren't so busy in those days either. Seems like you had the time to listen, that you really cared what I had to say."

"I haven't changed. I'm not any busier – or any less, if that matters. And I'm still here, waiting to hear how things are going at the factory."

"And I'd be quite happy to tell you – if there was anything to tell."

"Do you still enjoy your work? Has something happened to make it less enjoyable?"

"No, nothing's changed. Except, perhaps, they're filling the place up with young whippersnappers. Terribly exasperating that. They think they know everything, have nothing to learn."

"And you're feeling left out? Is that it, Everett?"

"*Left out?* Whatever gave you such a ridiculous idea? Good God, Maggie, is it any wonder I can't talk to you? Putting words in my mouth. You don't listen to what I have to say. I've gotten used to being treated that way at the factory but I still expect a little respect from you."

"They can't fire you, can they, Everett?"

"Fire me? Where did you get that outlandish idea? After all the years I've given them. Why? Have you heard something?"

"No, dear, of course not. It's just that you seem . . . well, worried about something. And I know, we both know, you are getting older."

"And you're not, I suppose?"

"Of course I am. That's hardly what I meant. But sixty. . ."

"Sixty-*smixty*. I won't be sixty till the year 1900 and that's a long, long ways away."

"Less than two years."

"I don't need to listen to this from you."

Maggie sat stunned as her husband angrily left the room.

. . .

"Act Five Scene One finds us on Pericles' ship.

Two sailors enter. Let's hope they don't trip."

The laughter echoed good-naturedly through the attentive audience. Lizzie sat back to let her readers finish the play without interruption. It had been a silly idea perhaps, but one that was overwhelmingly accepted. And not a single sleeper on either of the two nights!

LXII

July 1898

Maggie could remember when she used to anticipate Everett's coming home from work. Initially she had worried for him, unable to pinpoint what had changed, much less when, while sharply remembering his demand that she stop pushing him. It had stung as much as if it had been a physical slap.

Strangely, he still proved an excellent escort whenever they were in company. Just look at his attentiveness at the Shakespeare Club picnic! At least until they were alone in their carriage. Then he had turned cold and uncommunicative.

Deeply hurt and initially distressed, she now found release in the women's books that had recently flooded the stores. There must be many unfulfilled women, she supposed, for the market for these potboilers was proving to be huge.

Who were they, she wondered? And why were there so many? Had they all known the kind of love she and Everett had shared – once upon a time?

. . .

The Buffalo Public Library had been bustling ever since its telephone lines were installed. The jangle of the new bell irritated the ever-busy librarians.

Jo eyed the contraption with nervous apprehension as Lizzie retreated to the stacks with another pile of books.

In spite of her fears it was a quiet morning with a chance for the three to rest over a cup of coffee shortly before eleven.

"Lizzie, you've been moping around all week," Ardith began as she set her cup down across the table from her friend.

Jo looked up, surprised. "That's why," she paused to glance at Jo, the twinkle in her eye reappearing, "Jo and I have planned this outing – and you absolutely must promise to come. You will . . . won't you?"

"*Promise?* How can I promise when I don't know what it is?"

"Never you mind about that."

It struck her suddenly. Could they possibly be thinking of an excursion to that park on Lake Chautauqua? She had heard talk in earlier seasons of people going there to enjoy the bathing with time later for dinner and dancing. Now, according to what she had read in the papers, Midway Park had added tennis, croquet and even boating. Might that be what her friends had in mind?

"All right, I'll go along with whatever you two have planned. But do understand, please, that I do it with reservations."

"Nobody said anything about needing reservations, Lizzie. Though actually, Jo," Ardith turned from one woman to the other, "reservations aren't such a bad idea, are they?"

"No; and let's plan to stay after for lunch. We'll have time, won't we?"

"Absolutely. This is not a day I want to hurry through. In fact, I've heard about a new spot, *Monica's* they call it, which serves the most sinfully rich desserts."

"Count me in." Jo was well-known for her appetite for sweets.

"What are you two talking about?"

"Do we have your word you're coming, Liz?" Ardith was determined to get confirmation before letting her secret loose.

"I promise. After all this I wouldn't dare pass it up. So fill me in, please. Where?" Lizzie looked quizzically at her friend. "And when?"

"The *when* is up to you though, if it's agreeable, we'd like to set it up for this coming Sunday, the thirty-first."

"An auspicious ending to July, is that what you have in mind?"

"Then, or earlier –" Jo interspersed.

"Later, if need be," Ardith added quickly.

"Sunday is perfect. Now tell me please just what it is you're doing with me on Sunday."

"We're taking you to Lily Dale!" The two women looked at each other before both turning to gauge Lizzie's reaction.

"Lily Dale? You know I can't do that. Jack would never permit it."

"It's lovely there, Lizzie."

"Just wait till you see the lake –"

"Are you two trying to convince me you want me to travel all the way across western New York just to see a lake? Girls, have you forgotten Buffalo sits on one far larger?"

"Oh, Lizzie! That isn't the same at all."

"And you know it."

Lizzie hesitated. "I know it wasn't fearsome when you went before – but what if something went wrong?"

"What can possibly go wrong? We're talking about nothing more than an outing to the country."

"And, from what Ardith says, a fabulous lunch."

"But you are thinking of roping me into getting a . . . what do you call it?"

"A reading. That's all, Lizzie. A reading."

"Whatever it's called, you are going – and taking me – with that in mind. Yes? or no?"

Ardith hesitated momentarily. "Yes."

"We confess."

"Only it's fun, Lizzie. There's nothing bad about it."

"Please come. People go back time and again." Jo felt she was beginning to find a plausible argument. "They wouldn't if it were as awful as you think, would they?"

"You'll never know until you try it for yourself." Ardith happily supported her friend.

"So . . . are you in or out?"

"Friends?" Lizzie remained unsure.

"Lizzie, you know we are. We wouldn't dream of doing anything that might possible harm you."

She looked at Ardith and then Jo, lingering to study their

visages carefully before turning back to the head librarian.

"All right then, Ardith, I'll do it! What time shall we plan to leave?"

LXIII

July 1898

The swaying of the train tended to soothe the anxious woman as the cars headed west along the southern shore of Lake Erie. Ardith's prayers for a beautiful day had been answered. The waters shimmered in the bright sunshine, the sky a deep blue above them. The fields on the other side were lush green with row after row of grape vines, carefully trained to wires stretching as far as the eye could see.

It was no more than an hour before they alighted at the Dunkirk depot, standing momentarily in silence as the train pulled away. There seemed to be no one in sight.

"Can I help ya ladies?"

"Oh! Yes, please. Or rather, I hope so."

"We didn't see anyone at first."

"No sense settin' out in this noonday sun unless one has to, if'n you ask me. But I'm here now. What can I do fer yas?"

"We'd like to hire a carriage to take us to Lily Dale."

"I'd of guessed as much. You've come to the right person. Michael's the name. Old Bess and my rig are gist 'cross the road in the barn. Wait here. Be right back."

The women settled comfortably in the carriage and happily surveyed the countryside as they moved out of town, first following the creek and then slowly beginning to climb the hill they knew separated the higher Lily Dale from the Lake Erie shore. The steeple bells in Laona reminded them guiltily of the churches they had missed to make this a full day's outing.

Michael halted the buggy before Lily Dale's gates.

"Suppose you'll be awantin' me to come back and get 'cha after a spell?"

"Why, yes, please. It's just after noon now. We'd like to spend the afternoon here but still get back to Buffalo by suppertime."

"Got a brother gist down the road a spell. Wanna figure on meetin' here 'bout four?"

"That sounds perfect, Michael. Thank you. We'll be back here –"

"Right here –"

"At four."

The women turned and walked to the gate, pulling out pocketbooks to secure the money needed to purchase their passes. Lizzie stepped inside and took a deep breath. She could see the lake on her left, the far shoreline not too distant beyond. Straight ahead ran a path with cottages on either side.

"Come," Ardith began excitedly. "Let us show you around a bit first. Then we can talk about mediums and readings."

"But –"

"First things first, Lizzie. Jo and I want to convince you this isn't an evil place. That's Step One. Then, if you'd rather not, we'll find a place for you to relax –"

"They have a nice library."

"The library would be good. Or, perhaps, down along the lake. *Where* isn't of paramount importance right now. Let's just walk. Then Jo and I do want to visit a medium. What you do is up to you."

"Yes, Lizzie. No pressure. We promise."

"It's beautiful here! I don't know what I expected – a smaller Chautauqua perhaps – but I can already see they aren't the same at all. Not," she hurried on as if feeling an apology was necessary, "that I'm saying one is better – or worse – than the other."

"Lizzie, for goodness sakes, relax! You have nothing to fear." They had come to the next street in, a large grassy oval open in the center with houses ringing it. At the end stood a large amphitheater and, beyond, the shores of the upper Cassadaga Lake.

The women walked and talked and then, finding a bench

that overlooked the still lake, sat and talked some more. Suddenly Ardith, realizing how quickly the time was passing, jumped to her feet.

"Lizzie, stay here if you like. I know Jo is also eager for a reading. If you wish, we'll just plan to meet back here in an hour, maybe a little less."

"No, my curiosity is peaked. I'd like to go along – if you don't mind."

"Terrific!"

"Fantastic!"

The two women stumbled over words as each talked at once. Ardith had found Madame Eva to be a sympathetic match and eagerly looked forward to her third visit. Jo had not had as good luck with her first medium and now wanted to try the one Ardith recommended. They were relieved when she promptly answered their ring. She eagerly greeted her customers though looked less satisfied when they explained their time constraint. She felt she could do two readings by then, nodding to Ardith and Jo. Taking it as an immediate sign that her fortune would be a disaster, Lizzie started to walk away.

"Madame! Madame! Don't go like that. It is not bad news that I see –"

"But how did you know?" Lizzie turned back, completely stunned. "I didn't say a word."

Eva laughed gently. "One doesn't need to be a psychic to understand all emotions. It takes little training, simply keen observation to read a face such as yours."

"Then you are *trained?*"

"Of course! Becoming a medium – for that's our proper name – requires training, then rigorous testing. We're quite on the up and up, you know."

Lizzie blushed at the words.

"Oh, Madame, I meant you no embarrassment. You haven't been here, to Lily Dale, before?"

Lizzie nodded in silence.

"And you are curious?" The bewilderment crossing Lizzie's face was obvious to all three. "Your friend here," Eva nodded at Ardith, "has already asked me to do a reading for her and your other friend. If you intend to meet your carriage by four, there simply isn't time for a third, much as I would enjoy doing it for you. May I suggest someone else?"

Lizzie, still silent, looked to Ardith and then Jo for reassurance before turning back to the jolly heavyset woman who stood on the steps in front of them.

"Yes. Please do."

"It might surprise you to know that we mediums have our favorites, too. Andre would be my first choice, especially for you, madam. Come in and sit. It's much cooler inside. I'll have my daughter run over to see if he's there." She winked pleasantly. "Let's keep our fingers crossed."

The girl was back in minutes, smiling broadly as she handed Lizzie a card. Lizzie glanced down to read the name written in a fancy script: Andre Robson, Medium. She turned it over to discover a small map had been drawn on the reverse. Robson's home was apparently only a block down and around the corner. She assured them she could find it without trouble and agreed to meet her friends at the lake when their readings were over.

Lizzie walked briskly down the stairs as Madame Eva's door closed behind her. She turned right and headed for the corner, turned again and immediately saw Robson's house. Her steps faltered as she neared his porch. Her right foot rested on the first stair, hesitated and backed down to the walkway. She stood still for a moment, then turned and began to slowly walk away.

Had she heard the door behind her open? Lizzie felt certain she had stopped even before hearing his voice.

"Are you looking for me? I'm Andre, Andre Robson. I was told an attractive woman would be coming to see me. Oh, dear, I didn't know my words would make you blush. I am sorry. May I help you?"

"I . . . I . . ," Lizzie stammered uncertainly.

"Never had a reading before, have you? Please; don't be afraid. Come in. Let me explain what it is I do. And don't worry. I think you'll quite enjoy our time together."

. . .

"Can I get you another piece of the torte? Or more tea perhaps?"

"Oh, no, thank you. I couldn't eat another bite."

"Nor I."

"But it certainly was delicious, Monica."

"More tea then?"

"No. I'm afraid we're all full. Would you mind if we just sat and continued our conversation? It's positively marvelous out here on the balcony. Your view of the lake has to be unequaled."

"It is grand, isn't it? Please do, stay as long as you like. If you want anything else, give me a call. I'll be inside."

The three women smiled as Monica left them. Small boats plied the water; gulls occasionally shrieked overhead and the resident swans glided slowly by beneath them.

"Oh, I wish we never had to go. I wish I could stay here forever."

Ardith looked at Jo and burst into laughter. "That's probably the last thing we expected to hear from you, Lizzie."

"Or I to be saying, for that matter. But it's true. It's beautiful here. So peaceful. And quiet."

"No ghosts or goblins to get you then?"

"Oh, heavens no! You both must have thought me a silly dolt, the way I prattled on about how terrible I thought this place must be. Now I feel like a real ignoramus."

"Education, however instigated, has its values. Glad you came?"

"You know that already."

"But you haven't told us much about your reading. Or do you want to keep it to yourself?"

"No, I'd love to tell you. It's just that it all happened so fast, so much was said, that my head is still swimming. I wouldn't know where to begin. Tell me what happened with each of you. And I'll try to have my mind back in one piece by the time we're on the train to Buffalo."

The women talked happily until it was time to meet Michael and his lorry. They were surprised to find the road beyond the gate empty. He wouldn't keep them waiting, would he? Certainly trains from Dunkirk to Buffalo ran often enough that they shouldn't have trouble getting back but better not to have to worry at all.

The gateman exited his tiny shed. "Are you ladies looking for a buggy and his driver? Michael, I think he said his name was."

"Yes, we're the ones. He said he'd meet us here at four."

"And got a good railing for it, too."

"Why? What's the matter?"

"Nothing, ma'am. Only I'm afraid he took you in. Not that it isn't a pretty drive out in the carriage, just hardly necessary, that's all."

"What do you mean?"

"We have to get back to the depot in Dunkirk."

"I understand that, ladies; truly I do. It's just that taking a carriage isn't the most expedient – or cheapest, if you don't mind my saying so – way to get there. You don't mind walking a bit, do you? Just a short bit, I assure you."

"We've been walking all afternoon. What can a little more hurt?"

The gatekeeper directed them to the station nearby where, following the briefest of waits, they were able to catch a train from Pennsylvania going right into Dunkirk. A short delay later found them comfortably seated on their way back to Buffalo.

"Coming back to the real world yet, Lizzie?"

"Huh? Guess my head's still swimming."

"Anything you'd care to share?"

"Trust me, friends, I've no secrets. There's just so much I wouldn't know where to start. Besides which, I just realized how close we've been to Mother Knapp's. Should I feel guilty for not stopping to say hello? Or grateful we didn't run into her somewhere in today's journeys? I don't even have the answer to that."

"Well, I think guilt is out. We hardly had time for what we did –"

"And I wouldn't have passed up that heavenly chocolate

concoction for anybody's mother-in-law."

"Only too true."

"All right then. Let's put Mother Knapp aside."

"But that's the easy part."

"For starters, tell us, were you afraid at first?"

"I know you expected to be."

"At first? Yes, I guess I was. In fact," she paused to reflect, "I had just about decided to turn and run when Andre stopped me."

"What was he like?"

"I can't even imagine getting a reading from a man."

"Short and frumpy like Madame Eva?"

"Hardly! Tall. A little swarthy perhaps, mustachioed with the brightest eyes. Looking into them was like looking into a pool of deep water. One just wanted to be pulled right in." She stopped, realizing the absurdity of the words as she spoke them. "And a nice smile. Anyway, a nice man, easy to talk to. He seemed to know all about me before we were even seated. And that's just what it was – a talk. No crystal ball. No levitating tables, no –"

"Didn't we tell you, Lizzie?"

"I guess I expected something really spooky. Everything but ghosts and cobwebs. Not that seeing his house was all that reassuring. It could use a good coat of paint."

"So could a lot of them."

Ardith shot a glance at Jo. "Go on, Lizzie. Did he tell you anything of importance?"

"Mmmm? Oh, I know what you mean. Future, all that. No, just that everything looked good. In fact, he said he could see me finding a success greater than any I have known so far. Can you imagine? I have no idea what that would be. But it was amazing how much he knew about me, my background, Mother and Dad, the children . . . yes, he even mentioned Abram. Seemed to know all about him."

"You mean he mentioned Abram by name?"

"Yes, I believe so. No, I guess he . . . let me think now. He knew he was one of twins. And that we had named them for a fallen president. That alone would have made me a believer,

I assure you. Said that he would always be faithful to me, though he saw a cloudy future for the boy. Just – well, the boy always has been different, hasn't he?"

"Think you'd go back?"

"Oh, yes! I can't remember ever having had such an entertaining afternoon."

"Too bad there's nothing like that in Buffalo, isn't it?"

"That really would be something. Though, you know, maybe it's better this way. Having the whole experience, I mean."

"Even that sinful dessert."

Lizzie leaned back in her seat as the car swayed reassuringly. She had a lot to think about.

LXIV

September 1898

"I thought I knew her, that I could understand what she was likely to do. But this!"

"I confess I was pretty hurt when I first learned about it."

"You! Why, Ardith, it never, not in a million years, would have occurred to me that you wouldn't be invited. You've always been closer to Lizzie than I though, honestly, I can't imagine her doing such a thing and not including either one of us. You bet I was hurt."

"After all, we were the ones who took her to Lily Dale."

"Took her kicking and screaming as I recall. 'The great Andre Robson.' Do you think he could have cast some spell over her? Hypnotized her maybe?"

"I wish it were that simple. I wish there was an explanation, Jo, something that made sense to us, something that could excuse her behavior."

"I remember sitting with her on the train coming back. One of us said something about how much fun it would be to have a medium in Buffalo, to be able to go whenever we wanted. I glanced over at Lizzie then. I remember her face – it had the strangest look."

"Yes! She said something – what was it? *Entertaining?* Wasn't that the word she used?"

"Ardith, you're right! Maybe it was all just a great entertainment to her. Then she leaned back, into the seat cushion . . . She must have already had the idea."

"No, it couldn't have occurred to Lizzie that quickly. Though I wouldn't doubt for a minute that she was already seeing the possibilities. Just needed time to figure out how to pull it all together."

"Well, she certainly did a good job. She's absolutely the talk of Buffalo. I overheard two women gossiping about her reading afternoons. Some, I think, would just about kill to get in."

"Don't you think that was part of her idea? Part of the attraction? To Lizzie, I mean. Bring something that's new to the city, something one can assume will be a big hit, and then limit the number who'll be allowed to attend."

"With Lizzie being the one to decide who gets in – and who doesn't! Fiendishly clever."

"And she thought she was riding high when she was president of Shakespeare Club!"

"And then that paper of rhyme. To tell you the truth, I was ready to throttle her at the time."

"I'm every bit as upset as you are, Jo, but do give credit where it's due. She was a fabulous president and that program – well, she deserves all the praise she garnered. Not that she doesn't also deserve credit for this. I mean, bringing Andre to Buffalo was a touch of genius."

"Obviously, her select few can pay well for the privilege, too."

"You'd better believe it! No place on a list like that for two lowly librarians. Why, she's hardly found time to come in since this all began."

"That may be just as well, Ardith. I think I'd have a hard time knowing what to say to her."

"Well, we'll have to, sooner or later. It may kill us both but let's try to be gracious."

"Gracious? I'd rather wring her neck. Besides, it never would have happened without us."

"But neither would it have occurred to either of us to twist it into the social event of the season. We found the readings amusing. Helpful, perhaps."

"I thought mine was very encouraging."

"But parlor entertainment? It took a Lizzie to turn it into something like that."

· · ·

Maggie contentedly peeled and cut the vegetables as Janie worked on the rest of the evening meal, setting aside the bread to rise as she rolled out the crust for the evening's pie.

"Forgive me if I seem to be prying, Maggie, but as a friend I'm concerned. Coming alone to visit, of course, but also the faraway look I catch in your eyes. Are things that bad?"

"Good heavens, no. Well . . . no, not really. I'm not trying to hide anything; it's just that I can't explain – to you, any more than I've been able to understand it myself. I just know that Everett has changed, his attitude toward me, I mean."

"I can't imagine that. You've told me in just about every letter how he shares everything that goes on at the Larkin, how he's always welcomed your insight. If I remember correctly, some of his more successful ideas may have budded within you. I don't see how that could change."

"Neither did I. I always welcomed his news. I missed it terribly once he insisted I stop working; you know that. The church was a blessing and I wouldn't trade it for the factory –"

"I should hope not!"

"But I always believed I had the best of both worlds. And yes, I did have a good idea or two in my day."

"Are you saying that isn't true any more?"

"That's precisely what I'm saying. Why, if I so much as ask how his day went, he flies into a rage, accusing me of prying, even interfering. I don't know what to say to him any more."

"I'm so sorry, Maggie. I had no idea."

"Why would you? And, believe me, I was fully prepared to let it stay that way."

"Is it bad, for you I mean?"

Maggie laughed more easily. "Hardly. Part of me keeps believing those good days will return. Of course I do miss my *in* to the company. The only news I get nowadays comes from reading official releases in the paper. That hurts. Still, I welcome the free time I have now, certainly hours more than I ever did before. To tell you the truth – and I feel rather guilty confessing it – I have begun to read a lot and find it terribly enjoyable."

"Read? What's the matter with that? How can you feel guilty for enjoying the classics?"

"That's just it, I'm not reading classics. I'm into it purely for the joys of escape – Haggard, Twain, even some Kipling though I find his work uneven, Dr. Jekyll and Mr. Hyde – if you haven't read that do, Janie, right away – and now I've begun a story about a new detective, Sherlock Holmes. Great writing, all of it, and so much fun. I hate to admit it but once in a while I find myself barking at Everett for interrupting me! In fact, I had even begun encouraging him to find outside activities – especially sports – just so I could have more time to myself.

"Then one morning I woke up and realized there was nothing left. We're like two strangers existing side by side. I really don't even know what he does anymore, beyond knowing it doesn't include me.

"I think about Peter sometimes, more than I know I should. What is it they say about unrequited love? Perhaps it's easier to accept the dreams that never were instead of the ones that came only too true."

"You wouldn't do anything, Maggie, would you?"

"Do anything?" Her voice betrayed her puzzlement.

"Try to see Peter, I mean. You know that would be wrong. Oh, Maggie, to be a sinner . . ."

"Good Heavens! And I do mean Heavens, Jane. I may never earn my halo but no, adultery is out. It's not a real thing – with Peter, I mean. I don't expect I'll ever see him again, nor that my not seeing him will make any difference."

Vernon entered the kitchen on the heels of his daughters in time to see Jane hugging her friend. Maggie wiped away a stealthy tear and turned to greet him.

· · ·

"Dear, how would you feel about inviting some guests in? Or having a little party perhaps. It's been a while since we've entertained at home."

"I don't mind."

"But that isn't the same as saying you'd like to."

"It's saying I don't mind."

"But the symphony last night?"

"I didn't mind going with you."

"But didn't you enjoy it?"

"I didn't mind it."

"Do you have any idea how negative that sounds? Do you prefer I cut myself off from my friends?"

"See them . . . or don't. I don't mind . . . either way."

LXV

Spring 1899

Two crows cawed their warning as the men continued to trudge across the muddy field. The corn had been harvested before the first snowfall, leaving foot-high rows, now brown and brittle, to narrow their progress. The long-awaited January thaw had turned the icy tracks to mud. As they walked they welcomed the tangy scent as a sign of promises ahead.

"I can't tell you how grateful I am that you took this time to come visit. I was so sorry not to be able to get up to Buffalo to share at least part of the Holidays with you and Lizzie and the children but Mother seemed to need me here. Well, you can see for yourself."

"She's definitely failing. But you know, Charlie, she's an amazing old woman. In fact, I'm quite surprised how well she is doing. Hardly seems fair for you to be tied up here though."

"Don't think that. I love this old farm. Nothing that can't be done here as well as in Pennsylvania. Congress is in recess till the end of the month. I'll go back to Washington then but must confess I'm enjoying the respite."

"It hardly seemed like Christmas without you. Of course the children, as you keep calling them, are pretty much grown up and, for the most part, out on their own."

"So tell me about them, every single one. I didn't want to question you in front of Mother, knowing how exasperated she gets when she can't hear what people are saying, but I shall wait no longer."

"Grace celebrated her thirtieth birthday two weeks ago Tuesday. Quite a to-do, as you might imagine, though, my God, Charlie, it made me feel ancient. She's not a young girl any more but a proper matron. Doing well, too. Husband's making quite a name for himself and wait till you see their girls! Little charmers. Anne's not far behind in any category: good husband, good children, making Papa feel older by the day."

"And Ralph?"

"You'd be proud of the boy, Charlie. Must admit when he first got interested in these new-fangled telephone thingamajigs I thought it was a losing prospect. Called him a fool for ever leaving the factory. Larkin would have assured him of a good future. Shows how little I know, doesn't it? He's going great guns. Wouldn't be surprised if we all have 'em in our homes before it's over with. Too busy to get back to Buffalo though, even for the Holidays. You can imagine the letdown we felt."

"But Bessie was there – she was, wasn't she?"

"Of course. Thank God for good ol' solid Bessie. I can't convince her women have no place in the marketplace. She *wants* to work and, I must say, enjoys it thoroughly. Trouble is, near as I can figure, she's as damned good as any of the men in her office."

"Does make you wonder. And John, now that he's graduated, what does he intend doing? Always admired the head on that young man."

"Indeed. And I don't expect him to disappoint you in the future. He's taken a position clerking law though, just between you and me, I think he's already restless to get out and see something of the world. Meanwhile Clara's pushing sixteen very hard and keeping us all on our toes."

"And what about Abram, Jack? You didn't mention the boy."

"Abram? Phew! As useless as all get out. Has his nose stuck in a book, reading all the time, unless of course he's traipsing after Lizzie. Positively won't let his mother out of his sight, not when she's home anyway. Only good thing I can say about him is that he's apparently outgrown his compulsion to tease his sister."

"Poor boy. Wish I could do something there to help. But

Lizzie. How is she? I miss her high spirits. Think I probably would have married long ago if I could have found another woman like that."

"Guess it's all a matter of perspective, Charlie. You're probably better off as a bachelor."

"That's a terrible thing to tell your brother! Especially if it's meant as a slur against Lizzie."

"Nah. Let her be. She keeps busy with her own things. But, by God, it seems like there's a new project every time I turn around. I'm surprised even you haven't heard about this latest one. Seems all Buffalo can talk about. And talk about nonsense!"

"I assure you the news didn't filter this far."

"Should have. This is where it all started."

"Here? Fredonia? Cassadaga? Good Heavens, what is she up to?"

"Lily Dale, that's where. Bunch of garbage, if you ask me. Whole lot of charlatans. Fakes. And the biggest of them all sits in our parlor every Monday afternoon acting as if he had personally descended from Delphi."

"Jack, you're kidding! I can't imagine this."

"Imagine away. Every word I speak is the absolute truth."

"But what? How? How did Lizzie get mixed up with Lily Dale?"

"*Mixed up?* That's good. Yes, that's it for sure! To answer your question, her fellow librarians talked her into going to a medium for a reading. The one and only Andre Robson."

"Who's he?"

"Damned if I know – except the medium Lizzie met at Lily Dale. She thought it all so highly amusing that she decided to bring the charlatan to Buffalo to entertain some of her acquaintances. Let me tell you, you've never seen a group as select as Lizzie's. Why, she has the cream of our society licking her boots, praying to be admitted. She limited the number –"

"That sounds practical."

"Had to. Our parlor isn't that large. And I guess each reading has to take a certain amount of time. God knows, these ladies want their money's worth. But you can bet no one turns her down."

"How is she reacting to this new celebrity?"

"She's riding high, believe me. Sometimes it scares me, it really does. No, I don't mean I begrudge her this success. She's happy now and that's good. I just wonder what will happen once this is over."

"*Over?* Yes, I see. Perhaps you are right. It isn't the kind of act that can sustain itself indefinitely, is it?"

"I wouldn't think so. Lizzie does, of course. And with all those women clamoring to get in, who knows? For now, it's good. You must plan to get up to see us. Her radiance these days will make the trip worth while."

. . .

Standing in the powder room after the meeting of Shakespeare Club, Maggie had started to reach for her hat when she stopped to listen to the women still in the hallway.

"I heard she's only allowing sixteen women in."

"That's what I was told, too. Evelyn Burback didn't make the cut. Talk about being furious! I don't imagine she'll speak to that Lizzie Knapp again as long as she lives."

"Hmm. Wonder what went through her mind when she was deciding who was in and who, out. Imagine the nerve to do something like that!"

"Brazen, if you ask me. I used to think she was nice, really enjoyed her company here. Then this!"

"I can guess who you ladies are talking about. Did you hear that she even cut her closest friends, the two who work with her at the library? A lot of hard feelings there, I assure you."

"We were trying to figure out what criteria she used to select the ones she did. Any ideas?"

"None."

"To tell the truth, I'd have picked just about the same women."

"Dorothy!"

"Well, look at it. If you're going to do something like this, well, you can't let everyone in. They say a reading takes about ten minutes. I mean, it can hardly go on all afternoon."

"Do you really believe he can tell the future?"

"I don't know. I suppose it's possible. What do you think?"

"I think I may consider a trip to Lily Dale myself next summer. Care to come along?"

Maggie tied her bonnet and excused herself, dividing the clump to leave the hall.

LXVI
April 1899

Maggie laid the music aside to sit back and rest. She took a deep breath as her eyes skimmed the vacant church. It was just over three weeks until her big May recital. She felt prepared, all except the Buxtehude that continued to plague her. Funny, she'd been playing his music since her earliest days on the organ and had never found it particularly challenging. Yet somehow, now, this one wouldn't come. Well, wasn't that what practicing was all about?

Janie had promised she would try to come back to Buffalo for the recital, bringing Vernon and, if she could, the girls as well. She was as eager to have them there as Maggie to show them the sights. Talk about progress and growth! Maggie thought even the pragmatic Vernon would find the bustling city exciting.

Everett had seemed miffed when she told of the marvelous times they had shared during her visit to Erie the previous September. At the time he had shown a complete lack of interest but, on her return, seemed almost resentful. Or, she wondered, was it just a reaction to her deciding to go alone after he refused?

It would do them all good to renew these old friendships.

First things first, she scolded herself. Time later for dreams and happy anticipation. One last run-through on this pesky Buxtehude and then she'd be done for the day. She knew only too well that trying too hard just led to disaster. She played much better when refreshed.

Involuntarily her fingers began one of the Bach preludes and glorious music filled the sanctuary. She had tried so many times to explain those feelings that came over her at these moments, grateful for fingers that could speak when words failed.

Buxtehude could wait until tomorrow.

She shut down the organ, placed the music in its folder, and began to walk toward the back of the church, grateful for an April day warm enough to have permitted her to leave her coat at home.

Hard to believe it had dared snow for the Easter services just weeks ago! Ah, yes, Easter. There had been glory that day for the music of St. Paul's.

Maggie couldn't imagine wanting more. There was Everett, of course. A lot to be wanted there but – then again – what had life taught her if not to be satisfied with what she had? Some things could be changed, and . . . well, she'd work harder next time on the Buxtehude. Some things never disappointed.

How much, after all, did she really need beyond that? Four more months would see her thirty-seventh birthday. Hardly an age to be acting like a child filled with wishes and regrets.

Next year – 1900, was that even possible? – Everett would turn sixty. Now that did make her feel old.

Good Heavens! Was that the cause of his anguish? She had always heard that men tended to get *funny* as they aged. Was that what was happening to her husband? Was he pushing her away because of some fright he was facing?

Or, the thought forced itself into her consciousness and scared her even more, could he be exhibiting signs of some age-related illness? What did she know of such things? What could she do?

Nothing; that's what you do, Mrs. Hopkins. At least for now. You're happy with your playing and looking forward to your recital. It's spring. The air is full of birds and the scent, so long missed, of early blossoms. The sun is shining. Who knows? When you get home you may find everything just as perfect as it used to be, Mr. Hopkins racing in to eagerly share his day. Indeed, why be foolish enough to look for trouble?

She had reached the door and turned to look once more down the long aisle to the pulpit at St. Paul's. The fire! It would be eleven years since that fateful day, eleven years next month. Had anyone seen the connection when they asked her to do her recital in the month of May? Maggie would have to be sure somebody made a note of it.

Hat placed squarely on her head, she quietly pulled the door shut behind her, listening for the click of the lock, turned, and strode down the steps to the sidewalk.

Maggie crossed Delaware Avenue and began to head uptown, window-shopping as she passed all the great stores. The fashions were changing so quickly. Good for the young people, she reflected, though the old shapes were better for a woman her age. But now, take a look at that hat! Hats had always been her weakness. Bonnets and dainty shoes. No woman could have too many of either.

She turned towards home. The afternoon was fleeing. Then again, what did she have to go home to? There was always a new book to keep her amused but there was plenty of time ahead for reading. Better to stay out and enjoy the rewards of this early spring day.

She might walk all the way home. That was worth an hour or two. But what was served by wearing herself out? Her practice had been demanding enough. Of course! Why not reward herself with a cup of tea and a sweet pastry? Wright's was just around the corner and, certainly, no place offered more delectable treats. She'd take the respite, grab a bite, and perhaps, once refreshed, even look over that dratted Buxtehude before catching the trolley home.

In minutes Maggie had found a quiet corner table and sat now, the music spread before her, nibbling on a piece of apple strudel as her tea cooled. She put the fork back on the plate to tap her fingers to the music.

"No!" She recognized her mistake. "It's a B-flat down to G." Had she been playing an F all this time? That would certainly explain the dissonance, enough for sure to throw off the rest of that passage. Her left hand pressed the imaginary notes, once, twice, and yet again as the pattern started to impress itself into her memory. She studied the score, searching for a repeat of the mistakenly played notes.

Blessed with the gift to be able to hear the music even as

her fingers tapped the tabletop, Maggie sat fully engrossed in her study, unconscious of the activity swirling around her.

Slowly she became aware of a quiet figure standing at her table's edge. She recognized his presence before looking up. Peter was smiling down at her.

"Hard at work, I see." He nodded quizzically at the sheets spread before her. "What is it now?"

"Buxtehude. Don't know why such a familiar composer suddenly decided to give me trouble but I've been having a dickens of a time with this. Though I think I just found my mistake."

"Preparing for something special, Margaret?"

"Why, yes. Yes, I am. I'll be doing another recital at St. Paul's next month. I thought at first it might be too much of a burden, coming so soon after Easter and, well, I'm sure you understand the preparation needed for those services, but I've felt pretty confident except for these few passages. Think Mr. B. and I have it worked out now."

"It's good to see you smiling. How have you been?"

"Fine, Peter. Busy. Keeping busy. Still playing –" She blushed at her awkwardness.

"Would you mind if I join you? I confess I've hoped that I might someday run into you –" He understood the blush this time but hurriedly continued. "I've been hoping we might talk again some day, Margaret." He nodded at the table. "May I?"

"Oh? Why, of course. Here –" She started to fold the score, gathering up the rest of her music. "I certainly did spread out, didn't I?"

"Why not? It looks like the perfect spot for what you were doing. May I get you another cup of coffee? And would you like something to eat?"

"Tea. And no." She paused. "I'm sorry." Must she always sound so idiotically foolish? "I had a piece of strudel earlier. That was enough but I would enjoy more tea. I was having tea, not coffee."

"Stay there. I'll be right back."

She stared at his retreating figure, embarrassed to be

caught as he turned around to smile at her. He was back in moments.

"The waitress will bring our order over." He waited patiently – could he be enjoying her obvious distress? – until they were served. "Now, tell me about all you've been doing."

"*All*? For how many years?"

"All right then, let me make it easy for you. You're still playing the organ, that much is obvious. And I assume that means you are still at St. Paul's."

How had he known that? Yet what could be more obvious? Her recitals were always well-publicized. Had he attended without her being aware?

"And, judging from what I see here, may I assume it is still rewarding to you?"

"I honestly don't know what I'd do if I hadn't my music."

"Do you ever play the piano anymore?"

"We have one at home. Everett bought it for me."

"Ah! So there's still a Everett, is there?"

"Of course. And you?" What made her so brazen she could ask such a question? It sounded indecently personal, not what she had intended at all.

"Did you know I was married?"

"Why, no." Had she never entertained this possibility? "Congratulations. I suppose they're in order." Please, God, let her words stop stumbling so awkwardly.

"You misunderstood. My fault. I *was* married, but it was ages ago. And very short then."

"Then I am sorry."

"For what? Perhaps some things simply aren't meant to be."

They sat, sipping in silence, Maggie wracking her brain to think of something intelligent and safe, Peter apparently happy in her silence.

"So now, tell me what you've been doing, Peter." She hadn't forgotten the key after all! Egocentric as always, he filled the passing moments with tales of his endeavors as they drained yet another cup.

Entranced and bored as he went on, Maggie listened in grateful silence until she became aware of the moving shadows.

"Good Heavens!" Gathering her papers, she jumped to her feet. "Do you have any idea how long we've been here?" Another of her more brilliant lines. "I've got to get home, Peter. Everett will be wondering what's happened to me. I wouldn't want to cause him worry. You will excuse me, please." She reached for her purse. "Let me pay for my tea."

"Don't be silly. The pleasure was mine. I only wish we could do this more often." He stopped, gauging her expression. She had turned to look at him questioningly. "Margaret," he continued slowly, "may we?"

"What? What did you just say?"

"I merely asked if you, if we, might meet again for tea sometime. Sometime soon, that is."

"I can't do that. I'm a married woman."

"My dear, I was not suggesting an assignation – not yet, at any rate. Oh, come now, don't keep blushing so. I surmise you enjoy my company as much as I have treasured these moments with you. All I suggested was that we meet again – in a very safe, and very proper, place. I'll even let you chose it."

"No, Peter. I wouldn't dream of it."

"Then come see me, please. I haven't moved since those early days. You know where to find me."

He bowed quickly, turned and started across the room. She watched him go speechlessly, stunned as he turned to her one last time and winked.

"I'll be waiting."

LXVII

She felt his arms slowly wrap around her. How had this happened? It wasn't supposed to happen. But . . .

Slowly, very slowly, he drew her closer. Her head touched his chest, his vest soft against her cheek. She knew he was speaking but heard only a soothing murmur.

As her arms encircled his waist she was a little surprised just how natural the movement felt. The solidness of his torso was new to her and yet seemed . . . well . . . She welcomed the sense of familiarity washing over her.

It would have been all right to have remained curled in his embrace forever. She might have wished for nothing more. Well, she might of.

Now though, her body thrilled as she felt his gentle kiss on the top of her head, his lips quietly teasing her hair. She knew that when she pulled away – just enough to look up into his face, eyes searching eyes, knowing he would kiss her fully then. She shivered in anticipation.

The electricity that surged through her body came as a shock. She reciprocated hungrily.

She had her hands pressed against his back now, then flung about his neck in a tight embrace. His hands began to explore her body, welcomed at every step.

Was it supposed to feel this good?

"Margaret," he murmured. "May I stay?"

"I think it's time you came in," she whispered.

"What's that you said?"

Startled, Maggie looked up from the book she was reading to address her husband. "I'm sorry, dear; I must have been thinking aloud."

"That good, is it?"

"Hardly." She buried herself again in the pages. Had it come to this? Were the saccharin words of a poorly written bodice-ripper seeping over into her life?

She had considered these books a harmless form of escape. Daydreams were supposed to be benign. Well, weren't they?

She glanced over at her husband who had resumed his reading of the evening news. He seemed barricaded behind his paper. The reminder of her lonesomeness surged painfully. She missed the touch of his hand. Her body felt sere, unused. Was it like that for every woman nearing forty?

"Any news today?"

He didn't look up. "Huh? No. Nothing."

She turned back to her novel, realized the book had fallen and her place lost. She opened it randomly. Did it matter, any of it?

LXVIII

September 9, 1899

The music gave Maggie time to reflect on Peter's note and Everett's angry confrontation after he had intercepted the day's mail. An assignation? Hardly. What did he take his wife for? Anger momentarily surfaced, but was forgotten quickly as she recalled her excitement when he had finally thrust the printed words into her grip. It wasn't even an invitation, she had hastened to assure her husband. Peter's students were practicing for a competition, a very important one to young pianists, and at the last minute had lost the woman he expected to judge their performances. Maggie, he knew, would be an unbiased listener. She was quite excited at the prospect for she was certain he would present a nice string of talent.

Later, much later, she had had time to reflect on the scene, wondering then if she had appeared too eager. Should she have refused? Should she have given more weight to Everett's decidedly odd but angry confrontation? Perhaps she might play the scene differently if it could be redone. Then again, wasn't her openness the best possible proof of innocence? Nothing more than a participation in a musical competition. That was all.

Happy in having made the right decision, Maggie enjoyed watching Peter, quite unaware of her attentiveness as this man of talent worked with his students. She couldn't remember feeling so alive and yet so serene, so close. It wasn't until he had closed the door as the last student left and crossed the room to where she sat that she grew self-conscious.

"Oh, my goodness!" She jumped to her feet. "I must be going, too." She was halfway across the room before his words stopped her.

"You are glad you came, aren't you, Margaret? When I looked over at you I thought I saw a woman being blissfully entertained."

"I hadn't quite thought of it as *blissful* though, to be sure, it was marvelous entertainment. Oh, Peter, it was wonderful being here. I felt so . . . so stimulated. As I told Everett when your invitation came, I haven't been around young pianists much these past years. I had forgotten how exciting it could be."

"I assume then he didn't mind."

"Mind? Oh, Everett. Well, yes, at first – I guess he did." How, she thought, would she ever explain that? "No. No, he didn't. He knows how much music means to me. I'm just so very grateful you considered me. This has been a positively marvelous afternoon."

"Then it mustn't end so soon."

"Of course it must. Actually it's getting quite late and I should get home. I've got quite a walk ahead. In fact, I always wondered why you elected to live so far from the trolley lines."

"Perhaps I just like being isolated. It's never seemed to bother anyone else . . . But Margaret! There's no need for you to walk home. Let me drive you there."

She turned to him. "Well, will wonders never cease! After all this time you've gotten a carriage? I am surprised – and impressed."

"No, no," he laughed. "No horses for me. I've bought an automobile."

"A motor car? Why, I don't believe it! One has to be very wealthy to afford one of those."

"Perhaps some do. But I realized I was getting older and had very little to spend what money I have on. To be perfectly honest, I've been able to put quite a bit aside. So when I saw that automobiles were going to be the rage, I decided to be among the first – instead of the last, as I suppose I've always been. Now, do let me give you a ride home. Have you ridden in one before?"

"I can't say I have. Oh, I stood nearby when Everett was

given a ride. One of the men at work bought a Haynes and was eager to show it off. To tell you the truth, I'm not sure if he was impressed or not. I never expected I'd be in one."

"Then it's time. Come on."

"Are you sure it's safe? Have you driven it a lot?"

"Not too much. Actually, you'll be my first passenger. But such a lovely idea, isn't it? Of course it is."

He continued to reassure as he led her around his house to the garage. Should she be doing this, she questioned, very conscious of the feel of his hand as he guided her arm. She quickly chided her foolishness as she realized that he was as oblivious to his action as she had been aware.

He let go just before they reached the building. Maggie stepped aside as he proceeded to open the heavy door.

She couldn't control her gasp as the doors swung open and a slender beam of light fell across the front of the contraption. How it sparkled and glimmered. And how modern it looked!

"Here. Wait there while I bring it out." She watched in silence as he released the brake and pushed the vehicle out into the daylight. It was even lovelier than she had first imagined. The leather seats shone with obvious polished care, the rims on the tires so white she had immediately inquired if it were brand new.

Maggie grinned as he struggled to start it. No, he answered proudly. He had had it for almost three weeks now. Wasn't it a beauty?

"It cost me a bundle but it was worth it, don't you think?"

She nodded as they jerked steadily down the avenue. With no horse before her, she felt thrillingly unprotected as she stared forward. My goodness though, what if Peter should lose control and steer them into a wall? There was nothing at all between!

And yet, wasn't it marvelous to have such an unobstructed view? No horses' behinds in front. Nothing anywhere! Maggie looked to the left, to the right, and down at the street as it disappeared underneath. She tilted her head up, marveling at the trees above, farther, farther back.

"Margaret, are you all right?"

She nodded her head, and smiled.

"What were you doing?"

"Enjoying the view. It's a lovely ride, isn't – " Must every word sound like such childish gibberish? But she did feel like a child, didn't she? Oh, what absolute delight!

"Oh!" Bouncing in a deep rut she grabbed the side handle, inadvertently reaching out to Peter's knee as well.

"Are you enjoying the ride?"

"Oh, yes, indeed I am. It's just so . . . well, it takes a little getting used to, doesn't it?"

"I haven't gotten used to it yet myself. To tell the truth, I hope I never do. Quite a thrill. Whoops, sorry. I'd better stop talking and watch where I'm going. Say, would you mind if we took a turn through the park?"

"Oh, could we?" The exhilaration had quite overtaken her.

He turned onto Main Street. A horse whinnied in fright as they chugged past. Maggie sat up a bit straighter, feeling quite superior to the snorting beast.

Some pedestrians looked up at the noise, stopping now to shout and point. She waved back gleefully. A carriage driver cursed them as he passed.

She giggled as the automobile turned into Delaware Park.

Everything seemed amplified. Trees were bigger, flowers brighter. She felt certain the nearby birds sang lovelier songs even if drowned out now by the noise from the engine.

It was with distress that Maggie recognized the gate that would take them away from the park.

"Could we do it again? Would you mind terribly?"

Peter smiled and turned the vehicle into the left drive that would circle back into the park.

"And shall we do it again, Margaret?"

Had she detected a sneer in his voice? She turned to look at him questioningly, aware for the first time that her excitement had made her completely oblivious to his presence.

"Please, I'd like to go home."

The dark asphalt sped under their wheels as the automobile continued on its way. Maggie remembered how proud Everett had been of the many miles of streets Buffalo had paved for its bicyclists. They would be used even more now.

He helped her down.

He must have.

Maggie didn't really remember as she walked toward her front door.

LXIX

September 1899

Peter experienced deep feelings of disquietude as he drove away from Margaret. He knew now that she had been in his thoughts from the earliest moments of decision about the car. It was her approval for which he had been searching. The stares of passersby were valuable, but it was Margaret's opinion he wanted most.

And hadn't she seemed almost oblivious to the car? His automobile! Well, wasn't that just like a woman?

But darned if she didn't seem to be falling for him! He'd certainly never expected that.

He smiled now. She had seemed so happy riding up there with him, so free in a way he'd never seen before.

He would have liked her to pay a little more attention to the automobile but . . . well, Margaret was a prize, too, wasn't she? He'd have to see what he could do about that.

. . .

As she heard the stumbling footsteps, Lizzie hurriedly placed the novel she'd been reading on the table beside her chair.

The door swung open, hitting the radiator against the far wall. Jack tripped on the small Oriental rug as the door slammed behind him. He looked around hazily. Usually the house was quiet with everyone asleep by the time he got home.

He was aware of the unusual brightness coming from the library even before he saw Lizzie curled in the chair.

"Waiting up, were you?"

"Not at all, Jack. I got so involved in this book –" she nervously started to pick it up, "that I simply lost track of how late it was getting."

He started toward her.

"Did you have a good evening?"

"Harrumph," he grunted. "Do you really care what kind of evening I have?"

"Jack, I was merely trying to be polite." She watched him advance unsteadily. "Let me just say good night and I'll go up to my room."

She had nearly reached the door when she felt his strong grasp on her shoulder.

"Jack –"

She could smell his disgusting breath as he pulled her toward him.

"Please, Jack." She was surprised that her plea came out sounding like a whimper. "Just let me go."

She thought for a moment he might fall but he regained his footing. If she struggled he would tighten his clasp even more.

Letting go of her shoulders, he cupped her head in both of his hands and drew it to his lips, his teeth cutting her. The pain gave her added strength. She wrenched her body away with a cry of fury and hurting.

Angered now, Jack reached out again.

"What are you doing to my mother?"

"Abram, get out of here. This is none of your business."

"Father, leave her alone."

Jack loosened his grip, surprised at the threatening tone in the boy's voice.

"Abram, this has nothing to do with you. I order you to get away from her – now."

"Then let Mother go. I'll see her safely upstairs to her room."

Lizzie backed away as Jack now turned fully toward his son.

"Leave immediately or I'll beat you as you've never been beaten before."

"Try it." Abram's eyes blazed as he continued. "I'm not leaving. I'll do anything I have to protect Mother."

"Abram, go."

"No, Mother. I'll go nowhere till I'm sure you're safe."

"Get out of my sight, you little monster."

"In case you haven't noticed, Father, I'm a *little monster*, as you so delicately put it, no more. I turned eighteen this past June, not that I'd expect you to take notice, but you might have of the fact that I'm almost a head above you. Stronger too, if you want me to prove it."

"And as unrelated to a human being as you've always been!"

"Jack!"

"Shut up, Lizzie. You too, Boy. Go, both of you, and good riddance."

Lizzie didn't turn to look at Jack as she hurried by. She had never expected to need, or want, protection from any of her children but patted Abram's arm in gratitude now as they walked quickly toward, and up, the stairs.

"It was wrong of you to interfere. Your father had a bit too much to drink, that's all."

"But, Mother, he was hurting you."

"Abram, I'm his wife. These things happen." She took his hand in hers. "It was between your father and me."

"No!" His raised voice was adamant. "I won't let him – or anybody – hurt you, Mother. Not now. Or ever. Don't you know that?"

"Hush, Abram. You mustn't talk like that."

"But it's true, Mother. I'll take care of you." He turned. "Always."

"Go to sleep, dear." She kissed his cheek and turned toward her door. He spoke softly as he watched his mother slip inside and heard the door lock behind her.

"I'd die to protect you, Mother."

. . .

Talk about coincidences! Maggie had been in the middle of a letter to Janie when the postman brought hers to the door.

Everett had had so much to say when she had returned on Saturday that she had felt it better not to volunteer further information, especially since she was never sure what upset him most. Sunday had come and quietly gone.

But now, Monday morning, she was feeling ready to burst. As soon as Everett left for the office, she raced to her writing desk. She needed to explain her exhilarating adventure in the automobile to her best friend and she was writing furiously when interrupted by the ring of the bell.

Nothing else of interest caught her eye except the familiar stationery and script of Janie's letter. Maggie felt a tinge of curiosity as she slit the envelope open and removed the perfumed page.

"How are things in busy Buffalo?" she started to read. "The girls and I – and Vernon – were talking again just the other day about the splendid time we had when we visited last May. Your playing was a real treat for us all. I don't believe either of the girls had any idea they had an 'aunt' as talented as you. Blame me for not educating them properly!" Maggie smiled at her friend's ballooning exclamation mark.

Janie, Maggie reflected, was the same as she'd been when they first became acquainted, the same in print as if she were standing right there speaking to her friend. Hearing her rambling words reminded her how much she missed her.

Vernon had had an accident at school. Tripping over a bucket left by a hurried janitor, he had fractured his leg. The bone, she continued, was sticking clear through the skin by the time they got him to the doctor. The doctor had been able to set the leg and Vernon was getting around pretty well, her letter continued.

"Then Vernon began to run a fever. Doc says the leg's infected bad and may have to come off. I keep praying, hope you will too, but . . . well, the surgery is scheduled for next week and I'm asking – I really hate to, Maggie, but I don't have anywhere else to turn. Could you come take care of the girls while I'm with Vernon? It will just be for a couple days. The doctor says he'll do the examination next Monday with surgery, if it's really needed, Tuesday morning, so there's no sense coming before then. But if you could stay with the girls for two or three days – whatever it takes – till we're home again." The sentence seemed to simply peter out.

Janie hadn't used a closing, had even absent-mindedly forgotten to sign it.

Of course she'd go. She'd put it to Everett as soon as he returned tonight and have a reply ready for tomorrow's post.

. . .

Convincing Everett hadn't been as hard as Maggie had feared, replaying the scene now as she continued to pack her valise for the journey to Erie. The news about Vernon was upsetting. Janie seemed too young and vibrant to care for a cripple. How would she manage? Where would she find the right words when the time came?

She put in an extra lightweight blouse and then turned to pull a second sweater from the chifforobe. It was still warm for September but who knew what another day might bring? She didn't imagine she'd be going out much once she got to Erie so figured she'd need little but day-dresses, maybe one better – just in case.

There wasn't much more to be done when her reverie was startled by the ring of the doorbell. The postman had made his delivery earlier in the morning, so who?

She quickly placed the folded items in the valise, pulled the lid down and hurried to the staircase. She could see a tall figure through the glass.

Rushing down the front stairs, she hurried to open the door.

"Peter!"

LXX

September 18, 1899

"Hello, Margaret."

"What are you doing here? Did I forget something the other day?"

"No. I came because I wanted to talk to you. To see you again."

"I'm afraid I don't understand."

"I felt unsettled after you left. I've been thinking of little else these past ten days."

"I'm sorry, Peter. I still don't understand."

"You know what I'm talking about." He paused and glanced around.

"I'm sorry." She really didn't understand.

"That day. The way you acted. The things you said. I know it meant something to you, too."

"Yes, it did. I'm glad you realized how important it was. I'm afraid that I was so wrapped up in the experience, in my feelings, that I never properly told you how much it did mean."

"Then I didn't imagine it?"

"What?"

"How you felt. Your rapture. The afternoon. How special our time together was."

"*Special?* That's hardly the word for it. I can't remember feeling such exhilaration. Yes, that's the word. It was totally exhilarating. I can't honestly recall ever feeling such excitement. Why, I could hardly wait until I could write and tell Janie all about it."

"You told your friend?"

"I started to. I couldn't wait to tell her. To be honest, I thought

I'd burst holding all those feelings inside. I could hardly tell Everett. I really didn't think he would understand."

"I wouldn't think that thought would even occur to you."

"It was such a exceptional experience, I had to tell someone."

"I'm delighted you felt so strongly, my dear."

"*Strongly?* Oh, my, yes indeed. It has to be one of the high points – one of the very highest in fact – in my life."

"Why, Margaret!"

"I mean, well, life has been good to me. There have been special moments – great joy, elation, excitement – but little that can compare with the feelings I had last Saturday. Why, I believe I got quite carried away, quite forgot myself," she chuckled quietly in reminisce, "for a bit at least."

"I'm overwhelmed. I guessed it was special to you, but . . . well, hardly anything like this."

"I'm sorry I can't explain it better. I tried to when I was putting my feelings on paper but, once I reread it, it all sounded perfectly inane. All I know is it was very special. You understand, don't you?" Maggie paused. "But you must."

"Yes, dear, I believe I do."

"Sitting up there so high, with nothing to block my view in any direction, even being able to watch the pavement disappear right under the carriage, the air blowing through my hair, seeing all those people looking up as we passed."

"Hearing that means so much to me."

"And I just knew you had to understand when you suggested the second turn through the park. It was so dear of you to do that, Peter. I realized later I had hardly thanked you at all. Well . . . I pray you do understand. And will accept my gratitude."

"But it was more than that. I know I wasn't imagining it."

"Now you have me confused again."

"You told me you wrote to your friend Janie."

"Yes, I did."

"Are you trying to tell me you wrote just to tell her about a . . . a ride?"

" *Just?*"

"That all it meant to you was –"

"I don't understand."

"I don't believe you."

"Peter, why would I lie to you?"

"No need to sound offended. Perhaps the ride was as enjoyable as you say. But there was more than that. I know there was."

She had no idea what to say, how to explain herself to this confusing man.

"Tell me," he reacted with anger.

She took a step backwards. "I think you had better leave."

He followed her into the vestibule, closing the outer door securely behind him.

Suddenly Maggie was very much aware of being alone with this man.

Taking his eyes from her, Peter looked around the house, seeing it all for the first time.

"I've often wondered what your home would be like. What kind of furnishings you'd select. Whether it would be sparse, or cluttered with bric-a-brac. Ah, so much I never knew about you. But this . . . It's quite charming, Margaret. Very comfortable . . ." His words trailed off as he crossed the hall and entered the parlor. He picked up a figurine, an intricately sculpted Dresden doll, from the nearest table, looking it over carefully as he turned it, smiled, and set it back on the table. Walking to her piano he stooped to play a series of arpeggios. "I see you keep it well-tuned. Good for you; good for you." He glanced throughout the room before being drawn to the wall of bookcases. "And this is what you read?"

"What are you doing here?"

"I came to see you."

"You should go."

"Go? Not yet."

"I don't know why you came, or what you want, but I do think you should leave."

"No, Margaret. I'll stay."

"Please –"

"Why, what is the matter? You know I'd never do anything to harm you."

"I am not afraid, Peter. I just think it better – for both of us – if you leave. Now."

"Is that what you really want?"

"I think it's a good idea."

"But is it what you want? What do you want me to do? Do you really want me to go?"

"Yes. You should go."

"All right then, I will." He turned and took two long strides towards the front door.

"Peter, stop."

He turned to face her. "Ah, I should stay then?"

"I don't want you to leave in anger."

"I'm not angry."

"Upset then."

"Margaret, do you want me to go, or to stay? Make up your mind."

"It isn't a matter of my making up my mind. You've come here, taking me quite by surprise – you must agree your visit was unexpected."

"Ah, yes! Unexpected. But unwanted?"

"I was packing to leave –"

"*Leave?* You're leaving Everett?"

"Don't utter such nonsense. I'm not leaving my husband. My friend in Erie . . . Janie –"

"Ah, the letter."

"Yes. Janie's husband is facing a terrible operation tomorrow. She wrote last week asking me to come, to help take care of her daughters till he's out of the hospital."

"And you're leaving today?"

"That's what I've been telling you. I'm catching the late afternoon train so, you see, I really don't have time to visit."

"That's still two hours away."

"But I haven't finished packing."

"Half an hour. Can you spare a half hour for me?"

"Peter, I am sorry. To be honest I'm totally flabbergasted. I never expected to see you here. Here or anywhere, for that matter."

"Would you offer me a cup of tea? Please?"

"I can't. I have packing to do, preparations to complete before I leave."

"No tea then. You do drive a hard bargain, my dear. All right then, I'll go."

Peter walked resolutely to the door and reached for the doorknob. As it began to turn in his hand, he turned to face her once more.

"Marg –"

"Peter!" Her voice expressed the exasperation she now felt.

"I'll go. I promise. Just answer one question first."

"But –"

"No, you must promise."

"This is ridiculous."

"Shall I come back in then?"

"You simply have got to go. I have things to do. I have explained all this. Really, I have."

"One question and I'll be out of here."

"Wh –"

"I promise."

"Oh, all right. But make it quick. Please."

Having won the round, he hesitated. How unlike him, of all people, to stutter! And now, of all times. He knew what must be said but felt uncertain how to say it. When the words were blurted out, they sounded, even to him, as if each had been grossly over-rehearsed. This wasn't going at all as he'd imagined.

"I'll go. I promised – and I do keep my promises. I just want to hear you tell me first that you have never cared for me."

"*Cared?* Why of course I care. I've always wished you well."

"You've followed my career? Tell me you have."

"Peter! Years have gone by. I've been involved in my own life."

"So you forgot me?"

"Of course not. Our paths seem to keep crossing – your appearance at Chautauqua, the competition last Saturday –"

"But in between, you don't think of me?"

"I have lots to keep my mind busy."

"Never?"

"This is ridiculous! Of course there have been times when I've thought of you."

"With good feelings?"

"Why, yes, of course. I've known you for . . . well, for just about as long as I've been here in Buffalo."

"And you've cared for me all that time? Is that what you're saying, Margaret?"

"Peter!"

"Tell me."

"I'm a married woman."

"But you care for me?"

"Peter. I –"

"Margaret, you know how I feel. Certainly –" He took one step closer.

"Go."

"No. Not now. I've thought too much of you. Dreamed too long of this moment. Waiting for you –"

"Really, you must go. Now. Please, Peter. I don't want a scene."

"A scene? Don't be ridiculous. There'll be no scene."

"You dare call me ridiculous? Why, this whole thing is ridiculous! I'm married, Peter, happily married. I have always been true to Everett and always shall. In fact, he'd be terribly distraught if he even knew you were here."

"Aha! So he knows how you feel about me."

"I didn't say that."

"He doesn't then?"

"You're . . . you're . . . oh, Peter, you're twisting my words, confusing me so."

"There's no reason to be confused. I know how you feel towards me. Certainly you must know I return those feelings."

"Pe— No."

She spoke nothing further as his arms closed around her. She felt her body being gently drawn to his, his lips meeting hers, gently, oh, ever so gently. She let herself go into the pleasant dizzying blur. Had bliss ever been as tender? Surely she must have reached as eagerly toward him. Swirling. Forgetfulness. Was music playing? Could there be roses blooming?

Maggie felt herself opening within – to him. This was honest. They were beyond a place where right or wrong had meaning. Only *is* existed. And, for her, the *should*.

Was this what she had been waiting for all her life? Thirty-seven barren years, now awakening.

"Oh, Peter." She heard her gentle murmuring. And his words, sounding so natural. How right it all felt. His warmth. The solidness. His smell. That voice. So very right. Had she somehow known it would be like this?

Words she hardly recognized coursed through her mind – Elysium, empyrean, ethereal – what did they mean? Why should she care? Sinking into this awesome oblivion, everything else seemed to disappear.

Let it, Maggie thought. I'll enjoy the . . . rapture . . . bliss . . . oh, my, paradise . . . ecstasy . . . amnesia.

My God, what was happening? How had this thing happened at all? She had never intended to encourage the man. He had to leave. She had to finish her packing. Go to Janie's. Wipe this memory out of her mind.

Trying now to pull away, she was surprised to feel his grasp tighten once again. She tried to speak. He stopped her with another kiss, more forceful than before. He was becoming rough with her now. She could feel his hands at her clothes, unbuttoning her blouse, his hand squeezing her breast. No.

She had her hand against his chest now, eager to push him away. As she did, his hand slipped from her blouse as both reached around her to firmly grasp her buttocks. He pulled her close, pushing against her. The hardness of him terrified her. This wasn't the gentle man she had known.

"Peter!" she gasped. He kissed her mouth as she opened it to protest – hard – probing with his tongue.

She shoved him away. "Get out of my house."

"Don't be a child, Maggie. This is right for us both. You know it as well as I. Don't fight me. Don't fight yourself. There's time. This is the time for us . . . now."

"There's no time for us. There is no *us*. This is positively ridiculous. It's obscene. I want you out of here."

He loosened his grip as he backed up, staring at her. She could sense his anger but was too indignant to care.

"Can you honestly tell me you want me to leave?"

"You know I do."

"This isn't a game, Margaret. If I walk away now, I won't be back. There'll be no second chance."

"There shouldn't have been a first."

"Can you tell me – even now – that you don't care? That you don't love me?"

"Stop this nonsense. Leave now."

"Say you don't care."

"I'm a married woman, Peter."

"And?"

"And . . . I love my husband."

"I'll go then. Is that what you really want me to do?"

"Yes. Yes, it is."

She kept her eyes averted as she opened the doors and stood still, waiting until the sound of his footsteps lessened. Only then did she dare look up.

His motor car was parked at the far corner. Give him credit at least for having discretion.

She closed the door quickly, turning the latch until she knew it was securely locked.

Involuntarily she hurried to the parlor window, knowing he would not be able to see through the lace curtains hanging there.

In rapid strides he walked quickly down the street, turned once to glance back at the house, turned again and hurried on. She stood stock-still and watched as he climbed up into the driver's seat, waiting until he and the automobile had driven out of sight.

Only then did the tears begin.

She sank to the floor, hugging her knees tightly, and wept till she could cry no more.

LXXI

September 18, 1899

As instructed the two maids waited until the last of the guests had left the dining room before extinguishing the candles on the long table. It was a bright sunny afternoon, brilliant even by September standards, but Mrs. Knapp always insisted on having her family candelabra on the tea table. The dining room was, as she pointed out every week, a dark room at best, situated on the darker side of the house.

The sixteen guests had now excitedly left the room, eager to take their places in the parlor, awaiting only the arrival of Andre Robson.

Lizzie had lost few guests since beginning these gatherings just over a year ago. Because membership, a word she liked to use, was strictly limited to sixteen, few newcomers had been admitted. Therefore all of these women were well-acquainted with the routine about to begin.

Chairs had been placed in a large circle. Each felt a proprietary right to her own seat and would never dream of usurping another's.

Many of the husbands, Jack vociferously among them, had frequently questioned why weekly gatherings with this character – one of the kinder descriptions uttered – were deemed so necessary. How many times could one have one's fortune told?

Initially some of the women had protested. Now they silently accepted the chiding for the truth was they had come to depend on Mr. Andre's weekly advice for every action they took. If the Smiths were invited for dinner on Saturday, it was he who would tell Mrs. Jones whether poultry or a lamb roast was favored. Unbeknownst to many a husband, where and when they vacationed was now determined more often than not by this stranger to Buffalo. Likewise, the schools chosen for their youngsters, even frequently which restaurant they should favor or when to purchase that stunning new outfit, whether in scarlet or vermilion. Very few of the women were ever so sick that they failed to make it to the reading.

Now the level of sound rose imperceptibly as the hands of the clock passed two. Had something happened to Mr. Andre?

No, he's coming now!

The two maids, peeking from a slit in the closed doors of the dining room, exchanged dubious glances and returned to their work

. . .

The last of the sixteen had just left, gushing her appreciation at Mr. Andre's latest advice.

Lizzie handed the man his coat, unable to keep her eyes from the wad of bills he slipped into an inner pocket.

"Another successful afternoon, Andre. You know how much we all appreciate your making these journeys. And I thank you once again, speaking for all of us, I know. Do have a safe and pleasant journey back to Lily Dale."

"May I speak to you for a moment before I leave?"

"Why, of course."

"Come, let's return to the parlor. I'd like to know my words won't be overheard," he glanced furtively toward the closed dining room doors, "by anyone else."

They crossed the entry hall to the parlor.

"Please sit down," he instructed. Andre took a chair facing her.

"You act so mysterious, Andre. Is something the matter?"

He laughed gently. "Perhaps you should be the one giving the readings. You certainly seem perceptive enough today."

"What is it?"

"Lizzie, my dear." Leaning toward her he reached for her hand. "You know as well as I that it is difficult for me to make this long journey every week during the winter months."

"I suppose it is though I don't recall any occasions last winter when you weren't able to get through."

"No. The trains these days are quite reliable. It's just that – well, it is a long way to come. Just for this."

"I don't understand. I thought you were pleased with the situation. You asked for more money this year and all the women agreed without rancor. Without much discussion at all, if you want the truth. What else can I do?"

"Nothing, Lizzie. I appreciate everything you have already done. You must understand that. Your circle of friends is lovely and I do enjoy my afternoons here in your home."

"Then what's the trouble?"

"The *trouble*, as I see it, is simply that your gatherings are limited to so few."

"Few? Yes, I suppose sixteen is not a great number but, Andre, there is hardly room for more here in my home. Besides, as it is, your brief readings take over two hours. Pardon me, but I don't see what more you can possibly expect me to do."

"I'm not asking you to do anything more, Lizzie."

"Now you have me confused."

"Lizzie, I have nothing but complete gratitude for all you have done for me. These afternoons are special, as I said, and I see them going on for a long time." He checked himself. "I don't mean that as a prediction, although I suppose it could be. I merely meant that I hoped we would be able to continue this arrangement for many more years."

"Well, of course. But I don't see where you are heading with this."

"Be patient for just one minute more. Please." She nodded as he continued. "I fear I am not doing a good job of explaining myself." She waited quietly. "The point I am trying to make is that it is a long trip to Buffalo. I have to take the train from Lily Dale to Dunkirk and then, after waiting, it's another hour into the city. Patience, please." He raised his hand to beg her silence. "I know you are aware of my travel arrangements. What I'm trying to say, Lizzie, is that I come all that way, a total traveling time of around two hours, just to do brief readings for sixteen of your friends. A minute, please. I am well compensated, I agree, and certainly appreciate the increased generosity this year. But don't you see? I could make much more money – double it easily, perhaps increase it even further – by doing more readings."

"But . . . but I thought we just agreed that I have neither the room, nor you the time, to add more ladies."

"True – if the readings are done here. Truth is, I've made arrangements at the Union Hotel to do a group every Monday morning and then, if that proves successful – perhaps eventually to add an evening, possibly even staying over to continue on Tuesday. There isn't much going on in Lily Dale during the winter so if I can make a little extra here . . . well, it just makes sense. You do see that, don't you?"

Lizzie's face had gone white. "But you can't do that!"

"I'm sorry. What do you mean I *can't*?"

"Our arrangement – Andre, it was always an exclusive arrangement."

"You'll still have your afternoon. That won't change at all."

"But it will; don't you see that?"

"No, I'm afraid I don't."

"Andre, the women come here only because there is no other place for them get a reading. It's either my home – or that long trek to Lily Dale you just spoke of. This has been a success because there was nothing to compete with it. Why, because of you, Jack and I can't begin to keep up with all the invitations we get. But, if you start giving other readings, what will be left for me? The women you see here will feel free to come and go – with you, I mean – as they wish. Who then will even want to come to my house?"

"They're your friends. Of course they'll come."

"They aren't my friends. Don't you know that? They come only because of you. Only because they have no option. Take that away and I'll have nothing left."

"Lizzie, this is ridiculous. I've never been any good around crying women. You mustn't make a scene."

"I have no desire to do anything of the sort." She stood and walked to the window, her back to the confused man.

There was silence for a moment. Lizzie blew her nose and put the handkerchief back in her pocket. Suddenly she swirled to face Andre.

"No! I refuse to let this happen. I've waited all my life for a chance like this – I was born to it – and I won't have you, or anyone, take it from me now. You and I made a bargain. I expect you to keep it."

"But –"

"My God, man! Can you be that ungrateful? Have you forgotten so quickly what you were when I first met you? It was I who brought you here, I who introduced you to these people of power, I who made all this possible. You were one medium among many. It was no more than a lucky happenstance than I went to your door that day. Now it's *Mr. Andre* this and *Mr. Andre* that. For no reason except my determination to make these afternoons a success. No, I won't hear of your changing a thing."

"Lizzie, please –"

"There's nothing more to say. It won't happen."

"Listen to me. The arrangements at the hotel are made. There will be advertisements in the paper. It's settled, Lizzie."

"Nothing's settled. I refuse to believe anything of the kind."

"You're being unreasonable –"

"I'm being nothing of the sort. I –"

"Your tirades will have no effect, I promise you that."

"But –"

"No *buts*. Lizzie, come back and sit down again. That's better. I have tried to tell you how grateful I am for all you have given me. I know I wouldn't have gotten my start here without you. You opened the door."

"That's what I just said."

"And I'd be the last to deny it. But, Lizzie, the time has come for my operation to grow."

"Is it more money you want? How much? I don't know how much more I can get from Jack but I'll try. Is that what this is all about? Name your figure, Andre."

"No, Lizzie. I appreciate the offer. Obviously any of us can use more money but that isn't the point."

"Well, what is it then?"

"Reputation, I suppose. I have a chance to increase my clientele in Buffalo, to make inroads as a medium. And, believe me, being the first is important. It's a chance I may never get again. I know some of my fellows at Lily Dale have already questioned my success here."

"And that isn't enough?"

"No. Not now. Not any more. Look, what I told you is known to no others yet but it's – how do they say it? – a done deal. The room is reserved, the advertisements are written –"

"You did all this without a word to me?"

"It happened quickly. I don't actually believe I had thought about it until last Monday, going back on the train. To be candid, Lizzie, I initially thought your afternoon teas might be a quickly passing fad. I hadn't even honestly banked on this second season. Then, returning last week, I saw the women were more eager – *dependent* – than I had realized before. I saw I had a calling here, a chance to make a quick buck. But . . . well, something about striking while the iron's hot. I took an earlier train today, went to the hotel and made the arrangements. I'll start there two weeks from today, the first Monday of October. It seemed an auspicious beginning."

"No –" It was all she could sputter before he continued.

"I honestly believed you'd be pleased that I had this opportunity. I am grateful to you, Lizzie, and I always will be. You gave me my start and I will always be here for you – every Monday afternoon. You'll see. Nothing is going to change."

"No!"

"Lizzie, please."

"No. It isn't going to happen, Andre. These were my days. I won't allow you to change that. You must continue to come here every Monday, just as you have. If you want more money – robbery, if you ask me, but – well, if that's your demand I'll try to meet it. But all this talk about growing, expanding, whatever you want to call what you'd be doing – no, Andre.

It won't be."

"Lizzie, Lizzie. Quiet down. You'll be heard throughout the house."

"You think I care about that?"

"I should think you would."

"Andre, you aren't going to do this."

"I'm wasting my time here with you behaving like this. We can talk more about it next week, when you're feeling better."

"No –"

Coat already in hand, the tall man stood and reached the front door in quick strides.

She supposed the door had closed on her long before her string of epithets came to an end. My! She was surprised how many terrible words she knew. What a dreadful way for a proper lady to behave. But what a despicable man! He'd have to be stopped.

Lizzie turned and started back toward her parlor, glancing up in surprise to see Abram sitting on the top of the stairs.

LXXII

September 18, 1899

Maggie hurriedly paid off the buggy driver and rushed across the station to find the waiting train. She just had time to stow her bag and take a seat before the conductor's "All aboard" carried through the car. There was a jerk, a second movement, and the train pulled slowly away.

She still hadn't caught her breath. Was it, she wondered now, because of her rush, or was it something else?

No question that Peter's appearance had delayed her packing. She had left the house less tidy than she wanted but it was either go or miss the train and she had taken a moment to scribble a note to Everett to apologize for running out of time. Ready to seal the envelope, a moment's reflection saw her reopening the letter to add a reassurance of her abiding love for him. Then off, and just in the nick of time.

No matter how quickly the last hours had flown, how frantic she had felt as she hurried to reach the train, her overwhelming feeling was more real: the very pressure of Peter's kiss on her lips. She had heard of women swooning. Is this what they were whispering about? She wished she had a clearer understanding of just what had occurred. Sinking into that blissful oblivion – was that a condition others might have known?

She knew if she closed her eyes, now, just for a moment, the feelings would return. Desirous of wanting to let herself retreat into that warmth, Maggie pulled herself back with a stern rejoinder.

Whatever had happened with Peter had been an accident. She had not invited him, nor wished it so. And certainly it was a scene that would never be repeated.

Then again . . . she permitted herself the final luxury of dreaming again of those lovely moments. The early ones, of course. Toward the end his actions had frightened her. She knew she had been relieved to see him gone.

Or had she? Could she be honest, even with herself?

Would it have made a difference had he chosen any day but this?

Her eyes popped open. Better to stay in the here and now. The train was leaving the city behind, pulling into the lush farm country that lay between Buffalo and Erie. She could see the men and their wagons already at work on the early harvest.

Suddenly Maggie became aware of the man sitting across the aisle from her. Tall, rather swarthy, a foreigner perhaps? He was attractive – in a peculiar way. Hard to keep her eyes off him, now that she'd noticed him. Quite intriguing, actually.

As if aware of her thoughts, he turned and stared straight at her.

She flushed and diverted her eyes to her hands, still demurely folded in her lap.

"Pardon me." Was he speaking to her? "Do I know you?"

"Why, no. Or at least, I don't think so."

"I saw you getting on the train in Buffalo. I know quite a lot of women there – though I'm sure that isn't where we met."

"No, I'm sure we have never been introduced."

"May I then? My name is – "

"Excuse me. I don't mean to be rude. I'm sure what you do is very interesting but . . but –"

"Of course. I understand. You'll excuse me, please." He returned to his paper.

Interesting lady, he thought, eyes not registering the printed words before him. Seems so upset. Nervous. Suppose she's always that high-strung? Pretty though. Wonder if she's running away. Yes! Perhaps that explains it. A husband perhaps? Or a love affair gone sour? He had watched her last-minute dash to the train, sensing her relief as she took her seat. Seemed terribly upset, even more than just running to make a train. Wouldn't it be a gift if one truly could read minds? He'd love to know what he'd find behind that demure countenance.

She had glanced at him briefly as she passed his seat, averting her eyes quickly as if afraid he might see something unguarded. A curious woman indeed.

But a woman none-the-less.

And hadn't he had his fill of them, enough in one day to last a very long time.

He reached into his inside pocket and unscrewed the lid to his silver flask. He had almost left it home today. It had become his habit to have one drink, perhaps two, at the station before boarding and then another once they reached Dunkirk. That generally sufficed until he reached Lily Dale.

Maybe he knew his future even better than he'd give himself credit for! Nah, he doubted that. But, whatever the reason, bringing the flask today had been an excellent idea.

Not that there was enough alcohol in the world to wipe away that nasty scene.

What if she were right? That her only hold over those biddies was that they had no other way to see him? What if his meetings at the hotel did start to draw them away from her? Serve her right. He might even see fit to lower his charges if they came to him. No reason, except to spite her. But was any other needed?

He smiled to himself. One more sip couldn't hurt.

Oh! So she'd caught him at the flask. Another one. What difference did it make – did any of them make?

. . .

Maggie tried to read but her concentration was crowded out by all the recent thoughts. Peter. Everett. This stranger on the train.

The train.

And then, of course, she remembered where she was going. Janie and poor, poor Vernon. She imagined he would be restless at home – or would they put him in the hospital the night before his surgery? *Surgery*? Janie had never been positive they would take his leg. Was there a chance it might be saved? She would pray – though that seemed foreign to her now.

Maggie shuddered, feeling very much alone and frightened. She picked up her novel and tried even harder to concentrate.

. . .

He needed the drink, he told himself. Usually after a few he began to feel pleasantly light-headed. But the flask was empty now, the liquor he'd consumed in Buffalo equally ineffective. He'd stop at the tavern here in Dunkirk. Just a quick one. He knew the boys there.

He also knew Sandy – *Madame Cassandra* to his *Mister Andre* now that they were moving up in the world – would be waiting for him. What a doting sister! Truly a Godsend.

So then, all women weren't necessarily bad after all, now were they?

LXXIII

September 18, 1899

"Where have you been? I was beginning to get frightened." She glanced at the figure in the doorway. "Oh, Andre, you've been drinking again."

He stumbled through the door, catching himself on the table in the middle of the room.

"I've been celebrating, my dear."

"Celebrating? What have you – You did it then! Oh, Andre, did you really tell her?"

"I did indeed, my dear."

She rose to kiss him. "I'm proud of you, prouder than I can say. I thought I knew my baby brother as well as anyone, but, to tell the truth, I never thought you'd go through with it."

"I did. In fact, I did better than that."

"Better?"

"Sandy, I went to the Union Hotel first and made arrangements to rent a room every Monday, beginning next month, even checked on fliers and advertisements. I figure I can fill the mornings, possibly the evening – might just have to stay over, maybe add more clients the following day."

"And what did the lady say to that?"

"I'll give you credit for that one, dear. I still can't see why she got so upset –"

"I could."

"And you were right. Made a scene, if you want the truth. Embarrassing. It got quite messy before I was able to get away."

"But you'll go back?"

"Of course I will. I'm sure it'll be forgotten quickly – probably already if I know my women."

"I'm not sure you do, Andre."

"You're wrong this time. I learned today she uses me to gain social power among the hoi polloi of Buffalo. Can you imagine?"

"You? I don't believe it!"

" 'Tis true, my dear. 'Tis true. That's why she got so upset. Wanted to keep me exclusively for her chosen set."

"Then your announcement must have been a terrible blow. Even worse than I imagined."

"Nasty, that's all. But let's put that behind us. Look –" He reached into the inside pocket of his coat to pull out the wad of bills. They spread as they hit the table.

"I don't recall seeing so many before."

"You haven't. I told the ladies last time I needed an additional inducement if I were to make the trip regularly all winter long."

"Andre, you didn't!"

"But I did. And why not? There's little to recommend that filthy train."

"But to make so much in one afternoon? Didn't they object? Oh, Andre, I'm afraid you'll gamble once too often and lose it all."

"Silly sister. They'll pay through the nose. Why they've grown so dependent they hardly dare dress or go out without consulting me first. In fact, sometimes I feel my talents are utterly wasted on that group. The bigger things – *that's* what I could be telling them. But do they want to listen? Hardly! I spend four-fifths of my time suggesting what Mrs. Power should serve for dinner when the Biggses come."

"You're teasing! . . . You are, aren't you?"

"Believe it or not, I'm not."

"But that must be terribly frustrating . . . for a man of your talents."

"Oh, I'd prefer to do some deeper delving. To spend more time with the spirits, the real ones. But this is what they want – and it's a living." He nodded at the bills scattered across the table. "Want to help count it?"

"Don't tempt me. You can tell me later how much you got.

Right now, I'm off."

"Off? But I just got home."

"I know you did, dear, and I'm sorry to run out this way. To be honest, I'm feeling quite guilty about it."

"Guilty?"

"Yes. Funny, isn't it?"

"Ridiculous. I'm a big boy now, Sandy. Or haven't you noticed?"

"It just doesn't feel right. Maybe it's because you've been drinking."

"The boys at the tavern would miss me if I passed up a Monday night now that fall has rolled around again."

"But this is different. You don't normally come stumbling through the door. If the table hadn't been there, I think I'd have witnessed your falling right on your face. Really now, Andre!"

"All right. I did have more than usual. A little bit." He caught her eye. "All right, perhaps more than a little bit but I'm all right now. Agreed?"

"Well, yes, I suppose so. I've heated the stew and it'll be ready in just another minute or two. A good hearty bowl should settle your stomach – and head. Just promise you will eat."

"Yes, little mother."

"Promise me, Andre."

"I promise."

She checked the pot. "It should be warm soon."

He shook his head as if to dispel lingering cobwebs. "Maybe I have had more than I thought. Forgive me but I can't remember where you told me you were going."

She laughed. "I swear you'll never change. But fear not, this time it isn't your fault."

"But –"

"I only meant I never told you."

"A woman of mystery?"

"Hardly. Madeline invited a group of us over to play cards. You know how little there is to do in the Dale, what with fall setting in and most of the residents gone for the year. Some of us decided to organize a traveling card party."

"*Traveling?* That I've got to see!"

"Silly. Here, let me dish up a bowlful for you. But I expect you to come back for seconds. You need a good hearty supper, now even more than usual."

"While you're out *traveling* around?"

"That's hardly what I meant. It just means we'll take turns. Eight women, meeting twice a week, so each of us hosts the group once every –"

"Four weeks. See? The old mind is still working after all."

"I doubt if a barrel of liquor would slow down the part that's concerned with figures. Here, eat. Oh! I guess I should have warned you – darn it, Andre, couldn't you see it was hot? Give it a moment or two to cool. Then eat."

"Suppose I have time first to count the loot? Once you're on your way, I mean. Till then I suppose I'm going to have to put up with this constant niggling."

"I'm going, I'm going. Count your money, do. God knows you've earned it. But then – please, Andre, put it someplace safe. Out of sight. I do worry, you know. Are you sure you'll be all right?"

"Last I heard the days of the robber gangs were over. But, if it makes you feel any better –" He rose unsteadily and walked to the sideboard where he opened the top drawer. Sandy knew what was in there. As often as she'd complained about keeping a gun in the house – even the tiny double-barreled derringer – now she felt relief that he had it. She admired the pearl grips as he placed it in the center of the table near the wad of bills, looked at each in turn and then carefully spooned a sip of her stew to his lips.

"Go, Sandy; go. Can't you see I've got things to do?"

She wrapped her shawl about her shoulders and started to open the door. Turning back, she walked to where her brother sat and leaned down to kiss him gently on the top of his head.

"What?" he sputtered. "Sandy, you're behaving strangely."

"I'm sorry, I know I am. It's just that – well, I've got the creeps tonight. Everything feels so unsettled. Are you certain you'll be all right? I could stay if you'd like."

"Don't be ridiculous. Seven card players'll get nowhere. I'll be just fine. Go. Don't worry yourself about us."

"*Us*?" The word made her turn to face him once more.

"Us – me, my money –" He patted the pile complacently, "and my trusty little pistol."

"Andre!"

"Scat, Sandy. Your ladies await."

She shrugged, wrapped the shawl tighter around her shoulders and left him sitting there.

. . .

She knew the moon had been shining brightly when she set out. She hadn't thought a torch necessary for it was a simple matter to pick her way along the path. As the trees had sprung up here at Lily Dale the roots had grown as well, creating obstacles for the unfamiliar walker. Feeling smug with her familiarity, she had blessed the moon for its light, and hastened along her way.

Now, returning, she found it a more difficult trek. Heavy clouds hid the moon and she faced a darkness as complete as any she could remember. Sandy was pleased that Patricia lived in the same direction and had shown the foresight to carry her lantern. She gratefully accepted the offer to walk along with her friend.

They strolled slowly, watching their steps and talking happily about the evening. The women were all old neighbors and friends and played strictly for their amusement. There was no gambling, not even a rivalry over who scored the highest. She hadn't expected dessert to be served but observed the pleasure with which it was devoured. So she'd have to plan on baking before her turn next Monday. A large pot of strong coffee and maybe her prune cake. Women seemed to like that.

Had she been so lost in these thoughts that she had tuned Patricia out? Oh, dear, what was it her friend was saying?

"Yes, stop for a minute. That is an owl. Look. See it up

there? No, that tree. Look, follow my arm, where the finger's pointing."

They heard the big bird fly away as her friend aahed in wonder.

They had come to where their paths no longer went in the same direction. Patricia seemed particularly concerned about the darkness of the night. What if Sandy should stumble?

She protested weakly, secretly relieved when her friend insisted and turned with her toward the little frame house she had continued to share with Andre after their parents died.

"There, now. It's just down the path. Pat, I thank you, but I know every step the rest of the way. Trust me, I really do. I'll be just fine. See, the light's still on in the kitchen. Andre must have decided to wait up for me."

Final words were exchanged as Sandy agreed to join Pat and another friend for the wagon trip into Fredonia for the weekly groceries.

"I'll see you tomorrow, ten-thirty then."

Sandy stood still, watching as Patricia retraced her steps, her light bobbing unevenly along the path. She stopped to wave on reaching the corner, turned to the right and was quickly out of sight.

Sandy turned and hurried home. It wasn't like Andre to stay up this late. In fact, she might not have enjoyed her evening half as much had she known he'd be waiting up at home. What would he say?

Nonsense! She was a grown woman. Out with friends, people he too had grown up with. What was there to be said?

She was surprised to see the front door ajar. It had been warm for September, admittedly, but now there was a chill in the air.

She smelled the burn before her feet were on the stairs. What? Oh, no – but of course! She hadn't realized he'd had that much to drink. She should have stayed to be sure. For wasn't it obvious he had passed out, leaving her stew simmering on the woodstove? *Simmering?* Burnt to a crisp! Her nose was already warning her.

God, it was one thing to get to bed and then pass out. But right in the middle of the floor? Had he had a secret stash in the house she hadn't known about? Would he have gone and done more drinking after she'd left?

"Andre –"

. . .

The scream echoes through the sleeping village. Seven women, in various stages of undress, arrested their action to listen. Had they really heard what they thought they had?

Sandy screamed again.

LXXIV

September 18 & 19, 1899

Patricia's husband was the first of the men, wakened hurriedly by their alarmed wives, to arrive. Many of the women, less careful in their dress, were already there. He could hear Sandy's sobs through their circle as they surrounded her protectively.

His entrance caused few of them to look up. Patricia caught his eye, and nodded to the right. Only then did he make out the body lying on the floor. Andre, no question about that, and enough blood to make a closer examination unnecessary.

His eyes sought those of his wife. "Have the police been called?" he mouthed.

She shook her head.

"I'll ride into Fredonia for the marshal." He headed quickly to the stables to saddle his horse. It was a dark night for a ride such as this. The buggy might be safer, it had the light, but no, too slow, and this needed to be done quickly.

. . .

The police were still there in the morning. So too were the women.

All of them had been asked the same inane questions and who among them had an answer to any? Had that tall disfigured constable actually suggested Sandy might have had something to do with it? Sensing that, the women had refused to answer anything more. Finally, the sergeant realized what was causing the trouble and sent his officer off to inspect the grounds.

"Where?" he had sputtered at the command.

"Good God, man. Can't you see what you've done? Anywhere but here. Just stay away from these women. They're distraught enough."

So he had departed without fully realizing why he had upset them so.

The women were there to comfort Sandy. Nothing more to be done about Andre, poor thing, but his sister – well, she could use their support.

None could help hearing the talk about money. Apparently quite a bit of it, too, judging from the way the sister spoke. No, she told the officers she didn't know how much. Andre had planned to count it after his supper . . . and she had left before that.

The gun? Ah, yes, they whispered among themselves, what was anyone in the Dale doing with a gun? They were Spiritualists after all, professing a devotion to their chosen faith. And where was there anything in that about going armed? Sandy had felt it would protect her brother. And just look what good that had done.

The pearl-handled derringer lay near the door, across the room from the fallen Andre. The police buzzed that whoever had fired the gun had felled him immediately. Probably never felt the bullet. As if that was any comfort now to his grieving sister!

The police seemed pleased to have the derringer. God knew they had little else. The money was missing and no one expected that to show up anytime soon.

They had all heard Sandy relay, down to the minutest detail, each moment from the time Andre had arrived home until her departure. Talk about her stew and how hot it was, his drinking – yes, it was unusual; no, she didn't know why. Yes, unusual in amount, not that he was an abstainer. No, she didn't know how much. She had seen him stumble when he entered the house. If he had drunk more, she for one wouldn't have been able to guess where he'd gotten it. Those kind of spirits were not allowed in her house.

Food burned on the woodstove. Stew still in the bottom of his soup bowl. Spoon on the table.

It didn't take a detective to figure someone had entered, surprising him while he ate. Struggle? Some perhaps, not a great deal. He certainly wasn't done in at the table.

The women finally wended their way down the paths to their respective homes as the sun blazed high above the tall pines.

Reluctant to leave, the police stayed until they could think of no reason to further delay their departure.

They'd give Doc a chance to look over the body, recompose themselves a bit, and would certainly feel better – more chipper at least – after a good hot breakfast and bath.

Everyone at Lily Dale knew they'd be back.

· · ·

Scheduled to be admitted to the hospital this very evening, Vernon had used all his powers of persuasion to be allowed to wait with Janie to meet Maggie's train.

As soon as Vernon was at the hospital, Janie collapsed into the arms of her trusted friend.

When the crying abated she dared ask her question. "Then the news is as dire as you feared?"

"At least. Oh –" and the gulping sobs drowned out the rest of her sentence.

"Janie, Janie. I know this has to be difficult but you have got to be strong. Tell me . . . please, do . . . what has happened?" She hesitated momentarily as the thought struck her. "Oh, Janie. It's not Vernon . . . is it?"

It was a moment before the impact of the question reached her. "Oh, no, Maggie. Not that. At least I don't believe so. It's just that . . . well, the doctor says the infection's worse than he anticipated. I suppose we waited too long. The leg has to go – first thing in the morning. More, too, than originally thought. But Vernon? No. God willing, he'll pull through. Though –" She shuddered involuntarily.

"But, Janie, the good news is that his life will be spared. That is true, right? And is there really anything more precious than that?"

"Maggie, I swear you're a goddam – well, you're the

breath of fresh air we all need right now. You'll do the girls more good than I possibly could. You always know exactly what to say."

"I only wish I did."

"Come. We'll let the girls judge for themselves. You know they've been dying to see you. Sometimes, in fact, I think they're more excited about your visit than upset over their father."

"I'm sure that's not so."

"Might be good if it were. Come on now. Let's get this buggy moving. It's late."

. . .

By early afternoon the police were back, convinced now that the murderer must be among those living at the Dale. The sister – what was her name? Cassandra? Oh, yes; but didn't they call her Sandy? – seemed the most likely suspect. She had been the last to see him alive. Well, yes, one supposed the murderer must have come afterward. But who could that be?

The women weren't about to budge and the men grumbled. When questioned they turned out to be equally intractable. Their wives were guileless and, in most cases, the men were at home, either fast asleep, or waiting up impatiently. The latter heard the first screams, at least those living near enough. Turned out the breezes off the lake tended to carry the noises away so that a few claimed to have heard nothing till roused by their wives.

But motive? "You tell me," they answered in unison, shrugged and walked away.

. . .

It had seemed an interminably long day by the time Maggie saw Janie slowly walking toward her front door. She didn't need to call the girls for both had been waiting unbeknownst at an upstairs window and now rushed down to meet their mother.

Maggie couldn't help but notice her friend's ashen face. She said nothing until the girls, reassured, had run off to find their friends.

"Oh, Jane."

"Is it that obvious?"

"He didn't – I mean . . . that is . . .Vernon's all right. . . isn't he?"

"Oh, dear God. Oh, yes, Maggie; he's going to live, if that's what you mean. Oh . . ." She swooned into the strong arms of her friend. With difficulty Maggie was able to guide her to the divan and help her stretch out.

Slowly, torturedly, Janie relayed the day's details: the wait for the doctor, the sickening sweet smell of the ether, Vernon's screams in spite of it all, his delirious rantings, the tossings and turnings until at last he did awake – and the pain overtook him again.

Janie's talk slowly turned to a murmur, more and more difficult to discern, until her voice was stilled at last. Maggie stroked her tired brow, kissed her gently, and rose to find lights and something to feed the girls.

Over a quickly-prepared supper, she did what she could to comfort Vernon's daughters. As their concerns were assuaged, the glances and then the jokes returned in a rapid exchange. Maggie was startled and surprised when she recognized her own laughter.

Upstairs, she saw them tucked into their beds, prayers recited, and sat with them until they fell asleep.

It struck her suddenly that she been about the same age when told of the deaths of not one, but both, of her parents. She had lost it all. Not that she wished tragedy on anyone but she almost envied them . . . comparatively speaking. They still had each other.

Somehow, she felt, that was more than she would ever have.

· · ·

The September afternoon had turned unseasonably hot and, with it, the tempers of the local gendarmes. Experience taught that odds were the murderer was someone who knew the victim. Here they were then, surrounded by likely candidates and getting nowhere.

Who else, the men in uniform pressured, could be involved? Who else would have known of the money he carried? Which house was his? Or that his sister was out for an evening of cards?

The sun was lowering itself almost to the western hill across the lake. A crow cawed and was answered loudly by another nearby. Squirrels chattered. Something swooped through the trees, unseen, unsounding.

If the answer was to be found here, it could wait until another day. Time – a good time – to be getting away.

LXXV

September 21, 1899

Like many things which become common knowledge before one realizes it, the news of Andre Robson's death was soon shared by all the knowing Buffalo matrons. It had been just a small item, buried deep in the morning paper. Who had seen it? Who had notified whom? By Thursday noon, not one of Lizzie's women could even remember who had first shared the story.

Except, Lizzie knew damned well, it hadn't been she. And that irritated her even more than his passing. Even in death it seemed he was determined not to let her have an exclusive.

. . .

Andre Robson was buried Friday afternoon in the small cemetery on the grounds of Lily Dale underneath the towering pines. Winter population was always sparse but those there attended the service before trekking to the burying spot.

The police arrived just as the mourners returned from the glen. The locals looked at them warily, an expression mirrored by the new arrivals.

"Well? . . ."

The lieutenant ambled up to the man who seemed to be leading the pack. "I'm as sorry to have to return as you are to see us. We promise to make it as brief as possible."

"Who you after this time?"

"We just have a few more questions for the sister, Cassandra Robson."

Mumbles and grumbles followed about the sanctity of a funeral, the need to grieve privately and the irritating nuisance these interlopers created. The lawmen waited patiently.

At last Sandy was observed coming along in a group of mourning women. Spotting the lawmen, they separated. Knowing, she approached them.

"Sorry, ma'am. We didn't know about the funeral."

"So I assumed. Just what is it you want?"

"A few more questions, ma'am. All right if we ask them in – " he nodded toward her house, "private?"

She led the way.

The men, irritated by this invasion, wended their way in a group to the cafeteria where Edward was already preparing a fresh pot of coffee. The men, used to meeting this way, sat at the long table in their customary seats.

"Bad thing, all of this."

"I for one will be a lot happier once they're gone."

"Guess it can't be too much longer 'fore the fools realize whoever did it wasn't from these parts – "

"Then they'll go away."

"Not soon enough for me."

"Amen."

"Amen, brother."

"You know, I always did have mixed feelings about that young whippersnapper."

"Well, I'm sure even he didn't expect to cause us this much trouble."

"Don't think any of us knew for sure what he was going to do."

"Why couldn't he have . . . well, been just – "

" Just like the rest of us?"

"You got it!"

"Know exactly what ya mean."

"We keep to ourselves. Don't stir up trouble."

"Certainly don't angle for publicity."

"Happy to share our gifts, always have been."

"And don't mind a pretty penny either."

"*Pretty penny?* Young Andre was reaping in a lot more than a pretty penny."

"I don't know. He was ambitious –"

"Lucky, too, the way he latched on to that woman –"

"Though he always talked like she was the one done the latching on."

"Can't look down on a man gist cause he wants to make money."

"Agree."

"Yup. I envied him, wished I had it as easy, but there's no crime in that, I don't suppose."

"Don't rest quite right with me, even now."

"Why? What's the bother?"

"Not that what he did was wrong but – I don't know – gist figured our gifts should be used for more than . . ."

"Than what?"

"I know what he's saying – and agree. It is a gift, our communicating with the spirits. It doesn't always come easy –"

"Amen to that –"

"And requires serious training. And I 'spect should be used in the same manner."

"Right. Seriously."

"Then you don't think Andre was serious?"

"Oh, I think he was when he started. But all that money . . . and those women. From the little he said to me, I don't think any of them even cared about the world beyond. They only wanted to know what dress would look best at their next ball."

"You're right. You are, you know."

"And I think he stopped taking it seriously as well. They didn't need his gifts."

"Probably didn't even want them."

"Or know what could be done."

"Why, he turned the whole thing into a game –"

"A bloomin' parlor game, if'n you ask me."

"Lot of big bucks for very little."

"And don't each of us wish we'd hit on the idea first?"

A communal guffaw was followed by a moment of silent respect. Then the men turned to issues more topical.

. . .

"I can't believe you're back again." Sandy walked into the house and went straight to the most comfortable – her – chair. She knew by now the lieutenant would follow. Amenities seemed unnecessary, indeed unnatural.

"Said I was sorry, ma'am. Had no way to know about the burying. Can come back some other time if you'd rather." He hesitated just inside the doorway.

"No. Don't come back. Just tell me what you want this time. Maybe it will be the last."

"Hope so, ma'am."

"Though, as I recall, you said those same words yesterday." She couldn't refrain from smiling at the beleaguered young man. "So, tell me."

"We've checked everyone and everything around here. Including the tavern where your brother stopped in Dunkirk. Just one quick drink – if that helps any – and then he must've come straight home."

"You've been through all that before. Not the drink part but that's hardly a surprise, is it?"

"No, I guess not – though I supposed you might be glad to hear it."

"You didn't come all the way out here just to tell me my brother had only a single drink, now did you?"

"No, ma'am." His head bowed slightly.

"Well . . . Then?"

"I'm just trying to say we feel we've investigated everything there is to do at this end. The men –" his hand swept a wide circle, "don't seem to have any particular motive, and –"

"Are you saying you suspect me?"

"No, ma'am. Not that. Forgive my awkwardness. I just wanted to explain why we were giving up – at least for now –"

"Giving up?" Her voice registered her astonishment.

"You didn't let me finish. Giving up the search for the murderer around here. It just doesn't make sense."

"And it's taken you more than three days to figure that out?"

"Sorry, ma'am, but a complete investigation is necessary.

Surely you can understand that."

"I wish I could as easily understand just what brings you back here today."

"I'm trying to tell you, ma'am. The captain's decided we should check out your brother's whereabouts in Buffalo, the day he was killed."

"Buffalo? Why now, that is ridiculous. Andre wasn't killed in Buffalo –"

"Know that, ma'am. But we're thinking the killer might have come from Buffalo –"

"You mean followed him back here?" Sandy felt his story was becoming more ridiculous with every sentence.

"It is possible, ma'am."

"And just waited while Andre ate the stew I'd fixed?"

"Waited, maybe, until the killer saw you leave and realized your brother was alone."

"Oh . . . Oh, dear." Could the man possibly be making sense, she wondered. "Do you think that's possible?"

"Anything's possible. For now it's just a lead. But until we check it out, it may be the best one we have."

"No," she said firmly.

"No?"

"No."

"How can you say that? How can you be so sure?"

"Motive. Killers have to have a motive. Andre went to Buffalo to see a bunch of old ladies, at least that's what he told me. Can't imagine a less likely group to spawn a killer."

"Ah! You may well be right. Then again, who can ever know what truly lies deep in another's heart? I can't guess – though you have to admit the most likely motive remains the missing money."

"I'd forgot! Forgive me, lieutenant; I'm beginning to be rather impressed with the thought behind this new direction your investigation is taking."

"May be nothing, don't forget that. But, now you agree, it can't hurt to dig a little deeper."

"Indeed." Relaxing a bit, she suddenly roused herself to stare straight at the lawman. "Then why are you wasting time here? Why aren't you in Buffalo?"

He laughed, more gently than she had remembered. She was beginning to find his company rather pleasant. "Buffalo's a big city, ma'am. And we haven't a hint where to start looking. I'm here, hoping you can give us that clue."

"Clue? Of course. You want the name of the place he went, right?"

"You do have it, don't you?" She discerned a moment of doubt in his question.

"Not offhand, I'm afraid. He talked lots about the women, sixteen or seventeen of them as I recall, but didn't mention names much. *Lizzie*. Yes, I'm sure there was a *Lizzie*. He talked about her quite often."

"You wouldn't happen to know Lizzie Who?" She noticed just the slightest sparkle in his deep brown eyes.

"No, I don't recall ever hearing a last name."

"Well, then –" he started to rise, "I'm sorry for taking your time. I'll try not to bother you again."

"No, wait." Her hand flew out to restrain him. "I said I don't know her name and that's true. But it may well be among Andre's papers. Should I look?"

He gulped. "If you would – please."

She scurried up the rickety staircase to the room the lieutenant assumed had belonged to her brother. He could hear her footsteps overhead, then a strange creaking sound. He waited in silence, picturing her leafing through sheaves of correspondence and miscellaneous papers, wishing he might be given immediate access to them all. It wasn't more than a few moments before Sandy skipped quickly back down the stairs. She excitedly thrust an opened letter into the officer's hand.

A quick glance showed him a letter of inquiry. A Mrs. Knapp had enjoyed the reading he had given her at Lily Dale – he checked the date, rather surprised that it had been written over a year earlier. Would he, might he, consider coming to Buffalo to entertain a group of her friends? Preliminary suggestions were included, amateurish in their lack of detail. It was signed, he noted with pleasure, by Mrs. Jack Knapp.

She just had to be their Lizzie!

Sandy watched from the doorway as the policeman slowly retraced his tracks. She didn't suppose she'd be seeing him again and fought her mixed emotions at the prospect.

Time later though for such shenanigans.

She turned, once certain he was gone, and headed back up the stairs. Sandy had never gone through her brother's belongings and felt guilty doing it now. Somebody had to, she told herself. Besides, what she had seen looking for that letter had made her curious.

Yes, there they were. Official looking papers. Contracts of some sort. A room rental agreement with the Union Hotel. Of course! Andre had mentioned something – gloated in fact – about taking a room so he could run more meetings. Then this must be it. And a rough draft of what appeared to be a sketch for an advertisement. Newspaper, she imagined. She read it carefully, feeling as if she were seeing a side of her brother she had never known. So this hadn't been just another of his fanciful dreams.

Could this have anything to do with his murder? Was she wrong not to have shown it to the policeman? No, these were Andre's papers. His business affairs were none of theirs.

· · ·

The news of Andre's death brought deep consternation to the home of Lizzie Knapp. Servants were ordered to polish the silver one last time and pack it away, so certain was she that her regular Tuesday soirees were at an end. How inconsiderate of the man to die, she reflected as the hours slowly passed. Worse, of course, that somebody else should have done it.

Lizzie took to her room, stretching out on the chaise hour after hour. She was waiting. She didn't know for what except that there had to be something. There had to be a project in the works, some goal to give her direction. Something to keep her going.

Lizzie waited for whatever was coming next.

LXXVI

Late September 1899

Lizzie was again reclining on the chaise longue when her maid knocked softly on the bedroom door.

"Yes, Gertrude, what is it?"

"There's a policeman at the door, ma'am. Says he wants to talk to you."

. . .

Well, she'd wanted something to spice up the long days. She had made him wait, that was the fitting and proper thing for a woman of her standing to do, and was now pleased to see that he was well-featured and curly-haired. He rose as she entered the parlor.

She enjoyed the questioning since her replies came easily. He wanted information on her first meeting with Andre, confirming it was she who brought him to Buffalo – why was it so hard for this young man to understand Andre's appeal to women such as she? To comprehend precisely what it was that he did at her home.

How ignorant some of these people could be! And such a good-looking sergeant, too. But my goodness, she thought rather indignantly as the questioning began to drag out, no, of course tables didn't rise. Ghosts didn't appear. There were no voices from beyond the grave. They didn't turn off the lights, chant, do any of those strange things.

Terrible his death, of course it was. A great loss to her friends. She didn't imagine one like him could be replaced. What did her circle plan to do next? Why, officer, such an indelicate question! The poor man probably isn't even in the ground yet . . . oh, he was? Well, that's a figure of speech anyway. Certainly you don't think we'd be thinking of anything that crass – not at a time like this. Not yet, certainly. Of all the –

Why was he so curious about her? She grew uncomfortable with the direction his questions seemed to be taking. Here now, she'd been willing to cooperate. So why was this young man starting to treat her rudely?

What would she know about the circumstances surrounding his death? Had the little item that had appeared in the Buffalo paper even stated how he had died? In fact, she thought it strange when this man first mentioned a shooting. Why had she somehow assumed he had been stabbed? More than likely in a fight.

Had he been the type to fight? How would she know that? Really, officer, Mr. Andre came to my home for a few hours each Monday during the Season, got paid for his appearance, and departed.

How dare you question our relationship? Do you have any idea to whom you're speaking?

Look now, what good do you think threats will do? I'm sure it would be a simple matter for my husband to speak to your superior. Might be good to have you taught a few manners.

Oh, you're from Fredonia, representing Lily Dale, not a Buffalo regular? Well, how was I to know?

Look now. Coming back with more men – I don't care if it's two or two hundred – isn't going to make a whit of difference. I've already told you everything I know.

She was glad when he took her lead, rose and walked to the front door. She watched with a feeling of relief until he was out of sight.

What an impudent young man.

Lizzie trusted it would be the last she saw of him.

· · ·

"Oh, Everett! I was so afraid you wouldn't get my letter in time. It would have been dreadful if you hadn't been here to meet me."

She welcomed the embrace but quickly pulled away, eager to continue relating all that had happened.

He led her gently to their waiting carriage, Maggie never letting up as she described Vernon's depression after the leg had been removed and then his growing cheeriness as he returned home and was once again surrounded by his adoring family.

The girls had been a delight. Maggie now looked on them as close to daughters. They had promised to write regularly and she dreamt already of buying special gifts for each. Something for now first and then definitely Christmas presents – why, she'd find plenty for Janie's entire family! She and Everett had so much and, really, so few to share it with. Maggie excitedly prattled on as the carriage bumpily made its way through the streets and on to their home.

Everett held the door for her as she entered. The barrenness of the place struck her immediately.

What was happening?

She had been so eager to see her husband, so wound up with all she wished to share. So happy that he had known to be at the station for the right train. Forgetting that things between them weren't as close as they had once been. Forgetting everything except how happy she felt to be coming home.

It was chilly in here!

Maggie glanced around, her eyes falling on the parlor, its curtained window facing the street. Then she remembered the last time she had stood there.

A shiver ran through her exhausted body.

. . .

"How dare you continue to harass me?" Lizzie felt her temper rising as she was called a second time to face the sergeant from Lily Dale. "I've certainly told you everything I know. There is no possible reason for you to return."

"Sorry, ma'am."

She was startled at the second voice, believing the

beleaguered young officer had returned alone. "I'm Captain Drubbs, Buffalo police this time."

"But –? Why?" She allowed her questions to drift off as she stared silently at the two.

The men exchanged glances as if trying to decide where to begin. The sergeant deferred to his superior with a nod.

"I'm afraid I simply do not understand." Lizzie regained her composure quickly. "I know nothing about the death of Andre Robson and I believe I made that perfectly clear last time. I don't see what more you can want from me."

She seated herself grandly in the tall corner chair. She knew she was not involved. What simpletons men could be!

"You know we've questioned your servants," the captain began quietly.

She had known, of course. The sergeant had asked her permission in fact. "What could they possibly say that could help you? I've told you all I know."

"Not quite, ma'am –" The handsome sergeant stopped, cut off by a sharp glance from his superior.

"Mrs. Knapp, he means that you didn't mention the argument you had with Mr. Robson."

"Argument?"

"You deny that you and he exchanged words the last time he was here?"

"Oh, that." She leaned forward in the chair. "It was nothing. Really nothing."

"Hardly *nothing,* from what your maid told us."

"Well then, I guess you had better ask her."

"Did, ma'am."

"And?"

"According to her," he pulled a thick notebook from his pocket, "you and Mr. Robson were involved in a very heated exchange. Shouts. Perhaps tears . . . on your part, that'd be. She almost thought threats were exchanged."

"Threats? Nonsense!"

"Care to tell us about it then?"

"There's little to tell. Andre – Mr. Robson, had told me of an idea he'd had to increase his clientele here in Buffalo.

That's all it amounted to."

"Then why the fury?"

"My, do you all exaggerate so? There was no fury. No argument. We simply disagreed, that's all. He had some notion of hiring a room in a hotel – can you imagine? – and I thought he should continue his meetings here. That's all there was to it."

"How was it resolved?"

"It wasn't."

The men exchanged glances before turning back to her.

"His plans were hardly final. I imagine I expected he would bring it up at a future meeting – or perhaps, wisely, let the notion drop all together. We – those with whom he worked here – were quite wealthy and happily paid for his advice."

"A bunch of rich fools, if you ask me." The three turned in unison to see Jack standing in the doorway.

"And you?"

"Jack Knapp." He strode manfully into the room, knew immediately which of the officers was the superior, shook hands in order and turned to his flustered wife, reading the question across her face.

"Just came in and couldn't help overhearing my wife's last exchange. She told me you were here before. Mind if I ask what you're doing here again?"

"Would you mind, Mr. Knapp, if we ask you a couple of questions?"

"Me? I assure you, my wife knows very little, obviously nothing about that man's death, and I even less. Why, I hardly saw the man. Not sure I'd have recognized him if we'd crossed paths."

"Then you don't object to our questions?"

"Object? Why should I?"

"Did you know, Mr. Knapp, that your wife had had an argument with Andre Robson on the day he died?"

"An argument? What could she and he possibly have had to argue about? He came to perform a service, was paid well and departed."

"Then there was no personal relationship between the two?"

"How dare you?" Lizzie jumped to her feet. "Jack –"

"Quiet, ma'am. Now then, sir, could you tell us about the relationship between your wife and Robson?"

"There was no relationship, I assure you."

"But they did fight that day?"

"You say so. It's news to me." He turned to look at Lizzie who began to ease herself back down into the chair. She remained on its edge. "Was there a fight, Lizzie? Is what these men say true?"

"It wasn't a fight. I keep trying to tell them that."

"But he did stay after all the women left. That is correct, is it not, Mrs. Knapp?"

"Yes." She hesitated. "He did."

"Was he in the habit of staying?"

"No. Yes. It didn't matter. Sometimes there was something he wanted to talk about. Nothing important. We weren't . . . *friends*, if that's what you mean."

"Were you surprised when he stayed this time?"

"Not particularly."

"Had he indicated he wanted to, that he had something to discuss with you?"

"Yes, I imagine he did."

"And when was that? When he arrived?"

"No. As a matter of fact he came in late. All of us were waiting, rather impatiently if you must know."

"Was that what caused the later argument?"

"No, I already told you."

"Please tell us again."

"Every word as it happened, if you can, please."

"Every word? I doubt if I'd remember. It was really quite unimportant."

"Try, ma'am."

She sighed deeply. "All right. As I've already said, Andre whispered to me as the others were preparing to leave that he wanted to stay to talk. Just a moment or so, I believe he said. Yes, I remember now. He usually left with the women and I remember feeling awkward that he was making no motion to leave. I worried what the others might think."

"The others? Oh, the women."

"Yes."

"Go on, please."

"That's it. He stayed until all had left. Then he said he wanted to explain about a new turn his enterprise – I think those were the words he used though I really can't be certain now – his enterprise was going to take. I'm afraid I wasn't paying that much attention. I mean, what he did was his own business, hardly mine."

"But surely you can remember what he had in mind? The details, I mean."

"I'm not sure I can, officer. Something about wanting to hire a room, to be able to meet with people here in Buffalo. I'm not certain even he knew exactly what he planned to do."

"Is this what upset you?"

"I've told you. I wasn't upset."

"The maids heard you, ma'am."

"Well, I certainly didn't mean to get upset. Certainly not over something so trifling."

"Go on. Tell us what happened. Word for word. As near as you can."

"Really." She hesitated. The silence continued. "Mr. Robson had some notion of using a hotel room to expand his clientele here in town. When he told me about it, I suppose I did become upset. My women – the women who meet here every Monday afternoon – believed they had an exclusive arrangement with the man. They had been very generous, agreeing to every increase in pay that he demanded. That he *asked* for. I simply tried to explain that exclusivity was a necessary part of the arrangement. His services would be worth less if he offered them to all."

Jack smiled as he continued to watch his wife. "Why, Lizzie, I never imagined you with a head for business. Pretty astute reasoning, isn't it?" It was obvious he expected the officers to agree.

"Were you a party to this discussion, Mr. Knapp?"

"Or the argument which followed?"

"No, I wasn't, but, by Jove, I damned well wish I had been. Can't expect a woman to hold her own against a snake like that. Imagine! Taking advantage of a group of innocent women! I'm beginning to think he deserved what he got."

"Jack!" Lizzie gasped.

"Never did care for the man, if you want to know the truth. Didn't hanker to having him in the house much either."

"Jack, you never –"

"Didn't see any reason to discuss it, Lizzie. You had your mind made up." He paused.

"Go on . . . please."

"Go on? With what?"

"You obviously have strong feelings on the subject of Andre Robson. We'd be interested in hearing them."

"Told you, I hardly knew the man. Lizzie met him at Lily Dale – though God only knows why she ever went there in the first place. Apparently liked something about him. Got the idea of bringing him here – running these Monday afternoon readings. Near as I could figure, the man did very little for his money beyond telling the women exactly what they wanted to hear. Pretty slick, if you ask me."

"Just how did you feel when you learned that he was planning to . . . ah, expand?"

"Never heard anything about that until right now."

"You didn't know about your wife's fight with Robson?"

"No, of course not."

"She didn't tell you?"

"Don't suppose my wife and I talk as much as we might. Though, now that I think about it, I suppose she would have told me if she'd thought it important enough."

"You don't think his planning to expand his operation was important?"

"I'm trying to say I don't think Lizzie thought it so. Otherwise she would have mentioned it."

"Anything you can add, ma'am?"

"Goodness, no. I feel as if I've told you everything any number of times."

"And left out nothing?"

"And left out nothing."

The officers started for the door. "We'll be leaving then. Don't worry, we can let ourselves out."

Jack had already reached the front door, his hand turning the knob. "You're through with us, I assume? You must see we're eager to cooperate in your investigation." He paused. "But at the same time, these incessant questions do get to be a nuisance. May we assume you've finished here?"

"Sorry, sir. I can't promise that."

"What?"

"Try to see it from our side, sir. A man was murdered, leaving very few clues for us to work with. We questioned everybody who was at Lily Dale and got nowhere."

"But certainly – That is where he was killed, isn't it?"

"It was. Can't say, to be perfectly candid, that he'd have won any personality contests there but we haven't found any reason for one of them to want him dead either."

"Didn't I read that he had a large amount of money on him? And that it was missing?"

"True. And I suppose one of them could have been jealous enough to kill."

"Then why waste your time here, harassing us?"

"Not harassing, sir, just asking questions. I agree with you. Robbery could be the motive. Or jealousy. It's just that – well, I suppose you'd have to see the people who live there, neighbors and friends. Just not the murdering kind."

"You call that an investigation?"

"Really, Mr. Knapp, no need getting riled up. We did investigate."

"Thoroughly, too."

"And we're prepared to go back – if we have to. But, to tell you the truth, no matter where we turn all the paths keep leading us back here."

"Here?"

"To Buffalo, ma'am. You – and your friends – were just about the last ones to see him alive."

"Ridiculous! You're saying one of my wife's friends

followed him back to Lily Dale? And killed him?"

"I'm saying there's a good possibility someone in Buffalo did."

They turned and walked away. Jack could hear Lizzie bustling about the emptied parlor as he stood at the door staring in silence. What a fool he was! Why had he been so eager to disparage the man? He had read the look in the departing eyes clearly. If only he could remember now what he had told them.

LXXVII

October 1899

"Here, come sit with me, Everett. Oh, not there. Or, if you want to, let me move those newspapers. I keep meaning to go through them. You were so good to save them for me while I was in Erie."

"Stop frittering, Maggie. They'll wait. Better still, why not start on them now?"

"And ignore you?"

"Nonsense. I have papers here that need going over."

"Work?"

"Nothing important. In fact, they're about done. I won't mind a bit if you want to interrupt. If you find anything worthy of note, that is."

Each read in silence.

"Why, I met that man!"

"Hmm? What did you say?"

"Here. Look. This article, did you miss it?"

"Maggie, I'm not a mind reader. What article? What man?"

"It says he was murdered. How perfectly dreadful."

"And you met him?"

"Well, not really. But I saw him. He was on the train. When I went to Erie."

Everett leaned over her shoulder to reread the forgotten article. "Says he was returning from a meeting in Buffalo. Strange-looking character. Did he talk to you, Maggie?"

"No, of course not. Well . . . I don't think so. To be honest, it all seems hazy. I can't really remember him very well."

"I'm sure your thoughts were centered on Jane, and Vernon with his impending surgery. I'm surprised you'd even notice a stranger."

"Yes, now that you mention it, I can't recall why I did."

"Were there many on the train that day?"

"I don't think so. But I do remember this man. Had a rather haunting look as I recall."

"Maggie! Did you finish the article?"

"No. There wasn't time. Why?"

"According to the paper he must have been killed shortly after getting off the train in Dunkirk. And, look here, on the very day you saw him."

"How frightening!"

"Do you think you should go to the police?"

"Police? Why would I?"

"It says they're looking for possible witnesses, anyone who may have anything to help determine his activities on that fateful day."

"I could I suppose . . . No!"

"That sounds surprisingly final, my dear."

"And why shouldn't it? I have nothing to offer. He was just a stranger, a man I saw once on a train. They already know that – see, it says so right here."

"But what if you were the last to see him alive? I suppose it's possible."

"I'm certain there were others."

"Are you sure, Maggie? Absolutely sure?"

"Let's not talk about it any more. Believe me, I have nothing to contribute to any police investigation."

. . .

The plate slipped from her fingers, breaking into countless pieces as it smashed onto the floor.

"Oh! You scared me."

"Sorry. I thought you heard me come in."

"I guess I'm just jumpy today. Have been all day, as a matter of fact."

"That's not like the Maggie I know. Come sit down. Perhaps if you rest a bit – There, that's a good girl. Will it help if I rub your shoulders?"

She smiled up at her husband. "Can't hurt. Hmm, you know how good that feels."

"Why don't you tell me about your day."

"'Fraid there's little to tell, Everett. I'm just trying to get everything back the way it was before I left. How was yours?"

"Fine, dear. Quite grand, in fact."

"Anything new at work?"

"Actually there is. Exciting news, too. Here, let me hang my coat up – mighty chilly out there for October – and I'll fill you in."

Over a cup of hot tea and Mrs. Sirianni's genuine Italian biscotti, Everett brought Maggie up to date on the happenings at the Larkin Company. He described the doctor and dentist already on the premises and talk of a new gymnasium, also for the employees. Maggie's ears picked up when Everett described plans for an orchestra. There was a library. And scholarships for worthy employees and their children.

She shook her head in wonderment as her husband went on. "This all makes my head swim."

"That isn't even the whole of it. Why, just today, Maggie, I caught a glimpse of the plans for their building for the Pan-American Exposition."

"A whole building? I suppose he'll want the most up-to-date designs."

"Hardly. Larkin is full of surprises. It's to be totally classic, nothing new-looking about it. In fact, it's topped with a huge dome, Italian Renaissance they were calling it."

"Italian? I can't wait to see that. What exciting news!"

"I know I thought so. But your face just dropped. Did something I say disappoint you, dear?"

"Of course not. It's terribly exciting. Only . . . well, it makes me sad that I'm not still working there. It must be terribly stimulating, especially with so much going on now."

"Maggie! Are you telling me you'd trade your position at St. Paul's to work as a clerk again at Larkin's? If you're really serious, I might be able to find a place for you. Starting, of course."

"You rat! Stop teasing. Come; keep me company while I start dinner. You must tell me all the details."

"Need any help?"

"Of course not. Then again . . . how are you at scraping vegetables?"

"Git, woman. You scrape. I'll talk."

. . .

"I don't believe this! How dare you come back yet again?" The police had insisted on questioning the other sixteen women who had not taken the threat of notoriety kindly. Her reputation, Lizzie believed, had been sullied through all of Buffalo. And for what? "I know nothing about Andre Robson's death. I have told you that over and over and over again. Just how long do you plan to keep harassing me?"

"I am sorry, Mrs. Knapp. It's certainly not our intention to harass you –"

"Or anybody else, for that matter."

"But you must know you've absolutely ruined me. You saw how those women behaved. I can assure you they'll never return to this house. And for what? What have I done to deserve your punishment?"

"*Punishment?* Not by us, ma'am."

"Call it what you will. Just tell me what you want and then get out. I've had enough."

"No reason getting upset, ma'am."

"Is Mr. Knapp here now?"

"Jack? What on earth could you possibly want with him?"

"Just a couple questions, ma'am. Is he here?"

"Just a minute, I'll get him."

Their questioning was brief but thorough. The investigators apologized profusely but wouldn't Mr. and Mrs. Knapp please try to understand their dilemma? The killer logically was someone who knew Robson in Lily Dale. Of course they understood that. And, yes, the money was missing. And yes, they had questioned everyone residing there. It just petered out, that was about it. Motive, yes. Opportunity, of course.

But not reason, not a real reason. So, sorry, but the trail keeps coming back to Buffalo, to here.

Jack rose in anger.

"This is ridiculous! You tell us the people at Lily Dale had both motive – the money, I assume – and opportunity. And yet you continue to harass us, fifty miles away, we who had neither the means nor the reason."

Striding across the room, he turned abruptly to face them. "To be honest, I thought at first my wife was becoming hysterical over something too petty to be bothered with. Now, I'm afraid, I side with her. We have tried to cooperate; we have answered all your questions. We have treated you much better than you have treated us. And I, for one, have had enough.

"Come, my dear. I'm sure these men can let themselves out." He turned and walked rapidly from the room. Lizzie rose to meekly follow.

"Just another word, please, Mrs. Knapp."

"No. No more."

"I'm afraid I have to insist."

"What? How dare you?"

"Sit down, ma'am."

"I will not! I most definitely shall not. I have answered your questions and shall answer no more. You'd think you suspected me of killing the poor man."

"Yes, ma'am. I think we do."

Her mouth fell open in a silent gape as she stumbled to the nearest chair. She continued to stare at the two men. In time, recovering, her face grew flushed. The anger flashing in her eyes was unmistakable. At last she started to rise.

"Mother!"

The three turned as Abram rushed to his mother's side.

"Are you all right? What are these men doing to you? What have they been saying?"

The investigators feared he might strike them as he stepped between them and the stunned woman.

"Don't you dare hurt my mother. Get out of this house." His eyes blazed. "Now!"

Were they getting somewhere at last?

LXXVIII

November 1899

"Why, Grace. Anne! What a delight to be told you two were downstairs. I've gotten so I shudder every time I hear someone at the door. But that doesn't matter now. To what do I owe this happy occasion?" Lizzie glanced at her oldest daughter, then more quizzically at her second born. "It is a happy occasion? Do tell me that it is."

"Why yes, Mama, of course it is."

"I hope it is."

Lizzie turned quickly to Anne. "What's the matter?"

"Oh, Mother, we didn't mean to alarm you," Grace responded quickly.

"No, certainly not."

"Oh, dear, now I'm afraid Anne and I have gotten off on the wrong foot."

"Completely," Anne continued.

"Enough of your chatter. I can't imagine what you're talking about."

"Oh, Mama, I'm so sorry. It's nothing sinister, I promise."

"Or bad."

"It's just that we were quite dismayed –"

"Terribly –"

"When we heard of your refusal to join us at the Club for New Year's Eve."

"You aren't really going to boycott the party . . . are you?"

"You must come, you and Papa."

"Nonsense. We're too old for such frivolities."

"Mother, you aren't old at all."

"And you know how Papa loves parties."

"Besides, this is the Millennium."

"Grace is right, you know. It wouldn't feel right not having you there. Why, the whole family has to be together."

"Just think, Mama! The Twentieth Century! Can you imagine? I mean, *really* imagine?"

"Perhaps not," Lizzie smiled. "I'm not sure I ever thought I'd live to see this day."

"All the more reason you must come. You absolutely must."

"Oh, do. We'll all be there, you know."

"*All?*"

"Not little Clara, of course. This party is strictly for grown-ups."

"And I doubt if Abram would want to."

"Though I suppose he could if he'd rather."

"But Ralph and John are coming and they've promised to stay for the entire weekend."

"And Bessie positively refuses to go back to Vassar till after the Holidays."

"Besides, the Club has promised a lavish buffet. We shan't go hungry."

"And you and Papa and Uncle Charlie absolutely must be there."

"Charlie's coming?"

"Father thinks so. You must know he'd rather be out partying if Charlie's here."

"Why, yes. I suppose he would."

"Then you will go?"

"It's not that I don't want to be with you. And the party does sound nice, quite special."

"But?"

"Well, to tell you the truth, I'd feel terribly uncomfortable. You know how much gossip there's been."

"You mean because of Mr. Andre? But, Mother, that was months ago. The investigation has to be finished by now."

"There's never been an arrest, certainly not one that I've read of – or heard about. Yet, to be perfectly candid, I'm more afraid of the recriminations of the women who'll be at the party. They were quite angry when they left after being questioned by the police."

"Then you absolutely must come. Let everyone see you haven't changed. That you still value their friendship."

"Anne's right, you know."

"And what better time to turn over a new leaf –"

"Make a new start –"

"Than on New Year's Eve?" The sisters giggled as they finished in unison.

"Well, put that way . . . What you're saying does make sense. And of course you're perfectly right about your father."

The girls rose together to embrace their mother excitedly.

"You two!" She sighed. "I imagine you could talk me into just about anything."

"And it will be a wonderful evening. I know you'll have a marvelous time."

"Of course I will. Now that that's settled, may I ring for some tea? I think there's pie left from last night's dinner, too."

"Not today. Grace had agreed to come with me –"

"To shop for our new gowns."

"You do want the best-dressed daughters at the party, don't you?"

Lizzie was always lifted by their giggles. "Go then. Go find the prettiest dresses in Buffalo."

"Oh, we shall. We shall."

Kissing their mother, the girls departed in a whirlwind of plans.

"Now that I'm downstairs, I might as well stay." Lizzie sighed and rang for tea for one.

. . .

"Maggie, I've got to say I'm worried about you."

"Me? Why? What's the matter?"

"I wish I knew. I'm used to your spirits being high enough to buoy us both. But lately . . . well, I just don't know."

"I'm sorry, dear. I didn't realize it showed."

"Then you know what's troubling you?"

"No, I wish I did. I just seem to feel . . . well, unwell, if you will."

"That's what I mean. I thought at first it might be fatigue from your trip to Janie's. God knows, I'm sure that whole situation had to be a strain."

"Oh, Everett, do you really think it's been that long? Why, Thanksgiving is almost upon us. I went to Erie over a month ago."

"And came back somehow changed. Do you feel ill?"

"If I could answer that, trust me I'd have made an appointment with Dr. Bowman long before now. There are times, to be honest, I almost wish I did feel poorly. Then at least I'd know what to do. But this . . ."

"You do think you're sick then?"

"No. Honestly I don't. It's just that my usual energy's gone. I've tried getting more sleep but that doesn't help either."

"And you've been losing weight, haven't you?"

"Oh, dear, I hope not. Though I have noticed my clothes are fitting more loosely these days. Food just doesn't taste particularly good."

He had to laugh. "That's hardly my Maggie! I've gotten quite used to your robust appetite."

"But your dinners are still all right; they are, aren't they?"

"Of course they are. You're a fine cook. I meant no complaint. My only concern is for you. Thanksgiving, as you pointed out, is right around the corner. Then the Holidays will be upon us. And the Millennium."

"Oh, yes, Nineteen Hundred. I can remember as a girl dreaming of that date, wondering what the world would be like – wondering what *my* life would be like."

"And has it turned out as you imagined, dear?"

"Better, much better, if you want the truth."

"Now that the subject's come up, is there something particular you'd enjoy doing to celebrate year's end?"

"I have given it some thought but if you don't mind, I'd like to reserve whatever options we have until the date gets closer."

"Are you waiting for something else? A special offer perhaps?"

"Not at all. I just . . .well, right now I really don't feel up to celebrating. I'm just hoping I will by then."

"I'll second that, and the sooner the better. Here, you stay there and relax. I'll brew a pot of tea."

"That's a lovely idea, my sweet. Though if you don't mind, I'll pass. I'll be happy to sit with you; I'd enjoy that very much. But tea? Not today."

LXXIX

New Year's Eve 1899

Lizzie gasped as she entered the grand ballroom. Every square inch seemed to glisten or sparkle. The ceiling undulated with huge white balloons that she supposed would cap the midnight ceremonies. She had felt a tinge that surprised her when she first viewed Jack in his white coat and tails. Charlie was almost as handsome.

The hours sped by in a whirl of good will. The orchestra played a goodly selection of waltzes, always her favorite, and she was much in demand on the dance floor. Thank heavens for a handsome husband and a brother-in-law and two sons-in-law. Gentlemen all and, my, wasn't this fun?

The buffet was a feast of every imaginable food, each beautifully prepared. She was glad she had succumbed and gone shopping at the last minute for a new gown. She couldn't have found a more perfect outfit, she told herself now as she read the faces of the other women – and felt pleasantly surprised at the glances of approval registered by their husbands. Even Andre's death couldn't mar this occasion.

And just think: the millennium. *Fin de siecle* be damned! She had made it after all, felt as spry as ever. Bless those girls of hers for insisting she come. Especially since the sixteen had treated her so cordially.

How sad, she sighed, knowing it was twelve already.

Horns blared as the net holding the balloons was unfastened. A loud bang from somewhere across the room caused Lizzie to jump. Then she realized it was only one of the balloons popping. A man in front of her used his cigar to explode a few which floated too close.

She leaned toward Jack as he lighted her cigarette, catching his eye as he looked up from the match in his hand. Handsome man, indeed. How had she managed to forget how charming he could be?

"Think you'll be ready to go soon, Liz?"

"Go? Oh, must we?"

Anne and Grace had been approaching and were close enough to hear her plaintive lament.

"Then you are glad you came?"

"Glad? Oh, I'd never have forgiven myself if I'd missed a minute of this." Her head moved in a wide circle to take in the whole room. Turning again to her husband, she asked, "You weren't serious about wanting to leave, were you?"

"Me?" He had the pleasantest deep laugh. "You know me better than that. Given my druthers I might well be here till the sun comes up."

"Hell, you might have to carry me out if I stay that long."

All eyes turned to Charlie.

"You're not thinking of leaving?"

"Not yet, no. I figure I might as well stay. Don't expect I'll be doing much a hundred years from today."

"All the more reason to celebrate while we can." She hesitated. "Jack, would you be a dear?"

"Yet another glass of champagne?"

"You don't mind, do you?"

"Of course not. I'll get all you want."

More champagne. More food as the Club continued to restock the groaning buffet. And more dancing, at least until Lizzie realized the blister on her foot had broken and reluctantly called a halt.

"Or one more. Maybe two," she giggled at Charlie. "After a little more to eat and just, Jack, please, a little more champagne. Not a full glass, mind you."

But it was.

She relaxed in a swirl of couples twirling around her, enjoying the security of being held fast in Jack's arms while champagne corks popped between the doomed balloons.

Lizzie remembered the sleigh bells as the team headed back to Delaware Avenue, the warmth of the blanket across her knees, and Jack's strong arms around her.

She stumbled, grateful it was dark as they entered through the porte cochere. Over their protests Charlie had departed hours earlier. She noticed that his windows were dark.

"Want another to wrap up the night?"

"I really shouldn't."

"Well, I'm going to. Do as you think best." He turned to face her, glass raised in a salute. "Only I would be pleased to have you join me."

Lizzie shrugged. "Why not?" she tittered.

The liquid, brandy now, not champagne, felt warm as she swallowed. "Hmmm, that's good."

"Just a little more then?"

. . .

Judging from the angle of the sun streaming through the bedroom window, it was late morning when Lizzie stretched sleepily and gradually began to wake. Her movement caused Jack to turn toward her. She snuggled against his warm body as his arms tightened about her.

LXXX

January 1900

"Oh, I'm sorry. I must have dozed again." She slowly allowed her glance to circle the room, taking in the bright sunshine at her bedroom window. "Have I been sleeping long?" She wished he weren't there at all, that she might be allowed to sink back into the warmth of her last dream. He had been there, holding her securely, wonderfully. He had leaned down, ready to kiss her. And she'd woken.

"It's good for you to sleep, dear."

"Have you been here the whole time?"

"Since you dozed off? Yes."

"I'm so sorry. It must be terribly boring for you."

"Oh, Maggie, don't even think that. There is nothing I'd rather do; no place I'd rather be –especially now that we know you're carrying my baby. Just imagine! I still haven't gotten used to the idea. After all this time . . ." He allowed his words to drift off.

It had come as a shock when the doctor told Maggie her recent aliments were caused by nothing more serious than a pregnancy. After so many years of fruitlessness, they had given up ever having a child. And now, she thirty-eight and dear Everett almost sixty, a baby was on its way.

"May I get you anything, my dear?"

"Oh? No, no thanks. I think I'll try to sleep again." Sleep. She felt secure in her dreams.

In moments she lost all awareness of her husband in the room. He saw a gentle smile cross her lips, kissed her forehead, returning her sigh with a smile of his own before tiptoeing out.

. . .

The room was dark when Maggie woke again, all but the bare flame of the lamp burning on the table near the window. A wave of admiration swept through her as she saw Everett seated in the far corner, his head resting on his chest.

He snorted once and sat up with a jolt.

"You're awake!"

"Just woke, in fact."

"How are you feeling?"

"Quite wonderfully, to tell the truth."

He rose and came to her. "May I get you something to eat?"

Maggie couldn't remember the last time she'd had an appetite and the words began to form in her mind. "You know something? I feel famished. What have we got?"

She had always loved her husband's laugh. "Let me go raid the larder. Nothing in particular that appeals?"

"Anything. Anything at all."

He returned with a large tray laden with all sorts of Epicurean delights, also bringing the mail of the past two days.

"Here's a letter from Janie. Why didn't you tell me?"

"How could I do that, my little sleeping beauty? But go on, read it. I'm sure the food can wait."

"No, you open it. Please. I'm dying to know what she has to say – if the girls liked our Christmas presents and how they are all doing – but, to tell the truth, I'd much rather eat a little first. Better yet, would you mind reading it to me? That way I can hear and eat." Her fork was already raised.

. . .

"Why, yes, dear, I did read tonight's newspaper. It was positively full of news about that Hay man and his plans to open China to trade. I didn't make terribly much of it. Do you feel it will really affect us?"

"It certainly will. The world's getting smaller every day."

"Smaller? What do you – Oh! I see. Why, yes, I suppose that's true. Though I really can't see that anything China does – or doesn't do, for that matter, will ever cause us much concern. Certainly Mr. Larkin isn't planning to send soap over there?"

"Not that I've heard. Then again, Lizzie, you never know, not with that man. Still, I have to feel this new policy will prove a good one."

"If you say so. I meant to ask earlier . . . comment perhaps, on your early arrival."

"Early? Why I came straight home from work."

"Exactly what I meant. I can't recall the last time you did that. Seems you usually prefer the company at the Club."

"Why, yes, I suppose I did. Right now, however, I find I get a warmer welcome here at home. Ever since New Year's Eve – why, Lizzie, you're blushing! I never thought I'd see that day."

"It was just so unexpected –"

"But not unpleasant? I hope not."

"Jack! You'll set me blushing again. Really!"

"We are husband and wife. I'm just glad we can behave as such. Mighty proud, too, if you want to know."

"Why, I –"

"You didn't mind, did you, Lizzie?"

"Mind? No. Funny, I guess I never gave it much thought one way or the other. But mind? Definitely not."

"Then you wouldn't mind if I – well, say, paid a return call one of these nights?"

"I think I'd be quite happy to welcome the visit. But really, I do feel most uncomfortable discussing such things. What if someone were to hear us?"

"What if they did?" He looked up at that instant in response to a knock on the closed parlor door. It wasn't a question of privacy, simply easier to keep warm on drafty January days with the gas fireplace turned up high and the doors tightly closed. "Yes?"

"Sorry to interrupt, Mr. Knapp, ma'am, but the policeman –"

"Oh, no! They can't be back again! I really thought one of the reasons I enjoyed the party so much was due to my knowing all this was behind us. Now –"

"I know, dear. Well, Gertrude, what is it they want this time?"

"Or who?"

"Nobody, ma'am. And, sir, I can't say what they want. He just left this message. Said something about talking to you soon, that you'd understand when you read it."

Jack took the paper from her outstretched hand, scanned it rapidly, and slowly reread it word by word, a frown growing on his face as he continued.

"My God, Jack! What is it?"

He turned to her deliberately, speaking slowly as soon as Gertrude had left the room and secured the door behind her. "Nothing. At least I hope not. If you want the truth, I can't make hide nor hair of it."

"Let me see." Lizzie started to reach for the paper in his hand. "You don't mind, do you?"

"Of course not." Absent-mindedly he held it out for her grasp. He continued to stare into some indistinct space while his wife read the letter.

"I don't understand," Lizzie sputtered at last. "It sounds like they're all coming – and they want to interview us all, you and me, the entire staff and, yes, and Abram. What on earth do you think they're up to now?"

"I wish I knew, dear. When did they say they'd be here?"

"It says Thursday, January fourth. That's tomorrow night. Six o'clock. How inconvenient! You don't suppose they'll pull Cook away from her duties in the kitchen, do you? I know how we all get if dinner's delayed."

"I can't imagine dinner will be very important by then, dear."

"You're scaring me, Jack. Something in the tone of your voice."

"No point in doing that, Liz. Though I have to tell you I have a very bad feeling about this. I don't like it at all."

"What do you think we should do?"

"I don't think there's anything we can do. Except wait . . ."

"Till tomorrow."

"Till tomorrow."

. . .

"Read that last part again; would you mind?"

"Not in the least. Where is it – oh, here. Yes. 'Oh, Maggie, I wish you were here in person – you and dear Everett, too, of course – to see the changes that have taken place in Vernon. Why, he's as good as his old self! Not that his leg grew back or anything so magical – though, with my husband, even that wouldn't surprise me. No, I mean that his spirits have rejuvenated. If anything, he's even better. Do you think that's possible? I only mean that he's more loving – to the girls as well as me and, truly, made it the happiest Christmas we have ever known.'"

Maggie smiled at the good news. "Go on, do. Read the part about the girls."

Everett good-humoredly turned back to Jane's description of her daughters. "'You were the girls' Santa. They got no presents which thrilled them more. I promise they shall tell you so themselves – and very soon, mind you, but, being young girls, they are so involved in the spirit of these holidays that I would feel like an old biddy were I to deny them a moment of pleasure by forcing a letter from their hands. This new snow has brought all the neighborhood out for one sledding party after another. Snow used to seem a part of every winter here. Strange how so many now lack that magical whiteness. I've heard talk of a universal warming trend. It doesn't have anything to do with the Chinese and that Open Door – do you think?'"

"Janie always was a unique one, wasn't she?"

"And so, obviously, are those daughters of hers. Well, at least they received the presents and, I gather, genuinely did appreciate your efforts."

"As I appreciate your generosity, dear."

"Well, Maggie, it's not that I would want to deny you – or, through you, the pleasure of giving to your friends – anything. I trust you know that."

Her eyes widened as her husband sought the words to continue. "Oh, yes, I see."

"You do?"

"I think so. You're trying to say we need to save, what with the baby coming. Is that it?"

"That's not being terribly selfish, is it?"

"No, dear, of course not."

"So will you tell her?"

"Tell? Oh, you mean the baby? Actually, you wouldn't mind, would you, if I postponed any announcement for a little bit?"

"That's up to you, though I must say your decision comes as a surprise. Is there a reason? Good God, you don't know something you haven't told me, do you?"

"Of course not. It's just that . . . well, most women don't have babies – not first ones – at my age. If you don't mind, I'd feel more comfortable waiting, just to be sure."

He gathered her in his arms. "Anything you do is absolutely perfect with me. In fact, I guess one could say you've already done it."

He kissed her, then watched with deepening satisfaction as she dug into her food.

LXXXI

January 1900

"Jack, I'm sure I heard it strike six. Do you suppose they aren't coming?"

"I admit to issuing many hard prayers throughout the day but, no, I imagine they are simply late."

"It has been an awful day. I can't remember one dragging by so slowly."

"Work was pure hell. No matter what I did, I simply couldn't get my mind off tonight."

"It is terrible, isn't it? I mean, we both know we have nothing to hide. Yet, somehow all these policemen make me feel guilty. What do you suppose they want with us now?"

"I –" Jack's remarks were interrupted by a loud knocking at the front door.

"Let them in, will you please, Gertrude. And then have the rest of the staff ready whenever they're called. Oh, that this might be over and done with!"

Jack slipped his arm around his wife's waist as they turned to face the men entering the front hall. They recognized Captain Drubbs, the Buffalo detective, and Sergeant Siggins from Lily Dale. With them were three strangers, all in uniform. Introductions took place in a blur. Neither Lizzie nor Jack, they recounted later, was able to remember a single one of the new men's names. Being so outnumbered further increased their growing intimidation.

"See here now, should I have called our attorney to be present?"

"I don't think that'll be necessary, Mr. Knapp."

"Though you know you have that right, if you want to use it."

"Well?" The captain looked at him, waiting.

"No." Jack had made up his mind. "I can't imagine why we'd need an attorney."

"May we come in then?" There was no mistaking the voice of Captain Drubbs. "I believe the notice you received explained that we would want to examine your staff and your family as well."

"*Family?*"

"Just the boy, ma'am."

"You said he was the only other member of the family in the house that day. That is correct, isn't it?"

"Yes, I suppose I did."

"Well, is it correct or not?"

"Can you remember, Lizzie?"

"I remember that Abram was here, yes, most definitely. I just can't remember where Clara was."

"Then you have more than one youngster still living at home?"

"Yes. Abram is here. And our daughter Clara. She's in her last year of school and already excited about college next fall." She paused. "Surely this has nothing to do with her?"

"Don't believe so, ma'am."

"Or the boy, I don't suppose. Though –"

"Jack, don't start on him. Not now."

"You and the boy don't get along, Mr. Knapp?"

"You could say that."

"Jack!"

"Sorry, ma'am. I'll have to ask you to hold your tongue."

"But –"

"Quiet, Mrs. Knapp. Please."

"Now then, Mr. Knapp, would you be so kind as to explain exactly what you meant."

"Gladly, though I don't see what this has to do with your investigation."

"Go on, sir."

Lizzie struggled to stop her husband, caught the message in the eyes of the Buffalo captain, and sat back in resignation.

It was apparent to all that Jack had a great deal to say on

the subject of his youngest son.

"He should be out on his own, should have left long ago. Would have, if I'd had anything to do with it. But his mother . . . well, that's an unsettling situation in itself." He stopped to take a deep breath, began to continue, and realized he had aired all his complaints.

"Anything else, Mr. Knapp?"

"No, nothing that I can think of. But why so many questions? This certainly has nothing to do with your inquiry. Nor, for that matter, have you told my wife and me why you are here. All of you."

"Yes, do tell us, please. We simply can't understand why you came back, not after all this time. Oh!" Lizzie rose expectantly. "Why, I know!" She missed Jack's quizzical look. "Of course! We should have guessed, Jack, the minute we received their notice. You've come to tell us the case is solved, to apologize for all the trouble you've caused."

"Lizzie, you're brilliant. Of course that's it!" He faced the five men. "And I bet we were right all along, weren't we? It was one of that fellow's neighbors."

"We guessed that right away. Probably jealous when he saw so much money."

"'Fraid not, ma'am. Sorry, Mr. Knapp, but that's not the way things seem."

"We don't believe he was killed by anyone living in the Dale."

"How can you be so sure?"

"We've investigated all of 'em thoroughly, mind you. After we finished our questioning here – you and your staff and the other women – we even went back and dug deeper."

"Then I don't understand. Certainly you don't suspect me? Or my husband?"

"Well –"

"But what reason would either one of us have had?"

"That fight, ma'am. We think it was quite a bit stronger than what you'd have us believe."

Jack laughed uneasily. "So I hopped the next train and followed the man back to Lily Dale where I shot him, is that it? Is that what you think? Why? Just to shut him up?"

"Or to keep him away from your wife."

"This is insane. Why I've half a mind to –"

"Don't get so riled up, Mr. Knapp. You may have had reasons. Maybe you did. But we don't think you're the guilty one."

His smile disappeared as quickly as it had come. "Then what? Who?"

"Can't say I exactly understand what it was Robson was proposing that upset your wife so but your servants agree they had a pretty unpleasant scene."

"Are you suggesting that my wife would have followed this man to Lily Dale? Preposterous!"

"A bit far-fetched, to be sure, but women have killed for less reason than that."

"But to travel alone on a train for the purpose of committing murder? Really, I'm sure whatever they argued over wasn't that bad. Believe me, gentlemen, my wife is not a cold-blooded killer."

"No, we don't believe she is."

"You mean then, you think she went there to – to continue the argument? To try to persuade him to change his mind?"

"You have to admit, Mr. Knapp, there is a certain logic in that."

"Logic, perhaps. But horse manure! Utter nonsense, I tell you. My wife is incapable of killing anyone."

"Even in a heated argument?"

"Even if she failed to get her way, sir?"

Jack paused, then turned to Lizzie. "For God's sakes, tell the men you didn't do it. This is absurd." The silence that filled the room cried out for words. Anybody's words.

"Lizzie." She had begun to sob quietly. "Lizzie?"

She looked up to see Abram standing in the open doorway. Taller than his father, well-proportioned if not handsome, he made an impressive appearance. He glanced quickly around the room, taking in the strangers and his father before his eyes fell on his weeping mother. He rushed to comfort her, kneeling at her side.

"Mother dear, what has happened?" He turned angrily to his father, then to the five in uniform. "What have you done to make her cry?"

"Are you Abram Knapp?"

"Answer me! What have you done to my mother?"

"Answer the question."

"All right then. Of course, I'm Abram."

"And you're how old, boy?"

"Nineteen, I'll be nineteen in June."

"Do you work, Abram?"

This was a gentler voice. Now that was better. He liked that one and turned to respond to it. "No, sir, can't say that I do."

"But at nineteen? Eighteen?"

"I know what you're thinking. If you want the truth, my father would like to see me righteously employed – and out from under his roof, if you know what I mean – in a flash. Trouble is, I don't suppose I have many talents to draw upon."

"You don't mind then that you're still living at home?"

"*Mind?* Goodness no. Oh, of course not."

"But what do you do all day?"

"Do?"

"To keep yourself busy. Do you work around the house? Help your parents? You certainly must do something."

"If you can figure that one out, officer, you're a better man than I am."

"That's why they're called detectives, Father."

Jack rose angrily. "Don't you talk back to me, young man. I won't tolerate that sass."

"Yes, Father dear, of course."

Lizzie had stopped weeping but continued to sit with her head down, praying for this latest scene to end.

"You don't get along well with your father; is that true, Abram?" Ah, the gentle voice again. This sounded like a friend, someone he should trust.

"No, sir, I certainly do not."

"Any reason you know of? Anything you could tell us?"

"We just don't get along. Never have. Don't figure we probably ever will."

"Then –" This voice was more like a knife, warning Abram to beware. "I suppose it must hurt a young man to feel he's always had his father's disapproval."

Nothing dangerous in that. "What he thinks is of no concern to me."

Lizzie was not surprised at the lack of expression on her husband's face.

"Do you have a reason for feeling so strongly?"

"Yes. Yes, I suppose I do at that."

Abram felt proud as the thoughts sped into his mind.

"And?"

"My mother."

"*Me?*"

"My wife?"

"I hate it when you call her that, Father. She should never have to be a wife to you."

The quiet voice again. "What do you mean, Abram?"

"He's a terrible man. More times than I could ever count have I heard my mother weeping, and always because of him."

"That's not so. You've always had a hard time finding the truth, son. Liz, tell them the boy is making it all up."

Confusion filled her face. "Well . . ."

"Lizzie!"

"There were times like that. What he said. But not now. Not anymore."

"He's been beastly, Mother. Tell these men the truth."

"Those days are over, dear," she continued quickly. "Can't you see how loving your father has become?"

"A few days? Because you had too much to drink on New Year's Eve and allowed him in your bed?"

"Abram! That is enough." Jack's roar filled the room.

"Please, Mr. Knapp. Let the boy respond. Now then, Abram, are you telling us you felt your father . . . well, abused your mother?"

"Yes, certainly. I'm sorry, Mother, but it's about time

somebody knew the truth."

"And what did you do about it, Abram?"

"Do? There wasn't much I could do. Oh, God, but it hurt so much to see her crying."

"Would you protect her from others as well, Abram?"

"Of course I would. I'd defend her against anyone who tried to hurt her."

"And what would you do?"

"Whatever it took."

"Would you agree, Mr. Knapp, with your son's statement?"

"The boy speaks the truth as he sees it. I guess that's the best answer you're likely to get."

"Answer?"

"To your earlier inquiry. What he does around the house all day. Let's just say he protects his mother. At least in his perverted view."

"Abram, think carefully now before you answer. Can you do that?"

"Certainly."

"You said you would do anything to protect your mother." The voice was quiet now. "Do you feel you would be willing to kill to protect her?"

"Abram, don't answer that!"

"Why, I suppose so. There have been many times I thought – quite seriously, if you want to know – of killing my father."

"Why you mean little son-of-a –"

"Stop it! Both of you. Jack, you're being insulting to us all. And Abram, you don't know what you're saying. We don't have to answer any more of these terrible questions."

"That's true, ma'am, you don't. You can do it down at the station house if that would suit you better."

"We have nothing to hide, Liz. Let's get this over with, once and for all. Then, perhaps, these men will leave us alone. Can we all agree to that?"

"We'll do our best, Mr. Knapp."

"We are trying, sir. Now, Abram, just a few more questions."

"Do you want to hear how I planned to kill my father?"

"That can wait. Let's talk about something else first. Is that all right?"

"Whatever you want."

"Did you know Andre Robson?"

"Who?"

"Andre Robson. I believe your mother's friends called him Mr. Andre."

"Oh, you mean the fortune teller who kept coming to the house."

"You knew him then?"

"No."

"But you just told us you did."

"No. I just said I knew who he was. Can't tell you I knew the man 'cause I didn't."

"Would you recognize him if you saw him again?"

"What kind of a fool do you think I am? He's dead. I won't see him again."

"But you did see him? In this house? And you saw enough of him to know who he was."

"Yes. Yes. And yes."

"Why, Abram, I don't remember your being around on those Monday afternoons."

" Matter of fact, I made it a point to be around. Didn't like the man at all, if you must know the truth."

"Why didn't you like him, Abram?"

"Seemed like more of a shyster than anything else to me. Just played up to that bunch of ladies Mother gathered, got paid well and did damned little for his efforts."

"Care to elaborate?"

"Well, sometimes I'd tiptoe down and stand out there in the hall, listening as he made his rounds of the circle. That's what they did, you know. I peeked once when I was sure nobody would see me. Sit in a big circle and let him answer their questions."

"Do you remember what kind of questions, Abram?"

"What does this have to do with anything?"

"Please, Mother, I don't mind answering. Mostly they

wanted to know silly things, like whether to buy the red silk or the blue velvet, or to serve a pork roast or chicken for Saturday's dinner. I never understood why the man had to talk to spirits – that's what he claimed – to answer such trivial questions."

"Did you hate the man, Abram?"

"Not at the beginning."

"But you felt he made fun of the ladies?"

"That was their business. It made Mother happy and I guess the rest found him entertaining. I know they paid a lot. I heard their discussion after the last time he asked for more money. They seemed to feel it was worth it."

"And you didn't object?"

"Object? Why would I?"

"But then something happened, is that it? Something that made you hate Andre Robson?"

"He hurt my mother."

"Hurt her? What do you mean?"

"They had this big fight. It was terrible. I've never heard Mother angry like that. Not even with Father. She kept begging and begging and the awful man wouldn't listen to her. He kept refusing to do what she wanted. She was crying and screaming and . . . and he just turned and walked away. I wanted to kill him then."

"Do you think your mother wanted him dead?"

"Mother? Oh, no, she wouldn't. She couldn't. You mustn't ever think her a murderer. Not my mother. Why, she couldn't do any wrong. You do know that, don't you? That's why I have to protect her. To keep her safe."

"But you . . . you would have shot Andre Robson to protect your mother. Isn't that what you're saying?"

Abram stood silently. He turned to look at his mother, an unreadable expression in his face. Did these policemen really believe her guilty of murder? No, they mustn't. What would happen to her then? She mustn't be hurt any more.

"I'd do anything for her."

LXXXII

February 1900

"This is absolutely insane. You know that." She turned to face her husband. "You do, don't you, Jack? Abram isn't a killer. Why, Abram couldn't –"

"Think before you finish that, Lizzie."

"If you just hadn't said those awful things to the police!"

"Of course you're absolutely right. I don't know what came over me – though, if you want a semi-educated guess, I imagine I was so relieved when I realized we weren't under suspicion – they were going at it pretty strong there for a while. I never thought they'd take Abram seriously. I don't think I ever have."

"But you don't believe he really killed the man?"

"Lizzie, I know you love him. And he is your son. *Our* son, if you will. But you heard him. He confessed to it."

"I don't believe it. I won't."

"Why would he say such a terrible thing if he weren't telling the truth?"

"Don't you think I've asked myself that countless times, ever since they took him away?"

"For your sake, I wish I could believe there was another, that the real killer if you will, will be found soon. But, Lizzie, we have got to be prepared. The boy confessed."

"But to kill Andre? For me? No, I refuse to accept it."

"I imagine we'll both have to, dear. It shouldn't be long before the trial."

"Then there will be a trial? Maybe that's it! Then he'll change his mind, tell the truth, tell us all what really happened."

"I haven't spent much time yet with our attorney, Lizzie, but I don't believe that's the way things will go."

"How then? What else can happen?"

"I'm told it's all a formality. The boy will be questioned under oath, asked to confirm all he told those policemen last week, and then he'll be sentenced."

"*Sentenced?* Oh, God, I never thought of that. I've been so worried about him, alone in that frightening jail. What do you think they'll do to him?"

"I wish I knew, dear. Our lawyer says there's no evidence to make one believe the killing was planned in advance so he probably won't get the chair –"

"Electro – ? Oh, Jack! No. They wouldn't do that," she paused. "Would they? I'm afraid I've been living from moment to horrible moment, not even questioning the tomorrows."

"There, there, Lizzie." She yielded to his arms. "Don't despair."

"Oh, Jack, whatever shall we do?"

. . .

"Charlie! I don't think I've ever been so happy to see anyone in my life. How are you? More importantly, how is Mother?"

"Your news has been so distressing, Jack. Believe me, I would have been here the minute I heard – but . . . well, Mother isn't good at all. Forgive me, but I felt I had to stay with her."

"I understand, Charlie. Of course."

"Till I realized how serious your situation was. Good God, man! Why didn't you tell me everything right at the beginning?"

"Could you have helped? Really, I mean? I knew Mother was sick and . . . well, with Abram, there just didn't seem much hope. Guess I figured you were of more use where you were."

"I can't believe that. But tell me, how is Lizzie?"

"Better than you might expect. It hasn't been easy. Not for her certainly, not for any of us. I'm sure you can imagine."

"You seem to be holding up all right."

"For a man who's just had his youngest son sentenced to

life in prison, I suppose I am."

"And Lizzie?"

"She's never given up hope. I don't imagine she ever will. I know part of her doesn't accept the boy's guilt."

"But you do? Without question?"

"He said he did it. I suppose, in his twisted way, he had more reason than anybody else. Turns out the boy overheard the whole argument."

"So it's done with then?"

"The trial was blessedly short – at least, I suppose it was a blessing. You know, of course, that the boy offered no defense. He just stood, silent the whole time. Not an expression on his face, not even when the judge pronounced him guilty."

Moments later Lizzie entered the parlor to greet her brother-in-law. "Oh, Charlie, I've been so looking forward to your arrival, actually counting the hours. So how are you? And Mother Knapp?"

"In the best of health – and not doing too poorly. But you, Lizzie, how are you? I was explaining to Jack how terrible I felt not being here with you – both of you – for this awful ordeal."

"I know you had to be with Mother Knapp. Believe me, you've no idea how grateful we both are that you had the time to spend with her. I honestly don't think we could have dealt with anything else."

"You've had more than enough. But tell me, what have you heard from Abram?"

"Very little, if the truth be known. I visit every chance I get, though –" She whirled to face him. "Why didn't you ever tell me just how abysmally dreadful our prisons are? I go – of course I do – but . . . Charlie, it's terrible there!"

"Of course it is, Lizzie. They don't build prisons for the likes of us. But Abram? Tell me about him."

"I wish I could understand what has happened. I wish I could describe it to you. All I know is that he refuses to speak. I visit almost every day. He remains accessible. Some . . . of the prisoners do refuse to see visitors. It isn't that."

"Then he's not spoken to you at all since he was sent to

prison?"

"Not really, Charlie."

"Did he talk to you . . . before he was led from the court house?"

"Only very briefly."

"And what did he have to say then, Lizzie?"

"Oh! That terrible day! The judge passing that despicable sentence. I'll never forget the look on his face. Oh, Charlie, we needed you then. I took his face in my hands, tears streaming down his cheeks, mine too they say, and I kissed him. I kissed his eyes. First one, then the other. Then his forehead. Then one cheek. The other. Thinking back, I don't believe I said a word. 'Oh, Abram' perhaps, more likely not even that. Just stood and hugged him and kept kissing."

"I understand, my dear. But did he say anything to you? Anything at all? Did he offer any explanation for what he'd done?"

"Only that he loved me, that I should know he would do anything for me."

Charlie rushed to comfort her as the sobs began anew. "That was all?"

"All. 'Anything for me.' Or was it 'everything'? I can't remember."

"Lizzie, come, weep, if you think that will help. You knew – you had to know – that the judge would pass sentence."

"I suppose so." She paused to look into the eyes of her brother-in-law. "The real killer is still out there. Once they find him I know Abram will be set free."

"Liz! Do you honestly believe that? No, now stop . . . think what you're saying."

"I wish shaking my head would clear it. I wish, for that matter, I had answers for all your questions. No, I don't believe Abram killed Andre."

"But –"

"Don't say it. I know. He was devoted to me. Unnaturally devoted, if you must. That's what others are saying. And that Abram was not an ordinary child. No one can argue that but, Charlie, you've known him all his life. You've also, if I'm not completely mistaken, seen the good in the boy. Seen all that his father never could."

"But you do know that he was completely fixated on you. You do see that, Lizzie, don't you? Couldn't that be motive enough?"

"That's what the police said. That's what they want us all to believe. And I suppose . . ."

"Yes?"

"Well, just between you and me, the argument I had that day was pretty heated."

"I don't need to hear the details, Lizzie."

"I wasn't planning to give them to you."

"Touché. Go on, please."

"It's just that . . . well, it might make sense. He overheard us, realized how distressed I was – *really* was, Charlie . . . and went after the man."

"So the police are right?"

"Maybe. Maybe not."

"How can you still doubt?"

"It's simple. I love my son." She turned away as if to leave him, then turned back. "Besides, if he did do it, what happened to all that money?"

LXXXIII

Easter 1900

"Are you sure you feel up to this, Maggie?"

"Feel up to it? Everett, I wouldn't miss the Eastertide services for anything. There isn't a more beautiful time of the year. All right, I know you're going to argue Christmas. And I can't disagree, especially now that I, too, am with child. But, musically, my vote has to be with Easter. Sorry, love. I may be a mother-to-be but I've been an organist a lot, lot longer."

"Then you stubbornly insist on playing all the services?"

"*Stubbornly?* Everett! It's my greatest joy."

"And nobody at St. Paul's had the least objection?"

"Why should they? My choir robes hide my delicate position, as they are wont to call it. Nobody knows except those who need to. And, my dear, you know I feel perfectly fine. Better than that. As strong and as healthy as an ox." She giggled. "Though I can't say I've personally known too many oxes. *Oxes?* Oh, dear, you know what I mean."

"Of course I do. It's just that we've waited so long for a child – I suppose I'm still afraid something might go wrong. Women in your condition – even young women – are told to stay at home. Rest. That's what the word means. *Confinement.*"

"Confinement? Exactly! I know how much you want the baby, Everett. And, believe me, I do, too. But stay home? Oh, please. I don't want to be punished for the miracle we've been given. The wardens at St. Paul's have been wonderful to me. Don't be any less – please. I beg you."

"Of course not, Maggie. I only want what's best for you . . . and our child, of course."

"Very well then, we shall have it."

. . .

"Margaret! You look positively radiant tonight! How are you?"

"Peter! I hardly expected to see you here. Did you come for the evensong service?"

"Only as an excuse to see you again. I swear, you play more beautifully than ever."

"Why, thank you. Of course, if you want to hear the glorious music, you should come tomorrow morning."

"I considered it. Really I did. Quite seriously, in fact. But an old reprobate like me in church on Easter morning?"

"Last I heard, things were getting more liberal. I wouldn't expect the walls to fall, if that's what you were afraid of."

"Not quite. Then again, you never know."

How easy it was to laugh with this man! How easy to forget, erase the unpleasantnesses, all those things she didn't want to think about. All those things she couldn't deal with. Not now. But Peter . . . how to explain a warm corner of her heart that opened just for him?

"So what's the answer?"

"Hmm? I'm sorry, Peter, what was the question?"

"How are you? How is everything?"

"Oh." She looked down at her hands, waiting before answering. "Fine, just fine."

"Keeping busy?" He leaned towards her.

"If only I could find the extra hours I'd like." She sighed, reflecting. "But tell me, how are you?"

"Busy. Active. Students. Performances. Not enough to mean much, but keeping busy. Mostly, thinking of you."

She shook her head. "That's no good."

"No chance then?"

"None whatsoever," daring now to look at him.

"You're sure?"

"Absolutely."

She watched without feeling as he turned and started to leave.

"Margaret?"

"Yes?"

"I forgot to ask. How's Jane?"

"Janie? Why –"

"Don't you remember? Last time I saw you, you were packing to hurry to her side. Something about her husband, a leg. Damn, I'm sorry I can't remember. To tell the truth, all I could think about that day was you."

"Janie is fine, Peter. Vernon had his leg amputated. Spirits as good as new now and all's well." She felt safe enough to look deep into his eyes and almost regretted it. "Thanks for asking."

"Thank you. I'll be around."

"Don't be too much of a stranger, Peter." Maggie blushed at the forwardness of her words. "I mean . . . the church is always open."

. . .

Maggie looked up, relieved to see her husband at last. "I was beginning to worry."

"I couldn't get through the throng, dear, the masses waiting here to congratulate you. I thought you were spectacular. In fact, I could sense the excitement building throughout the congregation. Come on. Can I help with your music? I'm sure you're ready to fold up and head home for a quiet afternoon."

"Help accepted . . .with deep gratitude. Say, did you see the Knapps back there?"

"Can't say that I did. Honestly, I doubt if I took my eyes off you."

"They were back in their usual pew. Funny, even after all this time nobody else has dared sit there."

"How did they look?"

"About as you'd expect. Considering. He's as stiff as an old soldier, no sign of any emotion in that face."

"I'd expect that with a son guilty of murder. Guess one never knows what to expect from the ones next to him. Proximity, not emotional closeness. Hell, you know what I mean."

"I know I'm not used to your swearing, Everett. Do you find it that upsetting?"

"Suppose I do at that. Haven't known many murderers in my life."

"You know, dear, there are more times than you can imagine when I wish I had wings – big as I am – and could fly out around the congregation to get a better view at the people praying here. Still, I count the sermons and long prayers as my personal blessings."

"Are you going to tell me you don't pray with your eyes tightly closed?"

"Everett, if I did I'd never see anybody. Sermon of course, but by then, most of 'em have already found me more interesting that the rector."

"That's a terrible thing to say!"

"Hardly. That's the lovely part of praying, if you want to know the truth."

"Which is?"

"All those bowed heads and closed eyes. Why, I can gaze to my heart's content. And should I catch the glance of a pair of wavering eyes – and believe me, it happens more often than you might think, why I just have to look stern and the eyes clamp shut leaving me, of course, free to go right on checking out all the others."

"Maggie!"

"Everett!"

"All right then, Madame. So tell me, what did you see when you examined Mrs. Knapp?"

"It was upsetting, if you want to know. I saw a strong woman. Rigid. Silent. And yet I sensed a deep sorrow tearing her slowly apart. Know what I was thinking most of all?"

"I wouldn't even hazard a guess."

"I kept wishing I knew her better, knew her well enough that I could have rushed to her side. Well, probably not in the middle of the service. Not even at St. Paul's. But I so wanted her to know – somehow – that I understood her pain, that I would take it on myself, if I could, that . . ."

"Does any of what you're saying make sense to you,

dear?"

"Sense? The feeling was so strong her pain made me ache. Literally. And yet you don't understand, do you? No, I thought not. What was it you asked? If it made any sense at all to me? No, I guess not. Nor, I don't suppose, will it ever matter."

LXXXIV

Spring 1900

"There, now. That wasn't as bad as you expected. Admit it. It really wasn't, was it?"

"Yes, Charlie, it was," Lizzie sighed. "You may be a dear and, for all I know, an excellent attorney and certainly as good a brother-in-law as one could hope for, but to make me show my face on Easter morning – and in that church, no less – why, I never should have listened to you."

"Balderdash, Lizzie!" Jack interrupted vehemently. "It was time you got out of the house. Let people see you. Me, too, of course. Let them know we're still here. Whatever happened, it was hardly our fault."

"Well, I wouldn't say that . . ."

Charlie interrupted, "No, listen to him, Liz. Jack lacks a certain way with words, a finesse which I suppose would have come in handy many times over the years, but he does know what to say."

"What's this? A compliment from my own brother!"

"This isn't the time for frivolity, either one of you," she scolded.

"We're not being frivolous, Liz. Jack's a good man. I'm just not sure you always understand that."

"And Abram?"

"Ah, yes. Abram."

"Is there any hope at all?"

"I wish I could be more encouraging. I didn't think the judge would give him life without a chance for parole." Charlie hesitated. "To be honest, I did expect a bit of a show of leniency. The boy's never been in trouble before." He caught both pairs of eyes before their shields rose protectively. "Well, nothing at least to influence the courts. And I don't believe anyone's convinced it was premeditated."

"But wouldn't it be grand if we knew?" Jack asked.

"Why do you suppose the boy still refuses to talk?"

"I don't know," Charlie scratched his head. "I'd like – believe me, as much as the two of you – to make some sense out of this whole mess. Seems so unnecessarily tangled, and yet . . ."

"Your argument – what we heard in court – was that Abram went after Andre because of the fight we'd had. I don't imagine, not if he won't tell us, that we'll ever know exactly what was in his head. Was he trying to avenge me, as the court would have it, or perhaps simply attempting to get Andre to change his mind, to forget all that nonsense about hotel rooms and additional customers. Why did he go?"

"You're closer to him than anybody, Lizzie."

"I believe that. And yet . . ."

"He's said nothing to you at all?"

"Nothing, Charlie." She paused. "Well, that's not exactly true. Last time I saw him, he said something strange. Very strange."

"And you didn't tell me?"

"I would have, Jack, had it made any sense."

"What did he say, Lizzie?"

"Let me try to remember the exact words. Something about being strong. Oh, yes! That was it. But I tell you, it made no sense."

"Try, Lizzie."

"He said . . . and I'm pretty sure these are exactly the words he used, he said that if he was going to go through with it, that I had to be strong, that I had to stand up to . . . to . . "

"Yes?"

"To you, Jack."

"That is exactly what he said?"

"Yes. Only if I promised to stand up to, I remember, 'to Father.' Yes, and to be strong. Always to be strong."

"And you, Lizzie, what did you say to that?"

"What could I say? I said I would. Of course I would. He's

my son."

. . .

"Time for you to cheer up!" Charlie stretched his body full length in the rope hammock, giving it a swing as a smile crossed his face. "Now, Lizzie, all I need is a nice summery drink."

"And a stiff one for me, as well."

"Jack! You're home early."

"Hard to work on a midsummer's day as beautiful as this. I wanted to enjoy as much of it as I could."

"No problem getting away then?"

"None. Old Man Larkin must feel I have my hands full without having to worry more about his latest projects. Though, to tell the truth, I've never seen so many ideas percolating in any company at one time."

"I'm surprised he'd let you go."

"I'm not. He knows a good man when he has one. I'm a hard worker, always have been. And will be again."

"*Will be?*"

"Face it, you two. It's a little hard for a man to concentrate on premium desks and model furniture, much less the latest lines of soaps and perfumes, hard that is with a son in prison and a mother newly laid in the ground. I mean, what else can happen?" He glanced at his wife and brother, catching the unspoken message in both sets of eyes. "No, don't answer that one."

"Lizzie. Jack. I swear you wouldn't accept good fortune if it landed right in your laps."

"Good? A son in prison?"

"A mother just buried?"

"Some things, at times many things perhaps, we don't have much power over. You're doing everything for Abram you can. And Mother lived an extraordinarily long and good life. Healthy, out in the fields, visiting her biddy friends, right up to her last illness, and even that blessedly short. I'm not saying things couldn't be better. They always could . . . for anyone, I'm sure."

"Then?"

"I am merely saying that you're the parents of a budding talent – My God, a veritable genius, to read his reviews – and you're so wrapped up in the sorrows of the past six months that you can't give credit where it's due."

"Oh, Charlie, we aren't forgetting Ralph. Why, the girls speak of little else. And you should read the letters Clara sends home from college. That *Purple Peanut* has taken the juvenile market by storm. I don't think a new children's series has ever captured the imagination –"

"Or the purses –"

"Quite as quickly. We are excited for Ralph. It's just that
. . ."

"My point is made, lady. You have a very talented son whose literary abilities are being recognized far and wide, yes, even as we speak. *The Purple Peanut* series is finding its way into the hands of young American children throughout this wild and rugged land."

'It is quite wonderful, isn't it?"

"Wonderful? Watch your words, ma'am. Your son is more than wonderful. No, I'll take that back. All your children, my very precious nieces and nephews, are more than merely wonderful. And I'm sure each harbors a unique talent that I pray to God will in time be recognized. But, in the meantime, your older son, undoubtedly influenced by his two older and most fabulously brilliant sisters –"

"Charlie?"

"Hush. Let me continue for I do know that Ralph's series of children's books is leaping off the shelves in the stores as quickly as they can be rushed into print. Just goes to prove that the country was fed up to here with all the old morality tales. Long on sermons, short on action – or interest, as we all know now. Then along comes *The Purple Peanut*, hardly the name I'd have chosen for an imaginary friend but hey! I'm not pulling in the money right now either. My point simply being that our children – this country's children – were ready for books with imagination and adventure and, yes, folks, fun. Good clean fun. Why, I've read each book, short as they are, the minute it hits the stores. Can't say I've ever gotten tired of one either. The lad has a fanciful imagination. Magic, pure magic. Wish I'd listened more to him when he was a mere tad."

"I don't think you'd have found your Purple Peanut there."

"But the imagination?"

"He had to have that, of course he did. Looking back . . ."

"She's right, you know. She didn't see it. I didn't. Neither did you."

"A late bloomer, is that what you think?"

"Not necessarily. It's just that Ralph was quiet –"

"So quiet. Such an easy child –"

"And between the girls, John, and Abram –"

"And James –"

"Enough, you two. Let's not get morose again. Let's concentrate on the good. Ralph has found his gift. He's immensely talented and we're all able now to share his joy."

"If only . . ."

"No, Lizzie. Don't look back. Look here. What do you see in my hands?"

"What –?"

"That's our today. Yours. Jack's. Mine. Our day to appreciate. And I don't think we should wait. Go find your Kodak camera. We're going to take a long automobile ride out into the country."

"Charlie, you're a genius!"

"No, your son is the genius. I'm just ready to enjoy what purports to be a heavenly June afternoon. Hurry up now. Let's go!"

LXXXV

December 1900 through January 1901

"Oh, dear! You caught me dozing." Maggie rose quickly to greet her husband. "What a lovely surprise to see you home so early."

"It's easier to get away from the factory since Larkin cut back on the hours his employees are expected to work. That forty minutes a day makes a lot of difference – even to yours truly."

"Tell me, Everett, is it really working? You know, to pay the same amount for less work?"

"Surprisingly, it seems to be working perfectly. Morale's up and they all love the old man, even more than before."

"I can't imagine anyone working a mere nine hours a day. Makes me almost want to return."

"Maggie, you never were factory help. You always got better than that." He leaned to kiss her. "Deservedly so, too."

"But of course."

"So tell me, Miss Mama, how's our little angel doing?"

"I swear she gets sweeter every day. And such a good baby."

"I know. I peek at her and wish only that she could stay as little and sweet as she is today."

"I can't promise you the *little* part but I imagine she'll remain as sweet, certainly if she takes after her father."

. . .

"Lizzie, you've been handing out those Pan-American stock certificates as if they were worthless. Ten dollars each is still a bit of money."

"But, dear, you know it's for a good cause. And everyone here in Buffalo is investing. I haven't seen people so excited, so eager to rally for one cause. It is, isn't it?"

"Exciting? You bet. But –"

"Besides, I'm hardly throwing them away. Some to tuck in the stockings for each of the children and –"

"Your children are grown adults, Liz."

"But no one outgrows the desire for a Christmas stocking."

"I won't get into an argument on that, my dear. But the others –"

"Just the help, Jack. We always give them something at Christmastime."

"But a certificate? What if they prove worthless?"

"Oh, that won't happen. Why, everyone I talk to is positive the Exposition will be a marvelous moneymaker. Why would you, of all people, doubt it?"

"I don't. I just mentioned a bit of caution might not be out of place. But I imagine what's done is done. The staff should be pleased with your foresight if nothing else."

"Oh."

"Yes?"

"Well, I did give one other. Don't look at me like that, dear. I meant only good."

"And who was the lucky recipient?"

"Mrs. Hopkins. Actually, her baby."

"Hopkins? *Hopkins?* Do I know the name?"

"He works in your company, if I remember correctly, but no, you probably don't. They were in Shakespeare Club back when I was a member."

"And you favored the members with ten dollar certificates?"

"Don't be silly! Of course not."

"Then why Mr. Hopkins?"

"Not *mister*, dear, his wife. She's the organist at St. Paul's."

"Aha! Now I see! A late touch of religion then."

"Stop teasing. There's just something about her . . . I can't explain. Perhaps I've never really thought about it. She's nice."

"Nice? *Nice* is worth ten dollars nowadays?"

"Not that. She just seemed to go out of her way to commiserate when Abram was sent to prison. Not many did. But Maggie was so sympathetic I felt she understood my pain. Anyway, it's done. If you're upset, I'll try to find ten dollars of my own to pay you back."

"My, dear! Don't talk nonsense. It's a small price to pay if it pleases you so."

"It does."

"So tell me. Actually, the question was on the tip of my tongue when I came in. You speak of Christmas which means that other big date is just around the corner."

"I trust, sir, you are referring to New Year's Eve. Am I correct?"

"Indeed you are. I don't expect it to be as special as last year's – though we've celebrated that night quite frequently, haven't we, dear? – but I was rather hoping you'd enjoy going back to the ball at the Club."

"Oh, yes. We have so much to celebrate this year. I mean . . ."

"I haven't forgotten the boy either."

"I just wish there was something we could do."

"I think you're doing it, Lizzie, with your frequent visits, little gifts, all the things you do to let him know he isn't forgotten."

"I can't tell you how much it means that you have become reconciled to him, dear."

"*Reconciled* might be too strong a word."

"But you do visit. I know. I've heard him speak quite kindly of you, Jack. Why, he even seems proud now that you're his father."

"Proud?"

"You should have heard him – oh, I wish you could have – he went on and on after you were elected to the board of the new automobile club. That was a real feather in your cap, Jack. And then to be able to attend the show in New York

City –"

"First auto show in the country! Think of it, Lizzie!"

"We're all proud, you know that. But none prouder than Abram."

"It has been a good year. If I were a praying man, I'd be down on my knees thanking God for all the blessings we've received."

"Especially when I remember last Christmas, and then those terrible days in January. I honestly feared we'd be driven out of town, the scandal and all the gossip."

"Your women friends never really came back though, did they?"

"So what? Who needs a bunch of high-falutin' gossiping matrons? A waste of time, if you ask me. I couldn't be happier back at the library with Ardith and Jo. True friends are a blessing. I should have known that from the beginning."

"To an even brighter future then! Our friends, the good that lies ahead now that McKinley's wisely back in the White House, to life itself!"

"Indeed. To 1901!"

. . .

"Are you certain you'll be happy staying home this New Year's, Maggie?"

"With dear Rose, can you truly doubt it? We've had many years to party – though, as I recall, neither of us cared much for such shindigs even when we could."

"Not sure I'd care to be out on the streets this year anyway, not with that Nation woman and her ilk smashing away at our public bars."

"That was in Kansas, dear, hardly back in our civilized East."

"Then perhaps you'd better warn that brother of yours. I imagine Omaha is still enough of a cow town to become quite uncivilized at times."

"Well, I'll definitely advise him to stay away from wild women carrying axes. That should do it, don't you think?"

"Have you heard any more about his trip east?"

"He promised to give us a date early next month. I hope he doesn't postpone it again."

"He's a busy man, Maggie –"

"Of course he is. And so successful I still feel overwhelmed at his good fortune. But he's also uncle now to the loveliest little girl in all Christendom and I want him to ogle her properly. Besides, if he doesn't hurry up, she'll be running out by herself to meet his train."

. . .

"Lizzie. Lizzie! Are you here, Liz?"

"In here." She folded the paper quickly, laying it on the sofa as she rose to meet her husband. "Home again early, I see."

He glanced at the depression she had left in the deep upholstery and spotted the paper there. "Not interrupting anything, am I?"

"Nothing I can't get back to later." She kissed him. "Fascinating article though. I can't imagine living that long. Or doing so much."

"Whoa, there. Can we back up? 'Fraid you lost me."

"I'm sorry. I was just reading about Queen Victoria, all the pomp that accompanied her funeral actually. You know, I can't picture a world without her ruling the British Empire."

"The end of an era, I fear," Jack agreed.

"It's hardly an auspicious way to begin a new century, is it?"

"Aha! I see you've been converted, too."

"Converted?" Lizzie looked up. "Oh, you mean to the new definition –"

"New?"

"Well, new to me. Anyway, I don't see that it matters much when the Twentieth Century began. Though, yes, I readily accept it starting this month. In fact I'll take all the new opportunities I can get."

"I'm sure you would, dear."

"I was serious though."

"About what?" Jack asked. "Besides the Twentieth

Century, that is."

"That her death seems a most inauspicious beginning. Wouldn't it have been far better had she departed quietly with the old century?"

"Lizzie, I swear you'll never stop wanting to put this entire world into a strict order. People simply don't die when it's convenient. But why inauspicious?"

"I can't really put my finger on it. I just know I get the shivers thinking about it."

"About what?"

"New beginnings shouldn't start with death. Do you think there'll be more?"

"Is that what you're afraid of?"

"I wish I knew. I think so."

"My dear, I promise you there will be plenty." He faced her confused countenance. "Deaths."

"But –?"

"People die all the time, Liz, and they're sure to go right on doing it. Nasty habit, but it can't be helped."

"Now you're teasing."

"It's quite a silly thought, if you think about it. Or," catching a warning flash in her eyes, "am I misinterpreting what you're trying to say?"

"Perhaps. I don't know. I just have this awful premonition. That the Queen won't be the last major figure to die this year. Do I sound silly?"

"Let's hope you're mistaken. But you haven't given me a chance to tell you why I'm here."

"No, though I'd guess, from the look on your face, it must be good news."

. . .

Lizzie caught the gleam in her brother-in-law's eyes, returned his forthright smile and waited in silence until the table was cleared, the staff returned to the kitchen.

"And now, my dear, you must tell us the occasion for your return. Why, I could hardly believe it when Jack told me you'd be coming home with him for dinner. You will be staying, won't you?"

"For a while, yes, thank you. I should like that very much."

"But did you know – I mean, when you were here for the Holidays – did you know then you'd be coming back so soon?"

"Yes, Charlie, this time I confess to sharing Lizzie's confusion. Not that you aren't welcome, I hardly meant it to sound that way –"

"No offense taken, I assure you. Nor, trust me, did I come with any intention of being a man of mystery."

They joined him in laughter as Jack rose to open the bottle of brandy on the sideboard.

"Yes, thank you. All I'm trying to say is that . . . well, when I came for the Holidays I had no intention of infringing on your hospitality so soon again."

"Jack never meant you weren't –"

"I know that, Lizzie. It's just – well, I do have a career you know. It's just that, when I was here, I had an idea. Just a little seed which began to grow."

"But –?"

"Hush, Lizzie, let the gardener finish."

"The more I thought about it, the better I liked it. But, you see, I had no idea if it would work. If, for that matter, I'd be able to do anything."

"If you can't grease those wheels in Western Pennsylvania, who the devil can?"

"Turns out that was pretty much the case."

"You can be as slow as your brother when the mood moves you. Please hurry. What is it you're hinting of?"

"Simply this. I know how upset you've been with Abram in prison."

"Charlie, don't tell me you've found a way to get him out! Or –" Her face reflected her true puzzlement, "have you found the true murderer?"

"No, Lizzie. I don't imagine that person will ever be found – if Abram didn't do it and . . . well, we can't really be certain of that, now can we?"

"But you said –"

"Let the man speak, Liz."

"You asked if I had found a way of getting him out of prison."

"And you did? Oh! Is it possible?"

"Liz –"

"Lizzie, you must understand that he has to remain behind bars. The judge passed down that sentence and nothing has happened to overturn it."

"But what then?"

"I think you'll both agree that there is a question of Abram's mental health. Whatever his motivation, whatever happened on . . . well, that day, his silence and refusal to defend himself is hardly what one would call . . . well, sane."

"We all know he's –"

"Charlie, are you saying you consider my son insane? How could you?" Lizzie glared in anger. "And you his uncle."

"Lizzie, let me finish please. I know what people think of the insane. Maybe it is better to be a criminal. But it isn't better for Abram. Surely you can see that."

"But –"

"What is it you have in mind, Charlie?"

"I'd like to see him transferred to the State Hospital outside Warren."

"An insane asylum!"

"An insane asylum?"

"It would be better for him than prison."

"How can you even say that?"

"Think about it, Jack. Lizzie. Granted there are still bars on the windows and wardens at the gates. It wouldn't be a holiday but neither would he be locked away with hardened criminals. And your boy, whatever else he is, is a soft and naive young man. Really still more of a child."

"And you think he'd be better off – more protected – in an insane asylum?"

"I like to think so."

"But –"

"Think of it as a hospital, Liz. I've seen the place. Not

good, granted, and I'd discourage your visiting but it's close to home for me and I'll promise to do all I can for the lad."

"You're telling me I couldn't see him?"

"Lizzie, Charlie might have a point. We both know how much you love the lad but you always return from prison torn up yourself. Of course it's difficult. That's precisely what Charlie is saying. Let him visit for you. I'm sure he'd write frequently, to let you know how Abram's doing."

"I wouldn't be able to see him ever again?"

"Forever's a long time but maybe . . . well, once the boy is treated and becomes better . . ."

Lizzie eyes dropped to her folded hands in her lap. Jack and Charlie wisely waited while she mulled over this startling proposition. At last she looked up.

"I'm sorry. I didn't mean to get so distraught. It just came as such a shock. You do understand that, Charlie?"

"Of course."

"I don't know anything about your State Hospital. Personally, I think asylums must all be dreadful places. No, let me go on. Please. On that point I am grateful for your not encouraging me to see for myself. For, if Abram does go, I would like to rest in peace, harboring images of a good place where he can be happy and safe. I have to rely on your advice for that, Charlie. If you feel it's for the best, then I for one am willing to accept your decision."

"But will you be able to do it, Charlie? I assume a judge would have to agree? And across state lines? Is it even possible?"

"I wouldn't have brought it up if I hadn't done some pretty thorough checking first. The judge is quite certain to go along. You'll have to petition the court but, trust me, he's none too happy incarcerating a boy still in his teens. He'll be quite relieved to turn him over to another jurisdiction. No, I don't see any problem there. None at least that can't be easily taken care of."

"And the . . . the hospital?"

"No objection at that end, I assure you."

"But, Charlie, you are convinced it's better for Abram?"

"I'm sure that he'd be kept in a separate area. After all, he is being punished for killing a man."

"But he's not a threat to anyone –"

"I believe you."

"And it will be better for him?"

"That I truly believe."

LXXXVI

Spring 1901

"Margaret Hopkins, this time I honestly believe you have lost your mind!"

"That's a terrible thing to say to me, Everett. I merely said I wanted to return to St. Paul's. I miss my music, dear. I need to be able to play again."

"But our daughter's not yet a year."

"And she's doing perfectly well. She doesn't need me every single minute of every single day."

"Next I suppose you'll be telling me you want to return as the regular organist."

"Now that you mention it, I did say I'd like to take over my old position –"

"Maggie!"

"In the fall, dear, not until the fall. That's quite six months away."

"Then why now?"

"Not *now*, dear. The recital wouldn't be until June."

"But why not just wait until September?"

"Because the great man died before Christmas and, if we don't do a memorial service soon, it'll be much too late to do one at all. Besides, I already have to add a second name. If I keep putting it off, God only knows how many more there'll be."

"But why do you have to be the one who does it? I haven't heard many complaints about the organist they have now."

"And I don't imagine you will. He's amazingly good. But don't you see? That's my point."

"You lost me there."

"The position at the cathedral's been just perfect for me

and . . . well, I just don't want to lose it. Besides, an organist has to keep practicing or she'll forfeit the ability she has."

"But you have been practicing, I know that. Near as I can tell, you and Baby Rose spend more mornings in that dark church than you do in the park."

"Good heavens, you're not supposing I neglect our child, are you? She gets her sunshine, I assure you."

"Maggie, Maggie, calm down. You're a wonderful mother. You dote every bit as much as I and . . . well, just look at Rose. She couldn't be a healthier or a prettier baby. As perfect as . . . yes, as the flower."

"It was a good name, wasn't it?"

"The best. As is she. And her mother, of course. I only want you both to be happy – always."

"Then give me a kiss, dear, and let me get a blanket for Rose. It looks like a perfect morning for an outing."

"If you hurry, perhaps you can walk me to the trolley stop."

"Oh, may we? I can be ready in just a moment." She turned before leaving the room. "Never going to get you in one of those automobiles, are we?"

"Still can't see any use in 'em. Trolley's been there for a long time. Suits me just fine."

LXXXVII

June 1901

"You certainly do have your admirers."

"But, I haven't seen him in –"

"*Him?* I was referring to Mrs. Knapp, Maggie. Who did you think I meant?"

"Oh, dear, I don't know. How foolish of me. But isn't Elizabeth Knapp a dear? She's been so generous to us – and the baby. I'm sorry I didn't get to know her better when she was in Shakespeare Club."

"Do you – oh! That's she coming now, isn't it?"

"Elizabeth. Mr. Knapp. How good of you to come."

"We wouldn't have missed this for anything. Your playing was positively superb. Why, I was saying to Jack just hours ago that I would bet this whole idea was yours."

"Idea?"

"To do a commemorative recital honoring both Sir Arthur Sullivan and Giuseppe Verdi. *Music from A to V.* Terrific idea. And done so very well."

"It was my pleasure, I assure you. Their music positively flows."

"My wife is too modest to take the credit that's her due but, yes, the entire concept was Maggie's from start to finish."

"Then you must be –"

"I'm sorry. Elizabeth, you may remember my husband, Everett."

"I do indeed. And I'm the one who's been remiss. Maggie, Everett, may I present my husband, Jack, and his bro – Oh, where did that scamp get to now? I wanted you to meet Jack's brother. He has to be one of your biggest fans."

Moments later Lizzie identified him in the crowd, pointing

him out to Maggie and Everett. Maggie found it difficult to keep her eyes from this handsome stranger. Or was he? Something about him seemed so familiar. Or did he only remind her of someone else?

. . .

"Well, isn't this something? Here we are, all together again. And so soon. Everett, Maggie, and oh! this must be the baby. Isn't she lovely? Rose, isn't it?"

The child ran to her mother, burrowing her head between Maggie's knees. By the time the formalities were finished, Rose had forgotten her shyness, turning to stare curiously at the two strangers. At last, eyes locked with those of Jack, she broke into a big grin.

"It's obvious you're used to youngsters, Mr. Knapp."

"As a matter of fact, I am. But please, not Mister. It's Jack."

"Thank you."

"But why are we standing here talking? This is my very first visit to the Exposition and I'm dying to see absolutely everything."

"Ours, too – time to be here. It certainly is impressive . . . for Buffalo, I mean."

"For absolutely any place, if you want to know what I think."

"Shall we make the rounds together? We're hoping Jack's brother will find us later. He's supposed to be on his way."

"For a while then, though I'm sure you'll understand if we leave when Rose gets tired. She can hardly be expected to make it through the entire day."

"Nor should she be. Though I dare say I'd love to see her face when the lights come on."

"And Maggie's as well. Can't say either of us has ever seen such a display of electric lights."

"Who has? This display promises to put Buffalo on the map once and for all. Nobody will ever forget our Pan-American Exposition. Why, I heard even the President plans to attend."

"He should. I can't imagine a grander sight anywhere."

"Where do you think we should begin?

"I don't know . . . but of course. The Larkin Building. Jack says it's quite grand."

"Haven't seen it but, knowing the old man –"

"There. That has to be it."

. . .

"Everett, you could have described that building to me from now till doomsday without coming close. I've never been so overwhelmed in all my life!"

"What? With a demonstration of soap making? Come on, Maggie, you worked for Larkin, too."

"I was hardly talking about soap – though, now that you mention it, even that part of the building was crowded, wasn't it? Personally, I couldn't get over the columns around that huge dome. Who else would ever have thought of making the supports out of Larkin products? Perfume, powder, Heaven knows what else."

"I can't think of a better way to advertise –"

"Or a more subtle way, right? Your boss is a genius."

"Don't think that's ever been in doubt."

"Tell you though, I was most impressed with the rooms."

"Rooms? Oh, you mean the furnishings?"

"And all those accessories. Imagine being able to furnish an entire house with premiums earned just from buying soap!"

"As long as they keep paying me," Everett smiled, "I'll be happy to let you furnish ours anyway you wish."

"I knew there was some reason I loved you so."

"Is the baby sleeping?"

"I imagine we'll have to wake her for supper. That was quite a long outing."

"Let's take advantage of the peace. I'll fix some lemonade and meet you on the back porch."

. . .

"Now we know what time the lights go off as well. I haven't been up that late since –"

"New Year's Eve at least."

"Right you are!"

"I thought the place was magical in the daytime. Then all those lights!"

"And the Electric Tower. I couldn't have imagined anything near as grand. Those tiny fairy lights left me speechless –"

"*Fairy lights,* Liz?"

"You know what I mean. It was like seeing the entire tower covered in glittering jewels. And then – oh! When all those other lights came on! I was absolutely overwhelmed."

"Then I did spy a tear?"

"I didn't realize you were watching so closely, Jack. No, I won't apologize. Some things are worth shedding a tear or two for."

"How 'bout a brandy on the veranda? Lizzie?"

"No, thank you. I don't think I can hold my eyes open another fifteen minutes."

"We won't be long, Liz. Good night."

"Think I will take you up on your offer of a nightcap, Jack. Only, if you don't mind, I'd prefer a tumbler of Scotch rather than your brandy. I feel surfeited in sweets."

"Poured as you speak, sir. Would you mind if we took our drinks into the garden?"

"Eager to drink up even more of this perfect night, are you? Can't say I blame you, Jack. Will this do?"

"Further, if you don't mind."

"Aha! Methinks this man has purpose to his movement!"

"I always said you were the smart brother."

"But not a mind-reader."

"Has Lizzie said anything to you about Abram?"

"Why, no, she hasn't. Oh," Charlie paused. "I see. It should have been the first thing she asked; that's what you're getting at, isn't it?"

"I would have expected it to come up. She knows – as do I – that you'll tell us when you see the boy. Believe me, we both appreciate the time you're giving –"

"I wish I could do more."

"But he is all right? What is it like there?"

"I'll tell you, Jack, it's not what I expected. It's a pretty dire place, if you want the truth."

"But the boy – he's all right?"

"I suppose so. I keep telling myself it's better than prison. It has to be." Charlie took a long sip from his drink. "But it's filthy. Stinking. Too many prisoners – though they call them patients, and too few to look after them. Herding's what it is, not care."

"And the boy? Has he accepted it? Does he seem . . . well, happy?"

"Abram hasn't changed, Jack. I look at him and it's as if he weren't there. Like a shell with no inside."

"Sounds to me you're convinced he really is insane."

"I wish I could accept even that. He acts like he is, I suppose. The doctors believe it – though I doubt he's looked at by one even once a month."

"What then?"

"It's hard to explain. I've had time and the opportunity to watch him, to see him when he doesn't know he's being observed. Then – I don't mind telling you just thinking of it sends shivers up my spine –"

"Good God, Charlie, what is it? What do you see?"

"I get the strangest feeling Abram just made up his mind never to speak again."

"That's crazy! But why?"

"It's almost as if by keeping quiet, he can protect . . . no, it makes no sense. The horrifying part is that, if I didn't know better, I'd say he was as rational as you or I."

"As sane?"

"As sane, Jack."

LXXXVIII

September 1901

"That racket's enough to give anyone a headache."

"Sorry, Maggie; but we can hardly expect the workmen to stop. Larkin is a real stickler when it comes to finishing his jobs on time and, God knows, we've heard little else but his need for the expanded manufacturing area as well as new office space."

"But, Everett, this is huge!"

"Let's start at the top and work down. There'll be elevators running by December but –"

"No problem. Are those the stairs?"

Words grew fewer as the two climbed higher. As with all the other buildings John Larkin helped design, this would be completely fireproofed with all the interior walls eventually plastered and whitewashed. His feelings on the subject were well-known: that the brightness added to a general feeling of cheer and good health. As they climbed, Everett slowly expounded on the many innovations currently being installed: intercom telephones between departments, a female rest room, coffee kitchen near by – don't make the joke, Maggie, we've all heard it many times, even an in-house savings department to encourage the employees' thrift.

"Is that something we should look into, dear?"

"Already have. I signed up for an account for little Rose."

"I trust it will be a better investment than those terrible Pan-American stock certificates. I remember how dreadful Lizzie Knapp felt when they were declared worthless."

"She wasn't the only one to lose that time. But Larkin . . . well, his word is as good as gold. Besides, my dear, they're promising interest of five per cent."

"I suspect your daughter will grow up wealthy as well as beautiful. But what are the men working on over there?"

"That? Oh, that's where the ventilating system will be placed. They say that all the air in the entire building – yes, all two-hundred-thousand feet of it – can be changed in just three minutes."

Maggie cut Everett's explanation short. "Listen. Are those other voices I hear?"

"Ah, Elizabeth! Jack! Another man with the same notion, I gather."

"Good to see you again, Maggie. Everett. This is quite something, isn't it?"

"Positively unbelievable."

"We just ducked in so Jack could show me where his office will be," Lizzie replied. "Isn't the news terrible?"

"McKinley, you mean? I still can't get over it – shooting the President, and right here at that."

"What's the latest you've heard?"

"Nothing this morning."

"Of course yesterday was a bad day but, before that, he seemed to be recovering quite well. I'm sure the downturn will prove only temporary. Simply can't imagine a man so beloved dying. Not like this."

"Let's hope you're right. I can't recall seeing much else in any of the papers this entire week."

"Well, ladies," Jack interrupted. "We're back to the main floor which, as they say, completes your tour."

"I can't wait to come back once it's finished. You know, it does make me almost wish I were still working. There've been so many improvements over the years."

"Why, Maggie, I had no idea you were ever employed here. What did you do?"

"Just a lowly clerk, I fear, Liz, but I loved every minute of it. The people, the conditions, especially dear Mr. Larkin. If it hadn't been for his generosity I don't know if I ever would have been able to go into music."

"That's a story I must hear. Would you care to join us for lunch at the Club?"

"Is it all right, dear?"

"Of course, Maggie. Dare say we could all use a bit of cheer after this past week."

The foursome chatted as they crossed the large entrance hall, Jack stepping ahead to open the door to the street. They stopped dead in their tracks, suddenly aware of the cacophony of sirens and church bells.

"Oh, no," the four sighed in unison. "The President."

. . .

Maggie smiled to herself as she turned to the final page of the Toccata. Coming back to St. Paul's had been a godsend. She loved this church, finding a warmth in its cold walls she knew no other place.

Something was different.

Somebody else was also in the chancel. She didn't allow her playing to ritard as her senses scanned the room. Was there cause for alarm? Though Everett had frequently warned her about the dangers of being alone in such a place, she had never felt frightened. Not here.

Nor this time. She felt her body relax as his steps became audible.

"Hello, Peter." He had stopped, no more than six feet away.

"Hello, Margaret. I didn't think you could get better, proving once again how wrong I can be when it comes to you. Your Bach was positively magnificent."

She felt herself blush, silently chastising herself for letting his words affect her so.

"Thank you. I've been reading lately of your accomplishments. Your reputation continues to grow."

"So it does. But I hardly came to crow about me. How are you?"

"Well. Very well indeed. And you?"

"Much the same." His pause was heavy. "Margaret –"

"No, don't. Please, Peter."

"But I must, my dear. Do you know that it was exactly two years ago today?"

"Two years? What was two years?" She prayed her voice stayed steady, that her words sounded convincing to him.

"It was two years ago – exactly – that day I came to your home. You haven't forgotten. Tell me you haven't."

"But –"

"No. You wouldn't forget. What you gave me that day – albeit momentarily – I carry that memory still. I have never gotten you out of my mind for a minute. I've spent these past two years thinking of you and little else."

"Peter, you mustn't talk like that."

"Then tell me you don't remember."

"Of course I remember. But, Peter, I'm a married woman. I love my husband. I have –" She stopped herself. Did he know of the baby?

"Yes?"

"I have a good life, everything I could ask for." Was that a lie, she wondered. "Everything I need." That wasn't.

"Then there is absolutely no chance? For us?"

"None whatsoever."

He sighed as he sank to the bench beside her. "I so feared that might be your response. Margaret, dear, dear Margaret. I shall so hate to leave you."

"Leave?"

"I've been offered a position in Chicago." She could feel her heart pound but let him continue. "I'd be associated with the university there and have also been offered many more venues for performing. You know – or I imagine you should – that I am running out of places here to utilize my talent. I'll be teaching more – theory and composition, as well as having all the students I can handle. That's their promise and I have to admit it excites me."

"It sounds like a magnificent opportunity."

"It is."

"Perfect in every way, I should say."

"It's all I have ever dreamed of – except that I would have to go without you."

"But certainly you would return to Buffalo? Sometime."

"I don't know. There seems little left for me here."

"Peter, you've led a fuller life than that. Students . . . friends . . . certainly more to return to than just me."

"None of it matters."

"Isn't that being just a tad dramatic? I've hardly seen you these past years. You must be doing *something* to fill all those days."

"Besides dreaming of you? Oh, sure, I keep busy. But it's not enough."

"Then you will go."

"I'd stay if I thought . . . No. Then it's good-bye."

"Good-bye then, Peter."

As he rose his mouth opened, then closed. Whatever words remained would be left unspoken. He leaned to kiss the top of her head, thought better of it, patted her on the shoulder and turned to leave the organ loft.

Each footstep sounded like the blow on an anvil as Maggie watched him slowly walk up the aisle.

LXXXIX
Autumn 1901

"I guess I should be grateful we're not with Charlie in Washington."

"Why? Have I missed something, Lizzie?"

"From what I was reading, they've decreed the entire winter season to be, wait a minute, 'officially devoid of gaiety.'"

"*Officially?*"

"That's what it says. Look, right here."

"'The official mourning shall extend over six months and must be rigorously observed.' Good God! Then again, it does make sense, doesn't it? I mean, the people mourned Lincoln certainly but he was hardly loved the way our President was."

"And Garfield. I admired the man –"

"His death was a calamity."

"Enough indeed to choose his names for our sons."

"But hardly in the same league with McKinley. I'm quite relieved, however, that Roosevelt seems to be panning out."

"Quite. But we shall be able to have some festivities, don't you think? I mean, that is what we were talking about, isn't it? New Year's Eve?"

"Yes, of course."

"Just a little fete, nothing major."

"I'm sure the Club will be dark. Were you thinking of something here at home?"

"Would you mind terribly? It seems like ages since we've entertained. Formally, I mean. And it has been a good year for us, Jack. Your work with that automobile club has been very successful. Much as I hate to admit it, I can remember pooh-

poohing the whole idea at the start. I really didn't believe automobiles would catch on."

"It's an important organization, especially now that they're manufacturing Pierce Arrows right here at home. I don't have to repeat how proud I am to be on their board." He stopped himself with a chortle. "I'm meandering, aren't I? What did you have in mind for the holiday, dear?"

"If you wouldn't object I'd like to have a band playing jazz. They say it's the latest craze."

"No more Viennese waltzes? Ragtime instead? Why, my dear, welcome to the Twentieth Century!"

"You don't think it's being too disrespectful? Loud dance music instead of the dirges we've been hearing for so long? I for one am ready to kick up my heels."

"I'm all for it. Death – well, that's one thing. But damn, I, too, am ready to live."

. . .

"No! He has the talent. His books were published first. It simply isn't fair."

"Calm down, Lizzie. Nobody said the book business was a fair one."

"But, Jack, it was only a month ago we were toasting Ralph and his *Purple Peanut*. His series took the country by storm; that's what everybody said."

"So they did, but now somebody else has come along. You of all people should understand."

"Why? Because I work in the library?"

"You certainly must be aware of the fads, if you will, in books. Readers have always been reputed to be fickle."

"I know. And of course you are right. Some books are like shooting stars while others . . . well, like the very moon itself, apparently destined to shine on forever."

"A little poetic perhaps but accurate, I'm sure."

"It's just that Ralph seemed to have it all. At least until this Baum fellow came along."

"Think of our son as a comet then."

"A comet, Jack?"

"Certainly brighter than a shooting star. Lingering – to borrow your thoughts – like the brightest comet."

"Until it too disappears, is that what you're saying?"

"I'm afraid so though I'm sure Ralph has enjoyed his fame, fleeting as it may have been."

"But no more enchanted peanuts. I think that's the difference, Jack. These new books have real people – a little girl –"

"Ralph's characters were certainly likable but so, I'm afraid, are the tin man and scarecrow and . . . what was the other one?"

"And a wizard? Is that any different from a Purple Peanut? Really, Jack?"

"Aha! But don't forget the wizard turns out to be only a man, and quite a vulnerable one at that."

"And I imagine his star – all right, I'll grant him a comet, too – anyway, I imagine it will flash and disappear just as quickly as our Ralph's. Why, already the library is being overrun with new series: Peter Rabbit which actually has quite lovely drawings though I find no magic in the stories, and an imaginative series of *Just So Stories* about animals, even mysteries by a British writer."

"What's to say Ralph can't imagine another series that might be even more popular? To tell you the truth I'd like to see him write for a little more grown-up audience."

"Grown-up?"

"Not adults. Ralph has a special gift that touches the child in all of us. I would be devastated if he lost that. But I think his stories are good enough that he doesn't need to rely on the shtick."

"Shtick?"

"Invisible nuts. Talking animals. He's good with people. Let's try to encourage that in him. Stories for children, definitely, but a series that can be enjoyed by all ages. I do feel he has the talent. Yes, Ralph will come back."

"And I'll save a shelf at the library for that happy day."

XC

Spring 1903

"I swear, Lizzie, you're getting beyond me. I never know what I'll find when I come home from work. One day you're flitting about, happy as a sixteen-year-old, the next you're so morose I simply do not know how to deal with it."

"Well, that's a fine howdy-do, Jack. Got any other arrows in that quiver?" Her eyes blazed. "You seem to be in fine form today."

"I'm sorry." Jack bent to kiss her contritely. "It's been a long, and I might say, difficult day. Larkin's been a real bear."

"Our benefactor of humankind?"

"'Saint John' if you wish, but still a bear to those of us who are expected to carry out his mandates. And a bear with sharp teeth and a big growl on days like today."

"Sounds like a bad one."

"There've been better. I'm about to pour me one stiff Scotch. Can I interest you?"

"At this hour? Oh, why not? You didn't ask, but it's been a heart-wrencher of a day for me, too."

"You? Then the tears – they have a purpose? Not just another bad mood, is that it?"

"I'd resent that, Jack, really resent it – except this hardly seems the time for either of us to be picking on the other. I mean, really, when was the last time you came home to find me in one of . . . what you call, my *moods?* Be honest."

"I guess I remember the old days and get my hackles up without even bothering to ask if there's a reason for your being upset. I am sorry, Lizzie, truly I am. But there! I've said it. So there is a reason for the tears?"

She slowly pulled a large envelope out from beneath the spread covering her lap. Jack took one glance at the card and knew it was fancier than any he had seen. Gold leaf lettering, padded satin hearts and feathers, obviously real and from no bird that ever graced the northern hemisphere. It never would have occurred to him to purchase something so bizarre, certainly not for a wife.

"It's one of those Valentine cards, isn't it?"

"Of course it is, Jack. And by far the most beautiful I've ever laid eyes on. Don't you think so?"

"The sight has left me quite speechless. To be honest, I don't know what to say." He paused, hoping she would continue the conversation. Faced with an awkward silence that increased by the moment, he bumbled on. "It's quite – lavish, I should think."

"*Lavish* it certainly is."

"Well, I know I didn't send it. Never seen anything like it. Don't think I'd have picked it even if I had. No, I didn't say that to hurt you. By now you should know I'd give you the stars and the moon if I could. But . . . well, nothing like that."

Determined to make him pay, Lizzie glared in return with the most severe stone-face she could muster. Upon seeing his confusion and sorrow, however, she burst into laughter.

"That's worse! Don't laugh at me!"

"I'm not, my dear. It's just that . . .well, it is beautiful, isn't it? And also quite hideous. And yet so unbelievably touching that I couldn't help but sit here and allow the tears to flow."

"I think I'm beginning to understand. But how could he get the money? In a state asylum, I mean."

"Charlie told us they could have work privileges. Earn a little by doing extra chores; I believe that's the way he explained it."

"Well, my dear, that card certainly required a great many extra chores."

"Then do you blame an old mother for weeping?"

He bent to kiss her. "And what is Cook planning for dinner?"

. . .

"Tired, Maggie? Anything I can do to help?"

"No, though I appreciate the offer."

"Rose hasn't been giving you trouble, has she?"

"No . . . well, it's just that . . .oh, I don't know, Everett, this mothering business is so . . . so *constant*. Why, it's gotten to the point I can't even go to the bathroom without my little shadow tagging along behind me."

"You know I've offered – if fact, I've begged you to hire some help."

"It's not that I need help. Well, I do – but not to have more leisure here. I just need to get out, to get away from time to time."

"*Away?* But, dear, you have your organ playing. That was always enough before."

"Ah, yes. It was. But then I was also free to come and go as I wished."

"And where is it you wish now to come and go to?"

"That's not the point. I just need – well, perhaps to spend more time among grown-ups. Two-year-olds are delightful, please don't get me wrong. I enjoy Rose very much. And it isn't that we don't get out. Walks, the park, though even that grows more difficult now that winter's on its way. But, oh, dear, I should like to talk to an adult once in a while. I'm beginning to feel that my mind is turning to pabulum with every bowl I prepare." She sighed. "Am I making any sense at all?"

"Not especially. Good God, but I'd give my right arm to be able to spend more hours with our precious little jewel."

"Too bad that we can't switch positions. I'd find Larkin's, oh, so exciting."

"That isn't necessarily true, Maggie. Work can be – But aha! I think I'm beginning to understand. It isn't what you're doing but having to do the same thing day after day –"

"— after day. Absolutely."

"Then I do have an idea, love. Can we hire someone to take care of Rose next Tuesday and Wednesday?"

"Both days? Are we going someplace? It's terribly close to Thanksgiving, isn't it? Actually, now that I think about it, I don't know if I'd want to leave her alone that long."

"I meant for the days. Working hours mostly, maybe a little longer."

"Now I'm dying of curiosity. What is it you have in mind?"

"John Larkin is talking already of building a new office building –"

"Another? Why the new one's been opened less than a year."

"I'm not arguing that, Maggie. Neither do I intend to disagree with the old man. If he wants to build, so be it. I'm sure I've told you countless times that sales last year totaled . . . well, less than eighty thousand – *thousand*, mind you – under six million dollars. And that's up from just over one million five years ago. He may pave over every square inch of Buffalo before he's through. But the point – and here's where you can come in – is that I've been asked to be part of the committee to meet a new architect they're bringing from Chicago. I've heard talk that he's planning to build a couple of houses here at the same time so I'm sure other wives will be involved in his reception. How about it? Are you game?"

"Game? I can hardly wait. Next Tuesday, is it?"

"And quite possibly Wednesday as well. I know Wright is planning to be here for those two days. Will it be a problem to find somebody for Rose?"

"I'll see that it isn't. Oh, Everett, this sounds exciting. Come; keep me company while I get supper started. If Rose will continue to play I might get you to tell me more about this man from Chicago. Considering all the great architects Buffalo has, he must be something quite special."

. . .

"What's this, Jack? *Ourselves*."

"Oh, that. Yes, I was curious to get your reaction to it."

"Quite polished, if you ask me. But what's it all about?"

"Believe it or not, with everything else that's going on, J. D. has found time to set up a magazine for his workers. You're looking at the first issue."

"I'm quite impressed."

"It's a marvelous way to keep all his personnel up to date on the changes taking place within the company."

"That little self-improvement guide thrown in can't hurt either."

"I think it's positively wonderful. And I swear there's something for everyone." He paused. "Ah, you've found something. What is it, Lizzie?"

"*Margaret Hopkins.* That's Rose's mother, isn't it?"

"Everett Hopkins' wife? Why, yes, I guess so. Can't be many with that name."

"I didn't know she still worked for the company."

"Neither did I. Nor can I imagine that she does."

"I trust the child is still all right?"

"We saw them . . . what, earlier this month, wasn't it? Yes, Eastertime. She seemed perfectly healthy then. Why do you ask?"

"Maggie's written a column."

"I missed that."

"Here. Something about Larkin's latest ideas for another office building. She seems to have done quite a lengthy interview with the architect he's hiring. Hmm, looks like he'll also be building some houses here."

"Anybody we know?"

"Anybody you'd better know. Bill Heath, and the Bartons."

"Bartons? How did they get involved?"

"It says that Darwin Martin is hiring this fellow – Wright – to build theirs for them. Delta's Darwin's sister, isn't she? Martin seems quite taken with the fellow. In fact, I get the idea he's behind the whole plan."

"To build the office building?"

"If not, at least to hire the builder."

. . .

"I don't believe it!"

"I expected you to be surprised, my dear. I wanted it for Rose's birthday."

"Oh, I'm surprised. Believe me, I couldn't be more surprised."

"Pleased then. Why, how many years has it been since you first broached the subject of my buying an automobile? It seems you talked of little else when they first appeared on the streets."

"Everett, that was ages ago. I had quite resigned myself to a life of walking. I simply don't know what's come over you."

"Then come see for yourself."

He led her to the drive where the car sat. Before she could give it a thorough once-over, Maggie was distracted by shrieks of pleasure. Moments later Rose appeared, climbing over the front seat to recline in the back.

"Look at the pleasure just sitting in it brings her." Everett's voice reflected his pride.

"You do plan to take it out on the road?"

"Of course I do. We'll go for many long rides, you and Rose and I. Now that summer's here, what's to stop us from enjoying the warm weather in style?"

"It's just such . . . such . . . well, so unexpected."

"Get used to it. I think our Rose already has. Dear, if you go get yourself a wrap, Daddy'll take you and Mommy for a drive right away."

The child swooped off the seat into her father's arms. Whooping loudly she raced to the house, returning moments later with a light coat. Maggie remained transfixed.

"Well, dear," Everett lifted the child into the seat next to his before turning to his wife, "are you coming?"

XCI

July 1903

"You're a damned fool, Everett Hopkins!" Maggie kicked the tire on the automobile as she thought once again of her husband's extravagance. How he had scoffed at her when she had practically begged for one! Unnecessary, he'd called it. A toy of the idle rich. She was sorry she couldn't recall more of his epithets. Why, he had practically laughed in her face! What did it matter to him what *she* wanted?

But Rose? Ah! That was a different matter. Certainly there were other, less costly, means of eliciting those same marvelous squeals though, agreed, her heart had softened when she saw the joy that first ride brought to her daughter.

Maggie rubbed until the scuffmark from her kick disappeared. A lovely car indeed. *The Yellow Bug* Rose had named it immediately, over the loud objections of both parents. Much too dignified a vehicle for such a terrible name and, truly, closer to a golden yellow than a bug color.

Maggie let her hand run along the puffed velvet of the upholstery. How comfortable to sit in those seats. She would have preferred to be up front with Everett but, for safety's sake, Rose was given her place.

Sometimes . . . occasionally . . . she'd hold Rose on her lap so all three could enjoy the view from the front. But this was a hot summer, June and now July, with little chance of a break for another couple of months. Better to sit separately, to take advantage of the breezes their movement created.

She rubbed the red spokes, squeezed the hard rubber tire as she scraped a small insect off the bright red fender, and then stepped to the front to admire the gleaming brass headlights. She'd never heard of a Peerless until the day it appeared in their driveway. Weren't loyal Buffalonians being encouraged to buy the Pierce Arrow? Still, this was the one that turned heads.

Climbing up into the thick cushion for that first ride, Maggie had been overwhelmed with memories of the earlier outing shared with Peter. If only he could see her now. Better, she wished it were he sitting up there beside her. Feelings that had lasted only as long as it took before she registered Rose's first delight. There was no thought of Peter after that.

She stepped back for one final look. The red outlining on the side panels exactly matched the shade of the cushions. Some thoughtful artist had even drawn a green line beneath for additional accent. And that lovely, lovely wicker basket, attached by some unbelievably thoughtful designer and already filled with all the necessaries for their outings, even a change of clothes and – she peeked now – Rose's second favorite doll, dressed up and ready to go.

Thank you, Everett. You are a good man. Nothing wrong with wanting to please his daughter either.

XCII

November 1903

"I'm so glad you agreed to this ride, Jack. I can't tell you how eager I've been to see the house this Wright fellow has designed."

"Why, Liz, I didn't know you had such a great interest in modern architecture."

"I'm not sure I would, even now, were it not for the columns Maggie continues to write for *Ourselves*. You know, she can make even the most inane detail sound absolutely fascinating."

"From the little I've seen of his drawings, I'd say it has to be her writing that carries the subject."

"Now, Jack, that isn't fair. Or accurate. Part of the fascination, I admit, is the bickering that's going on within the company."

"Good God! She can't write that! She isn't, is she? Why? What have you been reading?"

"No, of course she can't come right out and say a lot of this pushing and pulling is really a power play between Mr. Larkin and – well, you know exactly who, probably even better than I. In fact, I imagine most of her readers don't even catch that part. Maggie can be extremely subtle."

"I should hope so. Larkin's done enough good for us all that I'd hate to see him pilloried by anyone. Or for any reason." He paused. "So what, exactly, it is you've surmised, shall we say, from our friend's writings?"

"Nothing much."

"Lizzie?"

"Well, that Martin's the one who got all excited about him, that Frank Lloyd Wright hasn't even had experience with office buildings, or large buildings of any kind. And, of course, that it took an entire year before he won the commission to build – and to superintend the construction, which seems to be separate and, I gather, even more important since so many of his ideas have never been tried."

"A year!" His wife could still surprise him. "Has it really been that long?"

"Almost to the day. Maggie says he first came to Buffalo last November eighteenth."

"Well, then, a year it has been. To be candid – though you must promise never to pass this on, my dear – there are rumors that Darwin has been promoting this new builder to prove he can get the upper hand over Larkin."

"Why, that's terrible! Though, now that you mention it, Maggie did hint at other internal discord."

"Is she hinting we shall no longer be making soap?"

Lizzie laughed. "Hardly anything that dire. It's just that apparently Mr. Larkin is upset that the mail-order business will be separated in this new building instead of remaining a part of the factory as it's always been. Something – you'd certainly know better than I – about acknowledging the two parts of the company as separate entities. She also seemed to hint that – well, perhaps, Martin and Mr. Larkin disagreed on where the company should be headed in the future."

"I don't think it's quite that. Though, now that I think about it, he might be looking further down the road – to what happens once John Larkin retires. Not that there's much chance of his grabbing the reins. Larkin has his whole family – sons, sons-in-law, grandsons, even nephews – ready to step to the helm. Personally, I sometimes think Martin feels the Larkin success is entirely due to his own brilliance. Though – Lizzie, you're a genius! – why, none of us have been able to understand why Martin pushed Wright so hard to move the junior Larkins' offices back to the old building. Not that it did any good. Larkin's no fool."

"Obviously not."

"Now where is this house you wanted to see? We'd better get a move on. The days are growing far too short."

"And cold. Up here to the corner. Take a right in another block and then down Summit. Yes, it must be along here somewhere. That's the Martins' present home on our left, isn't it?"

"Modest enough. Not something there to attract attention. I like that."

"Guess it isn't fancy enough for him anymore, now that he's the rising star in the company. Oh, look, Jack! That has to be it." She strained for a better view in the growing darkness. "I've never seen anything quite like it."

"You said this belongs to whom, dear?"

"The Bartons, dear. Darwin's sister. It isn't much, is it?"

"Guess that's all a matter of what you expected."

"Well, it hardly fits the neighborhood. Then again," she paused as her husband briefly slowed the car, "It is different, I'll grant that. But an ugly little thing, isn't it?"

"So squat."

"Yet there is a linearity about it that makes it stand out. Do you suppose we might someday get a glimpse inside?"

"Not sure I'd care to." He shook his head. "Makes me even more grateful for our home, Liz."

"Maggie writes that this is just the start of an entire complex Darwin intends to build. A home for himself, some outbuildings, even some kind of pillared garden."

"Perhaps all will look better in the daylight. It's far too dark now to make out many of the details. Though, now that I think about it, that may be a good thing."

"Oh, Jack! I hope they won't be that ugly when they're finished. I was just thinking . . ."

"My feelings exactly. Poor Mr. Larkin."

XCIII

New Year's Eve, 1903

"Come! Oh, do come. Faster. We mustn't waste a moment of this precious day."

Everett gasped deeply and followed Maggie to the edge of the Falls. Ice formed along their edges as the cold attacked his lungs. What had ever possessed him to suggest spending such a day in a place like this? Maggie squealed in delight, and he knew.

"Oh, what a darling you are! Why, I can't ever remember a day as magical as this."

"Then you are enjoying our little getaway?"

"Enjoying? I feel quite certain there will never be another day as extraordinary as this."

"I should certainly hope it would be a warmer one!"

"Are you too cold, my love? We could stop up ahead for a cup of hot chocolate, if you'd like."

"I would definitely appreciate a respite from this biting wind. Though must it be hot chocolate? I believe I'm ready for something a little stronger."

"As you wish. I'll be happy with a cup of tea. In here? Ah, that's better. I hadn't realized how cold I was getting either. But tell me now for you know you never have."

"My wife, who always talks in riddles. What are you talking about this time?"

"Today, silly."

"Today?"

"Yes, our whole reason for being here. Much as I adore you, you aren't particularly known for either wild ideas or extravagance and today seems to be overwhelmingly both."

"Wild ideas? What? To come to the Falls? What's

[437]

extravagant about that?"

"Your willingness to hire a woman to care for Rose – for an entire day, and on New Year's Eve at that. I know they charge extra for a holiday."

"Double, but so what?"

"And you didn't mind hiring a carriage? Why, we could have driven –"

"The roads could be icy by the time we leave for home, Maggie. Now that we're here, my original suggestion does seem quite *wild*, as you put it, but, to be honest, I hardly expected it to be so bitterly cold, even along the Niagara River. Do you think you can last the rest of the afternoon, or shall we head back to the city and find someplace a bit warmer?"

"We are staying out for dinner, aren't we? Though if you'd rather not, I'll understand."

"Don't be foolish, Maggie. We shall stay out for dinner – and dancing, assuming my legs thaw by dinnertime, and as much celebrating as you'd like. I told the woman not to expect us until well after midnight."

"And you don't find all this a – well, just a bit out of character?"

"You don't mind, do you? I know you had some reservations at first."

"It was simply so unexpected. But *mind*? My goodness, no. Why, I feel like a young girl again. Don't laugh at me, I really do! So carefree . . . oh, dear, is that so wrong?"

"To enjoy the time we have? Not at all. Are you ready to brave the frigid outdoors again?"

"Would you mind terribly?"

"Not at all, my dear. Ah, yes, another drink for me, please, and another pot of tea for the lady. Thank you."

. . .

"Still awake, my dear?"

"Just barely."

"Warm enough?"

"Oh, yes. Or," she giggled, "should I say no and hope we can cuddle closer?"

"We can try."

"Ouch! Not that close. I fear I ate much too much for dinner. There's something about Canadian food that always seems a little better than what we get on our side of the border. I think the vegetables are fresher."

"Explained, obviously, from their more southerly position."

"Don't tease. I'm serious. You can't argue that foods aren't presented more attractively."

"Nor that they really do taste better. We'll have to make a point of driving up more often once it gets warmer."

"I'd like that . . . very much. Though I shall miss those very much."

"You're doing it again."

"Doing what, my love?"

"Talking, and making absolutely no sense at all."

"It makes sense to me. Perfectly. What is it you didn't understand?"

"What 'thoses' you'll miss very much."

" *Thoses?*"

"Maggie, you said – and I quote as near as I can remember – you said 'I shall miss those very much.'"

"What? Oh! I was talking about the sleigh bells. I guess all these years they became so common a part of everyday life that we forget how pleasant a noise they do make. It's such a happy jingle, isn't it?"

. . .

"I got the woman safely into the carriage and both paid off."

"I checked Rose. She's sleeping soundly." She tugged her high shoes off and sighed as she sank into the sofa.

"Yes, my dear, what is it?"

"Would you mind – terribly – if I had just one glass of sherry before we go up to bed?"

"Maggie, you are a woman of surprises! Shall I pour that, or would you prefer a brandy?"

"Just sherry, please."

[439]

"Anything. Anything at all for the love of my life."

"Aren't you being the old romantic!"

"I do love you, Maggie. I trust you know that."

"Why, of course I do – and I love you, too."

"And you're happy?"

"Happy? Why, I'm positively delirious! I can't remember such a day– absolutely fabulous, every minute of it – even the chilliest ones. Oh, Everett, I can't thank you enough. This is a New Year's Eve I promise I'll never forget."

"Ready to go up? Or shall I pour another sip?"

She waited in silence as the clock in the hall bonged four times. "I had no idea it was that late. We'd better hurry. I don't suppose Rose will be willing to let us sleep in."

"Nor should we ask that of the child. But, Maggie –"

"Yes?"

"Just one kiss first. That's all right, isn't it?"

"Silly." She went to him, eagerly accepting his embrace. Maggie had always liked being held in her husband's arms. But no! Not like this. As his teeth pushed against hers, she tried pulling away and was alarmed to feel his strength wrenching her even closer. He was panting. Good God, was he about to suffer a seizure? He grabbed her roughly, struggling to undo the back of her dress.

"What in Heaven's name are you doing?"

"Loving, my dear. We need to love."

"But you were hurting me. That isn't loving. Besides, it's terribly late. Don't you think we should get some sleep?"

"Afterwards."

"No, not tonight. I'm exhausted. You're exhausted. We really need to get to sleep."

"We need . . . other things . . . more."

"*Need*? No, no other things, not tonight." His insistence confused her. She didn't think he had had that much more to drink. Yet she felt quite clear-headed, just in a quandary over the suddenness of her husband's unexpected ardor.

"Now."

"Everett, this isn't like you at all. Not tonight. Please. I mean it."

"*Now*, my dear."

"I do wish you'd stop behaving like this. It was such a lovely day. Please don't spoil it all now."

"But that's what it was all about."

"What was all about what? What on earth are you talking about?" She had pulled away and stared at him in rising anger.

"It was a lovely day. I wanted it to be . . . just for you."

"I don't understand."

"A perfect day. And then our love. And –"

"*And?*"

"Dear, you aren't being practical. Rose is already three and a half. By the time the baby's born, she'll be more than four. We really mustn't wait longer. It wouldn't be fair to her."

"'Fair to *her?*' But what about us? What about me?"

"Don't be so selfish. Think of what's best for Rose."

Maggie stumbled back until she collapsed on the sofa. She stared at Everett disbelievingly.

. . .

"One hundred." Lizzie put the brush down and turned out the light, closing the bathroom door behind her as she tiptoed into the bedroom. She had hoped Jack might still be awake, heard his deep breathing and reminded herself of the hour.

She slipped into bed as quietly as possible. Jack stirred and turned to his far side, leaving the bottom covers warmed for her. Tentatively she reached her hand out to touch his shoulder. She didn't wish to wake him, just wanted to feel his presence.

Lizzie rolled over on her back, stretched her legs out, then curled slightly and continued her thoughts.

It's always nice celebrating New Year's Eve with Charlie though Jack and I hardly needed to stay up so late to see in yet another year.

Charlie's been a dear, visiting him as regularly as he can, and he tells us as much as he thinks we should hear. I wish he'd be more honest . . .or do I? I pray my boy were home again.

Bless Jack! Amazing how he can turn in his sleep and pull me into his arms without even waking. How good he feels! . . and such a lovely smell. She smiled as she reflected. "You smell good," she had offered. "Honey, I am good." Please, God, keep him as he is right now. I couldn't ask for anything more.

Ralph would be marrying in the spring. Those weeks had long been marked on the calendar, actually as soon as Jack had brought the new one home. They'd go to Albany for the prenuptial activities, staying on for the breakfasts and receptions certain to follow the ceremony itself. She had managed to extract a promise from Jack as soon as the date had been announced that the two of them would continue on to spend a few days in New York City.

She had felt disappointed to miss the opening performances of *Rigoletto*. It had always been her favorite but Jack simply couldn't get away in the fall, not with all the turmoil around this new office building. Besides, hadn't he surprised her at Christmas with a Victrola of their own? Even recordings, opera of course, for her to enjoy whenever she wished? If she hadn't been able to attend Mr. Caruso's debut, it was almost as good having him come to sing for her!

She doubted that Ought-Four could bring any more exciting news than the year just past. Men flying through the air though people didn't belong in the air any more than under water. And moving pictures! Jack was looking forward to seeing *The Great Train Robbery* while in New York.

And Alaska! John wasn't really serious when he'd let that drop, was he? She'd reacted in such horror she assumed the topic would not be brought up again. Eastern New York was far enough from home for any of the children.

And a new Pope as well. Well, God bless him, too. She supposed He did already. Thank God none of her children were religious zealots like that. Episcopalian, that was enough. She'd promised Father Schuster that she and Jack would try to attend more regularly. She wouldn't commit to anything without Jack's knowledge and approval. Then again, it was a new year. It couldn't hurt to try.

A loose feather from the comforter prickled her nose as she turned to her side, legs pulled up tightly against her chest

Warm here. So comfortable. Perhaps if she kept quiet Jack would sleep on till close to lunchtime. She wouldn't be the one to wake him.

. . .

Jack raised himself on one arm and looked at his sleeping wife. It had obviously been light for many hours. He kissed her forehead, smiled as she did and listened to her soft sigh. He stretched a hand toward her, reconsidered, smiled tenderly once again and slipped from his side of the bed.

He'd better hurry. Sounded as if Charlie were already downstairs.

XCIV

May 1904

"Are you certain you don't want the window seat, dear? The view of the Hudson should be superb."

"Thank you, Jack, but I think I'll try to doze. We've certainly been through a busy time and, to tell you the truth, I'm bushed."

"Strange, it never occurred to me that May's family would be so much younger than we. I don't mind telling you there were plenty of moments when I felt my age."

"Jack! I haven't started calling you *old geezer* yet."

"I'll be turning sixty-three next month."

"Don't remind me for that makes me sixty in November. I can remember when sixty seemed positively ancient, can't you? But please, no reminders that I'm getting decrepit, too."

"You, Lizzie? Never."

"You don't feel it, do you? Sixty-three, I mean. I certainly don't think you look it. In fact, I thought you were just about the handsomest man there – next to Ralph, of course. And I didn't mind May's parents . . . terribly. Too much ancestor worship, agreed, though perhaps they were just trying to impress us. God knows, her family must already be completely versed in all those boring details."

"Ralph had warned us, I know, but I wasn't prepared to meet a direct descendant of Adam. It wouldn't surprise me if they had the papers to prove it!"

"The Revolution. Colonists. Even the Mayflower. And, I swear, most of them were in attendance."

"Think it would make a difference, Liz, if we out-pedigreed them?"

"I don't think I'd bring the subject up if God himself

[444]

carved our family tree on a stone right next to his message to Moses! But it was nice, wasn't it, Jack? The wedding, I mean. And all those parties. And most of the people. I quite enjoyed myself."

"I start laughing every time I think of Ralph's asparagus dinner. I mean, have you ever? I know there are all sorts of traditions that brides and grooms are expected to follow these days, but three courses of warm asparagus? Besides, I took it rather personally that anyone would even suggest a son of mine might need additional aphrodisiac powers."

"I thought it funny. Perhaps we should order an extra helping for you once we get to New York."

"Lizzie!"

"Just teasing, my dear. That's the last thing you need." Her attention wondered as she became aware of the passing scene outside the window. "Jack, look! On the road over there. What do you suppose that is?"

"Where?"

"It just disappeared around that curve. There! It looks like a bicycle, only it's moving much too quickly."

"Funny looking contraption, isn't it? I've heard of them – a motorcycle, they call it. Looks like fun, to tell you the truth. Maybe –"

"After we get home, dear, after."

"Oh, I wouldn't want to ride one in New York City. The driving there is already quite notorious. Too many cars. Too many people."

"And certain to be more, from what I've been reading. Just imagine! Cutting the rate to travel from Europe to just ten dollars a passenger. Why, our whole country will be swamped with foreigners in no time at all."

"Steerage, my dear."

"What?"

"Ten dollars only gets you a trip in steerage. I can't think of anything worse."

"And certainly the very ones we should most try to discourage. Is it gone?"

"What, my dear? The foreigners? I don't imagine so."

"No, the what-did-you-call it? That motorcycle? I'd like to have seen more of that."

"Then you'll have to come to our auto show."

"Jack, you know I wouldn't miss it for the world. Imagine, being able to put on an entire exposition devoted to the automobile! Are you going to have these motorcycles there?"

"Last I heard the Harley-Davidson Company has promised quite a display."

"Oh, good! I'd like to see more of them." She shifted in her seat. "What shall we do first when we get there?"

"I'm very curious to see the subway they're building. It sounds quite grand. European, if I might. Then, too, I'm hoping the railroad tunnel will be finished before we leave. I know it's out of the way but I'd quite enjoy taking the time to do it. Imagine, going right under the Hudson River!"

"I'll let you do that by yourself. You know how tunnels frighten me. Besides, I can't wait to go shopping and, yes, don't frown so, I know how tiresome that always seems to you."

"Lizzie, I work hard and it delights me – truly it does – to see you expending an equal amount of effort to spend what I've earned. And I promise not to say a single word, no matter how much you buy, if –"

"Yes, dear, what is it?"

"Just promise you'll pick up more of those bloomers for yourself. Must say, I do enjoy that new look."

"Why, you old reprobate! I'll do my best – *just* for you, of course. But I think I'll keep you far away from any more asparagus."

"Now, what happened to that nap you were talking about?"

"Are you saying I'm gabbing too much for you?"

"Just that you were the one to tell me you wanted to nap. That's the only reason I picked up this extra paper. But now – yes – now that I have it, I would like a chance to look it over. There's quite a feature here on the Panama Canal and their efforts to erase yellow fever down there. By Jove, the things this country seems capable of doing! I can't think of a more exciting time to be alive. You do share that feeling, don't you, dear? Lizzie? Hmm, must have been even more tired than she realized."

XCV

April 1905

I always knew life had been good to me and these days, the early part of 1905, were no exception. Rose is a healthy and happy youngster, full of spunk and obvious adoration for her doting father. Everett remains a dear though, truthfully, he seems to favor Rose while our time together has become less frequent and increasingly distant. Nothing's been quite the same since that dreadful New Year's Eve.

I am encouraged to present extra recitals as often as I feel comfortable learning that much new music (my ability to memorize does seem to be fading as I grow older). St. Paul's has a separate choirmaster now which is all right, too. He's a dear and we work well together.

Obviously, then, I have the right time to write about Mr. Wright.

I find myself growing cleverer as I spend more time with paper and pen. Besides, this man would keep anybody on her toes. Quite the little rogue – part pixie, part imp. Seems to think he's a true artist and thus answerable only to his impulses. Near as I can tell he fancies himself a man of the world and a real womanizer. I flirt a little – he seems perfectly safe – and am comfortable in our relationship. Also gives me access so that my writings for *Ourselves* carry more about his intentions than mere details of his work. People seem to like the personal touch.

Wrangling continues over the plans for the office building. Not only do the various officers have their own ideas of what should go where – Mr. Larkin eager to keep an eye on things and some of the others just as determined to put him far out of the mainstream – but it turns out this Wright fellow has a lot less experience than he let on at the beginning. Has the confidence to make up for it and doesn't seem particularly afraid of using his mentor's suggestions when he runs out of his own. Louis Sullivan is still recognized as one of the leading architects and his Guaranty Building one of the stellar attractions of the new downtown. Perhaps they thought they were getting someone of a similar ilk when they hired Frank Wright. As some are fond of saying . . . not exactly.

There's this spirit soaring inside him, fighting for all the world to be set free. He draws – I've seen the original sketches – what looks like any other modern building going up these days. Floor after floor of geometrically spaced windows with – or not – a bit of concrete to add exterior "design." Boxes. Big modern boxes. It's progress and I suppose it's good.

Only Mr. Wright can't stop there. He has to, simply *has* to, make it more different from the next box. He wants a fountain running right beside the Larkin Building and all sorts of huge open areas inside. Well, I mean, have you ever?

Personally, I hope they let him do it.

In the meantime, the house Mr. Wright designed for the Martins is getting closer to completion. I drove out with Everett and Rose when we had a break from those eternal snows that seem determined to continue all the way through spring and, I tell you, I couldn't believe what I saw. How does one begin to describe a soaring bird – or should I say floating? Cantilevered eaves to emphasize the low, flat profile that is in turn offset by long bands of small vertical windows.

I wanted to just sit there. The lines, the look, something so different, so new, my head was spinning. Everett scoffed. He never has cared for things modern or, now that I think about it, out of the ordinary in any way. Rose of course was much too interested in playing with her doll – Everett had just bought a new one as an Easter present, not, mind you, that there was anything wrong with any of her others. I have no idea, I tell you, where we'll find room for any of the gifts she's sure to get on her fourth birthday. And that just months away now, too.

Anyway, what they did really didn't matter. I just stood

– drawn, as by a spell, right out of the automobile – trying to drink it all in, wanting to remember every line, every view.

After that I'd find excuses to go by that house every chance I got. Mr. Heath was having another of Wright's designs constructed and, once I learned that, I circled by Bird Avenue, too. I'll be grateful once it warms up. It's unbelievably chilly for the middle of April.

I do ramble but I want to be sure you understand just how important Mr. Wright is. Terribly nice young man, too. Still, when I say our relationship has grown, I mean no more than that he recognizes me now and will agree to answer as many questions as I can ask – providing he isn't tied up with something else.

Still, I never expected to be invited to inspect one of his houses. And the Darwin Martin house at that!

I'd been so taken previously with the sharp clean lines that I don't think I had fully comprehended just how huge the place was. Funny, too, because the first feeling one gets on entering is of smallness. Mr. Wright told me he designed his homes with that in mind. A small entrance to make guests comfortable as soon as they arrive. He'd hold off on the *wows* until the guests were safely inside.

And wow it was! What a mind to fathom something so unique. Us with our parlors and sitting rooms and card rooms and room-after-room rooms. And he did away with it all! Just one big room which combined it all: living room, dining room and library all one, truly great – positively fabulous! You're scoffing, right? Nobody would want to live so exposed; that is what you're saying. Well, he thought of that, too, specifying that heavy drapes be hung to divide the areas when – *if* – absolutely necessary. A touch of the traditional even in a place as untraditional as this.

Today was the first time Mr. Wright had seen the finished sunburst in the fireplace brick in the reception hall. Gold leaf in the mortar between every single brick! Talk about a work of art!

Funny though, for all he did think of (and I'm sure I missed about as much as I can remember), Mr. Wright apparently didn't get very worked up about bedrooms. Without exception they're tiny. He explained and I do understand . . . and I suppose most men would be satisfied with the pleasure of stepping out onto the wide balcony. Lord of all he surveys, all that. Still, I don't think there's a woman alive who would be happy in such a cramped space.

My God, the windows! Leaded panes, some stained glass, all set in the most intricate designs. I wanted to hurry home to sketch the ones I could remember. They'd be lovely patterns for needlework. (I expect I'll have time next winter.) Strange, how that happened. They were so terribly impressive – as beautiful as anything I've seen – yet so much a part of the place that they seem to have faded from my memory right back into the whole.

Mr. Wright refused to let me leave till we had walked around the house so he could explain his ideas for the back. He's designed an open pergola that will go way out, gardens on each side, with the path leading directly to a conservatory, then off to the stables and garages. He's thought of absolutely everything!

On the other side is a path leading to the smaller house he had already built for Mr. And Mrs. Barton. That was the first actually completed. We circled it. I've looked at it before, of course, but always came away confused for it seems to completely lack all the things that make a Frank Lloyd Wright house so unique. It's just a little two-story box. Then I took another look at the large porch and began to understand the connection that had existed all along.

We walked back along Summit Avenue so I could see the real house (excuse me, Mr. Barton, but your brother-in-law has the jewel) with its porch – much grander, of course.

I figured by then we'd be ready to hurry away – my goodness, we'd already spent hours touring this magnificent edifice! But Mr. Wright first drew me back into the front yard. He seemed to be searching for something. The ground is still muddy but he didn't mind dirtying his boots and, well, you can be sure I wasn't going to complain.

Then, over in a corner, out of the way among other building

materials, he found what he was looking for. Obviously Mr. Wright considered this his crowning achievement but all I saw was a squat cement square with four openings on each side, two above, two below, capped with an oversized flat concrete roof. What on earth?

I didn't dare hazard a guess, fearing a wrong surmise might insult him.

"But, my dear," he said at last – after, mind you, laughing quite heartily at my obvious discomfort, "it's a bird house."

Trust me, I never would have guessed birdhouse. "A birdhouse?" See? Even words failed me at that moment.

"Well, I shan't make you guess further. It's a martin house." I remained dumb-founded. "Don't you see?" he continued, "It's a martin house – martins, birds – for Mr. and Mrs. Martin."

I think it was at that moment that I knew we were going to be friends.

XCVI

July 1905

"I simply cannot believe it, Everett!" Maggie had to raise her voice to be heard over the squeals of the young child. "What in Heaven's name got into you?"

"But –"

"I swear, I think you've taken leave – *complete* leave of your senses. How do you imagine me to –"

He laid his hand firmly on her arm. The stern look in his eyes ultimately stopped her ranting. "Listen to me, dear."

"But –"

"Please. This is Rose's birthday, and –"

"I know that very well." She shook her head in discouragement. "And I probably can't admit to being terribly surprised any more by anything you do. I swear! Last year, wasn't it that fancy doll – and, yes, I know – that not even for her birthday but merely as an Easter present? Other children, mind you, get candy, but your little girl got a doll few other parents could even afford. Not to mention its trunk and that complete wardrobe. And on her fourth birthday? Nothing but the fanciest tricycle ever seen in the city. And, no, I certainly haven't forgotten that either: the car, as if any little girl in this country didn't expect a car of her own when she turned three. But, Everett, this is too much! What do you expect a five-year-old to do with a dog?"

"A puppy, my dear. He's just a little pup."

"Who will undoubtedly grow into a dog. Judging by the size of those feet – muddy little rascal, isn't it? – he's going to be just this side of a horse. Whoops! Better not mention that. I'd hate to give you more ideas. Or is that already planned for her sixth?"

"Oh, Mommy, Mommy! Have you seen Buster? Oh, do come and play with us. Isn't he just the sweetest?" Rose shrieked in delight before racing from the room, the dog tight on her heels.

"Have you ever seen her so happy?"

"Has it ever occurred to you that she would be quite as happy with simpler, more ordinary, presents?"

"She's hardly a simple – or an ordinary little girl, Maggie. Why should her gifts be?"

"Why should you insist on making her feel so different from her friends?"

"She is different, my dear. She is our daughter . . . and, judging from the way things have been going, the only child we are likely to have."

"Don't start on that again."

"I'm sorry; I really didn't mean to bring it up. Not now at least."

"Mightn't you have at least asked about getting a pet before you made the decision? Or," she paused as she glared at her husband, "were you that sure I'd put my foot down?"

"Had I given it that much forethought, I'm sure I would have come to that conclusion but, if you want to know, I didn't."

"Didn't what?"

"Give it any thought ahead of time. I stepped out for lunch and happened to walk by a store that had a litter of these adorable puppies in the window. I mean, come on, Maggie, have you ever seen anything so sweet? Roly-poly, so chubby it practically waddles. And wait till you hold him –"

"Hold it? I?"

"Oh, but you must. Really, you have to. He is as soft as fur, and has the loveliest baby smell."

"Everett! Dogs smell like dogs."

"That's what I thought but we're both wrong. See for yourself. He's already captured my heart and is sure to win you over . . . if you give him half a chance."

"Tell me, Everett, do you even know what dogs eat?"

"The clerk assured me he would eat any scraps we had

left over."

"So –"

"Come on, Maggie. Don't you see? Already he can be a help, taking care of the leftovers you'd otherwise have to throw away. I bet he'll keep the varmints out of the garbage, too. Give him a chance. You can see how delighted this has made Rose. That isn't such a bad thing now, is it?"

"You know I didn't mean that."

"Mommy! Daddy!" The kitchen door snapped shut with a bang as Rose and Buster raced into the room. "You haven't played with Buster. Mommy, you haven't even met him yet."

"Ohhh!"

The three stood silently as the puddle grew even larger than the furry pup.

XCVII

August 1905

Grateful that the nanny had taken Rose to the park for the afternoon, Maggie glanced down at the pup sleeping at her feet, smiled happily, and opened the secretary drawer to retrieve a sheet of her best stationery. Her pen and blotter were always close at hand.

It was important Janie know how much her anniversary congratulations had meant. Twenty years! Impossible. In some ways it seemed only yesterday when she and Everett had celebrated the joys common to newlyweds. But . . . well, there were other ways, she reflected, that made her feel as if she'd been married forever. Tied to an older man, lacking close friends and seeming to fit in nowhere. Now, too, with Everett's demands and his more recent coolness, well . . .

He had remembered the date. Everett was not one to ever forget something like that. Flowers. Dinner. Fearful of what she expected might follow, Maggie had allowed her trepidation to wipe out any potential pleasure, relaxing only when her husband excused himself for bed, pleading an early morning and more than general fatigue. Nobody else had mentioned their milestone.

Shouldn't twenty years count for more than this? The flowers he'd brought faded quickly till only two stems retained any color. And his dinner – well, it was nice, but, really, couldn't he have agreed to leave Rose home just this once?

Buster, his head on her right foot, let out a little whimper, stretched and curled beside her, already deep in sleep again. She reached down to scratch his ear. Rose had predictably tired of the work entailed. The doll Everett had presented last Easter was the first thing Buster had chewed, tearing at the cloth body until stuffing flew, crunching its plaster head until Maggie had to retrieve the pieces to prevent the dog's swallowing them. Maggie was grateful the animal had been so easy to housebreak. A nuisance? Oh, he'd chewed one of her favorite slippers while the left-handed white kid glove had puncture wounds though, if she were careful, she might wear it still.

She scratched him again. He looked up, yawned, and went back to sleep. He was hardly ever more than a few steps away now.

Her eyes lit on the silver letter opener Janie had sent as their anniversary gift. Three pages written already and had she even mentioned it? She checked back. No! Talking of the dog and the day and her gratitude for such a friend but nothing about the letter opener. Not so far.

Closing her eyes for a moment, Maggie could almost hear the young girls she and Janie and Flo had been once. When did the tarnish start to blot out the shine? What changed? And why?

Was love lost to her forever? Her wisdom made her feel old while her hunger made her a girl again.

"Come on, Buster, time for your walk."

. . .

Buster brought the ball back enthusiastically, dropped it at her feet, and plopped down tiredly next to Maggie.

"Well, shall we give it a rest, old boy?"

He nudged her arm with his nose, tail wagging as he peered into her eyes with that unmistakable look.

"Again? Buster, I don't believe you know when to quit." She picked up the ball and hurled it across the grassy space toward the woods at the end of the park. "Oh, dear!" She was certain a man hadn't been standing there when she threw it. Quite an attractive stranger, too. Full beard, curly hair and eyes that positively shone.

"I'm so dreadfully sorry. Are you all right? I never meant to throw the ball at you."

"That's too bad. It's been quite a while since I was the object of such attention. As a matter of fact, I can't say I do remember the last time a lovely lady threw anything my way." He reached down to scratch the pup who had returned without his toy.

"Looks to me like we have a lost ball. All right if I help your dog search for it? You certainly can't go into the woods dressed like that."

Flustered as she looked up at the tall man, Maggie made no reply.

Moments later the two emerged from the side of the woods, Buster proudly carrying his trophy in his mouth.

"That's a fine looking dog, Ma'am. What's his name? He is a male, is he not?"

"Buster. And, yes, Buster's a boy."

"Well, I should hope so." They found it easy to laugh.

What a nice man. Then, aware of her circumstance, Maggie backed nervously away.

"Please don't go. I know we haven't been formally introduced but I believe you know my brother."

"Brother?"

"Yes, Jack Knapp. And his wife, Lizzie. I'm Charlie, Charlie Knapp."

"Then it's nice to meet you, Mr. Knapp."

"It's my pleasure to finally get a chance to say hello. I've admired you for quite some time. No, don't be flustered, please. I'm hardly a reprobate who dotes on attractive young women. Though, to be truthful, your red hair has always set you apart. You're one of the major attractions that pulls me to St. Paul's whenever I'm in town. You play beautifully as well."

"My goodness, Mr. Knapp, I hardly know what to say."

"A *thank you* will do for starters." He correctly interpreted her blank look and continued hastily, "For the compliment, I mean. On your playing."

"I'm sorry. You must think me a total dunce."

"Hardly." He chuckled. "No, not in the least. In fact, I've laid the law down with my brother that should you be doing another recital, I must be sure to be invited. Any chance there will be one any time soon?"

"Funny you should ask. It hasn't been publicly announced and I certainly have no idea what I'll be playing but I have agreed to do one more at St. Paul's before I retire."

"How serendipitous then that I should meet you just now! But retire? No, I trust that isn't what you said."

"I'm afraid it is, Mr. Knapp. To be honest, I'm quite looking forward to it."

"But why retirement? What do you plan to do?"

"This may sound silly but I want to be a writer."

"And you can't do both?"

"Oh, I suppose I could but – well, you see, music has been a big part of my life for so many years that, if I go on, it would continue to dominate. Habit, I suppose. I started writing a few years ago – on a whim, as much as anything – and have found I'm quite good at it."

"That doesn't surprise me."

"I find I'm able to really express myself. I had always thought I could do that through my music but this is quite different."

"Please," Charlie said, "go on."

"It was frightening at first, putting my opinions out where anyone could shoot them down."

"Then you have published?"

"Only in a minor sense. I write a column for *Ourselves*, a magazine put out for the employees of the Larkin Company."

"Margaret Hopkins!"

"Yes?" She felt puzzled again.

"Margaret Hopkins! I never connected the charming organist to Larkin's dazzling columnist. I should have introduced myself, Charlie Knapp." He reached for her right arm and pumped it.

"I know. Well, you told me that much. I guess it's my name we didn't get around to. But how would you know? Certainly you don't read *Ourselves*."

"Oh, but I do! I do!"

"But you don't work for Mr. Larkin. And you did say you only came to town occasionally."

"You have a great nose for reporting, I can see that already. I come only – well, mostly," he winked mischievously, "to visit Jack and Lizzie. We did already go through that too, didn't we?" Maggie had a hard time not laughing as she nodded in reply. "But you're wrong about what I read. Admittedly, every nuance of life within the Larkin Company can't hold my attention but you – well, I don't believe I have missed a single one of your articles. I especially like what you've written about Frank Lloyd Wright. Obviously he has a loyal admirer in you."

"Oh, but he should. His works are truly unique and so wonderful. Have you seen any of his buildings, Mr. Knapp?"

"Can't say I have. Heard a lot about them, of course. Personally I can't wait to see what the man does with this newfangled office building he's putting up."

"I'm afraid you'll have to wait another year for that."

"So I shall then. And look forward to keeping abreast of the progress through your articles. You do enjoy writing them, I take it?"

"I love it, positively, absolutely love it! I don't mean to brag, but I seem to have struck a chord. I feel I can speak and know others will listen. Goodness, that sounds pompous, doesn't it? Whatever it is, I know it makes me feel good.

"Oh, my goodness!" Maggie blushed as she continued. "Well, you'll never ask me another simple question, will you? I fear I've about talked your head off. And a stranger, too."

"Please don't call me that. I feel I know you – or should."

"I am curious, if you don't mind my asking, to know what you think of Mr. Wright."

"As I said, I've been waiting to see how the new office building turns out."

"But he's also building houses here. Certainly you knew that."

"Did indeed, though I haven't been in any yet. I know Jack and Lizzie have been in at least one of them."

"Then they told you all about it, I trust? You know how

great an architect he is."

"Not from them, I fear."

"Not – ? You must be mistaken."

"I wish I were . . . for your sake, certainly. But no, I'm afraid neither my brother nor Lizzie found much to admire in the place. Cold, barren, those were the adjectives that peppered their conversation."

"Then they didn't understand."

"Probably not. Though, if you want to know what I think, I think it more a matter that they've grown accustomed to their own surroundings, all the so-called fineries I gather your Mr. Wright has chosen to do without."

"Maybe I'll not make as good a reporter as I had hoped."

"Oh, please, don't let anything I say discourage you."

"It's just that – well, I fear I've been so blind I never allowed for the fact that some might see things differently than I."

"Precisely why I have enjoyed reading your work so much."

"And here I've been, babbling on like a . . . like a I-don't-know-what. So much for being at a loss for words!"

"It's a lovely distraction and I thank you, Miss Hopkins."

"Actually, it's 'missus' but call me Maggie, please."

"I'd like to . . . *Maggie.* Thank you."

She picked up the ball in preparation for her imminent departure. She had talked enough!

"May I throw the ball once for Buster?"

"Yes, of course."

The dog was on his feet immediately, straining to go as soon as the ball was released, momentarily confused that it could sail so much farther than any thrown by his mistress. Maggie raced after the bouncing pup, stopping to catch her breath when she caught up to him at last. She turned, expecting to wave to the nice man. The park was empty.

XCVIII

November 1905

"Oh, my!"

Everett looked up from his section of the newspaper. "What's that you say?"

"Oh? Oh! Nothing, dear. I was just looking at this . . . the advertisement here. I'm sorry. I didn't mean to speak aloud."

"No problem."

Maggie was relieved to see her husband already buried back in the column he'd been perusing. She glanced stealthfully around the room, feeling guilty even before her eyes returned to the small article. So Peter was returning to Buffalo!

Judging from the size of the publicity release, this was not planned as a major event. The Baptist Temple, Madison Street, early afternoon, Sunday November five, the year of our Lord nineteen hundred and five. She wondered if he'd be staying.

Everett set his portion of the paper down, stood and stretched. "It's getting late, dear, and I have a full day tomorrow. Think I'll turn in. Will you be coming up?"

"Just a few moments. There were some articles I didn't have time to finish. Don't wait. I'll be up soon." With any kind of luck he'd be asleep before she reached the bedroom.

If only . . . . .

Peter. Curled comfortably on her side of the bed, she allowed herself to remember the last time they had spoken. It didn't seem possible it had been more than four years until she began to reflect on all that had happened since. Yes, he had left just after President McKinley's murder. Long ago, indeed! The new President had already been elected to a full term. Meeting Mr. Wright and her subsequent writings for

Mr. Larkin. Would he even know? Rose's turning two, three – yes, the automobile! What would Peter think if he knew they had their own car now? – four, and now five. Even Buster!

Was there a day when Peter didn't intrude in her thoughts? Perhaps . . . now, yes. But she could remember only too painfully when not an hour would pass without some thought of the man.

He would have stayed had she offered the least encouragement. But she couldn't. Wouldn't. Not then. And not now.

. . .

"I'm sorry, dear, but I really must counsel against it."

"I'm sorry, Charlie, but I don't understand. Why can't I see my own son?"

"Lizzie, would you listen to Charlie? He feels it's for our own good. We did agree."

"I know, but that was almost five years ago and I've not seen him since."

"Lizzie, you must consider what's best for Abram."

"Believe me, Lizzie, I understand your pain. And so does Jack. To be honest, I'd love to get him out of that abysmal place. I just don't know what else to do."

Lizzie sighed unhappily as she acquiesced to the men's will.

Charlie remembered his initial promise to keep the two fully apprised of the welfare and condition of his nephew through frequent visits.

They had dropped from the early weekly occurrences to every few weeks, however, then monthly, and now less than that. It was true what he had said: Abram didn't know him anymore. Or didn't care. Either way, his being there elicited no reaction from the boy.

Boy?

Hardly. Tall and lank when he was admitted, he had grown huge, grossly overweight, lumbering, unkempt, dirty and completely unresponsive. Guilty or not, Charlie didn't suppose anyone would ever learn the truth now.

He had been adamant in pushing to be certain Lizzie gave up all ideas to visit the boy. He doubted if Lizzie would recognize her son, feared what it would do to her if she did.

He had earnestly – honestly – believed, and so convinced his brother and his wife, that their son would receive better treatment in the asylum than he had in prison. There would be doctors and care. Care? Charlie had seen the boy forcibly tied to his bed, days on end, with no food and no chance to be cleaned, or to clean himself. He had seen him bound so tightly he resembled little more than a struggling mummy. Then the chemicals, and the electric shocks. The doctors told him the seizures and comas were good for Abram.

Charlie had stood at the doorway watching the boy toss and turn, groaning in agony from the malaria ravaging his body, intentionally infected to provoke a brain-clearing fever. Abram had survived, much to Charlie's surprise, though some part of him never fully recovered. He had sadly accepted the derangement, convinced at least that there was nothing more that could be done to harm the lad.

Then this. He hadn't recognized Abram on his last visit, just the Tuesday past. His arms were tied to keep him from ripping off the bandages. But why, Charlie demanded, was his head swathed in cloths – bloody, filthy rags? What had happened?

It was the latest treatment for cases of this kind, the attendant assured him, the doctors slicing away a portion of the pre-frontal cortex.

Charlie hadn't gotten sick until he was well away from the grounds of the hospital but the guilt continued to wrack him. What in the name of God had he done to the family he loved?

. . .

She tiptoed up the stairs to the balcony, slipping into a corner seat conveniently behind a large pillar where she trusted she would not be seen. The church was only about half filled. Maggie wished better for Peter.

He played well, technically close to perfect though she

detected the same lack of emotion that always had rendered even the most passionate of his music sterile. She was sorry he had attempted to speak to the group. Why not simply print program notes if he felt something needed to be added? His jokes were lame and she found the silence that followed embarrassing. The applause was polite though uninspired.

She blessed this luxury to be able to watch him totally unseen. Emotions played havoc with her for moments until she began to realize how little emotion she did feel. Was this the man she had dreamt of for so long? The one she felt needed to be a part of her were she to truly exist as a fulfilled woman? How could she possibly have believed this one was a necessary part of her life?Disillusioned?

Perhaps, she reflected.

No, she smiled a wry smile, feeling as if she were seeing him for the very first time. Disinteresting. Such a dreadfully disinteresting man.

As the program wound down, Maggie found herself sitting tensely on the front of her pew, ready to spring and so escape before the general public, much less the performer, could reach the exit.

It could only be worse were he to discover her now.

She hadn't realized the door would slam behind as she made her furtive escape. The noise brought her momentarily to a halt. Then she wrapped her coat more tightly about her chin and hurried on.

XCIX

February 1906

"Wait up, you two!" Jack pulled the scarf more tightly over his mouth and, head down, forged into the howling wind. "Wait for me."

Turning, Lizzie and Charlie stopped in mid-sentence to let him catch up.

"Sorry you had to wait. I wanted to be certain the car was locked. Can't be too careful –," his head indicated an all-encompassing circle, " – around here."

"I'm sure you're safe, Jack. They keep the inmates locked up." Charlie stopped as he intercepted his brother's scowl. "Well, they're supposed to."

"I think we all know by now how much that means, don't we?"

The bitter air made speech difficult as the three continued back down the road their car had just entered. The final days of January had brought a most welcomed warming spell. Buds began to appear on the trees that in turn showed signs of reddening. The first leaves of the daffodils pushed upward into the short sun. The bright songs of the cardinals had been remarked upon back in Buffalo. Now though the harsh winds threatened to steal every sound beyond their own howls.

The three crossed the main road and continued on a too-well-worn path toward the creek. Once down its bank they reached a sheltered lee and stopped, happy to catch their breaths.

"I was telling Charlie about the Valentine Abram sent me."

"I was thinking of that, too, on the way down here. Hardly seems possible that it could have been four years ago, does it?"

"When I think of all the times I wanted to come . . ."

"It would have been better if you'd never come at all, Liz."

"Nonsense! I'm not a child and don't expect to be treated as one."

"Wanting to protect your sensibilities from the . . . well, the indelicacies of life is hardly treating you like a child."

"Nevertheless, I wanted to come, and I'm glad I did. Only I hardly expected it to be quite so . . . I guess *oppressive* is the word. Then again, I don't imagine any place would be very attractive on a day like this."

"I'm sorry – if you had to come here – that you couldn't have seen it under better circumstances. It isn't bad at all – especially in the summertime. Why, I can remember the first time I saw the Kirkbridge Center. The wrought iron balconies gleaming in the sun, bright canvas awnings over the office windows and those towers, really fine examples of architecture. You do remember what I told you about Kirkbridge, don't you?"

"I can't say I do anymore, Charlie. I know, at the time, it all sounded marvelous. Modern, up-to-date –"

"Sun in every window sometime during the day, a system of natural air conditioning, spectacular grounds with their landscaping and fountains, and – "

"Yes, I remember now. And promises of a library, even art lessons, weren't there, Charlie? Who for, for God's sake? Certainly not for Abram."

"Lizzie, he did absolutely nothing to cooperate. Not at his trial. Not in jail. And certainly not after I brought him here."

"You know Charlie's right, dear."

"Maybe if I'd just been able to talk to him –"

"Lizzie, stop blaming yourself. God made us all mortals and, God knows, we all make mistakes. But can't we – please – agree that we all did the very best we knew how to do? And let it go at that?"

"It's just that –"

"You wanted to see the place. Shall we walk along? The dampness off the water is beginning to get to me. If we must talk, I'd much prefer to do it where it's warmer."

"Later."

"What are you staring at, Lizzie?"

"Just watching the water swirl. Funny, when Charlie used to tell us about the creek, I pictured a small slow stream of water. Hardly anything as turbulent as this."

"It's a question of the seasons, Liz. In the summer the Conewango can even be used as a swimming hole."

"To swim here?"

"Why not? The waters then are practically still, not half so deep either. Really quite beautiful on a hot summer day."

"I'll have to take your word for that. And hope I never have to come here again, summer or winter. Is that the place?"

"I imagine it must be. The tire ruts look quite fresh."

"No chance of snow left here, not with all those footprints to stamp it into the ground. Watch out, Lizzie, it might be muddy there."

"Then I'll just have to clean my boots once we get to your home, Charlie. I've come this far; I want to walk all the way down to the water."

"Haven't you seen enough, dear?"

"Not yet. How long did you say the body was in the water before they found him?"

"I don't think anyone can answer that with certainty."

"He wasn't discovered missing until the final bed count of the evening but the attendants suspect he walked out earlier, perhaps even in the afternoon."

"Wasn't there a supper hour? Shouldn't somebody have noticed if he were missing?"

"One would think so but it wasn't reported. That's all I've been able to find out. They haven't found anybody – not as far as I know – who could say he was, or he wasn't, there."

"A strange way to run a hospital, if you ask me."

"Definitely a dereliction of duty, and they aren't denying it. The staff was at a bare minimum with many of the attendants gone off to hear a medical lecture. And they were full. That's six hundred and fifty patients with few to oversee what was going on."

"So nobody really knows?"

"Nobody knows."

"Lizzie, you keep going over and over this."

"I'm sorry, Jack, but I have to get it straight in my mind. Charlie's been wonderful – so patient, too – and I do appreciate it but . . . well, it was one thing hearing the news at home – and quite something else to be standing here – freezing as much as you both are, I might add – still trying to understand."

"Hurry it up then, Charlie. Once she's satisfied maybe we can scoot back to the car and head for someplace warm."

"It's only a few miles further to my house. What else do you want to know?"

"They discovered him missing about eleven then?"

"Between ten and eleven. It takes that long to cover all the wards, to check on every patient."

"And he was gone."

"Gone. At first, from what they say, no one was terribly alarmed."

"What? Are you telling me patients disappear all the time?"

"Don't be upset, Lizzie. It seems that many are not dangerous. Not all the doors are locked, so they can wander around – a bit."

"But you said they kept Abram bound."

"So I understood. That night there was apparently a new intern. He discovered the empty bed, made a note on his chart, but then continued his regular rounds. Even if they'd begun the search immediately, there's no guarantee anyone would have found Abram in time."

"No. I don't suppose so." She sighed loudly, bent to pick up a scrap lying on the ground, examined it and discarded it without further interest. "So it was about noon the next day – yesterday – when they found his body?"

"Closer to eleven, from what I've been able to gather. They did a perfunctory search the night before, decided there was little further they could do and waited for dawn."

"Or whatever you call it in this godforsaken winter."

"They called out the local fire departments and had a host

of volunteers combing the woods – after thoroughly searching the entire building first, of course. I don't think anyone thought he'd head toward the creek."

"And that's it?"

"I'm afraid I don't follow you."

"They found his body. They called you. You called us. Here we are, Abram wrapped up and ready to go home."

"What more can there be, Liz?"

"Lizzie, how many more questions can you think of?"

"Easy, Jack. Millions, and they're all the same. Why? Why? *Why?*"

"Perhaps we never really knew what was in Abram's mind, dear."

"Oh, I know that. But did he come here alone? Did someone else bring him? Or follow him? What really happened? And why?" Damn it anyway! She had promised there'd be no tears. Not here. Not now. Wasn't that part of her bargain to the men, in exchange for their letting her come?

"I wish I could give you answers, dear. I wish we could all know what happened night before last. But nobody does, I'm afraid, and nobody will."

"Just like the boy."

"What? What did you say, Charlie?"

"I was just thinking. Abram had many secrets and it looks like he took them all with him."

. . .

There was a small notice in the newspaper when the undertaker insisted it could not be omitted. Jack didn't suppose many in Buffalo would bother showing up for the funeral anyway. Abram's name must be all but forgotten by now. And the ghoulishly curious? Well, a church service might do them good.

Charlie had returned with them, promising to stay until Lizzie recovered. Having all the children there helped, too. In fact it turned into quite a festive occasion before it was over.

Not that any had forgotten Abram. Exactly. But no one had seen him for years, Uncle Charlie excepted, and, when birthday and Christmas notes went unanswered, well, it was easy after a while not to think about him. Isn't that what he had wanted, too?

It was Charlie who was most taken aback. When had Grace and Anne become proper matrons? Good God! Even thinking it added years to his own age, but, true enough, these were hardly blithe young ladies anymore. Somehow Elizabeth had fallen into middle age. When had she turned thirty? No mistaking the fuller body, the early tinges of gray. Clara – thank God for Clara, still hardly more than a debutante at twenty-two. But just look at the girl! Frumpier even than her older sisters, not that Charlie would be the one to point it out.

Nor that he had to. Leave that to John. Older than Clara and very happy to lord it over her – especially since all his exercise gave him the appearance of one much younger than his years. Thirty next year, he happily reminded one and all. And Ralphie. Sorry May couldn't make the trip with him – weren't rumors being bandied about that she might be pregnant? But just look what marriage had done to the boy! Settled into teaching and seeming quite pleased with his lot. Couldn't be happier at the school. Books? No, no more time for writing, not now certainly.

Charlie leaned back in his chair at the table and looked around, slowly, taking in each member of his family. When would they all gather like this again? Good God, please not another funeral. He was getting up there, Jack and Lizzie too –them in their sixties now and him about to turn fifty-nine. But fit? Hell! He expected to go on forever and knew his brother and sister-in-law shared the same optimism. Let's all live to be as old as mother – but perhaps manage to make it to those higher numbers with a little less crotchetiness.

A toast to Abram. Who'd figure he would have been the one to bring them all back together?

Strange lad. Always was.

He'd tried to be sympathetic, to find something in him to like. The boy made it damned difficult.

And then this whole murder business. Shouldn't have still

been home at his age anyway. What had gotten into Jack to allow it? Or Lizzie? He didn't imagine he'd ever understand women. Not that one anyway. Though she had acted pretty commendably at the hospital. No hysterics as he and Jack had feared. Too many questions. No, that was unfair. Just not enough answers.

And the killing. Couldn't the boy have spoken to someone before he died? That fortune-teller was supposed to be carrying a wad of money, isn't that what all of them had said? Had Abram taken it? He guessed the sister wouldn't be lying about something like that. Then again, who could know?

Charlie remembered Lizzie's anguish at the creek. "Why? Why? Why?"

Too bad life didn't come with simple answers.

C

June 1906

Maggie, that's not possible.

It was wrong to let it fester. She wasn't a fool. She knew what this resentment was doing to whatever feelings remained for Everett. Damn, but she had depended on him. Was it wrong for a wife to expect her husband to be at her side?

"That's not possible." That was all he had said.

Expect. Well, she could hardly demand. Besides, if she had pushed, he'd have simply said no. His mind was made up. Subject closed. No discussion. Her feelings be damned.

No matter how often Maggie reviewed the painful moments, her anger didn't diminish. She wanted to throw something. She wanted to cry. She wanted to hurt him as he was hurting her. And, thinking, she'd dissolve in tears, knowing he was beyond reach.

Never in her memory had St. Paul's banded so closely together in their enthusiasm to support an upcoming project. That it would be Maggie's final recital as organist added a deeper dimension of excitement to her own as she began choosing the music for the program. Accustomed to accepting the dictates of the higher-ups, Maggie was dumbfounded when the dean – the dean himself, could you believe it? – approached to seek her input on selecting the date. Together they settled on June third, a Sunday afternoon, with the music to start at four. That should be early enough to escape the oppressive heat of mid-summer and late enough in the day to give churchgoers a chance to eat and rest before returning.

The choir en masse had enthusiastically volunteered to host a high tea to follow while the members of the vestry asked if they might serve as ushers. She'd never been treated so regally!

Serious practicing resumed with the choir's return in early September. While the winter slowly passed, Maggie's stack of potential music dwindled as she chose some and rejected others, setting aside a third pile for further consideration and practice. It seemed the entire city of Buffalo had caught the excitement as near strangers stopped her on the street to inquire of her proposed program.

She had chosen her dress, a spectacular (and very expensive) gown, as soon as the summer fashions appeared in the stores. She recalled that day with pleasure, recapturing the surprise when she had first glimpsed her clothed figure in the full-length mirror. Her figure had returned to nearly what it had been when she was eighteen. Pretty good for a forty-four-year-old mother, she thought smugly. Occasionally she'd glimpse a strand of gray in her red hair, still few enough that each could be yanked out with a minimum of fuss.

She had considered it a blessing when Everett urged her to enroll Rose in early school. The girl would be six by the time the school year ended, certainly ready for the disciplines of the classroom. And she had been pleased with the change it made as Rose began to develop social awareness and to discover a world expanding beyond herself. She was a nice girl, Maggie admitted proudly, and becoming more of a joy to mother as well.

Everything seemed to be going so smoothly. Until . . .

"Everett, you can't mean it! You can't possibly be serious." By now the words were permanently sculpted in her mind.

"Maggie, I fear it is you who's being unreasonable. Think about it, please."

"I've thought about it all I need to. This is outrageous."

"Maggie, you aren't being reasonable."

"What does reason have to do with it? I'm your wife. This is my recital. In fact, it's one of the biggest events in Buffalo this summer."

"Then you'll hardly miss me if I'm not there."

"But you have to be. You're my husband."

"I'm also Rose's father, dear. This is her first school

pageant. Certainly you wouldn't think of having her perform without at least one of us in attendance."

"No," she had sputtered, her anger increasing as she realized the argument was lost.

"You have given many recitals, my dear. I have always been there for you. But this is Rose's first."

"And she'll have more while I may not."

"Maggie, dear, please think of what you're saying. I remember when I first began to attend your recitals. Long before we were married, wasn't it?"

"And it meant so much to me to know you were there. I don't think even then you cared particularly about the music –"

"No. I expect it never will be my forte."

"But you were there for me."

"Precisely my point. I was there when you needed me. Now it's Rose's time."

. . .

The months had passed, the pieces had been polished till she felt she could do nothing more, and now the great cathedral was filling to capacity. She could hear the scraping as folding chairs were set up along the side aisles and quickly occupied. Would some have to be turned away?

Two of her favorites from the choir stayed while the others were in the parlor preparing for the tea that would follow. Maggie had had a quick glimpse of the pastries and tiny sandwiches, always her weakness, and was struck immediately by the loveliness of the room. The long table was decorated with seasonal flowers entwined with strands of ivy that stretched its length. The silver was polished to a high glisten, the tea service on the left and the coffee urn set to the right. A tinge of sadness crept through her as she saw the sugar cubes. This was one time she'd be taking none for Rose.

She waited impatiently in the choir room as the small hand slowly moved toward four. There was a knock on the door, opened immediately by one of the women. Maggie looked up as she heard the gasp. Never had she dreamed the bishop himself might attend. He walked gracefully toward her, his red robes brushing the floor, hands outstretched. She took one in each of hers and reacted happily to his warm clasp.

"I hope it's all right. I wouldn't want to disturb you. But I did want to extend my best wishes even though I know you'll do superbly."

"Thank you," she stuttered.

He bowed slightly, turned and left as silently as he'd come. Only the aura in the room remained. Maggie looked at the two women who obviously shared her awe, realized all three mouths were agape and burst into laughter.

. . .

The reception room was so packed, Maggie reflected later, that she couldn't have gotten a bite to eat had the thought occurred to her. Later of course it did when she remembered those delicious delicacies stretched out before her – with only hundreds of people between her and the food. At the time, however, it was the people who occupied her mind. So many well-wishers! The bishop had quickly disappeared though she was assured he had stayed for the entire program. But here were Mr. and Mrs. Martin themselves stepping forward to greet her. She regretted not having time to discuss their magical house. And Dr. Park. Was there a man more esteemed in the entire city? Even Mr. Larkin, God bless him, getting up there in years but still charming with the elfin smile of a small lad. And the boys, Charles, Harry and John, Jr., with all their families. Just wait till Everett heard!

Damn! The balloon around her deflated as she remembered her husband's betrayal. Could she be wrong, she wondered. Should she have been paying more attention to her daughter? A woman, a stranger, tugged at her elbow, eager to extend her own compliments on a program skillfully executed.

Rose would have a lifetime to garner her own praise. Let this be Maggie's moment. She deserved it. She turned to the woman at her elbow, smiled and began to answer her questions.

It was many hours before the last of the well-wishers departed St. Paul's, even longer before Maggie, having changed into street wear so that she could help, was ready to leave. Only a few of the women remained, bustling in the kitchen as the last of the silver was stowed away.

"Go. Go, Maggie. It's been a long day for you. Time for you to get home and enjoy a well-deserved rest."

"Yes, dear. Put your feet up and relax."

"Or is Everett taking you out for a celebratory dinner?"

"Now that I think about it, dear, I don't remember seeing him here."

"Yes, Everett? Where was he?"

She hesitated. "I'm afraid he felt it more important to be with Rose this afternoon."

"Good gracious, no!"

"Is she sick, dear? Oh, how terrible to have to worry about that at a time like this!"

"No. No, Rose isn't sick. In fact, I've never seen her in better health."

"Then I'm afraid I don't understand."

"Rose is in school this year and . . . well, the Academy staged a pageant this afternoon. And . . . well . . .Everett thought he should be there since she was participating in it."

"How terrible for you, my dear."

"These things happen. Besides," she paused, "he's heard me play hundreds of times." Growing uncomfortable, Maggie reached for her light coat and started for the door. "Matter of fact, I suspect I should be on my way home. I've got to hear all about the afternoon at school."

"Wait, dear. Just a minute." The first woman looked at the second as if seeking confirmation and hesitated briefly before continuing. "We think you should take the flowers off the table, don't we?"

"Oh, yes. Especially since you didn't get any others."

Shaking her head no, Maggie turned to depart, hurrying before the tears could start.

She hardly heard the woman as she ran down the hall. "Don't forget to tell him all about the stellar performance you gave, my dear."

. . .

Funny, she reflected later. Not, in truth, that there was anything funny about the day. Not before, during, or after. It was just that – somehow – there never seemed to be the right moment to tell Everett anything about it. The bishop. The Larkins, her playing, any of it.

Everett had been full of Rose, more excited perhaps than the child who displayed far more eagerness to change out of her new dress, eat a hurried supper and be off to play. Maggie watched Buster race for the door Rose had just exited and the door snap back, almost striking the dog on its nose. She saw that he stopped short. He had learned. She guessed she would, too.

But Everett talked. She sat at the kitchen table, scratching Buster's ears, aware only of the stream of sound flowing over and around her. The children. Parents. Festivities and excitement as the school term stretched toward its end.

She tried to listen when he got to Rose – Rose, thumb in mouth, hair twisted around her finger, Rose in the back row, a flower of indeterminate origin, unable to perform any of the simple motions in time with the rest of her class. Rose, ever the star in her father's eyes.

She listened in silence. At last she rose, poured herself a half-filled glass of bourbon, and sat back down. The clock in the hall struck nine times. Had Everett eaten earlier? She knew she hadn't.

Maggie sat as he went on. As the final rays of the reddening sun turned dark in the western sky, Rose came in, volunteering to go to bed. Everett went up to tuck the child in.

He had asked no questions about her day. She didn't imagine he ever would. In time, she knew, whatever she had wanted to say would fade away and be forgotten.

Maggie, Buster at her heels, poured herself a little more and took the glass out on the back porch. She listened to the sounds of the night around her and found them comforting.

CI

August 1906

As the automobile slowed to turn, the driver glanced at his passengers in the rear.

"You did say Seneca Street, didn't you, sir?"

"Oh, dear, Everett, just look at the crowds. I knew we should have left earlier."

"Well, my –" He hesitated, knowing the battle was already lost. Rose had staged a last minute tantrum and Everett had insisted on remaining until she was quiet again.

"Oh, look!" Regretting immediately her mention of the earlier scene, Maggie hurried on. "That has to be it. A regular monolith if I've ever seen one." The huge building was indeed ponderous and forbidding in its seeming lack of detail. Appearing at first glance to have few windows, huge columns of brick rose massively toward the sky. "Can you see it, Everett?"

"Perhaps if you could explain what it is I'm supposed to be seeing –"

"The piers, for starters."

"Piers?"

She pointed to the columns running up the front of the building. "You know, it reminds me of Mr. Wright's homes. Only this is set on end!"

"I'll take your word for that. But what are those things on top?" He shielded his eyes from the sun, hoping for a better view. "Can it be? Has Larkin gone silly on nymphs?"

"Putti."

"What?"

"They're putti, figures of young boys. Actually they were very popular in European art, 'specially during the

[479]

Renaissance."

"But here?"

"Call it another of Mr. Wright's aesthetic considerations."

"Holding up the world?"

"The Larkin world, you can be sure." A tug on his arm led him toward the entrance where a sheet of water drew one's attention into a large pool. To its left a formidable staircase rose toward the entrance.

The silence inside was the first indication of the noise without. Surrounded by Larkin manufacturing plants, the neighborhood made no pretense but to be the industrial area it was.

"Maggie, you're turning in circles!"

"I can't decide which way to look first –" she glanced at the immense glass doors though which they had just entered. Turning again, she now faced the reception desk, apparently made of white marble. Three receptionists, sitting behind the huge semicircle, were kept busy answering questions from the curious visitors while a fourth, recessed further behind, worked at a switchboard. "I'm overwhelmed."

"Definitely a welcome one won't forget." He laughed as his wife continued to turn. "I confess the building looked rather like a bulwark when we were out there but it's quite light and comfortable."

"Maggie! Everett! There, Jack, I told you it was the Hopkinses." The couple hurried toward them. "Over here!"

"Lizzie! Good to see you again, Jack."

"Did you just arrive?"

"A few minutes ago," Maggie said. "I was admiring the facade. I want to drink it all in."

"This is the first time you've seen this building? Why, Maggie, I thought you followed Frank Lloyd Wright's every footstep."

"I would if I could, Lizzie. But no, I wanted to save this until it was completely finished."

"First impressions then," her friend pushed. "Are you surprised?"

"Surprised? Why, no. I'd recognize Mr. Wright's touch

anywhere."

"But it is quite ugly, don't you think? From the outside, I mean. All I could think of was a giant fortress. I told Jack it gave me the willies. And such a smelly neighborhood."

"I doubt if the Company can do anything about that. We certainly don't want them to stop manufacturing, now do we?"

"Oh, Maggie! You know what I meant. But it is . . . strange. Even you will have to admit that."

"Strange? In what way, Lizzie? Certainly you can't think the interior austere."

"To be honest, I've hardly had a chance to look around." A movement across the room caught her attention. "Say, could we meet later, over lunch perhaps?"

"Sorry to cut in on your plans, dear, but I believe we're expected – all of us – to eat here. There's a restaurant upstairs."

"We'll look for you there. I know Jack has somebody he wants me to meet now."

"And I'm dying to see the light court."

Everett watched Lizzie and Jack stop to visit William Heath, occupying the other executive desk in the middle of a large open court. "There's certainly no privacy here, is there, dear?"

"I'm sure that is exactly what Wright had in mind."

"I, for one, would find it terribly uncomfortable."

Hands akimbo, Maggie turned toward her husband in mock seriousness. "Why, my dear, are you telling me you're of the old-fashioned school who believes the top executives still deserve the status of executive offices, located somewhere in the uppermost reaches of the building?"

"That's what I'd like, not that I expect to rise that far, certainly not now, not at my age."

"I know what you're saying but, if I'm not mistaken, Wright designed this at the request of Mr. Martin and Mr. Heath."

"You mean they actually approved such an arrangement?"

"I mean they asked for it. Just one more step, if you will, to making the Larkin Company one big open family." As much as was practical the interior had been left open. Executives were placed in the center with secretaries around them. Farther on, rows after rows of desks, now empty would soon be humming with legions of young women entrusted with the work of running the Larkin mail-order business.

"Come over here." Maggie eagerly pulled him toward the area of the light court. "This is what everybody's talking about, isn't it?" She stopped, swaying backwards, to gaze up at the ceilinged glass high above her. Her eyes slowly followed the wide balconies between the columns; top floor, fourth, third, second and back to where they stood. "Oh, Everett, it is beautiful, isn't it?"

"It's certainly breath-taking. I never dreamed –"

"Funny – No." She began to laugh softly.

"What is?"

"Well, we know this entire building was designed for the administration of the mail-order business, Wright intentionally separating it from the manufacturing plants across the street." Maggie pointed at the file drawers which reached from column to column and on up to the windows high in the wall. "It just struck me that, in a way, the whole gigantic edifice represents one huge file cabinet. Look around. See what I mean?"

"I'm not sure. Well, yes, maybe I do."

A uniformed guide now directed them toward the west end of the floor where the offices for Mr. Larkin and his sons were located. So they hadn't been moved out after all! But it was immediately obvious the executives would definitely be lacking privacy for the walls enclosing the doorless spaces reached only halfway up.

"I think we'll all find this takes some getting used to." Everett's voice reflected his doubts.

"Oh, dear! I hope they don't give you a chair like those. It looks like a waffle iron with arms and wheels!"

"Uncomfortable, too. Here, try for yourself." Rising uncomfortably Maggie spied Lizzie and Jack at a distance.

They waved before joining the crowd to examine the directors' meeting room, unsurprising in its similarity to the Larkin offices.

Lizzie and Jack walked toward the staircase.

"Strange, but I almost feel this building is more of a tribute to Darwin Martin than to John Larkin."

"What do you mean, Jack?" Lizzie asked.

It was Jack's turn to remind his wife that it was Martin who had devised the card catalogue that kept the company running smoothly. With his card-indexing system, customer accounts could be quickly located and easily updated. His waved his arms in a wide circle. "Quite brilliant, you know."

"I'll take your word for that, dear. But what does that have to do with the building?" The words were no sooner out of her mouth than Lizzie began to understand. Mr. Larkin's side was the manufacturing part of the business, completely out of view in this building erected strictly for the processing of the mail orders, all the bookkeeping, and the maintenance necessary to keep the premium catalogue current. "Is that all they do here, Jack?"

"Hardly. There are also letters to be answered, even, I regret to say, a few complaints." He knew that mail would be sent to a separate office where it would be directed to one of the company's many correspondents. There a reply would be dictated into a graphophone which would record it on a wax phonograph cylinder. That in turn would be passed for transcription to a typewriter operator. "Once it passes muster, the response is mailed back to the sender. Pretty stream-lined, don't you think?" Efficient organization was a necessity with over two million customers already on the books.

"Do you remember seeing those little red flags that each transcriber could raise over her desk?" Jack continued.

"I saw somebody playing with one and wondered what it was for."

"When a transcriber runs out of work, she raises the flag as a signal to bring her more records. As soon as she has them, down goes the flag. A brilliant concept, isn't it?"

"Indeed, though . . ."

"Yes?"

"I don't know. It just seems to take an awful lot of steps, requiring, I might add, a great many people, simply to sell a bar of soap."

"You know better than that. We still sell perfume –"

"Well, I did know that."

As Jack began to recite a list of some of Larkin's current products – the soaps and cleansers, of course, coffee, peanut butter, macaroni, spices, vanilla, even puddings plus pharmaceutical products and cosmetics – Lizzie laughed and shook her head in wonder. By now they had reached the top of the gigantic building.

"Fifth floor, ma'am, no waiting."

She walked over to the balcony's edge. "I do rather fancy looking way down on all those desks. I can imagine the bustle when they're filled." She paused to take it all in. "You know, I almost feel I could touch the ceiling. But what do you think of all those inscriptions? *Intelligence, Enthusiasm, Control. Cooperation, Economy* – My goodness, nobody's going to forget for a minute what they're in here for."

" *Ask and it shall be given you* –"

"What, Jack?"

"Just reading the larger inscription over there. No, I have to agree. We are here, madam, for 'Action!' Had enough? I believe the restaurant is just over there."

"Perfect timing, I'm famished."

. . .

"I have to tell you, Everett, the more I see the more overwhelmed I'm feeling. There isn't a square inch in this entire building that wasn't designed with a specific purpose in mind. I've never seen anything like it. It's all so – so efficient."

"You wouldn't mind working here then?"

"Everett, you don't mean –"

"Good Heavens, no, Maggie. I was just comparing this to what it was like when you worked for Mr. Larkin."

"I'd find this much more edifying. I can't imagine ever

complaining about the drudgery of a mindless routine, not in these surroundings. Besides, did I hear correctly, that they are now providing noonday concerts?"

"You certainly did, dear. And lectures as well."

"Oh, what fun!" She clapped her hands enthusiastically.

"Don't forget, Maggie, that work, of course, remains its central function."

"It could be rather easy to forget, surrounded by all this magnificence."

"Undoubtedly why Wright hasn't seen fit to be subtle in his reminders. Did you see these?"

"Do you think anyone could not? Why, Everett, they're huge! 'Economy' 'Industry' 'Action' – not exactly toe-tappers, are they?"

She smiled as she took a deep sniff. "Hmm, we must be closing in on the restaurant."

Just then Lizzie and Jack approached from the opposite direction. They had eaten but Lizzie was eager to share her new information with her friend.

Maggie gasped as they entered the dining room. "It's huge. Funny, I wouldn't have expected the size."

"They told us up to six hundred could be fed at one time," Lizzie added authoritatively.

"Really? That doesn't seem quite –"

"I know what you're going to say, dear. But this is only half." A second dining room of the same dimensions lay across the atrium. Behind both to the north lay the kitchen where a chef oversaw the preparation of all the hot foods to be served while all breads, rolls and desserts were made on site in a bakery located at the south end of the floor. She continued, enthusiastically describing viewing the areas that would soon be flourishing roof gardens.

"I gather you're growing more impressed, Liz."

"Overwhelmed. And tired, I know that. But impressed? I'm not too sure."

"Look, girls, would it be all right if Everett and I leave you here for a while?"

"But Everett hasn't eaten yet."

"Don't worry about me, Maggie; I'll be all right. You don't mind staying, Lizzie?"

"I've never been known to pass up a chance to sit longer. Besides, I'd like to pick Maggie's brain to discover why she finds this place so intriguing." She smiled as she watched the other woman take a seat. "I should have warned you. The chairs aren't terribly comfortable. Why, I don't think the backs are anything but a board."

"Our Mr. Wright again," Maggie laughed. "I imagine he designed these chairs and tables, too."

"Oh, I know he did, Maggie. Our guide explained that. In fact, you'll never guess what the tables do."

"*Do*? What are tables supposed to do, Lizzie?"

"Well, the tops of these can swivel down to make benches. Can you imagine? We were told that over a thousand people at one time could be seated here for a meeting."

"That man hasn't wasted a square inch. I'm becoming more impressed the more I see."

"Wait till you've sat in these chairs a while."

"They can't be that bad. Come now, weren't you impressed with the folding chairs downstairs?"

"You mean those that fold up and slip under the desks?"

"Those. Just think, once they are all raised up, how easy it will be to sweep the office floors. Why, Lizzie, can you even begin to comprehend the labor involved in having to stack eighteen hundred chairs every night before cleaning begins?"

"But did you sit in one, Maggie? Jack insisted I try. They don't swivel far enough to really be comfortable and are as ungiving as sitting on a rock. And, speaking of rocks, how about those chairs in the directors' office?"

"I don't imagine you cared for the modern styling though I rather fancied their appearance."

"Then you didn't try to move one."

"I can't say I did."

"Well, Jack did. Talk about heavy! The bottoms, he learned, were made of cast iron. And then there were those three-legged chairs. I'm surprised nobody's gotten hurt yet on one of those."

"Hurt? Why, the place is hardly open."

"Tippy. Terrible. And those desk tops!"

"I thought they were gorgeous, Lizzie. You do agree on that, don't you?"

"Well . . ."

"Did your guide explain them to you? They're made from magnesite, a new building material Wright imported from mines in Greece. It's used throughout the building, like cement in a way but, because it can be mixed on site, it leaves no seams."

"I didn't realize –"

"I can tell you I was taken with that soft gray shade. And just look around. You've been seeing it on the desktops, the trim on their sides, cabinet tops, why even the floors are a mixture of it. I remember Mr. Wright's enthusiasm when he discovered this particular mineral."

"I'll grant you that one, Maggie. I do like the color and its coolness. And I imagine it should be quite simple to clean."

"Plus it absorbs sound and is completely fireproof – and you know how important that has to be in a building like this."

"So what do you think of the food?" She was eager to point out that the same menu served to the directors and most distinguished guests was provided for the lowest clerk with prices easily affordable to all. Though free for this special occasion, the board listed roast beef and mashed potatoes at fifteen cents a serving, coffee and cream at three and even ice cream for only three cents more. A full meal could be purchased for twenty cents.

"Good, too, and definitely more than I needed." Maggie could see that Lizzie was anxious to be on the move. As she rose, however, she suggested their foursome get together for dinner. Eager to let the day last as long as possible, Maggie excitedly accepted her offer, certain Everett would agree.

"Let's go look for our men. I do hope you aren't planning to spend the entire day here."

"Oh, Lizzie, I don't want to rush. I want to drink it in, every view, every piece of furniture. I've never seen a cathedral in Europe but I imagine I'd feel about the same there."

"Trust me, Maggie, this is hardly a cathedral."

"I know. But I imagine seeing one for the first time would also take my breath away –"

"Well, perhaps it might help if I could see more of it through your eyes."

"Looking for a conversion, are you?"

"Go ahead and try, my dear. Shall we be off?"

"I'm ready," she wiped her lips and set the napkin down. "I'm certain there'll be much more to see."

"More? Good God, are you serious? We've climbed to the top, Maggie, what more can there possibly be?"

"The annex, Lizzie, that's what."

"Annex?" She slumped to her seat in faux fatigue. "I didn't know there was an annex. Where is that?"

"You've already been in part of it, Lizzie."

"I have?"

"It's where you came in, at the front door."

"You're teasing! Then why call that an annex? It seemed like a perfectly normal part of the building to me."

"It does down there. In fact the first and second floors are continuous so you might not even notice the difference."

"Why is there one?"

"As you have undoubtedly noticed, the workers in this building have very little privacy."

"A nightmare, if you ask me. I know I'd hate it."

"Well, Mr. Wright realized that, too. With space in this office building for eighteen hundred people, to keep things civilized, there had to be places where they could get away."

"And work at the same time?"

"No, not work. But employees are allowed breaks."

"But why an annex? Why not just part of the main building?"

"Mr. Wright wanted to separate the work time from the rest time, to make the break a literal one."

As they had continued to talk, the two women had descended to the fourth floor. Questioned, Lizzie described what she saw. "Rooms. Classrooms mostly, if I were to guess."

"How does it feel? Like the rest of the building?"

"No." She felt a little nervous as she examined her surroundings more closely. "Not at all."

"Can you figure out why, Lizzie?"

"I feel almost cramped."

"That's it! Look up. It is cramped because the ceilings are only eight feet high. In contrast the working areas are sixteen feet."

"But how can that be, especially when the rest –"

"There's the genius of Mr. Wright! These floors are in between those of the main building.No longer able to see the main work areas, Lizzie's questions continued. "Then how does one get to them? How would an employee find her way?"

"There are steps. See, over here. But hardly large or even, I suspect, easy to find."

By now they had reached the third floor and entered a large employees' lounge.

"Well, I'll be –"

"Isn't this something, Lizzie? Isn't this a find?"

"Reclining chairs, no less! And is that a real fireplace? And, oh look! It's a player piano, isn't it?"

"All the comforts of home."

"Comforts, perhaps, but comfortable, hardly. I don't believe I've ever seen a room so stark. I certainly wasn't impressed with what I've seen of the exterior of the the Martins' –" She glanced at her friend's down-turned eyes. "I don't mean to say anything to hurt your feelings. I'm sure what he did is just fine – for somebody else. But, dear, I grew up and have lived all my life in Victorian homes. That's what I know. The American-Georgian style of architecture – now that is what I call rich, the turrets and towers and zigzags and all those interesting little additions that make each so attractive and, I might add, so unique. And this – well, you know how we live. Chintz, soft furniture that's comfortable, not this hard leather and wood, beautiful cut glass, all the . . . well, I started to say *finer* things. You do too, Maggie, and I'm sure you appreciate them every bit as much as I."

"Oh, I do indeed. And . . . well, I couldn't afford one of his houses anyway." She paused to think of the differences. "I know what you're saying. But it's just . . . well, there is something exciting in his work. A freedom. A spirit. I wish I could explain it. But, Lizzie, it isn't – it shouldn't be – a matter of one being better than the other. Think of it as a new kind of art."

"No conversion yet," she laughed, "but keep trying."

"These must be the stairs. Second floor coming up, ma'am."

"Or down, as you prefer. All right now, shall you lecture me on the aesthetics of a seemingly endless row of toilets?"

"Employees do need washrooms, Liz. But come over here. I suspect even you will like this."

"Why, yes, I do. This is almost cozy. Or am I just growing accustomed to it all?" Her eyes followed the railing along the small balcony where desks and chairs, admittedly still built in, provided a great view back down to the main floor. "But what's it for?"

"Care to hazard a guess?"

"I suppose recalcitrant employees could be sent here as a punishment. I remember isolation as a schoolgirl. Though, now that I think about it, it might better serve as a reward. But that's not it, is it?"

"No, and I don't imagine you could guess. These spaces are set aside for visitors. After a tour of the building, they'll be encouraged to stop here, to write a postcard perhaps – supplied of course –"

"Naturally."

"— to describe the tour of the Larkin complex they have just finished."

"Maggie, I'll admit you're right about one thing."

"And what might that be?"

"Your Mr. Wright certainly thought of every detail."

"Yes, I do believe he did. And designed it very specifically for the Larkin system and its staff. You may not like it, Lizzie, but I think you'll agree that it gives the visitor the feeling that the Larkin Company cares as much about its employees as it does about its customers. Stop for a moment and look back up there, the relief panel. See what it says? 'To establish order, harmony, excellence.' Pretty good, isn't it?"

"Pretty good indeed. But look, I see Jack and Everett over there." She looked closely. "I don't recognize the gentlemen to whom they're speaking."

"Nor do I but – Ah, here they come now."

"And how was the tour, girls?"

"Jack, dear, I am fully educated and elucidated and ready to go home to be recreated. Do you suppose we might meet these fair people later for a bite to eat? Maggie thought it a sublime idea."

"Sorry to disagree but we really need to hurry home, Maggie."

"But later, dear?"

"Not today. We've left Rose alone much too long as it is. Sorry, Lizzie, Jack. Rose doesn't take kindly to strangers. Matter of fact, we had a bit of a time getting away this morning. We've been gone enough for one day."

Maggie turned quickly to Everett, mouth opening to sputter her protest. The look in his eye changed her mind. She turned without saying a word to her friend and followed her husband out the door.

CII

August 1906

She settled back in the car as it pulled away from the crowded area. Maggie had continued to fume in protest at her husband's edict as they waited for the driver to get the car. Now, having had moments to reflect, she knew a lost cause when she met one and turned to a safer subject.

"How did you find Jack, dear? Did you men have a chance to talk?"

Relieved that a more neutral subject had been broached, Everett opened up eagerly and expansively.

"He seemed terribly quiet to me. Disinterested even, though perhaps that could be blamed on your Wright fellow and this latest design."

"I'd like to think it as simple as that."

"Why? Did Lizzie say something to you?"

"No." She paused to reflect. "I had hoped she might. God knows, she had enough opportunities but, well . . ." Her thoughts drifted into silence.

One would have had to be deaf and dumb not to be aware of the talk swirling through both the company and their society, not to be aware of the change that had come over Jack Knapp. It was Lizzie who had been so close to the boy, that's what confused those who continued to talk now. Lizzie who had carried the sorrow for so long, Lizzie who now seemed the epitome of stoicism and strength.

Jack's devotion – if that's what it was – seemed long overdue and, well, were one to be asked (and they weren't), rather misplaced. The boy hardly needed his affection – or sorrow – now. Better to devote his attention to that long-suffering wife of his.

. . .

"Well, Lizzie, surprise!" Jack's voice boomed as he strode purposefully across the parlor to where Lizzie sat sewing.

She set it down immediately. "Why, this is indeed a surprise. What happened?"

"They canceled the meeting at work. By the time I learned of it, it was too late to make other arrangements. So I decided to come home." He bent to kiss her. "I know you're always harping that I'm never home. Well, here I am!"

She looked up at him and smiled a little.

"Think there's enough food in the kitchen for one more?"

She momentarily hoped there wasn't as she realized how long it had been since Jack had taken her out for a dinner alone. Pushing the ungrateful thought from her mind, she started to rise. "Let me see what Cook says."

She was back in moments, a happier smile fixed on her face. "It may take half an hour or so. She says she'll have to add some ingredients but promises you'll not be disappointed."

"A half hour's hardly enough time, dear wife." He walked to the table where the tray of liquors and glasses sat. "It's been a hard day. Shall I get something for you?" She shook her head. "Then be a good girl and run to the kitchen for some ice – and a lager."

"With your whisky?"

"Certainly. It slows the whisky drinking and is actually quite a pleasant combination."

When Lizzie returned she saw Jack already drinking from a tumbler filled to within an inch of its rim.

"Shall I pour this in a glass for you?"

"Don't bother."

She crossed the room and handed him the bottle.

Before dinner was called he had finished a second whisky as large as the first. Lizzie couldn't see that the beer had slowed his drinking down at all.

He stumbled momentarily as he crossed the hall to the dining room, blamed it on a loose edge of carpeting, and took his place. Lizzie seated herself.

As the food was carried in, Jack boisterously demanded

that a bottle of burgundy be uncorked. Lizzie opened her mouth to protest, thought better of it, and remained quiet. She hoped all but this one woman had retired for the evening.

None of the staff was ignorant of Jack's heavy drinking. It had begun after they had buried Abram and the family had returned to their own lives. Children gone. Charlie back home in Pennsylvania. *Normal* lives, Lizzie reflected. She had thought once that perhaps even her life might regain a touch of normality after the death of her troubled son. Never had she expected Jack to be the one to fold.

"What's that?" Jack's question was muffled by the large piece of roll in his mouth. He pointed to a gravy boat that had been placed before him.

"Béarnaise sauce, dear. It's for the meat."

"Do I like it?"

"I should think so. It's quite good with the roast."

He poured about half of the contents of the bowl over his meat and potatoes. The first taste had him licking his lips. "Delicious, Lizzie, truly is. Why don't we have that more often? We should, you know." Jack reached again for the bowl and poured a sizable amount over his cold salad.

Lizzie continued to eat, taking small bites to savor the subtle flavorings of each dish, grateful for the small portion of sauce she had gotten for herself. Dinner proceeded silently.

As he reached for another roll, Jack knocked over his glass of wine.

"Oh, dear!" Lizzie unconsciously rose as she watched the majority of its contents spill onto his half-finished dinner plate. "I think Cook has gone to bed but, if you wish, I can get a clean plate and try to clean up some of this mess."

"For God's sakes, woman, stop fussing so!" He threw his napkin on the table, into the wine which continued to creep across the damask tablecloth. "I just wanted to eat in peace. Is that asking so much?"

He stood. "I expected you to be pleased to have me home. And yet what have you done ever since I walked through the door? Pick, pick, pick. What a sorry excuse for a wife!" Taking the bottle with him he crossed to the china cabinet for a clean glass.

"I'm tired tonight, Liz. Do what you have to do here and hurry up to bed. I'll be waiting."

"I'll hurry, dear, of course, but Cook is gone for the night and I can hardly leave – well, this."

"Forget the lectures. Just do what you have to. And hurry."

Lizzie enjoyed the newfound solitude as she slowly washed the dinner dishes, dried them and put them away. She rinsed the tablecloth well before taking it to the basement to soak. The table needed to be polished before the wine could strip the gleam from the wood. Wine had also dripped through the opening where an extra leaf fitted, forming a purple puddle below. Another cloth and a bucket of cool water took care of that as well as she could. She thanked the decorator for choosing burgundy-patterned carpets.

She extinguished the lights. The house seemed happily at peace. If only. . .

CIII

November 1906

Lizzie sat, staring sullenly at the windshield. A drop here, another raindrop there, slowly swelling until each began its slow race to the bottom of the glass. The day started off with a heavy snowfall but, by mid-afternoon, the sun had reappeared and now only slush remained in the streets. She thought now she might even have glimpsed an early star as she finished dressing and went downstairs to the waiting automobile.

"Did you find it?" She looked up as Jack hurried around the car, opened his door and slid in beside her. "Right on the bureau, just as you said. Thanks for remembering. I'd have hated to drive all the way out there and then discover we'd left our invitation at home."

"From what I hear, we'd never get in the front door without it, no matter who we know."

"I can't imagine Darwin Martin refusing us entrance. I've worked beside the man for more years than I can remember."

"If he tried, I'd be tempted to tell him where to take his ugly little house, and –"

"Lizzie, Lizzie! This bleak weather must really be getting to you."

"Don't you find it terrible, too? I won't believe you if you tell me it isn't bothering you."

"Of course it is, dear. It's been a beastly week."

"Winter."

"What?"

"Winter. A beastly winter and just begun at that."

"Whatever you say, dear. Perhaps I've just grown more used to it. Oh! That's the house, isn't it?"

"Oh, goodness! Have you ever seen so many cars? I wonder where we'll park."

"I don't imagine Martin would overlook that detail. Yes, here comes the valet now."

"Uniformed, too. Looks like it'll be quite an evening."

"Shall we go, dear?"

. . .

"Home, sweet home! I swear, I have never appreciated anything so much in my life. Why, I'd . . ."

"Kneeling to kiss the floor may be a bit much, dear."

"Even if I could, you mean? I'm sure I could get down but, oh, my, do you suppose I could get up again?"

"Let's not even try to find out."

"Did you have enough to eat there or shall I check the kitchen?"

"First time I've ever been served in a basement but the buffet certainly seemed adequate. You, too? Shall I fix you a drink?"

Accepting it gratefully, she sipped deeply and let out a strong sigh. "My, God, can you imagine those people actually having to live in that house? It's quite one thing to open it to a hundred – do you think there were more? – but imagine what poor Isabelle and Darwin must be feeling right now. Door closing on the last of their guests and turning back to face that empty – and I do mean empty – hollowed out hull of a building. If I were Isabelle, I assure you, I'd be in tears, and nothing, nor anybody, would be able to stop them. Short of moving me back into a real house. A home. Like that lovely one across the street."

"I really didn't find it that bad, dear. It is hard to imagine what it would be like without such crowds, admittedly, but it is a lovely building for entertaining."

"Oh, come on, Jack. How many times do you think the Martins, or anybody else for that matter, will be inviting a couple hundred in for a table of bridge – or a cup of tea? What would you do the rest of the time?"

"I'm just saying that perhaps it isn't *all* bad."

"Yes, my dear Jack, it is. Look around you. Here, just this room alone. What do you see?"

"I'm really not sure what you're getting at."

"Just look. The crystal chandelier, for starters. See how the prisms reflect the light? It's even lovelier in sunlight which we do get on occasions though lately I've begun to have my doubts."

"You're digressing. The room, if you please."

"All right then, chandelier. Look at the ornate paper on the walls, the lovely colors which your decorator picked up again in the draperies and of course in the carpeting and through all the upholstery, each obviously chosen to complement the other. Upholstery brings us to another point. What did you see in that house? Cushions, not very thick ones either, and furniture? Hardly! Why, I heard them saying that man built all their furniture. Even designed those terrible lamps."

"There I do have to disagree. I thought they showed a great deal of workmanship. In fact, I was quite taken with the colored glass."

"You're wrong. All right, I'll grant that maybe it worked in the windows – if, that is, you want your view of the outdoors blocked – but lamps? No. They made the rooms much too dark. And those colors! Or, I suppose I should say lack of color for everything seemed so terribly neutral. It was like entering a cave –"

"If that was a cave, it was certainly a large one. But let's not argue over something so unimportant. Here, I'll fill your glass."

He turned to the table, and then returned, handing the filled glass back to his wife. "Whether or not Martin and his wife are happy there, well, that's really up to them. What I think has little, if anything, to do with it. Way I see it, he's stubbornly staked everything on his faith in this Wright fellow. And, now that we've seen for ourselves just what it is he does, well . . . I can't help wondering what he'll want to do next."

"It certainly won't be anything like that house. As I recall, not even that new office building was this strange."

"Fascinating fellow, though, wasn't he, dear? Did you have a chance to speak to him? Certainly not lacking in ego."

"No, but I doubt if I missed much. Must admit, though, there wasn't much of Buffalo's society whom I didn't see somewhere in that expanse. Certainly was a crowd. And all those flowers – imagine! Finding so many so late in the season."

"Shouldn't be a problem for the Martins once their greenhouse is up and running. And I heard rumors they already had a conservatory."

"At the far end of the pergola, or so someone said. Not that one could ever see with so many bodies in between. I tried to get through but the crowds were too thick."

"So you missed the Nike?"

"The *what?*"

"I heard talk that Wright had insisted on installing a full-sized Nike statue at the end of the pergola. Rather like the one he'd done for the office building."

"Even in a house like that one, that seems a bit much. You do, don't you think? Why, I can't imagine anyone would allow a madman to go that far." She paused, drained her glass, and looked up onto her husband's eyes as he rose, hand already outstretched. "They wouldn't, Jack. Would they?"

"I'm afraid they just might."

CIV

August 1907

"And ice water for the gentleman, sir."

"Thank you."

"Still on the wagon, old boy? Well, bully for you!"

"I can't tell you how proud I am of Jack. Why, do you know it's been almost a year?"

"By George, are you sure, Lizzie? Even I didn't realize it had been that long."

"Then I trust it hasn't been a terrible hardship."

"Funny thing is, Everett, it never was. Well," he hesitated, "almost never. I can honestly say I've never regretted the decision."

Everett raised his glass. "Is it all right to invite you to join us in a toast?"

"No problem there. What shall we toast?"

"To our friendship, for starters. It's been a good year for us all, the year since the Larkin Company opened the office building."

"You can hardly call that an unmitigated success," Lizzie added.

"Look at all the criticism it's gotten –" Jack agreed.

"And those terrible seats, suicide chairs they were called before they were finally removed."

"Obviously Maggie's Mr. Wright never spent much time on a three-legged chair!"

"And I'm sure he won't now. But, really, we should be fair," Everett hurried to the defense of his wife. "The community has certainly accepted the building as a work of art."

"I'm not so sure about that. I've heard some – people whose ideas still count for something in the community, too

– call it an egregious mistake."

"Lizzie!"

"They are still arguing about the outrageous expense involved in its construction. How much good will would it take to justify all that wasted money?"

"I'd like to speak for Mr. Wright," Maggie interjected. "He adamantly believed that the fireproofing and clean air, not to mention the sanitary conditions, would contribute to the peaceful environment he deemed so necessary."

"And I know Maggie will tell you that Wright believed in cutting costs as much as anyone. He was always searching for the least expensive ways to accomplish his aims."

"Everett, Maggie, please!" Jack impatiently tapped his water glass with the fork still held in his hand. "You talk as if nothing has happened this past year except the opening of that one building. I'll grant you it's an important milestone but there's more to life than the Larkin Company . . . or even Maggie's Mr. Wright."

Lizzie snorted. "Hardly Mr. Wright to anybody these days, if what I read is true."

"Or is he Mr. Right to one too many? I know his present notoriety has caused some pretty big ripples through Buffalo society. You never had a clue, Maggie?"

"Sorry, Jack, I wasn't that interested in his personal doings. Not then, not now. The man's a genius. Maybe that makes him different from you and me."

As dinner progressed, Maggie glanced around the crowded dining room. She noted festive four- and six-somes filling the tables, each gaily attentive to their dining partners, and wondered if their dinner conversions were meatier than hers.

"Of course not, old girl." Jack's words held little meaning for her. "And I will try to make up for it next year. With Typhoid Mary finally arrested, I assume all of us can look forward to many more years of good health."

"It is amazing, isn't it? I mean how much longer people are living these days. And Rose! Just think of what the future holds for her! I know the average lifespan has increased, thanks largely to the advances in treating childhood diseases."

Everett did ramble so. Not that she minded the company of these kind people. Lizzie had quite a bit to offer and Maggie knew her husband admired the other man tremendously.

"Why, with the improvements we've seen in sanitation and housing, even nutrition –" How he did go on. " – not to mention our general standard of living, any one of us might live to be – why, who knows? Dare I say eighty?"

"I think that's carrying it a bit far."

"I wouldn't even want to live to be that old. Brrr! Just thinking about it gives me goose-bumps."

"Though I feel quite certain, my dear, you'd accept another ten years if it were offered."

"You bet I would. And wish the same for you – and Everett, of course. Maggie's so young she needn't worry." Jack winked at the younger woman. "Here, can we ask the waiter to fill our glasses one more time? I'd like to propose a toast to the future. To ten years from today."

I can drink to that. "Here! Here!"

"Yes, to nineteen seventeen!"

CV

June 1908

Lizzie switched on the ceiling light and quietly crossed the bedroom to her dressing table. Seating herself in front of the triple mirrors, she began to remove the pins from her hair. Long hair was such a bother, especially now that she was older, but Jack wouldn't consider allowing her to have it cut. She remembered only too clearly his consternation when she had brought up the subject early in the spring. Perhaps it was just the celebration of their anniversary that had made him so eager to cling to what had been. Still, forty years was forty years and, if he wanted her with long hair, then she'd let it grow until she was Rapunzel herself!

Picking up the silver hairbrush, she began to work the long tresses.

Oh, my! The reflection was certainly dismaying. If the light here did this, she hated to think how she must appear by the brightness of day. And wasn't this the season when those cruel days were the longest?

When had all those lines appeared in her neck? And around her mouth? My goodness! Just look how the lipstick ran in cragged cracks beneath her lower lip. Why hadn't Jack told her before they went out? She looked like a pumpkin painted for Halloween.

Nor could she any longer deny that her hair was gray. The change had been gradual and not unwelcome though she hoped it wouldn't be too many more years before it all turned white. Was there anything more attractive than a solidly white-haired woman, or man?

Funny, she still never thought of Jack as old. He took such pride in himself and that pleased her. Seems so few did at his age. He exercised daily, walked whenever he could and had taken to this new sport of golf with a relish she hadn't seen in decades. She was glad he didn't drink any more. His appetite – well, what other man would have eaten that much for dessert? Still, if he overindulged one day he sensibly cut back the next. She, on the other hand, was forced to watch every bite she consumed. *Matronly* was a kind appraisal, she honestly believed, though she remained determined not to let herself spread further. She had witnessed only too often what could happen to a woman in her sixties.

This was the first time she had noticed the folds of flesh dangling from her naked arm as she raised the brush. And all those lines and wrinkles!

"Jack! I didn't hear you. Have you been there long?"

"Just came upstairs, dear."

He looked admiringly across the room at his wife. Her long hair glistened in the light, her face as radiantly beautiful as the day he'd first seen her. He knew she took pride in her figure and was grateful for it. So many of the wives of the men he knew had let themselves go as they had aged. Yet here was his, a jewel among jewels. How could anyone turn away from a face like that?

Lizzie continued to brush as she watched her husband's figure, reflected in the mirror on the dressing table, cross the room. As he removed the studs from his shirt, one slipped to the floor. She was surprised how difficult it was for him to bend to pick it up. Straightening, he resumed his pace until he stood behind her.

"It was a lovely day, wasn't it?"

"Of course it was, Lizzie, though sometimes I believe you think every day a lovely one."

"Particularly in June. But I meant your birthday, dear. I hope it was good for you."

"Why wouldn't it be?"

"There was no party for one thing. Usually it seems that at least some of the children come home to help us celebrate. It seemed quiet, almost sad, without them."

"I've never seen so many notes and gifts. Why, Lizzie, I

feel exceptionally blessed to have such a fine family."

"Not a single one forgot you."

"I think that's quite special in itself. Don't you agree?"

"I would have felt disappointed – for you – had any of the children not remembered your birthday. It is a special day, you know."

"Sixty-seven? What's special about sixty-seven?"

"Not the year –"

"You mean simply that an old codger like me is still alive and kicking?"

"Don't talk like that, Jack. You're hardly a codger. Or old. No, I simply meant that . . . well, anyone's birthday should be extraordinary. I just hope this one was extra nice for you."

"You know it was. Here, may I brush for a while?"

"Oh! I'd like that very much."

"You do, don't you?"

"Do what?"

"Know that it was a perfect day, from beginning until . . . well, now. Even now."

"Wonder why it is that it always feels so much better when someone else brushes my hair?"

"I enjoy doing it, now that you mention it. Can hardly ask you to return the favor."

"'Fraid not, not any more."

"Know what I was thinking about as I climbed the stairs?"

"With you, Jack, it could be anything."

"Last August."

"Any particular reason?"

"Absolutely. I was thinking of the dinner we had with Everett and Maggie."

She glanced up at his reflection. "Strange couple, aren't they?"

"Strange? I thought you liked them."

"I do. It's just that – well, he's obviously so much older than she. I don't know, I find it hard to relate well to either one. Not that I don't like them."

"But Everett's only a year older than I," Jack added.

"And Maggie's still a young . . . well, she seems terribly young."

"I imagine she's getting closer to fifty than she'd like."

"Fifty! Here you are closing in on seventy."

"And you a mere lass of – what is it now? Sixty-two? I find it hard to remember."

"I always knew there would be advantages to a failing memory."

"Some compensation for the keys and pens I keep losing, is that what you're suggesting?"

"Something like that. And I'm really sixty-three but you can start counting backwards anytime you like."

"Are you afraid of growing old, Liz?"

"Afraid? I don't think I've ever thought of it, at least not in those terms. I do worry some. I guess that's fear. Of growing frail. Or going fuzzy in the mind. I've seen that happen and it terrifies me. Good God, what would happen if I needed somebody to take care of me? To clean up, to watch – to treat me like a little child. I'd rather be dead than have that happen."

"Lizzie, Lizzie. Calm yourself." He placed the brush back on the dressing table and reached down to massage her tightened shoulders.

"You forget, dear, I saw how it was at the end with Mother Knapp. Her mind was going, you know that."

"I do."

She let his probing fingers dig deep into her shoulders. She hadn't realized how sore they were. Bending her head forward, she was pleased he took the cue and began to gently rub her neck. "I know I want to go peacefully . . . before I become a burden to anyone."

"Let's hope that's a long way off. For either of us."

"Know something else, Jack? Sometimes I worry about you."

"Me?"

"What would happen to me . . . if anything happened to you? I've never lived alone and I can tell you I wouldn't want to begin now. Oh, Jack," she turned to face her husband.

"Promise me you won't leave me alone."

"Now you're talking silly. Turn back around and let me rub some more."

"Or poor."

"What?"

"I don't want to be poor, Jack. It was all right when we were young but I think I should suffer dreadfully if I had to do without all the comforts we enjoy now."

"Lizzie! Who said anything about being poor? Whatever put such a notion in your mind?"

"You know as well as I of the vagaries of the stock market. And I know it can go down just as well as up. Personally, I'd feel much safer with our money in the bank."

"Or, more likely, under the mattress. Really, Liz, there are times when I think you have to manufacture something to make you sad just to be happy. There is nothing wrong with the market. Larkin continues to prosper – and so shall we. Any other worries while we're on the topic?"

"Well, yes . . . darn!"

"What now?"

"I forgot what I was going to say." He continued the gentle massage on his wife, obviously lost in deep thought. Her head jolted up. "I'm sorry."

"Whoa, there! Sorry about what?"

"I interrupted you. I don't remember but I must have."

"Whatever are you talking about now, dear?"

"You told me that you were thinking of the dinner we had last August with Maggie and Everett. But you never completed the thought. No, I know I didn't forget that."

"It really wasn't that important. All I was thinking of was the toast: to ten years hence."

"Well, the first of those is almost gone."

"Indeed. And we've made in it health and, I dare say, a great deal of happiness. It's just that – well, sometimes that seems so far away. But then I realize how quickly time is passing and I imagine I'll be a tottering seventy-six instead of my present sixty-seven before I know it. Just as long as I do when the time comes."

"Would you do it all over again?"

"Do what?"

"Would you make changes if you could start over?"

"Can't say I've ever given any thought to that. I like the work I've done. Larkin is a good man to work for. Guess I wish I might have risen a little higher – wouldn't have minded an executive desk of my own – but, all in all, it's been a good life. I've been able to give you most everything you've wanted. I have, Lizzie, haven't I?"

"Of course, darling."

"And the children. All got college educations and seem to be doing quite well now."

"I do wish they weren't so far away."

"We both do."

"Do you worry about them, Jack?"

"Is this another case of your borrowing trouble? What's to worry about? I wish I'd hear from them more often. Certainly I'd like to see them more. But, as far as I know, things are all right."

"Of course they are. At least I imagine they are. I miss having the grandchildren around. They're like little strangers. Every time we get together we have to get reacquainted all over again."

"Lizzie! It's hardly as dire as that. Just look around you, all the pictures in this room. If living to a ripe old age does have its rewards, certainly these are ours. We have a beautiful family, much to be proud of."

"And –" She fell silent.

"Hmm? Oh. It's Abram, isn't it?"

"Do you ever think of him, any more I mean?"

"Of course I do. But I don't let the sorrow erase all our other blessings. He isn't forgotten, nor, I'm sure, will he be. Not as long as either you or I continue to live. But look around you, Liz. There's too much good here."

"Do you think we'll ever know what really happened?"

"With Abram? I know for a positive fact his mother will never be convinced he killed Andre Robson."

"No, I definitely won't."

"But he wouldn't defend himself, Liz. If he were innocent, why didn't he say so?"

"I used to think he did it to protect me, that he honestly believed I shot Andre. Yet, no matter how often I told him that was rubbish, he never changed."

"I'm afraid his secret went to the grave with him."

"I wonder . . ."

"Wonder? At what?"

"Well, if Abram didn't kill Andre, then somebody else must have."

"Yes, I'd say so. It didn't sound as if the poor bloke shot himself."

"Then what if the killer's still out there?"

"And creeping up right now to . . . to get you!"

"Jack! What if someone had heard me squeal like that?"

"You should do it more often, my dear."

"I should hope not!"

"The servants should get used to it!" He kissed her neck.

Lizzie leaned back, pleased at the solidness that was her husband. Bending down Jack kissed the top of her head. He glanced in the mirror to see a wide smile.

She reached behind her to circle his waist, felt the stings in her arms from muscles not accustomed to such motion and slowly rose from the dressing table instead.

If a murderer did remain at large, for now he would be hidden from the thoughts of one husband and wife.

CVI

I ran into the woods – what was I looking for? – when suddenly I was overcome with the most unspeakable horror.

Why? What is there to be scared of?

I had taken off at that first moment of fright, running as hard as I could, as fast as I ever have, until a stitch in my side forced me to stop. The pain! I leaned against a mossy elm, struggling to catch my breath, my chest racked with each inhalation.

No! I mustn't stop yet. I've got to keep going.

The woods aren't deep here. If I stand still I can see the sunlit green at the edge. The sounds of the players are close. Still trying to calm myself I looked up into the leafy umbrella that stretched overhead. The sky was the shade of the robin's eggshell I had found earlier in the spring, now among my treasures on the windowsill.

A squirrel chattered noisily.

At me?

Or was it telling them where to find me?

Should I hide? Or try to run again?

Run. Run. Faster. You have got to go faster.

Ouch! Clumsy. Watch your step. It's black as pitch in here. I can't see where I'm going.

What was that? Something moved . . . Quiet . . . Listen . . . Hush now. Don't panic . . . You mustn't let fear get the better of you . . . Listen . . . I don't hear anything behind me . . . But what?

There it is again! Over there.

That old owl's not going to hurt you, scaredy-cat. Stop shivering. It's hardly that cold.

What in God's name is happening to me?

Midsummer – hot – sun overhead and I'm pressed against this tree shaking uncontrollably! Why am I so afraid?

The clouds are parting. How bright the moon is. It's easy now to see the path. But if I can see it so can they.

Have they found him yet?

I've got to keep going.

Noise! Could it – yes, absolutely! It's the whinny of a horse.

But is it mine?

The sound's off to my right, not straight ahead where I think it should be. If it is my horse.

Yes, I'm coming. I'll be right there. I just stopped to listen to your laughter.

Such happy sounds.

Sorry, I didn't mean to be gone long. I was following the strangest bird song. No, I never did see it.

Horse. It has to be mine.

You're almost safe.

Just get away.

Faster.

CVII
June 1908

Exhausted, she rose from her bed and walked to the bedroom window. The first rays of morning's light were just appearing. Had she not dozed at all during the night?

Maggie looked back to where the child lay. She had thrown off the light blanket in her last fit of fever, tossing and turning so that at last Maggie had stopped trying to keep her damp body covered. She looked down as the youngster groaned now and turned, lost in fitful sleep. It had been days since Rose had recognized her own mother, days since she had taken any water or nourishment. The doctor, attending frequently as he made his rounds – so many sick now! – offered what words of comfort he could. Maggie knew that Rose lay beyond treatment. Just cool compresses and prayer, lots of prayer, until she could pull herself out of the devastating fever. If only she could rest.

Maggie looked with pity at the small body. Such a struggle for one so young. Thank God Rose had always been blessed with robust health. Certainly that would stand her in good stead now, get her through this when other children would perish.

His snort reminded Maggie that Everett had slept all night in the chair in the corner. She had begged him to go off to bed, at least for a few hours. What possible good did it do for them both to be here every moment? God knew, she was doing all that could be done.

What was Everett except in the way? Unable to make any effort to appreciate hers. And how he carried on! Why, hadn't he stood there, beside the bed, just yesterday, looking Maggie straight in the eye? "Do something!" he had ordered, his anguish obvious.

Well, so was hers. "What more, in God's name, do you want me to do?"

"There has to be something. Rose can't continue to suffer this way."

"The doctor was here this morning. You heard every word he said."

"Of course I did, but –"

"No. No buts. He's a good doctor. You've certainly had confidence in him up to now."

"You're right."

"Then be equally sure that we're in the midst of a raging epidemic. There is only so much anyone can do."

"But –"

"We're doing it, Everett. It pains me at least as much to see Rose like this."

"I look down at her and can't help but think of the happy child, the little girl who liked to play in the park with her friends, running after the ball –"

"Buster at her feet."

"As he is at yours now, my dear."

"I'm sure he's every bit as concerned as we are."

"Don't you think that rather ridiculous? Do you really believe a dog can worry?"

"I don't know if it's worry but he is obviously concerned. He won't leave her side."

"Or yours."

"Get some rest, Everett."

"I just woke up."

"Napping in that chair is hardly the same thing. Go ahead; I'll stay with Rose."

"No, you go. I'll stay."

Suddenly Maggie stretched – slowly, lavishly – and with it she felt the first fatigue she had known since Rose had fallen sick. She yawned. "I'm sorry. I didn't know how tired I was. Yes, if you won't, I think maybe I will lie down for a while."

The sheets felt cool. She stretched out, squirming into position until she couldn't feel the edges of the bed anywhere, hands and feet extended. She wanted to close them, remembering the motions she had used as a child to make angels in the snow. Angels.

Good God, what time is it? Maggie jolted awake, conscious that the room around her was dark. No. It wasn't possible she had slept all day. Had the doctor not come? Certainly that would have awakened her. But how good it had felt; how rested she felt now. Ready to face . . . Rose! Groggily she arose and crossed the bedroom floor, aware of the cool boards beneath her bare feet.

The lamp had been lit next to the bed where Rose still slept. Buster lay on the floor, now raising his head to acknowledge her presence with a wag of his tail. She saw that Everett was again curled up in the corner chair, eyes closed.

From the bathroom she went downstairs to the kitchen, turning on lights as she progressed. The house seemed ominously dark and silent. She'd have preferred milk with the sandwich she hastily prepared, opting instead for a cup of tea just to hear the happy whistle of the tea kettle.

Again, as still as a tomb. She shivered. The sandwich was finished before the tea had steeped. Carrying the cup she headed back to the staircase.

Everett must have risen while she was downstairs for he now lay on the bed beside Rose. How still she looked. How beautiful now. Then . . . the fever must have broken. Thank the good Lord! She would be herself again in no time at all.

Maggie walked closer, admiring the peaceful expression on the sleeping child. She placed her hand gently on her forehead.

Oh, God, no! Oh, no! It isn't possible. Please, God.

Everett woke as she shook the child.

"Maggie! What's the matter with you? Let her sleep. She needs her rest. Maggie! Stop it!"

He looked down now at the body of his daughter, asleep no longer.

. . .

"There shouldn't be funerals for children. It's not a time to be with others. Who can offer comfort? Not now."

"But Everett, they came to let you know how much they care – for you, for us."

"And how is that supposed to help? I don't care about them. I lost my little girl."

"They understand."

"No, Maggie, I don't think even you do." The coldness in his voice frightened her.

"What are you saying? She was my daughter, too. I loved her with all my heart."

"And your organ. Your writing. And your clubs. And your friends. And –"

"Stop it! That's unfair and you know it."

"I know nothing of the kind."

"I refuse to stay to listen to such nonsense."

He watched as she rose and began to leave the room.

"Going upstairs, dear? Do you think you can get away that easily? Escape the memory of our child by leaving the room?"

"I'm not trying to escape anything – except your very unpleasant mood. Why don't we just wait until you're feeling a little better?"

"*Better?* We just buried our daughter."

"Of that I am wholly aware. But that has nothing to do with my organ playing or – What other so-called faults did you throw at me? Friends? Clubs? What club, Everett? I belong to none but Shakespeare Club and you go to that as regularly as I."

"Are you saying I caused the death of my daughter by belonging to the Shakespeare Club?"

"I swear, you're practically ranting. I said nothing of the sort. Everett, I don't care how many clubs you belong to. It has nothing to do with what happened to Rose."

"But if you'd been here with her more, home as a mother is expected to be –"

"Everett, your daughter would have been eight years old had she lived until the end of the month. She was in school. She had friends. I was home, believe me I was, when I needed to be."

"Women – wives, mothers – belong at home. Seems to me you were always gallivanting about. Chasing after that Wright fellow. God knows what else."

"Stop it! I won't listen to any more of this."

"Nor will you have to."

She did a quick about-face. "Wha – ?

"I merely meant I was going to go to bed. I assume you still mean for me to sleep in the guest room." He turned angrily toward her. "Talk about misnomers! When was the last time this house saw a guest? The forsaken-husband's room. Let's call it what it is."

"Call it whatever you want, dear." She was beginning to realize the depth of her own exhaustion. She watched him slowly climb the stairs with a growing sense of relief.

How hideous this entire situation had become! Why, if they had any shred of love left for each other, they should be consoling one another, the earth still fresh over the coffin of their only child. And yet, look – well, wasn't it what she had come to expect?

She'd wait just till she heard no further movement upstairs. It would feel good to go to bed.

Instead, suddenly awake, Maggie decided to pour one small drink for herself while she waited. Maybe it would relax her, calm those jangled nerves, help her get to sleep.

How did anyone drink this awful tasting Scotch whisky? Her nose wrinkled up at the aroma even before she took the first sip.

She relished the slow burn as it passed her throat.

Motherhood hadn't been a hundred percent proposition with her, no denying that, but she had certainly loved her daughter. The park. Play times. Countless hours spent reading to her, her favorites over and over till the pages grew ragged. Helping with her lessons – well, Everett usually liked to do that and she was happy letting him. She had the days with the girl. An hour or two at night was the father's prerogative.

Father. Mother, she reflected bitterly as she filled her glass. Nobody had ever told her they were fighting words.

They had doted – together and happily – when the baby was born. Rose, like the flowers blooming in the late June garden. Everett had treated her like a queen then. Nothing he wouldn't give to the one who had given him the greatest gift of all.

. . .

Light was streaming in the windows when she woke. Shame surged through her body. What a way to behave just after her daughter's funeral!

She tiptoed upstairs, relieved to see the door to his room shut. Locking the door first, she bathed and then returned to her room to dress. Each step seemed to holler its squeaks as she tried to quietly retrace her steps to the first floor. She'd just fix herself two slices of toast with jam, maybe eat one of those oranges. If somebody didn't soon, they were certain to rot.

The house still quiet, Maggie decided to take Buster for a walk. She was happy to see him recover his usual robustness as they approached the park. Maggie reached for the ball in her pocket and threw it wildly. Funny, how those laughs sounded when they came at last.

She hesitated, unwilling to return to that house.

Church bells ring. The clock tower. Noon. The park was beginning to fill with the early strollers returning from church. She couldn't face so many people. Not yet.

Reluctantly she leashed Buster and the two headed back down the avenue toward home.

She was surprised how quiet everything was. Nothing in the kitchen had been touched. Certainly by now Everett should be up and eager for a hearty meal for hadn't he refused all nourishment last night?

She called his name. Once. Twice. Ever louder. Climbing the stairs now with determination, she hoped to make enough sound to waken him.

She saw no sign that he had been up at all.

"Everett." Nothing.

She knocked at the bedroom door. Getting no response

she tried the knob and saw it turned easily in her hand.

Still in his pajamas, he was stretched across the bed, breathing heavily.

Too heavily.

She walked closer, leaning down to feel his forehead, knowing before she touched him that the fever was already busily ravaging the man.

CVIII

June 1909

"And that's exactly what she said to me. Word for word. Can you imagine?"

Ardith and Jo exchanged looks of amazement before turning back to Lizzie. "Did she seem really happy, Liz?"

"If you want the honest truth, I think I'm more than a little jealous of her."

"You? Why, Lizzie, I always thought you and Jack seem so well suited to each other."

"No, Jack has been as good a husband as I guess any woman is likely to have, but . . ."

"He hasn't started drinking again, has he?"

"No, though, to tell you the truth, I almost wish he would."

"Lizzie, you don't mean that!"

"No, I don't. Of course I don't. It's just that – well, with his halo of sobriety, life has become a terrible bore."

"*Bore?* I don't believe it!"

"You wouldn't want him to start again, would you?"

Lizzie paused.

"Oh, Liz, I can't believe that."

"There are times . . . but, no. I confess I miss the highs but, then again, I'd never wish back those terrible lows. I just miss the fun now. Besides, I hardly see him anymore. Just when you think he'd be reaching an age when it was all right to slack off, he seems to have gotten even more involved with his work. What time he doesn't spend at Larkin's he's putting into the automobile club. Now it's their new magazine, *Buffalo Motorist*. Jack's discovered editing and he loves it."

"So you're sitting home alone much of the time –"

"And pouting."

"Girls, you make me sound like a spoiled child!" She looked from the eyes of one to the other, letting her words sink in as their quiet continued. "Oh, I see."

"No, maybe you don't, Lizzie."

"You mean I have a good life. Good man. Good family. Good home. And absolutely no reason to complain. That is what you're saying, isn't it?"

"I think it's possible to have – well, everything – and still be unhappy."

"You mean there's something the matter with me; is that it?"

"I think Jo's trying to say what you're feeling isn't abnormal. And it certainly isn't wrong."

"Or bad."

"Come on, you two. You've lost me. What exactly is it you're suggesting?"

"That you need a new outlet, new interests. I believe it's as simple as that."

"You just need to find a cause."

"Something you can pour all this extra energy and interest into."

"So what can I do?"

Ardith smiled. "She has the babies, you know –"

"I think Jo is a blessed saint to give so many hours to rocking those sick babies at the hospital. But I couldn't do that. It would break my heart. No, I don't want anything oppressive. Or even remotely depressing."

"Trust me, the babies aren't but I do understand. It isn't for everyone."

"I've an idea, Lizzie. Jo and I are going to a meeting tomorrow night to organize a campaign for emancipation. Why don't you come along?"

"Emancipation, Ardith? I thought we already freed the slaves."

"Not the coloreds. Us."

"We want to get the vote for women," Jo added.

"Certainly you've heard of the movement."

"I don't think I ever gave it much thought."

"Elizabeth Knapp, can you, for one minute, honestly tell me that you believe we women are unqualified to vote?"

"Why, no. Definitely not the educated ones. But what about all the others?"

"I can't believe you!"

"What good would it do to have a group of women voting if they had no idea what they were voting for?" Lizzie defended herself. "I can see where that might do irreparable damage to our country. Certainly you can't disagree with me."

"Can you honestly tell Jo and me that you believe every man is qualified and most women are not?"

"Lizzie, we're not talking the top echelon here. We're talking stevedores and bus drivers, laborers, even those not able to work. They are not inherently brighter than the average woman."

"Not that brightness has much to do with it. I think it's more a matter of being informed."

"Why shouldn't we be helping to elect our next President?"

"Let me think about it."

"It isn't that we're smarter than men –" Jo pressed.

"Though I just might be willing to debate that some other time –"

"Just that we – women – can be as well-informed as the average man. That isn't so hard to accept, is it?"

Lizzie shrugged. "I suppose I never thought about it. That's all."

"Well, think about it now."

"And come to a decision before tomorrow evening. Say the word and we'll pick you up on the way to our meeting."

"I can see you now, Lizzie the Suffragette!"

"Well, why not?" She smiled at the two. "Lord knows, I've tried everything else."

CIX

August 1911

"I never thought Vernon would learn to appreciate music but, Maggie, he was absolutely enraptured throughout your recital. Is it fair to add I thought it the best ever?"

"I'm grateful the cathedral would allow me one more chance. I'm afraid I hadn't realized how much I'd given up when I gave up the organ."

"Then you're going back –"

"You wouldn't think of leaving your writing, would you?"

"Good heavens, you two! No – and absolutely no. I love writing for Mr. Larkin. Yet this recital was something I wanted to do, something I've dreamed of these last few years, and I do know now that music must always be a part of my life. But these old hands," she stopped to rub them vigorously, "well, the doctor says it's arthritis."

"Oh, Maggie!"

"A normal part of aging, I fear. That's why it meant so much to be able to play today. But no, there are times to close some doors and open others a little wider."

"Any chance before you're deluged with those open doors that we could persuade you to return with us to Erie? We want you to come. Think, Maggie, it might do you good."

"I appreciate your invitation, Janie, really I do. Just give me a little while first. Candidly, I'd like nothing better than to sit in my favorite chair, put my feet up and read all the magazines that have accumulated while I did the practicing I had to do. Just time to unwind first."

"Of course! I should have guessed."

"Would two weeks from now be acceptable?"

"Vern?"

"Anytime's fine with me, Janie."

"Then two weeks from today it shall be."

"We'll be waiting at the station."

. . .

Run. Run. Faster. . . You have got to go faster. How can I? It's black as pitch in here. . . The clouds are parting. Yes. I can see the moon. . . What was that? It's the whinny of a horse. . . Can't stop now.

. . .

"Janie! Vernon! Over here!"

"My God, Maggie. You look like you've seen a ghost."

"I must have fallen asleep on the train for I had the most confusing dream."

"Can you remember any of it? They say that's a good sign."

"A good sign?"

"That, if you can remember, it may be possible to figure it out."

"I think my wife's been reading too many books –"

"But it *might* help, Vernon, really it might. Can you remember anything, Maggie, anything at all?"

"Strange! It seemed so real – right in front of me – and now it's gone. Something about running. In some woods perhaps."

"Were you being chased?"

"Janie, she's your friend; stop giving her the third degree. Let's leave the scary things on the train."

"What's that you said, Vernon?"

"I was merely expressing my hope that you would be able to leave whatever had scared you on the train, to put it behind you, and so enjoy your stay here."

"My God, Maggie, what is it?"

"Those words."

"What? Leaving your fears behind you? What's so strange about that?"

"It's what you said before, about leaving the scary things on the train."

"Before? Before what?"

She shook her head as if trying to clear cobwebs from her mind. "I don't know."

"Maggie! You're talking in riddles. What is it?"

"I just know I heard Vernon say those same words before. I think he did. I couldn't have dreamt that too, could I?"

"I can't say I remember, Maggie, but it shouldn't be that difficult to figure out. The only other time we met you was when you and Everett came together. But it wouldn't have been then, I don't imagine."

"No, I don't think so. It didn't have anything to do with Everett."

"But then – ?"

"What an expression, Janie! Are you remembering something we've both forgotten?"

"There was one other time we met Maggie here at the station."

"There was?" Maggie and Vernon asked in unison.

"And, now that I think about it, you were terribly upset then, too."

"You're absolutely right, Janie. Talk about good memories! That was – how many years ago?"

"I don't know. Decades, at least."

"All right, you two. I give up. What are you talking about?"

"Don't you remember, Maggie? It was your very first visit here. Back when Vernon needed his . . . the operation."

"And I did come for a few days. Of course! To help with the girls, to be home so you could be with him. But weren't you already in the hospital then?"

"On my way. Then you do remember?"

"I remember coming. Nothing about bad dreams."

"Oh, Maggie, you must! You were a terrible sight that day. Scratched. Your skirt ripped."

"One cheek was smudged," Vernon smiled now at the memory. "I thought it looked right cute."

"Vernon!"

"Well, I did. Though I admit there wasn't anything cute about your state of mind."

"I can't remember anything at all."

"Well, I guess we two can remember enough for all of us." He bent to pick up her suitcase. "Shall we be going?"

"No, wait a minute. Please. I want to hear more about this."

"There's really not much more to say. You looked a fright. You were terribly jittery –"

"Perfect word."

"And could offer no explanation."

"None?"

"No. Just said you didn't want to talk about it."

"And, believe me, by the look on your face, we both knew not to push."

"Nothing else that you remember? Nothing at all?"

"'Fraid not."

"No, there was one thing. Didn't think much about it then. Janie and I just figured she'd gotten your message mixed up."

"*Message?* What do you mean?"

"Janie told me you'd be in on the six-thirty train. We came down and waited . . . no Maggie. In fact we met every train well into the evening."

"Yes, I remember now. Vernon's right. I thought that I must have gotten the date wrong. We checked your letter one of the times we stopped back at the house but, no. So then of course we worried something had happened to you."

"It was quite a relief, I can tell you, when you did appear."

"I'm almost afraid to ask. What time was it then?"

"That was many years ago, Maggie. I'm not sure any more but I'd guess about eleven."

"Eleven o'clock? At night?"

"Or a little later."

. . .

It wasn't until much later, when Maggie had settled in for the night and was reviewing the busy hours just passed, that she realized Vernon no longer walked with even a limp. How marvelous the advances being made in these artificial prostheses! His spirits were as high as they'd been when she had first met her best friend's beau.

And the girls! Rosalie and Alice made short shrift of any such notions, returning after dinner to introduce their husbands and the three children they had already produced. And wasn't Alice about ready to have her second?

"Oh, Janie," she anguished when the friends had time later to talk. "We were their ages – just yesterday. What happened?"

"Father Time, old friend."

"But did it have to happen so fast? Looking at them makes me feel positively ancient. And yet, I don't, you know. I really don't."

"Well, good for you. That's the way I like to hear you talk. Your spirits have sagged for so long now." She hesitated. "You haven't mentioned Buster, Maggie. I know how you doted on that dog. What's become of him?"

"Another of those everyday miracles that have made these past months so special. Remember my telling you of the Knapps, Lizzie and Jack?"

"Hmm –"

"Jack also works for the Larkin Company though in a higher position than any Everett held. Hardly our social equals but Lizzie took a shine to us. And to little Rose."

Maggie had paused then to accept another cup of coffee from the pot Janie offered. "Come to think of it, I really don't remember how we did become friends. But we did. Not close, not really close. But we'd see each other maybe half a dozen times a year. Anyway . . . Janie, what on earth were we talking about?"

"I asked you about Buster."

"Buster! Of course! That's how we got on the Knapps. Funny, I never thought of either Lizzie or Jack as dog people but, somehow, it came out that I needed a home for Buster.

It hardly seemed fair to kennel him, knowing how much I wanted to travel now. This is much too long for a short story, the only point being that they offered him a home. He took to them both right away." She sighed deeply. "And that should answer your question. Before we both forget again!"

Seeing Janie yawn, Maggie checked her watch. "Good God! Look at the time! Vernon certainly has to go to work tomorrow and I imagine you have to get up early, too."

"Not this time," Janie countered. "He promised to let me sleep, just in case we did let our catching up carry us away. Still, if you don't mind, I think it's time I turned in. But there's no reason you can't sit up if you'd like."

"Nonsense. I can't tell you how much I'm looking forward to a good night's sleep."

"Wonderful then. I'll show you all the development that's taken place in Erie tomorrow and then, when Vernon is off, we'll go out to Presque Isle for a picnic. Maybe even a swim. The water's still surprisingly warm."

"I'd love that." She hesitated, then turned to her friend. "Thanks, Janie. Thanks for it all."

. . .

It seemed her eyes had only just closed when she became aware of the rhythmic bouncing of the train car. She woke with a start, soaked in perspiration. She had always thought the clickety-clack of the rails a soothing sound. Now the frightening noise resounded through the quiet room.

"I'm in Janie's house. All is safe." Maggie got up and turned on the bureau lamp for confirmation before sitting back down on the edge of the bed.

A train? Why should thinking of the train frighten me now?

Laying her head on the soft down pillow, she glanced once more around the tiny room before shutting her eyes.

Clickety, clickety, clickety. She could feel the sway in the car as it rushed . . . where?

Where was she going?

Why, here. To Janie's, of course.

She reviewed the short trip she'd made earlier that day from Buffalo. The car had not been crowded. She had enjoyed the scenery as they sped along the shores of Lake Erie before returning to the Kipling she had brought for amusement. She'd never read much of his work but, now that he'd won the Nobel Prize, it seemed a good time to start. She did have the time now, didn't she?

Clickety. Clackety.

She could feel her heart pounding.

Breathe. Deeply now. Take a deep breath. Again.

"Everything all right, madam?"

"What?" She was jolted by the interruption.

"I was afraid you might be getting sick. Everything all right?"

"Oh, yes. Of course."

The conductor passed on through the car, stopping just before leaving the far end, to turn and look back at this strange passenger. She caught his eye, cursed such luck, and kept her eyes on her hands for the rest of the trip.

. . .

"Janie. Janie! Are you asleep?"

"I won't be if you keep whispering. What is it?"

"Nothing. Just that your friend seems terribly restless."

"Then you've heard it, too?"

"It would be hard for anyone to sleep through that."

"She's certainly thrashing around and –"

"Those cries! What do you suppose is going on?"

"Let me go see if I can do anything."

The two women nearly collided in the darkened hallway, adding further to Maggie's obvious distress.

"Can I help?"

"No thanks. Hope I didn't disturb you. I don't know what's the matter tonight."

"Trouble sleeping? Could I fix you a glass of warm milk? They say that always works. Or cocoa, if you'd prefer."

"I think I'll just get a glass of water and try again. I really am tired."

Refreshed after her drink, Maggie returned to the guest room. She turned off the light on the table beside the bed and slipped back beneath the covers.

Please, she thought, no more nightmares. I just want to sleep.

Praying used to help. I can remember when I couldn't get through my prayers – all those God-blesses – before I'd be sound asleep. Maybe that's what I need to do now.

God bless . . . .

She continued to reflect on each person important in her life, praying for their needs as she saw them, giving thanks for . . .

She was back in the woods again . . .

Oh, no, please God. I'm so frightened there . . . But wait! It's different this time.

Wh – ? It's the light. It's brighter. Yes, daytime. Nothing to fear in the daytime, is there? I'm walking – slowly. Nobody's chasing me. Perhaps I'm just out for a walk.

It's even brighter up ahead. I see some sort of clearing. There are houses all around it.

How will I know which is the one I'm looking for?

Voices! I don't want to be seen yet.

It was a man's voice. "Don't worry about us."

"Us?" That was a woman.

"Yes – me, my money . . . and my trusty little pistol."

"Andre!"

"Go, Sandy. Your ladies await."

Andre! That must be the man I've come to see. There can't be too many with that name. Over here then.

She's going. Oh, this is easier than I expected.

. . .

"Well, you really were a sleepyhead! Good morning."

"Why didn't you wake me? Or did you plan to let me sleep the day away?"

"I figured you must be terribly tired to sleep so long. If so, I couldn't think of a better medicine than to let you go on. Besides, look what I've been doing."

"I didn't need to look, Janie. The aroma of those cinnamon rolls would have wakened me from the dead."

"Let me fix some coffee – or would you prefer tea? – and I'll get the butter. I wager they're every bit as good as they smell."

Janie smiled contentedly as she watched her friend reach eagerly for the first of the sweet rolls.

. . .

Later Janie tried to broach the subject again. More than a little curious, she was also distressed at the obvious strain under which her friend was suffering.

"Was there something you wanted to talk about, Maggie?"

"You know me. Always happy to talk, especially to you. Something particular you had in mind?"

"I just keep wondering about last night."

"Janie, most people can't recall what they've dreamt. I fear I fall into that category." She hesitated. "Good God! Do you think I'm lying to you?"

"Lying's a bit strong. And I don't mean to push but . . . well, I've always felt myself a good listener. Want to try?"

"It was nothing, I tell you. Just another silly nightmare."

"Yes?"

"There isn't . . . I don't know. Nothing made much sense."

"But it certainly upset you. Can you remember anything? Anything at all?"

"It was just a dream."

"And?"

"There was a man. I guess I was alone with him. And he tried . . . oh, it was awful. He was sneering, taunting me. When he came closer I could smell alcohol on his breath. Why, he must have been drunk!" She stopped.

Janie waited.

"Is that all?"

"I really can't remember anything but the ugliness."

"*Ugliness?*"

"His leering, the jeers. That awful smell. His laugh – oh, Janie! I was so afraid and he just kept laughing at me!"

"Don't cry, Maggie. That'll do no good now. You must be brave. What else can you remember?"

"Nothing . . . just what I've already told you. But it's so clear. I can see it all. The jeers. The drunken smell. His hands on me . . . "

"And?" She leaned forward.

"I was fighting him. Struggling to get away. And then . . . oh, Janie, I was running. Running into the woods. Running away."

"Then he didn't?"

"I don't think so. No, I'm sure of it. Somehow I got loose – maybe because he had been drinking, who knows why? – but I ran away."

Was it all right, Janie wondered, to push further? "Maggie, you told me – when you were describing the scene with this man that you could see him –"

"See him? No. Of course not. Don't be ridiculous."

"That's what you said. You said, I believe, 'I can see it all.'"

"The scene, I meant. Feel it. What it was like being there. With him."

"Then you've no idea who this man might have been?"

"No . . . no . . . none at all."

"Could it have been Peter? or Everett perhaps? Someone you knew?"

"Honestly, Janie! I don't think it was anybody at all."

"What?"

"It was all a dream. I told you that. Just a dream. Nothing more. Now, tell me, when do I get to see those charming girls again?"

. . .

The trip back was uneventful as time passed in a pleasant blur. Vernon and Janie had kept her hours filled and Maggie had enjoyed her stay, finally giving in to their entreaties and extending her visit for a full two weeks. By the end of that time she knew she was ready to return to Buffalo.

Cool air rushed out to greet her as she unlocked the front door and swung it open. What a refreshing change! The heat these past few days had been quite oppressive though hardly, God knows, as bad as the heat wave that now threatened the Continent. Her paper on the train had been full of the emergencies in London as the temperature hovered at one hundred degrees. There was much to be said for living along the cooling shores of Lake Erie.

She stepped inside, quietly closing the door behind her. The neatness of the house pleased her.

She walked purposefully through the rooms. The dining room was immaculately clean, the kitchen as polished as she'd left it – just waiting. Back into the hall.

So still. Everything was. Did she mind? She could always turn on her radio, now that she had given in and purchased one of her own. There'd be a great deal of music devoted to Gilbert, honoring the great librettist after his recent death. She'd enjoy that, especially the lyricism of Sullivan's operettas. And Mahler as well. Strange man. She didn't care for his music. Certainly haunting in its own way but so many bangs and crashes! No, she'd stick with the hummable tunes.

But no, not yet.

The parlor.

She walked to the window and pulled back the sheer curtain underneath the drapery. If she hurried she imagined she could catch a glimpse as he walked down the street. Ah, yes, there he was! She could still feel the burning of his lips from those passionate kisses.

Yes, Peter, I do love you. And I've sent you away. I had to, you do understand that, don't you? I didn't want to, God knows, I wanted you to stay, to hold me, to . . .

She sank into her reading chair in the corner. Should she have told him to go? It wasn't a question of loving Everett. Her husband had been a good man. But had there been a day in her life that she hadn't dreamed of Peter? wanted to be with her Peter? And then, having that wish granted at last, had sent him away.

Outside a passing car backfired.

What had she been thinking? Romantic dreams of Peter?

"Oh, yes. I knew where to go for the answer, didn't I? To get the advice I wanted so badly?"

She burst into uncontrollable laughter.

"For Peter."

CX

Spring 1913

"Lizzie, I swear you get more emotional every year. Throwing that book really made me jump." Rising, he gently rubbed her neck. "Hardly the way to treat your aging husband. Calm down and tell me what's upset you this time."

"I'm sorry, Jack. For upsetting you, I mean. It's just that –" she sputtered.

"You've been hunched over your desk most of the afternoon. What have you been working on?" He could feel the tension lessening as he continued to massage. "Anything you can share?"

"I wish it were."

"Can't you try? It might help."

"Oh, I didn't mean I refused. There's simply nothing for you to see. That's what has riled me so."

"But you've been writing – furiously, I might add – for hours –"

"And throwing every scrap of it in the wastebasket."

"Anything I can do to help?"

"You wouldn't mind if I had a drink, would you?"

"Lizzie, you ask the same question every night."

"I know I do, and you always answer it's up to me. I guess I just want your approval."

"Approval?"

"No, that's not the right word, is it? But I do want to be sure you won't mind."

"Any more than you mind my not drinking, dear."

She raised her glass in a toast. "Do you realize it has been over five years since you took your last drink, Jack?"

"Sixty-nine months, seven days, and . . . ah, let me see,

[534]

probably around twenty-one and a half hours. But, no, I hadn't any idea!"

"And I am proud of you. Have I told you that?"

"Only about sixty-nine thousand, seven hundred and twenty-one – no, make that twenty-four times. I'm glad you are, Lizzie, and even gladder I've been able to stick with it. It was surprisingly easy, after those first days. You know, I can still remember with perfect clarity how dreadful I'd feel after . . . well, after one of those nights."

"Words I've certainly heard before. I know you want me to stop, too, Jack. Perhaps someday. If the time were right. But it isn't now." She leaned back and sighed. "Bless you, Jack. You are a good husband. I suppose I should appreciate you even more than I do. Particularly when I get a day at home alone with you."

"But your suffragette friends might take exception?"

"Oh! Fiddle on them!"

"This does sound serious. What's the matter?"

"They wanted me to write a tract before their next rally. Honestly, you should have heard them. Lizzie: the Shakespeare member, librarian, college-educated – can you believe that, after all these years? – Lizzie, the only one capable, it seems, of writing up our needs."

"And?"

"It sounded simple so naturally I agreed. But now – what? Hours and hours and not a word to show for it." She rose from the desk, throwing her pen down in protest. "Everything sounds so bromidic. It's pointless."

"Lizzie, Lizzie . . ."

"I'm sorry. I know I'm getting terribly upset over something that really shouldn't be all that important. It's just that they are counting on me, and –"

"Why not just tell them you can't? Or won't? I'm sure your ladies will go right on protesting whether you're there or not."

"I didn't mean I wanted to back out. It's just that . . . well, it's this writing business. I can spend as many hours as I want – days even –"

"I have an idea, Liz," Jack interrupted. "Your friend Maggie's a writer, isn't she?"

"Going into it full-time last I heard."

"Well, then –"

"But she doesn't believe in this voting business, at least she didn't last time we talked."

"Who knows? Perhaps she's changed her mind. For that matter, maybe you can change it for her – though it doesn't mean she can't help you."

"It doesn't?"

"Good God, Liz, you don't think writers believe everything they write, do you?"

"I guess I'd never given that much thought. Perhaps you are right. Be a dear, love, and pour me another. I'll see if she's free."

. . .

As the winter months had come and passed Maggie had thrown herself into her writing. She continued to follow Frank Lloyd Wright as the now-famous architect offered the world ever-new and imaginative buildings. Mr. Larkin personally received all her manuscripts and had never so much as uttered one word of criticism before they were printed as submitted. Although remuneration was comparatively slight, because of the columns her name was becoming better known wherever Larkin employees worked.

Now she stood silently, face against the windowpanes watching the torrent of raindrops rush down the glass. Easter lay just days ahead. If this rain kept up, the lawns would be entirely snow-free by then. It had been one of those hard winters when the cold seemed to want to hold on forever. She couldn't think of a single soul who wouldn't be happy to see it pass.

The months had brought work to keep her busy and, with it, contentment. She was pleased to realize she hardly ever thought of Peter anymore.

Peter! She recalled that last recital and wondered if she'd ever felt real passion for the man. Hard to believe.

There had been the dreams. Dreams for which she felt she had to have an answer.

It had all seemed so logical – then.

Peter had left; she had finished packing and hurried off to the station, making the train with no more than moments to spare. Then it had occurred to her. There was an answer. She had heard the women talking about Lizzie Knapp and the amazing Andre Robson. Didn't he live in Lily Dale? Everett had taken her there and she remembered it well. And, if this Robson fellow could help her straighten out the confusion she felt about Peter, well, why not stop on the way? Go see him.

Lily Dale wasn't far from Dunkirk. She would hire a carriage, better yet, maybe a horse – it was unseemly but Aunt Fil had taught her to ride . . . besides, who in God's name would recognize her in a little town as out of the way as Dunkirk? Trains ran frequently. She'd simply catch the next – or the one after that – and hurry on to Janie and Vernon's. She could tell them she'd missed her scheduled one out of Buffalo. No time to let them know. Terribly sorry – but what did that matter as long as she could get an answer about Peter?

. . .

"Have you given up your organ playing entirely? Really, I do think that would be a pity. Not to mention a great loss to Buffalo as well."

"Oh, no, Lizzie! I couldn't do that."

"Then you do still play? We'll look forward to your next recital. They're always so exciting. Really, Maggie, you possess a unique talent."

"My goodness, I'm quite overwhelmed! Thank you. But I fear you'll be disappointed if you wait for me to give another recital."

"But you said –"

"I said I'm still playing. I'll substitute at St. Paul's when they need me and they're terribly gracious about seeing I have lots of time to practice but . . . well, I guess there are just too many other things that interest me now more than music."

"I find that hard to believe. Truly."

"Lizzie, look at you. You've gotten yourself all immersed in this suffrage business. That's new, isn't it?"

"Why, yes. But I don't see –"

"The only point I'm trying to make is that we grow as we pass through life and, as we do, our interests change. It's just a natural part of the progression. At one time music was my life. I needed it then. Then – well, marriage, Everett, then Rose, each filling another need in me."

"And now?"

"Now I believe it will be my writing."

"Of course! But certainly those articles for *Ourselves* can't take up all your time. Not that they aren't good. Jack reads every one, as do I. In fact Charlie has insisted we keep each issue for him. And I've always found what you have to say about Frank Lloyd Wright interesting, even if I don't necessarily understand – or agree."

"I know you don't, and that's quite all right. But, actually, while I'm still writing for *Ourselves,* I have also begun a book."

"On Wright?"

"Not at all. I hope this doesn't sound too silly but I decided to try to write a novel. I only began a few months ago. Have no idea how far I'll get, if one day perhaps I'll wake and decide it was a foolish thought and that'll be that – or if I'll keep plowing on. But for now it's challenging – and fun."

"Oh, dear. Then you're much too busy to help me."

"You? Never, Lizzie! Not if I can. What kind of help did you have in mind?"

During lunch Lizzie repeated the difficulties she had had composing a satisfactory exposition for her woman's group. Between the salad and the dessert she pulled out the last drafts she had made. Maggie looked them over, asking many questions while making copious notes.

"I think I can help. You've done a good job, Lizzie. But look here. Move this paragraph down to . . .yes, there. If you add a little more explanation in there . . .see? Like that . . . and then let's finish up with . . .ah, yes. Something like that."

"You make it look so simple I feel like a dunce!"

"Nonsense. I've just had more experience at this sort of thing, that's all. You write well. It'll come easier after a while. In the meantime, we can go over your pages in detail after lunch or, if you prefer, let me take them home and work on them for a day or two."

"Would you? Oh, please do. I can see what you're doing and I'm sure I could learn but, to tell you the truth, right now I'm so sick of those papers I'm ready to scream. Can we put them away . . . and talk of nicer things?"

"If you'd like."

"I've been dying to ask what you think of the latest house Larkin's built for his family."

"I don't really know much about it."

"But you've seen –"

"Only from the outside. It's quite lovely, isn't it? I always have admired the Colonial style, if one is going to stay traditional, that is."

"And so big! Do you like the white brick?" Lizzie continued.

"I found it quite stunning, didn't you?"

"Why, yes, of course."

"Though . . . well . . . "

"Yes?"

Maggie replaced her cup on its saucer. "I don't mean to criticize Mr. Larkin and I'm sure he did what would please his wife but . . ."

"But what?"

"Well, I admit I was quite dismayed that he would choose such a heavily wooded lot to build on. Certainly there must have been other sites that wouldn't have required such major clearing. I know we are practically overrun with trees – it has to be one of the reasons I love Buffalo so – but . . . well, can you think of anything more beautiful?"

"Honestly? Yes." She burst out laughing. Maggie turned to see what had caught her eye and began to giggle at the sight of the rotund man returning to his Model T. Costumed from head to toe, his duster almost swept the ground as he strode forward, cap perched jauntily on his head. Watching as he pulled the goggles down over his eyes, both women began to guffaw.

"Oh, say something sad or I fear I shall burst!"

Maggie thought for a moment before speaking. "Titanic."

"What?" Lizzie giggled again.

"The Titanic. Fifteen hundred lives gone and so tragically. After that disaster I don't believe I would ever want to go to sea."

"Well, if you do I hope you'll take that abominable Taft with you."

"Lizzie! You don't care for our President?"

"Not when Teddy Roosevelt's opposing him. Now there's a man with character."

"I do know what you mean, but I should think you'd prefer Taft over that Woodrow Wilson and I really don't see much other choice."

"Well, I certainly do. I'd be all for Roosevelt and his 'Bull Moose' ticket . . . if. See, Maggie? You've got to help us women get the vote."

. . .

Lizzie settled back in her chair as she reflected on the afternoon. She felt as if a major load had been lifted from her shoulders. Wise move having Maggie agree to do the writing for her. She had enough to think about, goodness knows, without that, too. Especially when it seemed such an easy exercise for Maggie.

She looked up as the waiter appeared at her side, gleaming silver coffee pot in hand.

"May I freshen your cup, madam?"

"No, thank you. I think I'm about coffeed out."

"As you please, ma'am." He turned and began to walk away.

"Waiter."

"Yes, ma'am."

"I believe I'd like to order a drink. You don't think it's too early – oh, what difference does that make? Bring me a Scotch and – no, just Scotch. On the rocks. And make that a double."

"As you please, ma'am."

She was pleasantly surprised that the second drink burned as deliciously with her first sip, the comfort of it warming her body. Hadn't this been a pleasant day! Maggie was a smart one to recognize her talents, her abilities.

Oh, my, had she ever felt so alive? So glad she had taken the time to expound her own theories in so much detail, knowing she was smart enough, good enough, to rival Maggie any day. Why, I should be running the local organization, not doing busywork. It's a waste of my good time to be writing these simple tracts. Just wait till they see what I can do. Then they'll recognize my abilities for what they are.

"No. Thank you. I'd really like one more – all right, just one more – but then I'll have to go home."

Sad, though, to think of going home. What she really needed was somebody to celebrate with. Somebody who would understand.

What was at home? Just dull old, sober old, Jack.

. . .

He had tried not to look aghast as she poured another glass once dinner was over.

"You don't understand. You probably don't even care, do you? Sorry then, it's your loss. Because I feel absolutely marvelous. And nothing you do is going to take that away. Absolutely in control. It's a great feeling, Jack, really marvelous."

"Then go right on being marvelous, Lizzie. God knows I wouldn't want to stop you. But I'm going to bed."

"No, please don't. I want to talk. I don't want to be alone. Stay a little while longer. Please sit and talk to me. We seem to spend so little time together."

"It's no use, Liz. Your speech is already garbled. You're making no sense at all."

She sighed in resignation. "Go to bed then."

"Good night, Lizzie."

A curtain of sadness descended as she watched him leave

the room.

"Damn you, Jack Knapp." The glass hurtled across the room, striking the marble front of the fireplace and shattering into hundreds of shards on the hearth where it reflected the red from the last burning embers.

CXI
June 1913

"I don't know, Charlie. There are times when I'm not sure I know much of anything any more."

"Old age catching up with you, brother?"

"I wouldn't be at all surprised . . . but, no, not this time. Unless you're referring to the old age of having been married to the same woman for forty-five years."

"I envy you that, Jack; really I do. I know you think she's giving you trouble now –"

"Damned right she is! First, all these shenanigans about voting rights for women. Then darned if she hasn't gone and discovered the pleasures of alcohol. Turned into a damned lush, she has. If it isn't one thing with her, damned if it isn't something else. Marriage? No, I swear, Charlie, you're the one who's to be envied."

"Jack, I really can't understand what's gotten you so upset. Give her time – and a little patience. I'm sure this, too, will pass."

"*Time* you say? Patience? Good God, Brother. I'll be seventy-two in a couple of months. How much time do you think I have?"

"I bet it's a lot more than you expect. You're not going to change her, at least not right now, so let's forget about it and . . . Well, let's go have some fun."

"*Fun?* Two old goats like us?"

"Speak for yourself, Billy. I haven't reached the old goat stage yet – nor do I plan to. Come on, let me give you a ride."

"Another new car, Charlie? By God, I can't believe it!"

"Not much else for an old bachelor to spend his money

on."

"What is it this time?"

"An American. Snappy little car. A 22-B. Come on, see for yourself. Tell you what, I haven't been out to see your new bridge yet. Suppose we could do that now?"

"Bridge?" A quizzical look passed his face. "Oh, the one to Canada. Peace Bridge. Sure. I need to get out of this house anyway. While we're driving I'll fill you in on all the struggles it took to get the damned thing erected."

"So you were in on that, too?" Charlie shrugged. "Why should I be surprised?"

"The Auto Club did it. I was merely part of that. But talk about an idea long overdue. Tell you what, we'll drive over to Fort Erie and have lunch there." Jack patted his brother on his shoulder. "Let's get moving. Hate to have to explain to Lizzie."

. . .

"Flo!"

"Then you haven't forgot?"

"You? Never! I can't tell you how often I've wondered where you were. What you were doing. In fact I can honestly say that there hasn't been a time when Janie and I have gotten together that we don't talk about you."

"Then my ears should be burning."

"Except there's been nothing to say. I fear we'd both given up ever seeing you again. So tell me everything. Is it still George?"

"George indeed. And coming up on twenty-four years of marital bliss; can you believe it?"

"Must say you look superb. Life must be treating you exceptionally well."

"I do feel blessed, Maggie, very blessed."

"So what brought you back to Buffalo? And how on earth did you find me?"

"Your music, Mag. I remembered you were – had been, I guess now – organist at St. Paul's. The rest was easy."

"Well, come in, come in."

She laughed. "I wondered if I were going to be expected to pay my entire visit on your doorstep."

"Oh, Flo, I am sorry. It's just such a surprise. Let me give you a big hug. And do come in, please. Here, sit down – wherever you'll be most comfortable. May I fix you a pot of tea? Coffee? Good. Oh, come on. Keep me company while the pot boils and tell me what brings you back after all these years to Buffalo."

"Actually, George is on his way to a convention in New York City. I decided to come east with him – hoping of course to be able to find my two best friends."

"What does he do?"

"He's with a company that manufactures zippers."

"Well, bless him! I can't think of a new invention I've appreciated more."

"Be surprised then, Maggie. They were actually invented way back in 1891."

"But –"

"I know. It took all of twenty-two years to find a market for the things. Now of course – well, as you say, how could any of us live without them?"

"Then you can stay?"

"For a few days. I'll need a place of course –"

"Right here, obviously."

"Oh, Maggie, I couldn't. I never intended to inconvenience a friend."

"*Inconvenience?* Oh, Flo! This is a marvelous surprise. Now where is your valise?"

"I left it at the depot. I really didn't know if I'd be able to find either one of you."

"Well, now you have. Let's send for it immediately. Better yet, let me drive you down."

"You? You drive?"

"You bet I do. That was my present to me for my fiftieth birthday. Decided to enjoy life while I could."

"It's easy to see Fil's influence lives on. Let me finish my cup, wash up a little if you don't mind, and we'll be off. Oh, Maggie, this is so very good of you."

. . .

"Did you see her, Charlie? Did you see her? I swear, I'm far too old for things like this."

"Jack, Jack! The only one getting riled is you. Of course I saw her. She's an absolute delight."

"Delight? She's wild! Smoking in public! Waving those – what did she call them? elephants? right under my nose and –"

"Camels, Jack."

"What?"

"Camels. Her cigarette. From what I've read they're the first brand to become known nationally."

"Camels. Elephants. None of them belongs in the hands of a woman!"

"Women have been smoking for decades, dear brother."

"Not my women. And the dancing! Did you hear the way she was talking? Weasel trot –"

"Fox, Jack. She called it a fox trot. Honestly, I don't know what to make of you. Dancing is hardly a sin. My only regret is that I never had the opportunity to learn all these fancy new steps. It really does look merry."

"The whole world's going to hell. Automobiles being put together on an assembly line just so all the poor people can run into each other on our already crowded streets, the government trying to force through that immoral income tax bill, dancing, smoking. And harrumph! Just look at her! Thirty years old, unmarried and not even a prospect in sight."

"Speaking of –"

"*The devil?* Dad must have been talking about me. Good evening, Uncle Charlie. I'm so glad you're here for a few days. I always enjoy visiting with my favorite uncle."

"Only uncle, too."

"It's good to see you, Clara, very good. And yes, I regret to report that was your father's discussing his baby daughter."

"Don't tell me you're going to start on me, too!"

"I wouldn't dream of it, dear."

"Good. One in this family is enough. If you ask me, I'm afraid Father is getting a bit too rigid."

"Blame it on my age; everybody else does."

"I'll blame it on nothing, and just keep hoping you'll soon see the light." She kissed each man on the cheek and waltzed to the parlor door. "I'm off again. Going out with some of my friends. Yes, Father, I imagine we will do a bit of dancing and I might just possibly smoke one of those – beasts, as you call them. Who knows? I might even have a drink. They haven't made that illegal – yet. 'Night, you two."

"Good night, Clara."

"Good –" But the door had already closed behind her.

"What, in God's name, are you smiling at, Charlie?"

"Just thinking. If I were surrounded with life that lovely, I don't think I should ever grow old."

"She'll put me in my grave, just you wait and see."

"Only if you let her, Jack. She's a darling. She'll settle down –"

"But she's already thi –"

"When she's ready."

"Women! All of 'em. You have to wonder what God was thinking of when he made 'em."

"He just wanted to keep us on our toes, Jack."

"Or see us in our graves."

CXII

June 1913

"Two pieces in one day! I'd forgotten how good the peaches back east are. Only now I'm afraid I've eaten the last of your wonderful pie, Maggie."

"I'm just sorry I have no more. Shall I bake another tomorrow?"

"No, please don't. But tell me what you do. From what you say, you are hardly idle. Many of the women I know wouldn't know what to do with so much time on their hands."

"I can't imagine ever being bored." Maggie took the two plates to the sink. "Right now, I dream of the day I can find time to read that stack of books over there."

"You've set yourself quite a task."

"I promised I'd take time and read every one, cover to cover, just as soon as the first draft of my book is finished."

"Tell me more about it, Maggie. I find that very exciting to know someone who has written a book. And you say it's almost finished?"

"Almost. It's been a long time coming but now it excites me, too. I fear I expect everybody else to feel the same."

"Well, count me in. I promise to buy a copy as soon as it comes out – but I want it autographed, please."

"Friends! You've got it – hot off the presses, I promise."

"May I ask what it's about?"

"Shall I give you the five-minute version or would you prefer the all-nighter?"

"Maybe somewhere in between. I think some sleep would be welcome before dawn."

"Then let's get comfortable – porch or parlor?"

"It's a beautiful night but, if you don't mind, I think I'd

prefer the parlor. It's been a long time since I've been in a city and . . .Well, the noise – "

"Strange, I never hear it. Let me get a pitcher of lemonade and we'll see how long I go before I've bored you to tears."

As soon as they were settled, Maggie began to spin her yarn.

. . .

"My story takes place over one summer, long ago, back before there were automobiles or telephones, any of the inventions we take for granted nowadays. Not even much electricity. It was coming, you see, but not widely accepted. It's all about what happened to one young girl. Alone in the world, considerably naive, actually much too much so for her own good, she led a solitary life – working hard to support herself, devoutly religious, et cetera, et cetera.

"Well, one day during this hot summer so long ago our girl – I call her Virginia – met a man, the kind of man I'm sure you hoped your daughters would never meet. Dashingly handsome of course, suave, very much at home in this world, as much a part of it, in fact, as our Virginia felt outside it. For reasons she couldn't fancy, this man – Pierre –"

"Oh, a Frenchman! I love it already!"

"Second generation, if the truth be known, and no touch of foreignness beyond his name."

"I still like it."

"Anyway, Flo, this man – your Frenchman, if you wish – took an immediate fancy to Virginia. She, as you may well imagine, having had no experience with matters of this sort, was absolutely overwhelmed.

"Here was a man too good to be true – you are getting the short version, you see; we can cut the long courtship – and yet seemingly head over heels in love with her. She searched for chinks in his armor but found none. She reassessed herself as honestly as she could and simply couldn't see that she measured up to her Pierre's inflated estimation.

"Now this went on through much of the summer. Where another than Virginia might have been blissfully happy, she simply couldn't be anything but tormented. Something had to be wrong. Why couldn't she put her finger on it?

"What should she do?" Flo shook her head at Maggie's offer of more lemonade.

"As fate would have it, one day she picked up a newspaper – literally; a nice touch I thought. You see, the paper was blowing down the street when she was coming home from work. One section actually wrapped around her leg. Bending down to remove it, her eye caught an article about a fortune-teller. Remember – well, sorry, I forget you weren't here. They had tents pitched at all the entrances to the Pan-American Exposition. Get your fortune told. Learn the future. All that. Well, it so happens there is also a whole colony of them living about fifty miles outside Buffalo at a place called Lily Dale. Clairvoyants, they call themselves. Mediums. Don't laugh. We've all heard the jokes about sizes.

"Anyway, our Virginia carried this paper home and read it and then reread all about this man's extraordinary powers. Intrigued initially, the more she thought, the more she decided that he would be able to provide the answers she by now so desperately sought: Was Pierre on the up-and-up? Could she safely trust her heart to him?

"Before she could reconsider, she was on her way. This little girl who had never done anything out of the ordinary was now off on her own to find the answers she believed she could find nowhere else.

"By the time she arrived at Lily Dale it was growing dark. She remembered the name of the medium who'd been featured in the newspaper article – Andrew Robertson – and immediately set out to locate his cottage. As luck would have it, a woman was leaving just as she approached and called him by name. Unseen, Virginia only had to wait until the woman was out of sight.

"Now, for the first time, she grew frightened. How silly she had been to come alone to a place like this! What did she really expect to learn from a stranger? Why not just turn around and leave as quickly as she had come? She intended to do just that. Really, she did. Instead, she heard her hand knocking on the cottage door.

"'Yeah? Who's there?'

"She wanted to run.

"It was a gruff voice that answered. 'I said come in.'

"Quite involuntarily her hand turned the knob and the door swung open.

"He was seated at a table in the middle of the room, facing her, his plaid shirt unbuttoned. She could see his yellow-stained undershirt beneath.

"She felt his eyes burning into her, as she stood speechlessly, aware now of the food still in the bowl before him. She began to take in more of the room.

Also on the table was a large pile of bills. Money! And then she saw it. Next to the cash lay a tiny revolver. Pretty little thing. That was actually her first thought, Flo. Then the incongruity of this beast eating what was obviously his supper with the money and a gun on the same table struck her.

"'Come on in, pretty lady.' She felt herself drawn further into the room.

"'Not often one as pretty as you just lights on my doorstep. Come on, pretty lady. Tell me what I can do for you.'

"She must have let go of the door for she suddenly heard the click as it shut behind her.

"'Yeah?' he'd repeated.

"She stared at him speechlessly.

"'Doesn't matter. Sit down. No, over there.'

"She remained standing, her eyes riveted to this man.

"'I said sit down. Well, don't then. Suit yourself. Wadda ya want?'

"To get out of there, that's what she was wishing for. To turn and run, run while she still could. Only, try as she might, she couldn't move.

"'Nothing,' was all she could answer.

"'You came all the way out here because you wanted *nothing*? Don't play with me, little lady.'

"'Mr. Robertson?' She felt she had stuttered as the words were pronounced.

"'Well, I know who I am. That's why you're here, isn't

it? To see the great Andrew Robertson. Or *Mister Andrew* depending on which circles you move in.'

"What a terrible mistake she'd made! She should never have come. How could somebody like this possibly help her?

"'Some give me credit for reading minds though I do do better with a clue. Tell me what you're here for.'

"'I'm sorry, sir. My name is – '

"Well, Flo, before she knew it, he had risen from his seat and started toward her. She tried to back to the door but he was too quick. As he grabbed her she could smell the liquor on his breath.

"'You've been drinking!'

"'Ah! So who's the clairvoyant around here?' He laughed at her, cruelly.

"She attempted to break free but of course that only made him tighten his grip. What an ugly laugh! Frightened beyond words, she sensed that he was enjoying her discomfort.

"'Cat got your tongue?" he taunted. "Bet I can loosen it up.' It was then that he bent to kiss her. She remembered the pain of his ugly abusive embrace, the terrible scent of his breath, the odor of his worn clothing. She felt his hands – roughly – groping her body.

"Oh, God! This couldn't be happening. Not to her.

"Suddenly she thought of Pierre. Pierre, the man who loved her. Pierre, whose embraces she had always rejected. Pierre, whose embraces she had wanted. Virginia – well, Virginia was a virgin and, expecting to remain pure until her wedding night, she had always turned Pierre's advances aside. Now here was this . . . this monster! clawing at her clothes. No! She wouldn't allow it.

"He pushed her backwards until she felt the edge of the table pressing into the backs of her legs as he bent over her, pressing her down. Her arm reached out, flailing, feeling . . .

"Now she had it! It had been many years since her hand had cradled a gun. This one felt cold as her fingers curled around it. Once long, long ago, she had gone with her father and an uncle and been permitted to shoot at tin cans on the back rail fence. The familiarity of the weapon came to her as if that long-ago day were only yesterday.

"He grabbed her hair to pull her head back, his bare teeth biting against the tender skin of her lips. His knee dug against her thighs as he tried to separate her legs.

"She never remembered the report, only her disgust at the ugly sound this man made, his lips now just inches from her ear. Then the surprise as his grip loosened. He swayed backward until she had nowhere to look but directly into his face. Such a look of stunned astonishment! Whatever he was trying to say came out as little more than a strange gurgle. Still pinned to the table by his body she felt him slip down along her torso, falling at last with a loud thud to the floor."

"Good God, Maggie, what happened then?"

"In my story she ran into the woods. Dark woods. Night woods. Running as fast as her feet would take her. She feared her heart must be ready to explode, finally stopping near a big old tree. She collapsed to her knees, then sat, back pressed up against the tree.

"It must be all right! No one was following her. Only then she realized no one could know what direction she had run.

"She sighed a loud sigh of relief – then hushed herself immediately, the better not to take any chance. That terrible man!

"She felt deep gratitude that she had been able to escape. Escape with her honor. Escape with her life. Still trying to calm both heart and breath, now she began to wonder exactly what had happened. Why had he let her go?

"She could still feel his repulsive body pressing on hers. He must have weighed twice what she did. How had she –? Why had he –?

"Virgina stood slowly. As she brushed the leaves from her coat, she felt something large and heavy in her pocket. She didn't remember . . . Her hand pulled out papers, one after another, wads of them. What? Why, they had been on the table, *his* table. How –?"

Maggie paused to gauge Flo's reaction.

"I make practically a whole chapter out of her escape.

Building suspense, you know." She eyed Flo. "But then – she finds her horse, exactly where she had hidden it.

"She gallops north now, back toward the big lake, back to where the trains run. She tries to clean herself as well as possible at the station and then learns that the next train – horrors! she has to wait here – alone – for over half an hour. What if –

"But Virginia knows now that there can be no thoughts of any *what if.* A lone woman in the station at this hour would likely attract unwanted attention. Besides, she remembers, she has things to do.

"Slipping back into the darkness, she follows the now deserted street to the lake, hearing the lapping of the waves before she can make out the water. There is just enough light for her to see the long municipal pier that extends out into the water. It is deserted.

"She slips out, kneels at the end, and begins to toss her papers – for by now she knows it has to be the money she saw on the table next to Andrew Robertson – into the water. Nightmare follows nightmare as the first papers float.

"Kneeling at first, then forced to lie prostrate, she takes each paper and holds it beneath the black water until, logged, it surfaces no more. Once that onerous burden is passed, she rises and retreats to the shore.

"The moon slips out from behind a cloud then, just long enough for her to see with relief that nothing remains floating on the surface.

"She turns again, brushes her skirt off and hurries back to the station as the train pulls in.

"And that's it. That's far as I've gotten."

"Maggie! I'm speechless. Why, it's fabulous. And so real, the way you tell it. I felt like I was almost there myself. But what happens?" She waves off the offer of anything more to drink. "What happened to Virginia? Did she escape? Did she marry her Pierre? Tell me they lived happily ever after. But, no, if she killed a man, they had to catch her."

"That's the wonderful part of writing your own story, Flo. You can give your characters whatever endings you wish. No, Virginia was never caught. Funny though, I do have her marry her Pierre, only to discover he's a monotonous churl. Not worth any of the effort she expended on him. Here now, may I get you a cup of cocoa, or a sip of sherry perhaps, before we turn in? I imagine it's gotten terribly late. You shouldn't have let me go on so."

"And stop that riveting story of yours? No way! But I'm still a bit confused. Murderers aren't supposed to get away with their crimes, isn't that practically an unwritten rule? Even in fiction?"

"You don't like it? Well, I told you I haven't written the ending yet. But I guarantee she won't be caught. Besides, it was hardly murder. Just a – well, call it an unfortunate accident."

"No investigation? There must have been police. It couldn't have taken place that long ago. After all, you do have a train in your story."

"Oh, yes, there were police. Indeed, they even arrested a man for the killing."

"That's terrible! What happened?"

"Funny, I think he actually confessed. Case closed."

"Brrr! I get the shivers, Maggie, just thinking of such things. How did you?"

"How did I what?"

"How did you ever get the idea for such a convoluted plot? You, of all people!"

"I don't know. It just came to me – as if in a dream."

"But it must have been based on fact, at least part of it. Was there a similar crime, perhaps here in Buffalo? There must have been something that got you started."

"No. I can't say there was. It's fiction, pure fiction. I can't imagine anything like that really happening. Can you?"

CXIII

August 1914

"My God, Jack. Is there anything in Buffalo that you don't have your fingers in? Whether it's Larkin or the Auto Club, you seem to find ever more projects with which to fill your time – and at an age most men would be content to put up their feet and sit back, to enjoy the fruits of their labors."

"Full of flowery phrases today, aren't we?"

"Can you deny it's true?"

"No, and I can add a hearty *thank the good Lord* it isn't. Seventy-three, and half the men I know are in their graves with most of the rest teetering on the brink. Is that what you'd wish for me, Charlie? I don't want to slow down. Why should I? I find reward in each and every one of these *projects*, as you call them. It's better than rotting at home with a sot of a wife. And I'll tell you something else while I'm at it, I'm happy, Charlie. I love what I'm doing. I hope I never have to slow down – or give up a single one of these activities."

"But to take on a new one? And something so huge? Besides, to tell you the truth, from the way you've explained it to me, I'm beginning to think old J.D. must be losing a few of his marbles. Maybe more than just a few."

"Nonsense. His employees love him. That's what makes this concept so exciting. Can you think of any other company where so many of its employees would fight for the chance to volunteer? To give up their free time and what I'm certain will be great amounts of effort – well, just for an entertainment? He gives to them and they happily give back."

"But so many –"

"Charlie, that's precisely the point I've been trying to make. You have a writer, a song-writer, God knows how many will be involved with special efforts and costumes – and you can be sure there'll be nothing shabby about those costumes – plus what? Last I heard they were figuring on a cast alone numbering over five hundred. And their families, of course. Plus the secretaries."

"Secretaries? I hadn't heard about them. You mean the stenographers from the office?"

"Hardly. My dear boy, in Larkin parlance a secretary is the link between factory and home, the one who hosts the parties where the goods are sold to the customer."

"But I thought mail order –"

"That's still important but it's the personal touch that wins the ladies over. Yes, the lucky five hundred who have achieved the best sales records are to be honored at the masque."

"All brought to Buffalo?"

"And entertained at Larkin's expense. The talk is that the top saleswomen will be given quite lavish prizes to boot. Is it any wonder people are so happy working for him? One would think he had no business other than thinking up new ways to reward his employees. And yet the company continues to expand and prosper."

"So this is where it'll all take place? I wondered why you were so adamant about bringing me back to Delaware Park."

"The city had to give permission for us – the Larkin Company – to use the park but . . . well, you can understand that there were no major hurtles there. See that man? He's Larkin's top engineer, sent out by the company to find the best site for the pageant. I'm told they're leaning toward that grassy expanse near Rumsey Road. Quite nice, don't you think?"

"Nice and level till it drops over there toward the lake. Or are you planning a water ballet, too?"

"Not that I've heard of. Just a pageant –"

"With your cast of thousands. Is the theme a secret?"

"I doubt it."

"Well?"

"If you're asking me to share, I'm sorry I can't."

"But you just said –"

"It isn't a secret, Charlie, but I don't know what it is. I know they've chosen Hazel Mackaye to write the script and someone else to do the music but I don't think they've agreed on a theme. Though you can bet it'll have something to do with the development of the Larkin Company."

"And this is going to be produced when?"

"Two years from now. I'm not sure a date has been announced though I do know it will take place sometime during that summer of 1916."

"Well, I certainly hope so. I can't quite picture five hundred snow bunnies, no matter how ardent they are in their employ. And let's hope, too, that it's a drier season than the spring that almost washed out the Pan-American Exposition."

"I'll be sure to pass your suggestions on. Now come along. I want to see this for myself."

"Jack! I swear I have a terrible time just trying to keep up with you!"

. . .

Demurely she walked up the front steps, unlocked her door, entered the vestibule, and carefully latched the door behind her.

"Whoopee!"

She shouted it again. And once again!

Pulling the letter from her purse, Maggie sat down on the chair in the hall. "Whoopee!"

She read it again though the paper was already showing wear and she knew every word of the letter by memory. It was true, the happy termination to all the hopes she had borne these past long months. Her book had been accepted for publication, the date uncertain though the letter-writer expressed deep hopes that it would come out in time to be considered among the purchases for the Christmas season.

Maggie looked round the house, deathly silent except for the ticking of the grandfather's clock in the parlor corner. Where were people when you wanted them most?

. . .

"Awful chilly for August, isn't it?"

"Strange weather lately."

"Does one blame that on the Germans, too? I hear talk they might have just the weapons to do something like that."

"Nonsense! I'm sure we'll still have our share of hot days. Let's just keep our fingers crossed that they don't get too hot."

"Talking about the war, are you, Father?"

"Why, Clara, I didn't see you in here. Actually, I think we were talking about the weather though apparently every subject these days seems to begin, or end, with the war in Europe."

"Europe hardly seems appropriate any more."

"What do you mean? Has something more happened? Enlighten your dotty old uncle. Please do."

"Dotty never, Uncle Charlie, though fortunately a little too old to be involved."

"Why, we're all involved, Clara."

"Of course we are, Father. I only meant that you and Uncle Charlie won't have to worry about going off to fight."

"Nor, I trust, will any American boy. Let the Europeans fight it out among themselves. No sense our getting involved."

"Hear! Hear! But what did you mean when you said it was hardly appropriate to refer to it as the European War? That is what you meant, isn't it?"

"It is. The papers say that Japan has declared war on Germany and that seems to mean Austria will declare war on Japan any day now."

"It is getting serious, isn't it?"

"Do you think the United States will get involved? I know thirty-one is considered old for a soldier but I would hate to see any of my friends sent off."

"Don't trouble yourself, dear girl. I admit to feeling relief when your father told me you had postponed your trip to the continent so, in that sense, I suppose we are involved. But no, it's much too far away. The fighting will never cross the Atlantic and we'd be damned fools to want to fight for someone over there."

"Well, well, we'll see, I suppose, who the damned fools really turn out to be."

"Mother!"

"Lizzie! I didn't realize you were up."

"Come join us. We needn't dwell further on this war business."

"Why not? Unsuitable talk for a lady? Come on, you two, that kind of protectionism went out long ago. Though I must say I heartily disagree with your appraisal of the situation."

"What would you know of it, dear?"

"I have my sources."

"And they're telling you –"

"There will be an even greater war – and we will all end up involved."

"Preposterous!"

"Really, Mother. I know you still do see some of your old friends –"

"Mighty few are very receptive to her any more, don't like the way she's changed, near as I can tell."

"Father, that's unkind."

"Just the truth, dear."

"Come on, all of you. This isn't the time or place for that."

"I know she drinks, Uncle Charlie. Feel free to talk in front of me."

"Well, not in front of me. Not if that's the way you're going to carry on."

"But, Liz –"

"Ah, let her go, Charlie. Nothing you say will make a bit of difference."

CXIV

Christmas Eve 1914

The last chords of the organ could still be heard as the large congregation hurried out of the cathedral and into the brisk night air. Church bells around the city pealed their welcome to yet another Christmas Day. Yawning children, dragged along by tired parents, hurried down the stairs as all dreamed of the near arrival of old Saint Nick himself.

For reasons not explained to her husband or his brother, Lizzie had suddenly stopped drinking. An occasional sherry but one, two at the most, Jack noted with true relief, had been all for the past weeks.

"Look, Liz. Isn't that your friend Maggie over there? I don't believe I've seen her in two or three years – My goodness, Jack. What did I say? I didn't know Lizzie could move that fast any more."

"Maggie! Maggie! Over here!"

"Lizzie!" Her eyes searched the crowd behind her rapidly approaching friend. She caught herself and turned back to the woman, ashamed that she had even thought of the brother-in-law. "Merry Christmas, Lizzie. It's good –" She had automatically reached out to embrace the woman, shocked at having her outstretched arms rudely slapped away. "Why –"

"How dare you? How dare you even think of showing your face in this holy place?" By now Jack and Charlie had reached her side.

"Lizzie, what is going on?"

"I've been waiting to meet this killer."

"This *what?*" Jack was stunned.

"Killer. Murderer! I've been praying for just this chance, Maggie. I waited to tell you to your face – no, I spit in your face!"

"Lizzie! My God, Maggie, I do apologize. I'm afraid I don't know what's going on here, Lizzie, but I think you should start by apologizing to your friend."

"*Friend?* Ha! She isn't my friend. Or yours. Or yours either, Charlie. She's a scheming double-faced, a . . . a . . . *murderer!* Why have I stopped drinking, you asked. Well, you didn't, but perhaps you should have. I've been locked up in my room – only figuratively, Charlie, though her book is as captivating as any lock and key –"

"Why –"

She turned now to her husband and his brother. "You two really must read our dear friend's book."

"I don't see what Maggie's book has to do with any of this, though I believe she should be congratulated on its publication. That's quite an honor – "

"Don't speak to that unspeakable *canaille*, Charlie. Not in my presence."

"Lizzie, would you please tell us what's going on? Maggie has always been your friend."

"She never was a friend – not to me, not to you, not to any of us."

"Lizzie –"

"She killed him. And she killed our son as well."

"You can't go around saying things like that. Your behavior is irrational –"

"Oh, it is, is it? Then you just march on home – give up one or two of your precious meetings – and read what she's written."

"But, Lizzie –"

"Don't *but* me, Maggie. It's all there. Certainly you can't deny that."

"I'm sorry, Lizzie –"

"As well you should be. But it's much too late for being sorry. A word or two isn't going to bring them back from the grave. Either one."

"I wish I knew what you were talking about, dear."

"Read the book, Jack. Read her goddamned book. Read

every poisonous page of it. Then you'll know the truth just as she does . . . and as I do, too."

"Lizzie, I'm terribly sorry –"

"Don't apologize to me, you witch –"

"I wasn't apologizing, Liz. I am trying to tell you that I don't know what you're talking about. I wrote a story. That's all. I really don't see what any of this has to do with you."

"A story? A story of your murders. And why wouldn't that have *everything* to do with me? One of those you killed was my son!"

"Lizzie!" Charlie's face turned ashen.

Jack stretched out his hand in a useless attempt to restrain his wife. "Now really, Liz, this has gone much too far."

"You don't believe me, Jack? You either, Charlie? Take my copy as soon as we get home though let me fill you in on the highlights now. How that harlot can stand there and pretend to be Little Miss Innocent is beyond me. Even right down to getting the sympathy of the two men who should hate her the most. Oh, yes, you'll see. They will, won't they, Miss Maggie?" Eyes gleaming, her words had become little more than a snarl. "What I don't understand is how you ever thought you could get away with it."

"Lizzie, my head's awhirl. Get away with what? I'm sorry . . . no, please let me finish. I simply don't understand what any of this is about."

"Then permit me to enlighten you – and these two men who are obviously so very much in the dark. Did you or did you not write about the death of a fortune-teller?"

"Why, yes, I did. That was the central part of my story."

"See? She doesn't even deny it! And did this fortune-teller of yours live or not live in a place called Lily Dale?"

"He did."

"Another strand of your fiction, I assume?"

"I still don't understand."

"This Lily Dale – you made that up, too, I suppose?"

"You know better than that, Lizzie. There is a Lily Dale, a colony for fortune-tellers, mediums if you prefer. Why, as I recall, you hired one from there yourself."

"Oh, you *recall*, do you? You know damned well I did."

"Really, Lizzie, I find no excuse for that kind of language." Jack's efforts seemed to have no effect. "Especially here on the steps of St. Paul's. And on Christmas Eve. I think you should apologize –"

"Jack! You don't know what you're saying."

"I know what I'm hearing and that's enough."

"Wait till I'm finished. Nice little story, Maggie. Man killed – shot too, wasn't he? – at Lily Dale and who's blamed for the murder? The police arrest the half-wit son of a prominent Buffalo family. He refuses to defend himself, is sent out of state to an insane asylum, where he ultimately dies a rather, as I recall, hazy death. Was it murder? Or suicide? Carelessness? Or just his plain bad luck? Well, Maggie, what was it?"

"Now I see." She reached out toward the other woman. "I am so very sorry. I never dreamed –"

"*Dreamed?* Dreamed what? What do dreams have to do with any of this?"

"I'm afraid that dreams played every part. I dreamed up the story. The pieces just fell into place as I went along. Slowly, and over a great many months. I had completely forgotten about your son, the killing at Lily Dale, all that. I know I shouldn't have but I did."

"But all this – everything that Lizzie's said –all of it's in your book?"

"Why, yes, Jack. It is."

"And you just made it up? Based on nothing more than a . . . a dream."

"Afraid so, Charlie. I'm sorry now, more sorry than I can say."

"For what, Maggie? What do you have to be sorry for – if, as you say, there is no connection between this and what actually happened."

"I'm very sorry I didn't remember the horrible time you all went through. I don't know why I didn't. It's not like me to forget something that important – to all of you, I mean. I just got so wrapped up in my own project, and . . . well, I am sorry. Terribly sorry."

"If you think I'm buying one word of that, you –"

"Lizzie, word calling will get you no place. Maggie has explained what happened –"

"And you believe *her*? Over me?"

"It isn't a matter of choosing sides, Liz. She says –"

"I heard what she said. I didn't miss one single perfidious word."

"Let's get her home, Jack. We've gathered quite a crowd and I find this entire confrontation very unpleasant. Right now I don't know what's true, or false, but I don't believe anything will be resolved by standing here and shouting at each other."

"And exactly what is it you propose then, Charlie?"

"Let's just go home – quietly. No more outbursts. Yes, Lizzie, I will read the book. Give it to me and I'll begin tomorrow afternoon."

"No, Charlie. Not tomorrow. Tonight."

"All right, whatever you want. I'll start it as soon as we get home. And that, dear, means the sooner we get going, the sooner I can begin."

"Come."

"Good night, Maggie."

. . .

She entered the dark room, glanced at the dark tree in the corner, threw her coat on the nearest chair, and ran upstairs. Just minutes later, Maggie was sobbing to herself, praying for the release only sleep could bring from such a nightmare.

CXV
Christmas into early 1915

She was aware of the burning in her eyes before growing fully awake. Bad enough to have to spend another Christmas Day alone, though Heaven help her if she hadn't gotten used to that by now. But to have a friend turn on her like that? No, it simply made no sense at all.

Maggie had replayed last night's scene many times over before finally drifting into a troubled sleep. She knew the rumors of Lizzie's drinking and was, admittedly, a little shocked by her gaunt appearance. Then again, it was the Holidays and, she had first imagined, a time of stress with a family as large as hers. Not, now that she thought about it, that she had seen any of the children at St. Paul's with Lizzie or Jack. Just Charlie coming more and more often as the family aged. Well, good to see him anyway.

But Lizzie! What had happened there? What was she talking about? Worse, she had been so angry, frightfully ugly to turn on Maggie. And for what?

As Maggie struggled to get out of bed, she asked herself yet again what had gone so awfully wrong. She felt she was innocent. But what was the crime?

. . .

"Talk about getting the year off to a rotten start! Just the twelfth of January and our cause is already doomed."

"I expected nothing else; did you really, Liz?"

"How can you say that? The cause is just – and completely sensible –"

"To all, apparently, except those hardheads seated in

Washington."

"I wish Charlie were still down there. I really believed Congress would pass our bill this time."

"Don't worry. They will . . . one of these years. Then they'll know the power they've unleashed."

"Once the ballot is placed in our hands." Lizzie raised her glass in a toast with her friend. "And why not? What was good enough for the slaves certainly should be good enough for us women."

"Slaves of another sort, perhaps."

"Oh, once maybe. When I was younger." Lizzie stopped to reflect on all the changes. "Have to admit there are advantages to getting older."

"And freer."

"*Freer?*"

"Of course. Nobody but ourselves to answer to, isn't that what all of this is about?"

"Can't say I thought of it just that way but . . . yes, now that you mention it."

"So is Jack expecting you home at any certain time?"

"For dinner. I don't mind that – though he whizzes in and out so fast I wonder why I bother. But that isn't for hours. What did you have in mind?"

"As if you didn't know. Up to it?"

"Me? When have I ever said no? Oh, waiter . . ."

"And a double for me, too. Good. Here's to us."

"And the vote!" Lizzie sat back and sighed, grateful for such a friend. "Ahhhh, that's better. Yes, much better. You know, a little sip and life seems almost bearable."

"Oh, I think it's better than that. We don't need those fools in Washington –"

"Or our husbands –"

"Or anybody! Right?"

"Right! Whatever it is, we're fully capable of handling it ourselves."

"Me, too." She giggled. "Shall we? Oh, hell, why not? Oh, waiter . . . "

. . .

"Jack! This is a surprise. I can't tell you how happy I am to see you. Come in. Please do. These past two months have been dreadful. I've been so upset ever since that awful scene on Christmas Eve."

"I'm sorry, Maggie, but that isn't why I'm here at all."

"But you can explain it, can't you? What happened, I mean. I've replayed the scene so many times over and it never makes any sense. Your wife standing there, calling me a killer, and . . . well, whatever else she said. It was frightful! Do you understand what it was all about?"

"I think I do –"

"Then, for God's sakes, you have got to tell me. Please, Jack, help me."

"Maggie, I read the book just as Lizzie asked. We all have. What do you expect me to say?"

"The *book?* My book? What does that have to do with anything?"

"Good God!" He shook his head in disbelief. "How can you look me straight in the eye and ask that?"

"I'm sorry; I don't know what you mean."

"You're not a stupid woman. Haven't you read your own book?"

"Well, of course I have. But what –? Oh, no." Jack could read by the expression on her face that Maggie was beginning to see what Lizzie had already discovered. "You think . . . You mean Lizzie believes that what I wrote was *real?* That I killed that man? Oh, God! That I would let your son suffer for something he didn't do? Jack, you can't imagine anything that outlandish could possibly be true."

"It certainly had the ring of authenticity to it. I'm surprised the police haven't been around to question you though I suppose it's better to keep a closed case closed." He sat down next to her. "Maggie, I don't know if what you wrote is true or not. But, even if it isn't, you must have realized touching on such a painful subject was bound to hurt Lizzie, and all of us who care for her. Didn't you ever think of her?"

"Why can't you recognize that it's just a story? Pure fiction. I wouldn't have done anything to hurt Lizzie, or you, or anybody. To be honest, it never once occurred to me that it might."

"But you skirted the truth all the way through. How can you look me in the eye now and say that's *just a story?*"

"The ideas came like a series of dreams. I assumed that's where most authors get their inspiration. All I did was write it down. And, once finished, found I had spun a darned good yarn, if I say so myself. Obviously, many others have also found it intriguing."

"Not those who know us. Why, Maggie, I don't believe you ever gave Lizzie a thought."

"I didn't know I needed to. I'm sorry, Jack –"

"You should be."

"No. That *isn't* what I meant. I'm sorry if Lizzie read things into my story that were never intentionally put there. I sorry if she used it as any excuse to . . . well, for new reasons to be upset. But I am not sorry I wrote the story. It was a figment of my imagination and I'm entitled to that."

"I'm afraid some of us may disagree." He rose and started for the door.

"You said that isn't the reason you came. Maybe you'd better explain why you did before you go."

"Getting forgetful, aren't I? I was sent on business. Strictly business."

"Business? About the Larkin Company?"

"There's been a terrible accident and, well – since Mr. Wright was your project, J.D. wanted you to write the column."

"What happened?"

"The engineers haven't finished their investigation but, near as can be determined, a large chunk of one of the exterior ledges broke loose and crashed into an office beneath the skylight. All the way down from the fifth floor."

"How frightening! What a blessing that nobody was hurt."

"I didn't say that, Maggie. In fact, a young telegraph operator was killed at her desk."

"God! And a tragedy for the Company as well. Why, I can't

imagine one in the entire state with a better safety record. And now this!"

"You'll write it then?"

"Of course I will. Give me the poor girl's particulars and I'll start with her. I'm sure that's of paramount importance. Looking into any possible faults in the building will come second."

"Thank you. You know the faith J.D. places in you."

"I do. And I'm sorry you can't as well."

"Not yet, Maggie. Let's give it some time."

"If you feel we must. But I'll be here. You can tell Lizzie that – if you think it would make any difference."

"If – when I do, you can be sure I'll pass your message along. Good day, Maggie."

. . .

"You don't want a drink, Jack? After that terrible accident, I'd think you'd be more than ready for a sip of bourbon. Rye. Or Scotch. Anything you like."

"No, Liz. The bottle is the farthest thing from my mind just now. I keep thinking of that young lady, hard at work one minute, dead the next."

"You knew her then?"

"No. Not even the name was familiar. Still, to happen right there . . ."

"Well, I'm going to pour myself a stiff one. I can tell you there is no easier way to erase such bad thoughts." She took a deep draught. "See?" She sipped again. "Everything already seems a little better."

"But it isn't. I'd think you could see that. Have you totally lost contact with the truth?"

"This is my world and, believe me, it is absolutely real. This just makes it all a little easier to bear."

"Does drinking really make you happier, Liz?"

"Of course not."

"Then why – ?"

"It makes me forget." She raised her glass. "Forget how sad I am."

"I know I can't tell you what to do, my dear, but I do wish you'd give it serious thought. The advice is good – remember, I've been there."

"I hear you. And I see you, see you stumbling through your sober life. If that's what you want, I wouldn't try to change you. I only suggested the drink because I could imagine what a terrible day it's been. But if sobriety works for you, well . . . fine."

"But it can't for you, is that what you're saying?"

"I don't want it to. I stopped for a while; remember? It was terrible. The sadness was overwhelming. Life completely lost its effervescence. I'm too old to want to live like that. All I ask is a little joy. It's just about all that's left and I don't want to give that up. Never again."

. . .

"I swear, time really does fly when you're here visiting us, Maggie. Three days already!"

Grateful that her agent had been able to arrange book-signings in Erie, Maggie had arranged a longer layover as her cross-country tour began. The flowers in Erie were a welcome sight for it had snowed in Buffalo just before her departure. She was enjoying her stay, treasured the moments spent with both girls and their families, and felt deep satisfaction at finding Janie and Vernon in such good health.

She had shared their laughter at her initial naïveté. Wasn't an author finished once the contract was signed? Certainly no one had ever told her about tours and signings. Still, armed with a healthy advance and a new wardrobe, she looked forward to this latest challenge. Initially disappointed when told her tour would only take her as far as the Mississippi, that was immediately sweetened by the offer to end her trip in Omaha.

Just think, she had excitedly told Janie, enlightening her friend on Bert's latest news. After all these years Bert was getting married. Initially impressed with Orva Lee seven years ago, she looked forward now to really getting to know her new sister-in-law.

"You know Vernon and I both hate to see you go. We have talked of coming to Buffalo. A lot. But there's just so much here – always. The school, the girls. And, if you want the truth, I just can't see me gallivanting around the way you do. Oh, don't take that as a criticism. I wish I could be more like you, Maggie. I envy you your freedom. I really do. Not that I'd want to give up what I have but . . . well, I hope you know what I mean."

"Of course I do."

"Sometimes when I try to explain something I feel like I'm just digging a deeper and deeper hole for myself."

"I hope you don't feel that way with me. Ever, Janie. After all that's what friends are for."

"You wouldn't mind then if I asked you something really personal? You can always refuse to talk about it, if you'd rather."

"I can't imagine anything I wouldn't feel able to talk about with you. What's on your mind?"

"Just something I've been wondering and wondering about, ever since I read your book. It is very well written, you know. That's what everybody says. But . . . well . . . weren't you afraid someone would find out?"

"Find out what?"

"The truth."

"Janie, you're speaking in riddles. What on earth are you talking about?"

"Your book. What really happened. That horrible man. All of it."

"I'm sorry, Janie. You must be confused. I really have no idea what you mean."

CXVI

October 1915

"God, I hate these dreary Bach things. They do go on and on. And talk about slow! It's goddamned morbid."

"Shush, Mother. Somebody will hear you."

"So what if they do? I can't imagine anyone else finding this any more uplifting than I. The man said nothing and took forever to get it out."

"It isn't nothing. Look; here is the new translation. Perhaps if you follow it you'll find the music more enjoyable."

"*I've had enough.* That's for sure. It's just beginning and at least two of us have had enough."

"Mother! People are turning around. Just listen. Please."

> I've had enough.
> Today would not be too soon.
> I could happily depart this life.
> I've had enough.

· · ·

"But, Mother, you don't understand."

"Well, apparently I don't. I don't know what the Germans were thinking of, to fire on a passenger ship. So many good people lost, and for what? Why, I can't imagine Roycroft without Elbert Hubbard there. And now you're telling me you knew a young man –"

"Yes, Mother. He has a name, Jimmy. Jimmy Charles. James."

"Was he a special friend, Clara?"

"Very special. To me. Jimmy and I had talked of being

married when he returned."

> I want to be released
> From all the pains of this world.
> If only God would take me
> I'd shout to the heavens:
> I've had enough.

. . .

"So they've put her in prison. If you ask me, it's about time."

Grace and Anne exchanged looks of exasperation.

"Mother! You wouldn't say that if you knew the facts."

"What facts? People like that woman don't deserve to be free to walk our streets."

"But she's the one who said no woman could be free," Grace argued, "until she could decide for herself whether or not to become a mother."

"And," Anne added, "she also said a woman had to be in control of her body before she could call herself free."

"Yes, Mother," Grace went on, "I thought you were the one who fought so actively for women's rights. What happened to your suffrage marches?"

"Voting is one thing, girls, and I have no doubt we women will eventually be granted that right. But to extend that to procreation – well now, that's something else entirely."

"No, Mother, it isn't."

"You'd turn the human race into a bunch of harlots. The whole idea is unthinkable."

"Personally I don't think more than half have much of a chance of becoming harlots –"

"I didn't know you wanted to make this into a joke, Grace."

"Try to understand, Mother. Margaret Sanger is fighting – why, she's even willing to go to prison – to be sure everyone has the same rights. Not all women want children, you know."

"I'm certain she wouldn't feel that way if she'd stick to one man."

"Mother!"

"Well, it is true, isn't it? Two husbands already and who can keep track of her lovers? No wonder she's willing to campaign for immorality. Going around trying to promote birth control? That is what she terms it, isn't it? And abortion?"

"Mother, really! She cares about *all* women. She watched her own mother die slowly, pitifully, after eighteen pregnancies. Can you even imagine such a thing?"

"Strikes me there'd be few children born at all if it were left up to choice. Why –"

"I hope you're not about to confess either of us was unwanted."

"*Unwanted?* What's unwanted? Women had babies – period. Nobody talked about wanted, or unwanted. It just happened. And when it did . . . well, it did."

"You know that isn't true. The educated and the wealthy have always had access to the information they needed. There are products on the market right now."

"But what about women who can't afford more children?"

"Or are too weak physically?"

"Or who get pregnant out of wedlock?"

"See? That's really what it comes back to, girls. It's all a ruse to protect the whores."

"Honestly, Mother. Anne and I were hoping we might carry on a sensible conversation."

"Go on, I'm listening. Though I think I'll get a drink while I do. Can I fix you one?"

"I'll wait till a little nearer lunchtime."

"Suit yourselves."

My eyes are heavy. I long to sleep,
To escape into a world of dreams.
There is nothing here for me.
I dream only of sweet release.
Bitter unhappiness engulfs me daily

My struggle seems so futile.
I pray for a better world,
A blissful place of peace.

. . .

"I always suspected women were irrational but this is something else entirely!"

"Jack, Jack! You mustn't let yourself get so riled up. What's happening in New York won't affect us any more than what's going on in Europe."

"Bulgaria attacks the Serbs and all of a sudden Europe is in flames. It's getting bigger, Charlie. And I'm not supposed to care?"

"Of course you care. So do I. But there's a difference between caring and letting the stress destroy you. I don't want to see our world engulfed in war. I know what Wilson says but, damn it, man, if this keeps spreading it'll be harder and harder to keep us neutral. He's so wrapped up with the Widow Galt, who knows what he has his eye on? To tell you the truth, I'm scared to death."

"Well, then –"

"But I also know there is nothing I can do, Jack. Your women want the right to vote. Half the time, I can't blame them. At least they have the gumption to march for what they believe."

"But so many! Nobody should ever allow twenty-five thousand women to gather together, no matter what their cause. It's scary, I tell you, downright frightening."

"As is the war being fought in Europe."

"As is the war. So where's the connection?"

"At least the women are doing something, Jack."

"You planning to go march, Charlie?"

"Don't be a fool. Though, to tell you the truth, I'd march all the way from here, from your living room to New York – even Washington – and back again if I thought it would make any difference. Think twenty-five thousand marchers would keep us out of the war over there?"

I wish I were already in Heaven.
How much longer must I wait?
I want to be loosed from this place
With its drudgery and fears.

. . .

The last of the golden leaves were still clinging to their branches as the taxi turned down her street. The tour had been extended as the popularity of her novel ballooned. If this kept up, there was a chance, the publisher had wired, she might even enter the realms of the top sellers!

But home.

Well, it wouldn't take long to get rid of the dust. The piano would have to be tuned – though, really, it wasn't as bad as she'd feared. How loudly the notes reverberated through the silent house!

Seating herself at the keyboard, she picked up one of the latest pieces of sheet music she had acquired in her travels.

"Keep the home fires burning . . . ."

CXVII

April 1916

"Charlie, this is a surprise! I can't tell you what it meant when you called to say you wanted to stop by. Do come in, please."

"Thank you, Maggie."

"You know, I was thinking after you telephoned it wasn't that much over a year ago when your brother came to see me. I had hoped then he would be able to help heal the terrible gulf between Lizzie and me, never dreaming he was coming to tell me of that awful accident at the office. You aren't bringing more bad news, are you?"

"No. At least I don't think you'll find it bad."

"Then –" She opened the door wide. "Please come in. Would you like a cup of tea? Or coffee? Brandy perhaps?"

"No. No." He laughed gently. "I'm afraid this isn't a social call. Exactly."

"Oh, dear. Perhaps I should fear any visits from the Brothers Knapp."

"I hope it isn't as bad as all that either. I only meant there was a reason for my coming." His uneasiness grew obvious as he struggled to find the wanted words. Maggie almost believed she saw a tinge of color brighten his cheeks. "Good God! I'm prattling like a schoolboy, aren't I? Forgive me – please. Actually . . ." He crossed to the sofa and sat down, his hat twirling slowly in his hands. "Yes, thank you. I do believe I'd like a cup."

"Anything in particular, Charlie?"

"I'm making a fool out of myself . . . aren't I?"

"No, it was wrong of me to tease." She seated herself in the nearest chair to face him. "Maybe it would be better if you just told me why you came."

"Yes, I think it would. It's Jack –"

"Nothing's happened to him, has it? Or Lizzie? I really was quite fond of her, you know."

"No. No. They're both all right. Well . . . considering. Lizzie, I mean. She isn't very active any more and Jack – well, he's getting up there, too, not that you'd know it. Busy, near as I can tell, near every hour of the day."

"Oh, my –"

"Says it keeps him young and I can't find any cause for disagreeing. Point being that there is no one at home to care for Buster. The staff adores him, of course – who doesn't? – but . . . well, Jack felt he needed a home. A real home. And he was –"

"You mean *me*? Oh, do you, Charlie? Really?"

"He wanted me to ask if you'd be willing to take your dog back."

"I would give anything to have him back again. I can't believe you felt you even had to ask."

"To tell you the truth, I've grown very fond of him myself. Never much cottoned to animals before, never had the time, but . . . well, yes, there is something special about Buster."

"Then you –?"

"No. That would hardly be fair. Not that I haven't given serious thought to moving here permanently, but – no. He was yours first and should be yours again – if you want him."

"Just tell me when can I get your – It's *my* now, isn't it – my dog?"

"Would tomorrow morning be convenient? Jack thought that should work well for him."

"So long? I was secretly praying he might be out in your automobile right now."

"I hate to disappoint you, even if it is just a matter of hours, but I fear I must. Jack wanted to tell Lizzie of his decision before Buster left. At the same time he didn't want to say anything until he knew whether or not you would take the dog. Furthermore, he feels the best time to speak to her would be first thing in the morning. Perhaps you understand."

"I'm afraid so."

"But then, if you agree, I'll bring Buster right over."

"What if Lizzie decides she wants to keep him? I know how she doted on him and Buster would be a very hard dog to have to stop loving."

"Maggie, I assure you this was in no way a conditional offer. Jack intends that Buster go tomorrow. There'll be no changing minds about that. On the other hand, he does want that much time to prepare his wife. I trust that's acceptable to you."

"Anything! Anytime! Oh, dear, I don't suppose I shall sleep at all tonight."

"I'm glad it's going to work out so. Must confess, too, that it does my heart good to see you so excited."

"Thank you." She hesitated. "Oh, my!"

"Is there a problem?"

She laughed. "No problem though I did forget. You said you would like something to drink and I was about to get it. Only – how silly I feel – I cannot remember what you told me."

"Call us both sillies then for I don't remember either. Tell you what I'd like better – It's a magnificent day for early April. Would you like to walk to the park?"

"I was hoping to get out before the weather changed again. This has been a perfectly frightful spring, hasn't it?"

"Absolutely. Why, I hear reports that it could officially be the wettest spring since they began keeping records of Buffalo's weather."

"That wouldn't surprise me at all. Shall I get my wrap?"

"You might want to check outdoors first. I don't think you'll need anything more."

"That warm already?" She walked to the door. "My, so it is! Why, this looks to be a lovely day." She turned again to face her visitor. "I'm glad you came, Charlie."

"Yes. I, too."

"You said Jack was keeping busy so I trust his health remains robust."

"Indeed. He puts us younger men to shame."

"And Lizzie. How is she?"

"Not good, Maggie. In fact I fear she's failing pretty fast."

"Failing? Oh, no! Certainly it can't be as bad as that."

"I'm afraid it is. To be honest, I don't think you'd even recognize her. Not that there's much chance for she hardly leaves the house. Too much bother, she says, to get dressed, though Jack suspects she's grown so gaunt nothing would fit anyway. I find it quite alarming."

"Alarming? In what way, Charlie?"

"As I said, she has lost a frightful amount of weight. Why, she hardly eats at all. It's either drinking, or sleep. Her arms and legs are nothing but skin and bones. And, well . . . I shouldn't be talking like this. Not outside the family."

"But I was her friend, Charlie. And Jack's. Yours too, I like to think. I promise not one word will go beyond us. You're safe saying whatever you want to me."

"I don't need to be told that, Maggie –" He hesitated.

"But what?"

"Nothing." A wave of his head pushed her away.

"Tell me. It can't be as bad as all that."

"It was a very hateful thought."

"About me?"

"It was just one of those irrational notions that pop unexpected into one's head. Usually at the most inopportune time."

"Then you must tell me. I promise not to be offended. To tell you the truth, I don't believe you're capable of harboring bad thoughts."

"I don't think I am. Not usually, certainly. No – well, now I've forgotten exactly what was said between us. You wanted to know more about Lizzie and I hesitated."

"Yes?"

"Then you promised whatever I said would remain between the two of us, and . . ."

"Oh, my God. My God!" She turned and walked away from where Charlie stood. "You know, I really thought when I wrote my book I was accomplishing something – well, something good. I felt quite proud, if you want to know the truth. And then to have it published –"

"And become a major success; you mustn't slight your accomplishment."

"But that's it, isn't it? That's what you were thinking. Perhaps I wouldn't tattle to another – but no guarantee that the strictest confidences wouldn't end up in my next novel. Oh, Charlie, I am so very, very sorry. Not that I can – well, what good would my promise do now?"

"It was a terrible thought, Maggie; unworthy of you – or me. And I do believe you are a close enough friend that you wouldn't do anything to hurt any of us . . ." He hesitated.

"Again. Is that it?"

"Look. That subject is over and done with. I really don't think there's more to say. You call it a coincidence. Well . . . I suppose I can try to accept that."

"I appreciate that, perhaps more than you can know."

"Shall we resume our walk? And yes, I will tell you about Lizzie, not that there's terribly much to relate. She still drinks of course . . . but the very worst part is her demeanor. She's become so nasty, why, you wouldn't believe it was the same woman."

"Lizzie? I do find that difficult to believe."

"Sadly, it is the truth. In fact," he paused, "I suppose you should be warned. She's developed this new far-fetched notion. As I said, she sees few friends and I doubt if the servants pay her any heed but . . . well, perhaps you should know. Just in case . . ."

"You make it sound ominous, Charlie. What could possibly be that bad?"

"You have to understand her entire life is now filled with little but spite. Hatred for everyone around her and, I suspect, hatred most for herself. No, don't say a word. Let me finish. You can undoubtedly guess why some of that hatred flows onto you. I'm not saying it's justified, just asking you to accept the fact that it's there. In any case, somewhere along the way Lizzie did some calculating and figured out that your little Rose was born almost exactly nine months after Andre Robson was killed. So –"

What an absurd notion!

"I just wanted you to know the kind of poison she is capable of spreading. Nothing either Jack or I can do about it. Though, in a way, I think she's already her own worst punishment. I swear, her mouth has turned down into a permanent scowl and – well, her eyes are so cold it's frightening! I honestly believe part of her is already dead."

"And you – or Jack – are powerless to intervene?"

"She could be hospitalized but Jack feels that would be futile. She's already in her seventies, probably wouldn't live much longer under the best of circumstances so, he feels, why not let her do as she wishes?"

"But Jack's in his seventies, too. And you say he's healthy and active."

"No sense trying to compare the two. And, as I said, Jack keeps busy every possible hour."

"I wouldn't like that if it were my husband."

"Lizzie used to hate it – and hate him for it. But now her drinking is so well known that Jack would have no social life at all if it weren't for the work he's doing. And with the Larkin, too, of course. He still keeps his fingers in that pot, doing a lot in fact for the masque this summer. To tell you the truth, I think he's taking a personal delight in seeing those plans through to fruition."

"For any special reason?"

"This probably is a secret, Maggie, for I know Jack would want nothing to overshadow the festivities that J.D. Larkin has worked on so long. It is – and will be – Larkin's day. But, strictly by happenstance, J.D. picked the date of Jack's seventh-fifth birthday."

"You don't say! The twenty-ninth of June!"

"Exactly! As I said, it mustn't become common knowledge –"

"But certainly Jack intends some kind of gala celebration."

"I don't believe he does. Not with Lizzie as she is . . ."

"Something though –"

"Oh, some of us will take him out for dinner, do something

to mark the day. Of course Lizzie doesn't care at all."

"That is so sad."

"I'm sure he'll make a happy day of it. But, as I told you, of primary importance is that nothing interfere with the Larkin Masque."

"Have they let you in on many of the details?"

"Quite a few actually. And you?"

"I've been asked to write –"

"Of course! You're still doing a series for *Ourselves*. I can tell you I've read every word. Even that extra article you did on Frank Lloyd Wright and the hotel he's building in Japan."

"The Imperial," she replied.

"That's the one. Gets around, doesn't he?" Maggie couldn't control the blush. "I wasn't referring to his personal peccadilloes."

"It shouldn't matter, Charlie. I've been following the man for decades now. He remains a very gifted artist. I truly believe he sees things others don't. Maybe that does extend to his personal life. It shouldn't matter. Certainly it shouldn't affect his reputation as one of America's foremost architects. Why, I found him quite charming myself."

"But you . . . you didn't. You wouldn't . . . Mercy!"

"Oh, heavens no! Shame on you for even thinking such a thing, Charlie Knapp. He was quite a bit younger. Reminded me a lot of my brother Bert, in fact. Then again," she smiled at the tall man walking beside her, "he wasn't *that* much younger than I."

Charlie took her by the elbow to escort her across busy Delaware Avenue. "I do seem to find my thoughts all mixed up when I'm with you."

"Funny, I was just thinking how relaxed I feel in your company. I am enjoying our walk very much."

"This is the site for the masque, is it not?" Charlie asked.

"Do we get the trumpets now or later? Ta-ta! 'A New Vision: A Masque of Modern Industry!'"

"Ah, yes, madam. May I escort you to your seat? Right over here perhaps. Let me spread my jacket. Or would you prefer a box seat? I see an available bench over there."

"Thank you. This is perfect."

"Then may I tell you that you are about to witness – yes! prepare yourself now! – a triumph of Imagination – and make that with a capital *I* – over the forces of Ignorance. Another *I*"

"Shame on you, Charlie; you're making fun of Mr. Larkin's grand vision!"

"He didn't write it."

"I know that, but you know it came from his heart. Indeed," she giggled, "he wanted it to be a dramatization of the virtues of, ahem, enlightened cooperation in the work place."

"Heaven help those who try to promote unenlightened cooperation – or should it be enlightened uncooperation? Is there such a word, do you suppose?"

"You're horribly hopeless. Look! Isn't that Industry appearing? Over there by that shrub."

"*Industry?* Indeed! Wearing his Capital *I* for all the world to see. Good thing he didn't get it on sideways. He'd have gotten himself stuck between those two trees."

"Charlie! My sides are aching from laughing so hard. Please stop."

"Not likely, ma'am, the play is only beginning. Why, look over there – yes, there. It's the Creative Energies of the World – lots of caps there as well – summoning our –" He wet his finger tip, drew a long vertical dash and dotted it above with a click of his tongue "—*Industry.*"

"Nice capital *I* there, sir."

"My goodness, looks to me like the author got stuck in the *I* pages of the alphabet. Guess that makes her semi-literate, am I correct?"

"You're hopeless, Mr. Knapp, absolutely hopeless."

"Well, hopeless or not, here comes *Ignorance.* Hiding behind that tall elm over there."

"I'm glad you called it a him. Of course."

"So now what, Maggie? You've seen a copy of the script."

"Well, so have you, that much is obvious. Do go on. I only thought I knew the plot. I confess it was nothing like this when I read it."

"Ah-ha, my dear. This will be our little secret. But, yes, we must advance. Looks like our *Industry* is a very hard worker but not . . . well, how do I put it delicately? Not terribly bright, shall we say? For the first thing Industry does is ask Ignorance to join him. Together, says our *I,* the good one – yes, the not-so-bright one – we'll run all the things needed for a modern factory. See, right on cue, here come Steam and Electricity, now Machinery and oh, yes, good old Labor. Lots more caps, of course."

"Indeed."

"Ready now? You must prepare yourself for the tragic part of this drama."

"Oh, dear, tragedy, too?"

"But of course. For Ignorance takes over and, wouldn't you know it, everything ends up in chaos."

"And what should happen then?"

"Imagination – should we be surprised it's another *I*? – comes to the rescue. See there? Out goes Ignorance with all his helpers –"

"Let me guess. Strife. Greed. Sloth and Disorder. Did I get it right?"

"Somebody, my dear, has been peeking at the script. Anyway, they all exit stage left – or shall it be right? One way or the other – out they go. And from the other side, here come Order, System, Ambition, Service and Cooperation to the rescue."

"Just in the nick of time."

"Were you terribly frightened?"

"Of course! Are you saying you weren't?"

"Well, being a man . . . Besides, I'm betting good – whoops, *Good* will prevail."

"This must be where the kettle comes in."

"I'm afraid I've only heard of that. Perhaps you're up on more of those particulars."

"On that, indeed. They're calling it a Golden Kettle – capital letters, naturally –"

"Certainly –"

"It's close to twelve feet high, gold of course –"

"Well, I should certainly hope so"

"And spews steam."

"Steam?"

"Oh, yes. Mr. Larkin's had the best engineers working on that night and day. They were having a terrible time finding a boiler that would produce an ample amount of steam quickly enough. Absolutely necessary, you know."

"Absolutely. I'm betting it will be as perfect on the day of the performance as all the dancing sprites waiting in the wings."

"Have you seen the costumes, Charlie?"

"Can't say I have. Jack isn't privy to details of that sort. Why? Are they as lavish as the rest of this spectacle?"

"Lavish isn't the word that immediately pops into my mind but of course you're right. They asked the head of the Art Department to design the dresses for the dancers. I'm told he was even sent to New York City to buy costumes for the principals."

"How many people can possibly be involved in making a few dresses? They are dresses, aren't they?"

"Most. Remember, over five hundred bodies have to be clothed. But it's much more than just *dresses*. The Pageant of Products has been designed to represent the twenty-two countries who contribute to the making of the various Larkin products. I've been hearing about efforts to beg, borrow or steal authentic clothes from each of those nations. Then too, all the other costumes have to be dyed to their appropriate colors."

"Stupid me! I should have realized plain old muslin would never do."

"Never, never do. Charlie, did you know that there is a Muslin Underwear Department?"

"As part of the Larkin Company?"

"Yes indeed."

"Good God! And I thought Jack had let me in on all his little secrets! Just wait till I ask him about this! So what is it? Are they turning out muslin underwear for all five hundred dancers? Somehow that sounds gross."

"Well . . . not quite, though I do wonder at the final effect."

"So what is it this top secret department is doing? And do the Germans know about it yet?"

"I don't know about the Germans but what they are planning is to dye every one of those costumes. Apparently someone in the company scouted around and found all sorts of sample dyes that had been stored away in the back of some closet or other. So now out they all come!"

"Unbelievable. But tell me – in strictest confidence – you said earlier you wouldn't call them lavish. The costumes, that is. Just what adjective did pop into your mind?"

"Strictly between thee and me? I think the whole thing is utterly silly. The plot, if one could call it that, the dances and especially all these employees prancing around in their diaphanous muslin. I hope I can sit way in the back – preferably behind a tree, or maybe that wall over there – for I would hate to embarrass myself by giggling so loudly that someone might hear. And I'm afraid that's exactly what I should do. And, Charlie, we haven't even gotten to the dancing Soap Bubbles, or the Perfume Bottles – they dance, too, along with the balloons and spinning wheels and . . ."

"It will certainly be one spectacle such as Buffalo has never witnessed before."

"Perhaps that's just as well."

She grew silent as she attempted to interpret the strange look that had crossed his face. Then, feeling uneasy as if she had peered into something she was not supposed to see, she hurried on, saying whatever words came to mind.

"Oh, I think this shall be a grand day for Mr. Larkin and his company. Just think, Charlie, they're expecting an audience of several thousand. And the orchestra. All the music's original, too, just like the script . . . But you know all that, don't you?"

"Yes, Maggie, I do."

"What is it? Did I say something wrong? Something to upset you?"

"You? Never." He reached over and patted her hand. "To tell you the truth I found myself wishing I could be hidden behind whichever rock or tree or wherever you decided to hide with your giggles. I can't think of a lovelier way to experience the masque."

"But –"

"Lizzie has promised Jack to attend the festivities with him. In fact, I believe some of the children – I guess I will always think of them as children – are coming home, too. This is very important to Jack. The birthday, too, of course, but also the masque itself. And having Lizzie there. He's doing everything he can to make it good for her as well."

"It's all right, Charlie. I understand."

"But –"

"You belong with your family on such an occasion. That's all. It's very understandable."

"It is?"

"Why, of course it is. Come now, I think it's about time for you to walk me back home. I have some preparations to make before you return Buster tomorrow."

They walked across the park and down Delaware Avenue in an easy silence.

"Maggie?"

"Yes, Charlie?"

"Already thinking about Buster?"

"You bet I am."

He paused. "Thank you, Maggie."

CXVIII

June 29, 1916

"Do you suppose an umbrella would do any good?"

"In the midst of five thousand or whatever Dad said were expected? I hardly think so. Perhaps this rain won't last."

"I wish I had your optimism, Ralph. It's been drizzling all morning long."

"But it's not yet noon and the showers do seem to be lessening. Let's hope for the best. What do you think, Annette?"

"Oh, I shan't care one way or 'tother. As long as they do the masque, that's all I care about. They will, don't you think?"

"For my little girl, you bet they will."

"Are we almost there?"

"Just around the corner."

"Ah, here we are. Shall I run in?"

"Let me do it, Ralph. Perhaps I can help Mother Knapp. Pinning on a corsage – I'm sure your father ordered one – or maybe with her dressing."

"You will hurry though, won't you? No sense upsetting Father on a day as special as this."

"It's Grandpapa's birthday. I know that!"

"You're right, little one. I'll be back in a minute – with Grandmama."

Father and daughter continued to talk as Ralph watched his wife ascend the portico steps. A magnificent woman, even after two children. Of course he'd like more but with this Sanger creature haranguing the wives – well, what was a husband to do? He was surprised to see her return alone.

"Anything the matter?"

"I think you'd better come."

"Is Grandmama sick, Mum?"

"She'll be all right. You wait here – like a big girl. We won't be long."

"Yes, Mama."

"My goodness, May. You've turned ashen. What's happened? It is Mother, of course."

"I'm afraid so."

"Where is she?"

"Upstairs. Here. In her bedroom."

Ralph gasped as he glimpsed the prostrate figure of his mother. As he rushed to her and knelt at her side, he was relieved to see that she was breathing. "Mother! Mother!"

"Yes . . . Oh! It's you, Ralph. Is it time already?"

"Yes, it is. Are you all right?"

"We need to hurry or we'll all miss the masque."

"First things first, May. Do you think you're all right, Mother?"

"Of course I am. Help me up, Ralph. Now, over to the chaise. I just need to sit a moment."

"How do you feel, Mother? Do you think you hurt anything in your fall?"

"Nope. Bones – arms, legs – everything feels the same."

"Do you have any idea what happened?"

"Well, I assume I fell."

"But I mean why you'd fall."

"No. No, I don't. I don't think I even remember. Don't know what I was doing –" She glanced down at her slip and stocking, feet still clad in feathered mules. "I'm a sight, aren't I?"

"That doesn't matter. It's your health we're concerned about."

"My health concerns me, too. But, for the moment, I believe I'm quite healthy enough. Your Father's big day, isn't this?"

"We hope you're excited, Mother Knapp. Both the Masque and the birthday celebration."

"May I help you find your dress?"

"I'm here to help too, Mother Knapp. Just tell me what I can do."

"Good Heavens, you two are circling like vultures! I'm quite all right. And still capable of dressing myself."

"I only meant –"

"It doesn't matter, May. What time is it, Ralph?"

"Not quite twelve, Mother."

"And the rains have stopped, have they?"

"For the moment. Are you feeling better now?"

"Much. If I can just rest a little longer . . ."

"But Annette's waiting in the car downstairs."

"My goodness, that will never do. You go on. Let me lie here until I catch my breath. Don't worry, I'll be fine. I'll have the chauffeur drive me over."

"Are you certain?"

"I could stay with you, Mother Knapp, while Ralph takes Annette to the park."

"Stop fussing. I'll be perfectly fine. I have plenty of time – you said so yourself. Go enjoy yourselves. I'll be there before you know it. Hush. Not another word."

"I don't feel right leaving you like this, Mother –"

"Stop fretting. I know your father is counting on your help. Get going, both of you."

"If you're sure."

"I am."

Ralph turned to his wife as they retraced their steps down the front stairway. "Do you –"

"Hush! She'll hear you. Wait till we're all the way down. There. That's better."

"I was simply going to ask if you thought she really was going to be all right. I thought she looked terrible, so pale and weak."

"She'll be fine."

"What do you suppose happened? She seemed quite dazed."

May turned to her husband angrily. "What's the matter with you? I could smell the liquor the minute I entered the bedroom. Of course, she'll be all right. Your mother just needs time to sober up. Let's pray, for your father's sake, that she can do it in an hour."

"We needn't mention this to Annette, do you think?"

"I'll just tell her Grandmama isn't feeling well this morning but that she promised us . . . and you, my dear – that she would come in time for the performance."

"Oh, I do hope so!" the child responded. "I have been looking forward to seeing her again. Grandmama is so wonderful, you know."

"Yes, dear, we do."

. . .

What a foolish thing – to fall like that! I wonder what Ralph thought. Or that pathetic excuse for his wife? Well, they're gone. Time to get dressed. Jack had that outfit sent in from New York City, just so I'd look my best today. That's what he said. He's not blind. I know how I look. So? Why should I care? I'd like to tell him – no. No need to spoil his big day. Any other . . . then again, on any other he wouldn't care if I lived or died. Just so I put in an appearance today.

Up. See? I can do it. But my! Didn't realize I was so unsteady on my feet. Must be the new shoes. Won't matter. By six o'clock I'll be – free – again. Let's go do this for Daddy.

She crossed the room unsteadily, grabbing the doorframe for support as she entered the bathroom. The image in the mirror gave her a shock. Better not to look. She splashed cold water on her face until she felt the first stirrings of alertness. Combing her hair by rote, she dabbed lipstick by feel as well and started to cross back to the closet where the new dress hung.

What tripped me that time? Got to get up. Have to get dressed.

Should she call her maid for help?

God, no! That prissy little thing would make even more of a fuss than Ralph and What's-Her-Name. If I can just get over to the bed – yes, there. Up. Up again.

Dress – up and over! Whoopee! On it goes. Damn, who designed a dress with buttons down the back? No way. I'll just wear a coat. Now, where is the new brooch Jack bought? Generous of him. Outlandish. Well, if he wants to flaunt his

3

wealth . . .

There. All eyes will be on that. Might be a good thing for I can't say I look very good.

It's going to be a long afternoon. Perhaps I should take a little fortification now. Certainly won't get the chance later. Just a wee one.

Almost forgot the hat. My God, what would people say were Lizzie Knapp to show up on such an occasion hatless? They'd say she'd finally gone and lost her mind – and are you surprised, Minerva? Why, no, Zelienople, I always figured it was just a matter of time.

But not yet, dear friends. Not yet. There's still life left in the old Lizzie.

Hat – sideways? Tipped? That way? Oh, who cares! Pin it on and – oh, my, just look how late it's getting. Better call for the car now.

One more quick one. Indeed. It helps. Out to the hall and down we go.

Ooh! Forgot my gloves. Yes, I hear you. I'll be right down. Now which drawer? . . . These will do. Who's going to notice?

Didn't realize there was a little left in the glass. Ahhh. That's good. And away we go.

She staggered as she crossed the hall to the grand staircase. Her hand reached out to clasp the banister and missed. The last thing Lizzie Knapp remembered was the beginning of her fall.

. . .

"Are you all right, Father?"

"Of course I am. What do you expect? Damned rain. It's pouring out there."

"It's supposed to rain for funerals, isn't that what they always say?"

"I'm just glad the weather cooperated for the Masque. Oh, I'm sorry."

"A little undiplomatic, Anne, but I do understand. Yes, I'm sure if J.D. had an in up in heaven he wouldn't have been able to order better weather. Just enough blue sky to alleviate any fears and enough clouds to make it bearable."

"I hadn't thought of it that way."

"Too much else on our minds then, I suppose."

"I see Father Rutledge motioning to us. It must be time to go in."

"The Bishop isn't here? I was sure he said he'd officiate."

"Then I'm sure he will, Father. But it doesn't take a Bishop to show us to our seats."

"My God!"

"What is it?"

"Why, the place is packed!"

"What did he say?"

"John just said to look at all the people who turned out on such a miserable day."

"I never expected –"

"Nor I either."

"Well, it just shows how highly the community esteems Father."

"*Father?* You don't think –"

"That they came out of respect for Mother? Hardly. At one time, perhaps, but no, this has to be Father's influence."

"I'm terribly impressed."

"I'm sure I'll never see a funeral this grand when I go."

"Give yourself another thirty years, Bessie. Who knows what you'll be by then?"

"Not like Mother. At least I pray not."

"We all do, children; we all do."

"Uncle Charlie! I didn't see you come in."

"Little late, I fear. Sorry. The parking was impossible."

"We could have –"

"Don't worry, dear. It's all taken care of now. You, Jack. How are you holding up?"

"Fine, Charles, just fine. To tell you the truth, I've been much too busy to even have time for proper reflection. Her death wasn't any great surprise. The timing – well, then again, leave it to Lizzie to mess up my birthday celebration."

"Father! That's a terrible thing to say!"

"Nonsense. Perhaps I just knew her a little bit better then any of you."

"Differently, I'm sure, Jack."

"Differently, definitely. Sad part is, I haven't been able to grieve for her. Not really."

"I understand, Brother. Don't worry about it. I'm sure your feelings will be straightened out with time."

"By God, I hope so."

"Shush, you two. You're worse then the children!"

"Hush! All of you. They're beginning the procession now."

. . .

"I was so sorry to hear of her death, Jack. But it was a lovely service, wasn't it? I felt almost as if Lizzie had had a hand in making the final arrangements."

"I shouldn't be at all surprised." He took her hand. "Thank you for coming, Maggie. It's good to see you."

"I hope you mean that, Jack."

"Well, I can echo my brother's sentiment and I know I mean it. How are you, Maggie?"

"I'm fine. Certainly much better than this weather. I'm sure you – and your forecasters – got your record for the wettest spring. But must you try for the entire summer season as well?"

"Good Lord, I certainly hope not! Here, can we duck in here for a minute? I'd hate to see you any wetter."

"I appreciate that, Charlie. Though once one is soaked through I'm not sure what's left. I suppose I should get home and dried out before I catch a chill."

"Then I won't hold you up. To tell you the truth, I was hoping I'd see you here today."

"Lizzie was a good friend. Once. Did you enjoy the Masque? The beginning, I guess. To tell you the truth, I wasn't even aware of Jack's being called away."

"Thank God for that. It would have been a double tragedy for him had Lizzie's death also ruined the Larkin Masque."

"They don't think –? No, I'm sure not."

"The doctor felt quite positive it was an accident. She'd been drinking. Ralph confirmed that. To be honest, I simply cannot understand what kind of thinking goes on to make a person behave like that."

"I suppose her thinking stopped somewhere before the end. So, you say she was drinking and –?"

"Started for the car. She was completely dressed, right down to her hat and gloves. Apparently just missed the top stair – and, well, the servants found her at the bottom of the staircase. Already dead. Tragic, of course, and yet . . ."

"Yes. I understand."

"Well, we got this conversation turned around and all gloomy, didn't we?"

"I'm sorry, Charlie. I just wanted to know what happened. I did care."

"Of course you did."

"Well, then –" She turned and started for the vestibule door.

"Maggie –"

"Yes?"

"Would it be? . . . Do you think anybody would mind? . . . Would you mind? –"

"Charlie!"

"Have dinner with me, Maggie."

"Tonight?"

"Is it too soon? Is that what you think?"

She hesitated.

"Then why not?"

"You won't be needed at home? With Jack, I mean?"

"All the children are there. Who's going to notice one absent bachelor uncle? Say yes, please." Seeing her indecision, he continued quickly. "If not for my sake, then for Buster's."

"For Buster? What does he have to do with it?"

"Give me a chance to see him again."

"Charlie Knapp! Are you planning to take Buster out to dinner? Or me?"

"You wouldn't mind if I said hello to him first, would you?"

"You're incorrigible," she laughed. "Do you know that?"

"Sounds good to me. Besides, I just might be able to save a little of my steak for my favorite dog. No promises, mind you, and you mustn't tell him –"

"I would be honored to go out with you, Mr. Knapp. Would eight be all right?"

"Eight is great. That'll give me time first with Jack. I look forward to seeing you then."

"Till then."

CXIX

She awoke quickly, oddly aware of the sun coursing her face as it searched the westerly slopes. Joltingly, the train rounded a bend and the light was lost.

But not its luminesce. Feeling still spotlighted and now totally awake, Maggie caught herself reliving glimpses of the figures of the past. Each seemed so vivid she caught herself to inquire if this was the same sensation they attributed to the last moments of a drowning victim.

How would one know? How *could* one know?

Death. So much death.

Her parents. Hannah. Fil. Oh, what a driving force that woman had possessed! Theodore and Rose.

Were there others?

Forgotten perhaps.

And a wave of guilt swept over her as she tried to recall the names of those she had forgotten.

Still . . . . .

Maggie shrugged. Hers hadn't been a particularly good life. Or a bad one.

Certainly no different from most others. She'd had more privilege of course. In the beginning, and then . . . yes, of course, now. And what were those in-between-years if not justified – fodder perhaps – for the here and now.

No better. No worse.

Pointless perhaps.

Ah, yes. That was it.

What was the point? If point there was. And did anyone these days still believe in there being a point after all?

Were we not born to struggle, to do our best or not . . . did any of it really matter?

The train. She . . . Those mewling about her?

Was life as set as the clackety clacking on the rails beneath her? A steady cadence. What was that beautiful line? Ah, indeed. *Signifying nothing.*

Was there a point? A reason?

.   .   .

Now the interior was mirrored by the dark beyond her window.

Nighttime. One more day gone by. One more night closer to her final one.

Maggie became quickly aware of the growing hunger building within. When had she last eaten? A real meal, not just a cup of coffee and a piece of toasted bread on the run. Food. Real food.

It was nourishment she craved.

She smiled then secretly. So the old woman wasn't so lost after all. Well, good for her.

She looked up again as he approached her seat.

And smiled.

ACKNOWLEDGEMENTS

The original impetus for HRFB came from a display my husband and I attended at the Buffalo and Erie County Historical Society. Showcasing what was then to us an unheard of company, Buffalo's own Larkin Company, I was flabbergasted at the "modern" innovations John D. Larkin provided for his workers. Medical and dental care, schooling, even noontime concerts – all were in use long before the end of the nineteenth century. When these dates coincided with family letters recently inherited, I knew I had the germ of a historical novel. Not being a novelist, I passed my suggestion along to Lauren Belfer who had recently published her own book on Buffalo in the same era, City Of Light. Admitting to being "quite entrenched in a negative view of Frank Lloyd Wright", she suggested I write the book. So I did.

Having set my manuscript aside for a number of years, I now confess to being more than a little rusty when it comes to thank yous and acknowledgements. My apologies to any whom I have inadvertently omitted.

Any newspaper, magazine, TV show or whatever that dealt with the decades immediately before or after 1900 added to my factual knowledge of that period. Of specific value were John D. Larkin: A Business Pioneer, Daniel I. Larkin; Frank Lloyd Wright's Larkin Building, Jack Quinan; Frank Lloyd Wright's Martin House, Architecture as Portraiture, Jack Quinan as well as Dr. Quinan's personal encouragement and suggestions on selected pages of my manuscript; The History of Chautauqua County, New York, Andrew W. Young; Three Taps of the Gavel, Alfreda L. Irwin, "Public Opinion", Chambersburg, PA, June 12, 1890, "Western New York Heritage" Vol. 3, Number 1, and a tour of Buffalo's homes built by Frank Lloyd Wright. Conde Nast Traveler, March 2000, featured "The Wright Stuff" while An Architecture for Democracy by Aaron G. Green, further increased the adventure that was Frank Lloyd Wright. The 1910-1911 edition of the Encyclopedia Britannica proved that there was wisdom in keeping old books. I also consulted "The Fredonia NY Souvenir Historical Book 1829-1979" by Marie E. Reinhoult and "Yesterdays . . . in and around Pomfret, NY," Book III, a series of weekly columns in the Fredonia Censor by Elizabeth L. Crocker. Episcopal Life/Church Facts added to my knowledge of the history of beautiful St. Paul's. I am further indebted to the Warren

PA County and the Fredonia NY Historical Societies. Also Joyce at the Chautauqua NY Library for her help with Susan B. Anthony. This would be drastically incomplete without mentioning the private letters of my great-grandparents, Charles Warren and Elizabeth Moorhead Stone. They opened doors into an era I could only imagine.

Dr. Spock's Baby and Child Care proved invaluable to my development of the twins from start to finish. Interviews plus the ceaseless attention given now to post-traumatic stress disorder (PTSD) helped bring those chapters to life that dealt with forgetting what is too painful to remember. Grant Cooper translated the German Bach to English; I translated Grant.

Over the years I have received a lot of encouragement when I needed it most. Else, this book would still be scribbles in a loose-leaf notebook. So thanks for setting me straight, helping when I goofed on facts, increasing my knowledge or just telling me it was worthwhile to continue the journey: Nancy for medical information, Jane for her criticism and inspiration, Emmy for the same plus allowing me to use some of our *Pericles* poetry, Peggy, Mary & Mary, Kay, Anne, Sheila, Fred, even the medium at Lily Dale who helped me understand Spiritualism as well as anticipate my eventual fame.

A special note must be made about the wonderful people who guide and continue to rebuild Wright's masterpieces at Graycliff and, especially, the Darwin Martin House. Every visit refreshes me and increases my appreciation for the beauty that existed once . . . and is being reclaimed even now.

Mostly of course my deepest gratitude to my husband, Bob, who stood by me as I struggled with the "bubbles" where my people lived and that were allowed to become this book. Though at that time he often didn't understand the vagaries of the temperamental writer (perhaps he still doesn't completely), he was always there beside me, ready to help and assist and support whether I knew I needed it or not.

I may have forgotten names but not my gratitude. It still amazes me this tome got written.

Sometimes we cannot help but alter the path of another, whether we desire it or not.

16746683R00369

Made in the USA
Middletown, DE
21 December 2014